Nicholson Baker's new novel is the story of Arno Strine, a temporary typist, who has perfected the knack of stopping time in its tracks and taking women's clothes off.

He is hard at work on his autobiography, *The Fermata*, which proves in the telling to be a very provocative and altogether morally confused piece of work.

Nicholson Baker was born in 1957. He is the author of three highly acclaimed novels: *The Mezzanine, Room Temperature* and *Vox*, and a work of non-fiction, *U and I*. He lives in Northern California with his family.

THE
FERMATA

Nicholson Baker

Chatto & Windus
LONDON

First published in 1994

1 3 5 7 9 10 8 6 4 2

© Nicholson Baker 1994

Nicholson Baker has asserted his right under the Copyright,
Designs and Patents Act, 1988 to be identified as the author
of this work

First published
in Great Britain in 1994 by
Chatto & Windus Limited
Random House, 20 Vauxhall Bridge Road, London SW1V 2SA

Random House Australia (Pty) Limited
20 Alfred Street, Milsons Point, Sydney,
New South Wales 2061, Australia

Random House New Zealand Limited
18 Poland Road, Glenfield
Auckland 10, New Zealand

Random House South Africa (Pty) Limited
PO Box 337, Bergvlei, South Africa

Random House UK Limited Reg. No. 954009

A CIP catalogue record for this book
is available from the British Library

ISBN 0 7011 5999 5

Printed and bound in Great Britain by
Mackays of Chatham PLC, Chatham, Kent

FOR MY FATHER

THE FERMATA

$\widehat{\cdot}$

I

I AM GOING TO CALL MY AUTOBIOGRAPHY *THE FERMATA*, EVEN though "fermata" is only one of the many names I have for the Fold. "Fold" is, obviously, another. Every so often, usually in the fall (perhaps mundanely because my hormone-flows are at their highest then), I discover that I have the power to drop into the Fold. A Fold-drop is a period of time of variable length during which I am alive and ambulatory and thinking and looking, while the rest of the world is stopped, or paused. Over the years, I have had to come up with various techniques to trigger the pause, some of which have made use of rocker-switches, rubber bands, sewing needles, fingernail clippers, and other hardware, some of which have not. The power

3

seems ultimately to come from within me, grandiose as that sounds, but as I invoke it I have to believe that it is external for it to work properly. I don't inquire into origins very often, fearing that too close a scrutiny will damage whatever interior states have given rise to it, since it is the most important ongoing adventure of my life.

I'm in the Fold right now, as a matter of fact. I want first to type out my name—it's Arnold Strine. I prefer Arno to the full Arnold. Putting my own name down is loin-girding somehow—it helps me go ahead with this. I'm thirty-five. I'm seated in an office chair whose four wide black casters roll silently over the carpeting, on the sixth floor of the MassBank building in downtown Boston. I'm looking up at a woman named Joyce, whose clothes I have rearranged somewhat, although I have not actually removed any of them. I'm looking directly at her, but she doesn't know this. While I look I'm using a Casio CW-16 portable electronic typewriter, which is powered by four D batteries, to record what I see and think. Before I snapped my fingers to stop the flow of time in the universe, Joyce was walking across the carpeting in a gray-blue knit dress, and I was sitting behind a desk twenty or thirty feet away, transcribing a tape. I could see her hipbones under her dress, and I immediately knew it was the time to Snap in. Her pocketbook is still over her shoulder. Her pubic hair is very black and nice to look at—there is lots and lots of it. If I didn't already know her name, I would probably now open her purse and find out her name, because it helps to know the name of a woman I undress. There is moreover something very exciting, almost moving, about taking a peek at a woman's driver's license without her knowing—studying the picture and wondering whether it was one that pleased her or made her unhappy when she was first given it at the DMV.

But I do know this woman's name. I've typed some of her tapes. The language of her dictations is looser than some of the other loan officers'—she will occasionally use a phrase like "spruce up" or "polish off" or "kick in" that you very seldom come across in the credit updates of large regional banks. One of her more recent dictations ended with something like "Kyle Roller indicated that he had been dealing with the subject since 1989. Volume since that time has been $80,000. He emphatically stated that their service was substandard. He indicated that he has put further business with them on hold because they had 'lied like hell' to him. He indicated he did not want his name mentioned back to the Pauley brothers. This information was returned to Joyce Collier on—" and then she said the date. As prose it is not Penelope Fitzgerald, perhaps, but you crave any tremor of life in these reports, and I will admit that I felt an arrow go through me when I heard her say "lied like hell."

Last week, Joyce was wearing this very same gray-blue hipbone-flaunting dress one day. She dropped off a tape for me to do and told me that she liked my glasses, and I've been nuts about her since. I blushed and thanked her and told her I liked her scarf, which really was a very likable scarf. It had all sorts of golds and blacks and yellows in it, and Cyrillic letters seemed to be part of the design. She said, "Well thank you, I like it, too," and she surprised me (surprised us both possibly) by untying it from her neck and pulling it slowly through her fingers. I asked whether those were indeed Cyrillic letters I saw before me, and she said that they were, pleased at my attentiveness, but she said that she had asked a friend of hers who knew Russian what they spelled, and he had told her that they meant nothing, they were just a jumble of letters. "Even better," I said, somewhat idiotically, anxious to show how completely uninterested I was in her mention of a male friend. "The designer picked the letters for their formal beauty—he didn't try to pretend he knew the language by using a real word." The moment threatened to become more flirtatious than either of us wanted. I hurried us past it by asking her how soon she needed her tape done. (I'm a temp, by the way.) "No big rush," she said. She retied her scarf, and we smiled quite warmly at each other again before she went off. I was happy all that day just because she had told me she liked my glasses.

Joyce is probably not going to play a large part in this account of my life. I have fallen in love with women many, many times, maybe a hundred or a hundred and fifty times; I've taken off women's clothes many times, too: there is nothing particularly unusual about this occasion within which I am currently parked. The only unusual thing about it is that this time I'm writing about it. I know there are thousands of women in the world I could potentially feel love for as I do feel it now for Joyce—she just happens to work at this office in the domestic-credit department of MassBank where I happen to be a temp for a few weeks. But that is the strange thing about what you are expected to do in life—you are supposed to forget that there are hundreds of cities, each one of them full of women, and that it is most unlikely that you have found the perfect one for you. You are just supposed to pick the best one out of the ones you know and can attract, and in fact you do this happily—you feel that the love you direct toward the one you do choose is not arbitrarily bestowed.

And it *was* brave and friendly of Joyce to compliment me that way about my glasses. I always melt instantly when I'm praised for features about which I have private doubts. I first got glasses in the summer after fourth grade. (Incidentally, fourth grade is also the year I first dropped into the Fold—my temporal powers have always been linked in a way I don't pretend to understand with my sense of sight.) I wore them steadily until about two years ago, when I decided that I should at least try contact lenses. Maybe everything would be different if I got contacts. So I did get them, and I enjoyed the rituals of caring for them—caring for this pair of demanding twins that had to be bathed and changed constantly. I liked squirting the salt water on them, and holding one of them in an aqueous bead on the tip of my finger and admiring its Saarinenesque upcurve, and when I folded it in half and rubbed its slightly slimy surface against itself to break up the protein deposits, I often remembered the satisfactions of making omelets in Teflon fry-pans. But though as a hobby they were rewarding, though I was as excited in opening the centrifugal spin-cleaning machine I ordered for them as I would have been if I had bought an automatic bread baker or a new kind of sexual utensil, they interfered with my appreciation of the world. I could see things through them, but I wasn't *pleased* to look at things. The bandwidth of my optical processors was being flooded with "there is an intruder on your eyeball" messages, so that a lot of the incidental visual haul from my retina was simply not able to get through. I wasn't enjoying the sights you were obviously meant to enjoy, as when you walked around a park on a windy day watching people's briefcases get blown around on their arms.

At first I thought it was worth losing the beauty of the world in order to look better to the world: I really was more handsome without glasses—the dashing scar on my left eyebrow, where I cut myself on a scrap of aluminum, was more evident. A girl I knew (and whose clothes I removed) in high school used to sing *"Il faut souffrir pour être belle"* in a soft voice, to a tune of her own devising, and I took that overheard precept seriously; I was willing to understand it not just in the narrow sense of painful hair-brushing or (say) eyebrow-tweezing or liposuction, but in some broader sense that suffering makes for beauty in art, that the artist has to suffer griefs and privations in order to deliver beauty to his or her public, all that well-ventilated junk. So I continued to wear contacts even when each blink was a dry torment. But then I noticed that my *typing* was suffering, too—and there, since I am a temp and typing is my livelihood, I really had to draw the line. Especially when I typed numbers, my error rate was way up. (Once I spent two weeks doing nothing but typing six-digit numbers.) People began bringing back financial charts that I had done with mistyped numbers circled in red, asking, "Are you all right today, Arno?" Contact lenses also, I noticed, made me feel, as loud continuous factory noise also will, ten feet farther away from anyone else around me. They were isolating me, heightening rather than helping rid me of my—well, I suppose it is proper to call it my loneliness. I missed the sharp corners of my glasses, which had helped me dig my way out into sociability; they had been part of what I felt was my characteristic expression.

When I started today, I had no intention of getting into all this about eyeglasses. But it is germane. I love looking at women. I love being able to see them clearly. I particularly like being in the position I am in this very second, which is not looking at Joyce, but rather thinking about the amazing fact that I *can* look up from this page at any time and stare at any part of her that calls out to me for as long as I want without troubling or embarrassing her. Joyce doesn't wear glasses, but my ex-girlfriend Rhody did—and somewhere along the line I realized that if I liked glasses on women, which I do very much, maybe women would tolerate glasses on me. On naked women glasses work for me the way spike heels or a snake tattoo or an ankle bracelet or a fake beauty spot work for some men—they make the nudity pop out at me; they make the woman seem more naked than she would have seemed if she were completely naked. Also, I want to be very sure that she can see every inch of my richard with utter clarity, and if she is wearing glasses I know that she can if she wants to.

The deciding moment really came when I spent the night with a woman, an office manager, who, I *think* anyway, had sex with me sooner than she wanted to simply to distract me from noticing the fact that her contacts were bothering her. It was very late, but I think she wanted to talk for a while longer, and yet (this is my theory) she hurried to the sex because the extreme intimacy, to her way of thinking, of appearing before me in her glasses was only possible after the less extreme intimacy of fucking me. Several times as we talked I was on the point of saying, since her eyes did look quite unhappily pink, "You want to take out your contacts? I'll take out mine." But I didn't, because I thought it might have a condescending sort of "I know everything about you, baby, your bloodshot eyes give you away" quality. Probably I should have. A few days after that, though, I resumed wearing my glasses to work. My error rate dropped right back down. I was instantly happier. In particular, I recognized the crucial importance of hinges to my pleasure in life. When I open my glasses in the morning before taking a shower and going to work, I am like an excited tourist who has just risen from his hotel bed on the first day of a vacation: I've just flung open a set of double French doors leading out onto a sunlit balcony with a view of the entire whatever—shipping corridor, bay, valley, parking lot. (How can people not like views over motel parking lots in the early morning? The new subtler car colors, the blue-greens and warmer grays, and the sense that all those drivers are leveled in the democracy of sleep and that the glass and hoods out there are cold and even dewy, make for one of the more inspiring visions that life can offer before nine o'clock.) Or maybe French-door-hinges are not entirely it. Maybe I think that the hinges of my glasses are a woman's hip-sockets: her long graceful legs open and straddle my head all day. I asked Rhody once whether she liked the tickling of my glasses-frames on the inside of her thighs. She said, "Usually your glasses are off by then, aren't they?" I admitted that was true. She said she didn't like it when I wore my glasses because she wanted my sense of her open vadge to be more Sisley than Richard Estes. "But I do sometimes like feeling your ears high on my thighs," she conceded. "And if I clamp your ears hard with my thighs I can make more noise without feeling I'm getting out of hand." Rhody was a good, good person, and I probably should not have tried to allude even obliquely to my Fold experiences to her, since she found what little I told her of Fermation repellent; her knowledge of it contributed to our breakup.

Well! I think I have established that there *is* an emotional history to my wearing of glasses. So in saying that she liked them, tall Joyce—who as I sit typing this towers above me now in a state of semi-nudity—was definitely saying the right thing if she was interested in getting to my heart, which she probably wasn't. You have to be extremely careful about complimenting a thirty-five-year-old male temp who has achieved nothing in his life. "Hi, I'm the temp!" That's usually what I say to receptionists on my first day of an assignment; that's the word I use, because it's the word everyone uses, though it was a long time before I stopped thinking that it was a horrible abbreviation, worse than "Frisco." I have been a temp for over ten years, ever since I quit graduate school. The reason I have done nothing with my life is simply that my power to enter the Fold (or "hit the clutch" or "find the Cleft" or "take a personal day" or "instigate an Estoppel") comes and goes. I value the ability, which I suspect is not widespread, but because I don't have it consistently, because it fades without warning and doesn't return until months or years later, I've gotten hooked into a sort of damaging boom-and-bust Kondratieff cycle. When I've lost the power, I simply exist, I do the minimum I have to do to make a living, because I know that in a sense everything I want to accomplish (and I *am* a person with ambitions) is infinitely postponable.

As a rough estimate, I think I have probably spent only a total of two years of personal time in the Fold, if you lump the individual minutes or hours together, maybe even less; but they have been some of the best, most alive times I've had. My life reminds me of the capital-gains tax problem, as I once read about it in an op-ed piece: if legislators keep changing, or even promising to change, the capital-gains percentages, repealing and reinstating the tax, the rational investor will begin to base his investment decisions not on the existing tax laws, but on his certainty of change, which mischannels (the person who wrote the op-ed piece convincingly argued) in some destructive way the circulation of capital. So too with me during those periods when I wait for the return of my ability to stop time: I think, Why should I read Ernest Renan or learn matrix algebra now, since when I'm able to Drop again, I'll be able to spend private hours, or even years, satisfying any fleeting intellectual curiosity while the whole world waits for me? I can always catch up. That's the problem.

People are somewhat puzzled by me when I first show up at

their office—What is this unyoung man, this thirty-five-year-old man, doing temping? Maybe he has a criminal past, or maybe he's lost a decade to drugs, or: Maybe He's an Artist? But after a day or two, they adjust, since I am a fairly efficient and good-natured typist, familiar with most of the commonly used kinds of software (and some of the forgotten kinds too, like nroff, Lanier, and NBI, and the good old dedicated DEC systems with the gold key), and I am unusually good at reading difficult handwriting and supplying punctuation for dictators who in their creative excitement forget. Once in a great while I use my Fold-powers to amaze everyone with my apparent typing speed, transcribing a two-hour tape in one hour and that kind of thing. But I'm careful not to amaze too often and become a temp legend, since this is my great secret and I don't want to imperil it—this is the one thing that makes my life worth living. When some of the more intelligent people in a given office ask little probingly polite questions to try to figure me out, I often lie and tell them that I'm a writer. It is almost funny to see how relieved they are to have a way of explaining my lowly work status to themselves. Nor is it so much of a lie, because if I had not wasted so much of my life waiting for the next Fermata-phase to come along I would very likely have written some sort of a book by now. And I have written a few shorter things.

I'm typing this on a portable electronic typewriter because I don't want to risk putting any of it on the bank's LAN. Local area networks behave erratically in the Fold. When my carpal-tunnel problem gets bad, I use a manual for my private writing; it seems to help. But I don't have to: batteries and electricity *do* function in the Fold—in fact, all the laws of physics still obtain, as far as I can tell, but only to the extent that I reawaken them. The best way to describe it is that right

now, because I have snapped my fingers, every event everywhere is in a state of gel-like suspension. I can move, and the
air molecules part to let me through, but they do it resistingly,
reluctantly, and the farther that objects are from me, the more
thoroughly they are paused. If someone was riding a motorcycle down a hill before I stopped time "half an hour" ago, the
rider will remain motionless on his vehicle unless I walk up to
him and give him a push—in which case he will fall down, but
somewhat more slowly than if he fell in an unpaused universe.
He won't take off down the hill at the speed he was riding, he
will just tip over. I used to be tempted to fly small airplanes in
the Fold, but I'm not that stupid. Flight, though, is definitely
possible, as is the pausing of time on an airplane flight. The
world stays halted exactly as it is except where I mess with it,
and for the most part I try to be as unobtrusive as possible—as
unobtrusive as my lusts let me be. This typewriter, for instance, puts what I type on the page because the act of pressing a letter makes cause and effect function locally. A circuit
is completed, a little electricity dribbles from the batteries,
etc. I honestly don't know how far outward my personal distortion of the temporary timelessness that I create measurably
spreads. I do know that during a Fermata a woman's skin feels
soft where it is soft, warm when it is warm—her sweat feels
warm when it is warm. It's a sort of reverse Midas touch that
I have while in the Fold—the world is inert and statuesque
until I touch it and make it live ordinarily.

I had this idea of writing my life story while within a typical
chronanistic experience just yesterday. It's almost incredible
to think that I've been Dropping since fourth grade and yet
I've never made the effort to write about it right while it was
going on. I kept an abbreviated log for a while in high school
and college—date and time of Drop, what I did, how long in

13

personal minutes or hours or days it took (for a watch usually starts up again in the Fold if I shake it, so I can easily measure how long I have been out), whether I learned anything new or not, and so on. You would think, if a person really could stop the world and get off, as I can, that it would occur to him fairly early on to stop the world in order to record with some care what it felt like to stop the world and get off, for the benefit of the curious. But I now see, even this far into my first autobiographical Fermata, why I never did it before. Sad to say, it is just as hard to write during a Fermation as it is in real time. You still must dole out all the things you have to say one by one, when what you want of course is to say them all at once. But I am going to give it a try. I am thirty-five now, and I have done quite a lot of things, mostly bad, with the Fold's help (including, incidentally, reciting Dylan Thomas's "Poem on His Birthday" apparently from memory at the final session of a class in modern lyric poetry in college: it is a longish poem, and whenever nervousness made me forget a line, I just paused the world by pressing the switch of my Time Perverter—which is what I called the modified garage-door opener that I used in those days—and refreshed my memory by looking at a copy of the text that I had in my notebook, and no one was the wiser)—and if I don't write some of these private adventures down now, I know I'm going to regret it.

Just now I spun around once in my chair in order to surprise myself again with the sight of Joyce's pubic hair. It really is amazing to me that I can do this, even after all these years. She was walking about thirty feet from my desk, across an empty stretch of space, carrying some papers, on her way to someone's cube, and my gaze just launched toward her, diving cleanly, without ripples, through the glasses that she had complimented, taking heart from having to pass through the optical influence of something she had noticed and liked. It was as if I traveled along the arc of my sight and reached her visually. (There is definitely something to those medieval theories of sight that had the eye sending out rays.) And just as my sighted self reached her, she stopped walking for a second, to check something on one of the papers she held, and when she looked down I was struck by the simple fact that today her hair is *braided*.

It is arranged in what I think is called a French braid. Each of the solid clumps of her hair feeds into the overall solidity of the braid, and the whole structure is plaited as part of her head, like a set of glossy external vertebrae. I'm impressed that women are able to arrange this sort of complicated figure, without too many stray strands, without help, in the morning, by feel. Women are much more in touch with the backs of themselves than men are: they can reach higher up on their back, and do so daily to unfasten bras; they can clip and braid their hair; they can keep their rearward blouse-tails smoothly tucked into their skirts. They give thought to how the edges of their underpants look through their pocketless pants from the back. ("Panties" is a word to be avoided, I feel.) But French braids, in which three sporting dolphins dip smoothly under one another and surface in a continuous elegant entrainment, are the most beautiful and impressive results of this sense of dorsal space. As soon as I saw Joyce's braid I knew that it was time to stop time. I needed to feel her solid braid, and her head beneath it, in my palm.

So, just as she started walking again, I snapped my fingers. This is my latest method of entering the Fold, and one of the simpler I have been able to develop (much more straightforward than my earlier mathematical-formula technique, or the sewn calluses, for instance, both of which I will get into later).

She didn't hear the snap, only I did—the universe halts at some indeterminate point just before my middle finger swats against the base of my thumb. I got out my Casio typewriter and scooted over here to her on my chair. (I didn't scoot backwards, I scooted frontwards, which isn't easy to do over carpeting, because it is hard to get the proper traction. I wanted to keep my eyes on her.) She was in mid-stride. I reached forward and put my hands on her hipbones. It felt as if there were cashmere or something fancy in the wool, and it was good to feel her hipbones through that soft material, and to see my hands angling to follow the incurve of her waist, which the dress had to an extent hidden. Sometimes when I first touch a woman in the Fold I tense up my arms until they vibrate, so that the shape of whatever is under my palms keeps on being sent through my nerves as new information. I never know exactly what I will do during a Drop. To get her dress out of the way, I lifted its soft hem up over her hips and gathered it into two wingy bunches and tied a big soft knot with them. It had seemed as if she had a tiny potbelly with the dress on (this can be a sexy touch, I think, on some women), but if she had, it disappeared or lost definition as soon as I pulled her panty-hose and underpants down as far as I could get them, which wasn't that far because her legs were walkingly apart. (Also, before I pulled down her pantyhose, which is a smoky-blue color, I touched an oval of her skin through a run in the darker part high on her thigh.) And then I was given this sight that I have before me now, of her pubic hair.

I'm not normally a pubic-hair obsessive—I really have no ongoing fetishes, I don't think, because each woman is different, and you never know what particular feature or transition between features is going to grab you and say, "Look at this—you've never thought about exactly this before!" Each

16

woman inspires her own fetishes. And it isn't that Joyce has some ludicrous Vagi-fro or massive Koosh-ball explosion of a sex-goatee—in fact her hair isn't thicker really than most. It's just that it covers a wider area, maybe, and its blackness *sparkles,* if you will—its curving border reaches a little higher on her stomach. A little?—what am I saying? It's the size of South America. To think that I could have died and not seen this— that I could have picked a different temp assignment when Jenny, my coordinator, told me my choices a few weeks ago. What is exciting about its extent is maybe that, because it reaches higher than other women's pubic hair, it becomes less and more sexual at the same time—the slang for it, like "pussy hair" and "cunt hair" (I flinch at both those words, except when I'm close to coming), doesn't apply because it is no longer, strictly speaking, "pubic" hair at all—its borders are reaching out into soft abdominal love-areas, so love and sex mix. I wanted to feel it, the dense sisaly lush resilience of it, which makes that whole hippy part of her body look extraordinarily graceful. It is a kind of black cocktail dress under which her clit-heart beats—it has that much *dignity.*

But rather than holding it immediately, I deprived myself of the sight of it for a little while and instead gently placed my hand on her braid, which was cool and thick and smooth and dense, a totally different idea of hair, so different that it is strange to think of the two orders of hair as sharing the same word, but which follows the curve of her head in the same way that her pubic hair follows the curve over her mound-bone, and when I felt the French-braid sensation sinking into the hollow of my palm, which craves sexual shapes and textures, I then went ahead and curled the fingers of my other hand through her devil's food fur, connecting the two kinky handfuls of home-grown protein with my arms, and it felt as if I were hot-wiring a car; my heart's twin carburetors roared into life. That's all I did, then I started typing this before I forgot the feeling. Maybe that's all I will do. That sexy, *sexy* pubic hair! I'm noticing now that its contours are similar to those of a black bicycle seat: a black leather seat on a racing bicycle. Maybe this is why those sad sniffers of comic legend sniff girls' bicycle seats? No, for them it isn't the shape, it's the fact that the seat has been between a girl's legs. They are truly pathetic. I have no sympathy to spare for compulsions other than my own. I would, though, like to rescue the correspondence between pubic hair and narrow black-leather bicycle seats from them.

All right, I think that is enough for now. I've been in the Fold for, let's see, almost four hours and written eight single-spaced pages, and the problem is that if I stay in too long I'll have jet lag tomorrow, since according to my inner clock it will be four hours later than it is. Usually I don't spend nearly this long in a Drop. I am going to put Joyce's clothes back in order and smooth out her dress (I would never have tied a knot in it if she wore a cotton dress, because the wrinkles would show up too much and puzzle her) and I'm going to scoot back to my desk and finish out the day. The good thing is that if she brings me a tape to do later this afternoon, I will be much more relaxed and therefore likable than if I hadn't partially stripped her without her knowledge or consent. I will jest knowingly and winningly with her. I will compliment her on today's scarf—which isn't, honestly, quite as nice as the Cyrillic one. (Maybe when she was getting dressed this morning she put on this knit dress and then remembered that I had admired her scarf, and maybe she thought that wearing it again as well would be too direct a Yes from her; but then again maybe the reason she was wearing the dress this soon again was that she had liked my complimenting her on her scarf and wanted to allude to that compliment indirectly by wearing the same dress with another scarf.) This new one is a Liberty pattern of purply grays and greens, definitely worth smiling at and even acknowledging outright. But I don't want to get into one of those awful running-compliment patterns, where I have to mention her scarves every time she wears one.

The other thing I should say is that under normal circumstances I would probably give serious thought to "poaching an egg" at this point, but because I have written all this, and because this is, I believe, going to be the very beginning of a sort of autobiography, I can't. What a surprise, though, to find this Casio typewriter acting as chaperon! (Maybe what I will do is go ahead, but not mention it.)

2

I WAS BORN WITH A KNOT IN MY UMBILICAL CORD, A SIMPLE pretzel knot. I doubt that this fact of my birth has anything to do with my later chronanisms, but I will put it down here just in case it does. I am proud of having set immediately to work art-nouveauing the functional furnishings of my intrauterine deanery. Somehow I was able to form a loop and then swim right through it. I tied a knot *in myself.* Like many child prodigies, however, I fizzled early. The Fermata, first unfolding itself for me in fourth grade, has been a lifelong distraction. I have wanted to keep it a secret, and as a result it has swallowed up large chunks of my personality. But I hope that will change now.

Once, following a long lull, I found a way to get back into the Fold five or six times after I smashed my head into a parking meter in Philadelphia. I was thirteen or fourteen. We were staying at the Barclay Hotel; as a treat I was allowed to drink some watered-down wine with lunch. I drank more of it than the adults knew and found myself acting wild and flaily on the street during our afternoon walk. I ran ahead, hid between two cars, intending to spring out on everyone. I sprang, shouting, "Boo!" But my mouth and the side of my face met a parking meter that I had forgotten was there. The collision made an enormous bony sound in my head. The meter had only a minute or two left, I noticed, staggering; the red thought-balloon saying EXPIRED was just about to dawn. I saw a pattern of squirming diamonds that would have made very nice Wiener Werkstatte wrapping paper. Twenty minutes later, as the bed made sloppy figure eights around the hotel room (where I had been left to convalesce), I pinched my swollen lip and noticed that all traffic noise stopped. I realized I was in the Fold. I walked downstairs to the motionless hotel bar and back to the kitchen and ate two huge shrimp that a motionless cook or cook's helper held as he arranged a shrimp cocktail. I was amazed at how good the cocktail sauce tasted. I sucked on a piece of lime and threw it out in a can behind the bar. I felt steadied. I went out into the lobby and sat down next to a woman on a couch and smelled the collar of her coat deeply. At first I thought it smelled like pickles, and then I realized that it smelled like cigarette smoke, and I was very surprised to think that pickles and cigarette smoke were allied smells. (Is that what people mean by a "sour" smell?) Then I went back upstairs and pinched my lip again the same way I had, a little to the right of center, until it hurt a lot, to turn the Barclay Hotel and the rest of the planet back on, and I went to sleep. I still feel bad about stealing those shrimp—not only because of the theft, but because the kitchen helper may to this day be troubled by that bit of strangeness all those years ago, when he had held one in each hand and had them suddenly disappear.

There—that was a typical early Drop. I know that I could probably make much better use of my gift than I do. For me it is just a sexual aid. Others might put it to fuller avaricious or intellectual use: government secrets, technological espionage, etc. Surely over the centuries a few individuals have developed this ability and used it to consolidate power or to liquidate enemies. J. S. Bach, for instance, could not have cranked out a cantata a week without some sort of temporal trickery: he was probably seventy-five when he died, not sixty-five, but he had borrowed the last decade of his life and used it up piecemeal in earlier Drops. I was reading Cardano's autobiography not long ago, to see how one is supposed to write one's autobiography (it's harder than I thought!), and I had a suspicion at one point that he had discovered a way into the Fold, but was not going to reveal that fact to us. Something he said about preferring solitude is what alerted me. He said, "I question the right of anyone to waste our time. The wasting of time is an abomination." In my place, some would toggle time and cheat on their Ph.D. orals or simply take money from open cash registers. Cheating and stealing don't tempt me, though.

Or maybe I just think it is wrong to cheat and steal and so don't do it. When I was desperate for money a few years ago and I found a way to drop into the Fold by writing a certain mathematical formula on a scrap of paper, I gave serious thought to walking around the city stealing one dollar from every open cash register. It would have taken me months to amass a few thousand dollars, so I would have worked for my loot in a sense, and I would have been stealing a trifling amount from each business. But I found that there was something horrible about the sensation of pulling a dollar bill that was not mine from under that springy clamp that held it down with its own species. There was misery in it, not excitement. I was behind the glove counter at Filene's trying to steal my very first dollar and I could not do it. Instead, I stood behind the motionless glove salesperson, a woman of twenty or so, very close to her, and squeezed her hard, so that I fancied I could feel the tiny cysts in her breasts as well as the ribs beneath her shirt. (I always find that it is good for me to hug a woman like this because when I feel her ribs I know she is human. Ribs inspire pity and tenderness and the sense that we are all in the same sparred boat.) She was an Italian woman, I think, who looked as if she had taken a few courses in beauty school and had had her natural esthetic sense injured by the experience. She wore a big engagement ring with an oblong diamond. She was a person who would never be physically attracted to a person like me, just as I would never be physically attracted by a person like her. This total incompatibility made me able to feel a surge of momentary sympathy for her which was almost like an infatuation.

I pushed the diamond on her finger back and forth. (Her nails were cut short, but polished—perhaps short because she liked trying on the gloves she sold?) Then I slipped her engagement ring off and looked through it. It said 14k on the inside. On a whim, I knelt and held her hand and slipped the ring gently back on. "Will you?" I said. I had not been aware before that moment of the straightforward erogenousness of a ring: it suddenly occurred to me that the sides of the fingers are sensitive in an upper-thigh sort of way, and that the singling out of that fourth vulnerable shy finger, the planet Neptune of fingers, which otherwise gets no unique treatment in life and does very little on its own except control the C on the high school clarinet or type the number two and the letter X, to be held and gently stimulated forever by an expensive circle of gold is really quite surprisingly sexual. The resistance of this Filene's woman's slender finger-joint, where her skin bunched momentarily before giving way and allowing the band I held to slide home, was in an inverted way like the moment of resistance or dry fumbling before the groom's unpracticed richard moved smoothly in. Getting engaged was thus an obscenity. "If you fingerfuck this ring for me now, darling, I vow that I will fuck you regularly for the rest of your life." That's basically the arrangement. Why does it take me so long to understand such obvious things, things everyone else probably picks up on right away?

Another more pertinent question might be, If I think that it is wrong to steal a dollar bill from an open cash register, and if I feel guilty about stealing two fresh shrimp from a hotel restaurant, why don't I have qualms about hugging an otherwise engaged glove saleswoman at Filene's? She doesn't know me; she doesn't know that I'm hugging her and mock-proposing to her. Do I really think I have the right to hike Joyce's wool dress up around her hips and tie a knot in it? How can I be sure that she would want me to have my fingers in her pubic hair? The question of my wrongdoing is a fair one, but I'm going to table it for the time being and instead sketch in a few more of my early Fold experiences—not because they will explain anything, but because when I try to imagine defending my actions verbally I find that they are indefensible, and I don't want to know that. I honestly do not feel as if I have done anything wrong. I have never deliberately caused anyone anguish. In fact I have with the Fold's help saved a few women from small embarrassments, adjusting the occasional awry slip before an important sales meeting and pushing a vagrant underwire in a bra back in place, that kind of thing. I mean well. But I know that meaning well is not any kind of satisfactory defense.

I first stopped time because I liked my fourth-grade teacher, Miss Dobzhansky, and wanted to see her with fewer clothes on. She might not seem beautiful to me now, but I certainly thought she was beautiful then. Everyone did. She had shorter hair than was usual for elementary-school teachers in 1967, and she was an enthusiast of stop-sign-red lipstick—she must have worn down a stick every fortnight, so full were her lips. She also had one of those wide soft tongues that just naturally like to rest a little way out of the doorstep of the mouth, beyond the teeth. (Not that it lolled!) She always smiled with her mouth open. She wore long, droopy, soft-looking navy-blue cardigan sweaters over sleeveless dresses. I listened to her with great attention as she described the system of locks on a nineteenth-century canal and the Indian technique of manu-facturing a dugout canoe. In sharp contrast to Mrs. Blakey, my talented and demanding third-grade teacher, whose loose arm-flesh flapped around in chaotic rhythms as she wrote on the board, Miss Dobzhansky's chalkboard arm was revealed to be fine and firm, gracefully fitted at the shoulder with a flame-shaped muscle, when in the afternoons she removed her sweater and draped it over the back of her chair.

I didn't feel lust for her, really. In fact, that word, *lust,* is too abstract and intransitive and preacherly to apply even now to my feelings for Miss Dobzhansky or any other woman. I never "lust for" or "after" a woman. I want to do specific things: have dinner with, make smile, hold hips of. I didn't even, in the beginning, imagine that I wanted to see Miss Dobzhansky in a state of undress. What first made me want to stop time was that after Christmas break she changed the original seating arrangement of the class. I had been in front and now I was all the way in the back. A kid who wrote words backward sat at my old desk. I understood her reasons, but still I was a little hurt. And I noticed then that I couldn't see the chalkboard as well as I had.

It was not a question of my being unable to read the words or decipher the figures. It was merely that I could no longer tell at a glance, as I had been able to in my former seat, whether Miss Dobzhansky was using a piece of newly broken chalk with a sharp edge that sometimes briefly left a faint second parallel line, or whether she was holding a more rounded piece that she had used before. I wanted to know exactly what was going on on the surface of the chalkboard—I felt I was missing out on the physical reality of her writing, as opposed to what it meant. When I was in front, I had been able to monitor the chalky ghost of a word she had several times erased; now that was almost always impossible. Two other kids had already gotten glasses, and I knew that glasses would help me a little, but what I really wanted to do was to stop the whole class, the whole school, the whole school district, for a few minutes whenever I needed to walk up to the board and inspect its surface at very close range.

My big Christmas present that year was a figure-eight race-track and one blue and one brown race car that drove around it and occasionally flipped off. I played with it for a week or two. The problem with it was that there weren't enough segments of track to make an asymmetrical race-course, and I strongly preferred asymmetry in race-courses. Soon the track got dusty and the cars began to halt suddenly when their bushings lost contact. I pushed it under my bed and thought instead about meat thermometers and toads who can hibernate for years in dried desert mud.

But after Miss Dobzhansky had moved me to the back of the class, I woke up in the middle of the night and let my arm drop to the floor between the bed and the wall. I was in the habit of doing this fairly often; I did it to prove to myself how nonchalant I was, how certain I was that there were no crustaceans under the bed. This time, though, my hand brushed against something warm. It was the transformer for the racetrack. It was still plugged in, still on, still transforming. I got out of bed and pulled the track out. The transformer had a red faceted light that glowed faintly. It also had a chrome toggle switch. I turned on the light in my room, so that I could see better, and held the transformer. It was very heavy, with rounded corners, and it had a finish that seemed to have been made by dipping it in thick black paint and then blasting it with hot air so that the paint formed a texture of tiny wrinkles. It had a silver UL label on the underside. "Underwriters Laboratories"—a racy, vaguely underwearish name. The hum that the transformer made was almost inaudible. I touched the toggle switch, then flipped it off, and suddenly I knew that this was the machine I needed, and that the next time I turned the transformer back on, it would stop everything.

I smuggled it and an extension cord into class in my lunch box. I did nothing with it all morning. As the rest of the students were lining up for lunch, when Miss Dobzhansky stood halfway out the door, I hastily plugged the extension cord into the outlet under the long table against the back wall, which was only a few feet from my chair, and hid the transformer in my desk. Over lunch, though I was quite keyed up, I gave nothing away. I casually discussed with my friend Tim what it would be like to be an agitator BB ball in a can of green spray paint, as if it were an ordinary day. We agreed that it would be fun to dig into the pigment at the bottom of the spray can and then fly up through the pressurized froth and clack around—better perhaps than descending in a spherical space vehicle into the chemical storms on Saturn. Tim contended that there were sometimes two agitator BBs in a single can of spray paint, and I disagreed, arguing that it only sounded as if there were two when you shook it fast.

I had not expected anyone to notice the cord leading into my desk, since I was in the back corner, and nobody in fact did. I let half an hour go by, watching Miss Dobzhansky discuss a kind of slitted sunglasses that the Eskimos whittled from bone to avoid snow blindness. She began to write the old spelling of *Eskimo*, with a *q*, on the board in white chalk. My hands were deep in my desk; my fingertips touched the wrinkle-finish black paint and the smooth toggle switch. As she embarked on the letter *m*, her back to the class, I flipped the switch. She didn't finish the *m*. She and the class were without sound or motion.

I said, "Hey." I said "Hey" again. Nobody turned toward me. Far from being eerie or disturbing, the silence was, I found, quite comfy. This acoustical coziness, which is a consistent feature of the Fold, is the result, I think, of the relative sluggishness of the air molecules that surround me. Sound diffuses outward only a few feet, as far as I can tell. I'm often reminded of a line in the first stanza of Keats's "Eve of St. Agnes": "And silent was the flock in woolly fold." My Fold *is* woolly.

Presently ("presently" is right!) I flipped the toggle back to the off position, deactivating the machine. At once everyone and everything took up where they had left off. The world expanded, sounding once again as if it were recorded in stereo. Miss Dobzhansky finished writing *Esquimaux*. She gave no indication that she was aware that anything out of the ordinary had just happened; and as far as she was concerned, of course, nothing had happened. She turned toward us and began talking about a thin strip of land that she claimed had once joined Alaska and Asia, over which tribes had traveled, giving rise not only to the Eskimo, but to the American Indians of the lower states. I must have been looking at her with an expression of unusual attentiveness, or even of rapture, because her gaze landed on me and she smiled. I knew we had a special understanding. I knew also that she might be the most beautiful person I would ever know. 1 knew that she knew that I sometimes didn't raise my hand to give answers to the questions she asked even when I knew the answers, because I wanted to give her the option of drawing out other kids, of calling on me only when she needed to, as a backup. Her explanation of the waves of Asian migrations across the Bering Strait interested me, so I let her finish before stopping the universe for a second time. As soon as she turned toward the blackboard again, to write *Bering*, I flipped the switch and took off all my clothes.

The air is quite close in the Fold and takes a little getting used to, although as long as you wave your arms around every so often there is no real risk of asphyxiation. I was very conscious of my breathing as I walked up the row of desks and chairs, naked, and reached my lovely teacher. "Miss Dobzhansky?" I said, standing right behind her, though I knew that she couldn't hear me. My plan, as I had conceived it in a flash when she had smiled at me a moment before, was to take off all her clothes and then sit back down at my desk and click time back on—that is, turn the time transformer off.

When she felt the cooler air on her skin and discovered that she was entirely nude, she would turn toward us, confused and startled, but not really flustered, since I had never seen her flustered—her serenity and ability to adjust to any eventuality in the classroom was an important part of what made her so lovely to me—and she would meet this challenge with her usual aplomb. She would turn toward us with her hands shielding her breasts and look inquiringly at our faces, as if to say, "How, class, has this happened?" Her eyes would seek out mine, because she knew she could trust me to help her through difficult moments, and I would look back at her with an ardent, loving, serious expression. I would stand and shush anyone who dared to snicker at the fact that both I and Miss Dobzhansky were completely naked, and I would walk up to her and nod at her as if to say, "Everything will be all right, Miss Dobzhansky," and collect her sweater and her dress, which I would have left neatly folded on her desk. She would say, "Thank you, Arno," in a voice that communicated how grateful she was that I was in her life and was able to help her through this moment. She and I would retire to the cloak-room for a few minutes, where I would hand her her clothes one by one as she got dressed. She would do the same for me. When we re-emerged, I would take my seat and she would continue her social studies lesson. The class, docile with shock, would have remained silent through our whole absence.

That was my plan, but I soon found that I had to modify it. Miss Dobzhansky was wearing her navy-blue droopy sweater and a simple white shirt buttoned at the top with a blue enamel Saturn pin covering the top button. The sweater was already unbuttoned, so I left it alone. But when I reached up to undo the enamel pin (or "brooch" I guess they are called)

I felt that this was not something I wanted to do at all. What if, once I got her totally naked, I chickened out and didn't want to proceed? Would I be able to pin the pin back in place precisely as it had been? I worried about possibly breaking its little catch, or putting it on crooked. If it wasn't replaced exactly right, she would sense a sudden slight displacement at her neck when I turned the classroom back on and she would suspect something, and because of my recent look of rapture she might connect me with her odd sensation, and if she asked me directly, I didn't think I could lie to her and tell her that I had had nothing to do with it.

By this time I was standing between her and the blackboard, very close to her. Her breasts were my horizon line. I decided that I could at least safely undo several of the middle buttons of her shirt to see what all was underneath. In the cottony silence of the idled universe, I undid two buttons. My fingers trembled, of course. And even now, twenty-five years later, my fingers sometimes tremble when I watch them at work undoing a row of a woman's shirt buttons, especially when her shirt is loose, so that once you have finished unbuttoning it no more is revealed to you than when you began, and, as a separate deliberate act, you have to part the still-overlapping sides of the shirt with the backs of your hands like a set of curtains. I peered into the oval world I had just created. What I could see of her bra was very interesting. It had little X's sewn along the borders of the two side-pieces that attached to the round bosom-holding parts, and the bosom-holding parts had perfectly sewn seams running diagonally up over their curves, like a napping cat's closed eyes. I reached up and pushed gently on one of her bosoms with the palm of my hand. (I called them "bosoms" then, and really it isn't such a bad word for them.) The shape was unexpectedly soft and quite warm. I unbuttoned another lower button so that I could now comfortably surround my whole head with her shirt. Her skin glowed in the shadowy cloth-diffused light. I felt like a daguerreotypist, crouching and covering my head with a camera cloth to see my subject more completely. I saw her stomach, which was extensive at this close range. In the middle of it was her belly-button.

This I hadn't reckoned on. It was the big moment. I had never seen anything so womanly, so grown-up-looking, at such close range, in my life. Miss Dobzhansky's belly-button did not look like a child's belly-button at all. There was a sort of stretched proscenium of skin over the top, a bell curve, similar in a way to the epicanthic eye-fold on Asian people (like Esquimaux), whereas the slope below led the eye right into a little private sanctum elegantly cupping something that looked like a tiny piece of used chewing gum or the knotted part of a balloon. What was impressive was simply how wise and experienced it looked, how profoundly *oval* it was. I passed my knuckles lightly over it, awestruck. Then I emerged from her shirt for a second to get a rounded piece of blue chalk, which I gently twirled in it, as if I were chalking up a pool stick, except the other way around. I left only the most imperceptibly small trace of chalk dust, brushing the excess away. Feeling by then that I had had more than enough for one afternoon, I buttoned her shirt back up. As an after-thought, I replaced the white piece of chalk that she was holding as she wrote the word *Bering* with the piece of blue chalk that I had used on her. Then I went back to my seat, put my clothes back on, arranged myself so that I was sitting exactly as I had been, and turned the time transformer off. Its chrome switch was almost painfully hot to the touch.

The class came alive. The blue chalk broke—perhaps I hadn't put it in her fingers properly. Miss Dobzhansky looked at it for a second, puzzled, and then she picked up a piece of white chalk and went on writing. "Once these tribes got to Alaska, they had to decide whether to settle there or keep going . . ." she said, and she continued the lesson. There was a faint smell of something burning. I tugged surreptitiously on the extension cord until its plug dropped out of the wall socket; I drew it little by little into my desk. I noticed, glancing down casually as if to pull my chair up, that the blades of the plug were a dull carbon black.

And that was exactly how it went the first day. Nothing bad happened. All went well. I left the transformer in my desk overnight, and I tried it again the following morning, with big plans, but unfortunately this time, as soon as I flipped the switch, the fluorescent lights in the ceiling fluttered and went out. There was an even stronger smell of burning. Miss Dobzhansky sent for the custodian. Time flowed on without interruption. After school, I carried the ruined transformer home in my lunch box. It was totally wrecked. The red jeweled light was partially melted, and there were whitish heat marks around the lower edge of the unit. Just to be sure, I plugged it in in my room one last time after dinner and flipped the switch, but I got no response. The cat continued to lick between the pads of her paws. The traffic lights at the corner colored segments of the big double icicle outside my window red, then green, then orange. It was over. I had only been able to pause the universe twice, for a total of maybe six minutes.

On the other hand, even six timeless minutes was pretty good. I adjusted remarkably quickly to the idea that I had seen as much of Miss Dobzhansky as I was probably ever going to see. My next task, to which I devoted the ensuing spring and summer months, was to develop an alternate, non-electrical way into the Fold. I explored a number of experimental possibilities, courting the unnatural. I sprayed some new mock-orange leaves with green spray paint to see whether they would become permanent fakes, since I had always found the notion of bronzed baby shoes mysterious and suggestive. I grafted a very fast-growing thistle to our magnolia tree, wrapping the conjoined wounds with heavy-duty thread, theorizing that the mingling of incompatible growth hormones might have chronoactive effects. I heated six marbles on a baking sheet in a slow oven and then spooned them one by one into a glass of ice water which I held quite close to my eye. Into the glass I had first placed a fossil crinoid and a snip of my fingernail. (Now that I think of it, the sound of my ex-girlfriend Rhody using a fingernail trimmer in the morning in the bathroom, the extremely brief and high-pitched chirping sound of the smiling snipper blades meeting after they had snapped through her nail, which I listened to in bed as some listen to real birdsong, is one of the most satisfying memories that I possess of that relationship.) I fully expected time to stop at the moment the interior of each hissing marble suddenly crazed itself with decorative cracks, but it didn't. I used the butane torch my father had bought for a refinishing project to heat a notched stainless-steel serving spoon until it turned a deep orange. Though it looked soft and slightly swollen, its edges rounded like the edges of a stick of butter, I could not get the spoon to melt. Then I put a small oval pebble in the same spoon and played the torch flame over it, hoping for some lava. The pebble exploded with a snap, sending a stinging fragment of rock into my T-shirt. All of these experiments, and many others I performed during that period, were inconclusive and, frankly, disappointing. It wasn't until the summer after fifth grade that I was once again able to Drop in, with the help of our basement washing machine and some thread.

3

MANY TEMPS DON'T LIKE DOING TAPES; I DO. NATURALLY
I like transcribing some tapes better than others. In the early
eighties I worked in the office of the head of a big company—
well, why should I suppress the name?—in the office of An-
drew Fleury, the head of Noptica. He had a three-person WP
staff who did nothing but type his gigantic output of correspondence, speeches, interviews, Q-and-A sessions at stock-
holder meetings, and so on. I think he must have had political
ambitions even then. I worked there several times. One long
tape of his that I did included a letter ordering a case of some
rare sort of Armagnac from a local liquor wholesaler. (It was
a personal letter, let me say.) I didn't know what Armagnac

was, and, guessing, I typed *Armaniac.* Discovering this, Fleury flew into a rage. I heard him laying into one of the two co-office managers—"Paula, tell me what is wrong with this paragraph!" The letter was returned to me with the following marginal scholium: "An alcoholic beverage, not a crazy Armenian!! Don't guess, look it up!!" Well, maybe he was right—I should have looked it up. But once Fleury caught the error, he could have at least passed on the fact that the word had a *g* in it. I lost five minutes flipping around in a dictionary. Most of the time, though, salaried people expect so little from temps that any slight awareness of a letter or memo's context or intent fills them with joy, and they are as a result very easy to work for.

But why is it that I so like typing tapes? I've seen word-processing operators throw their headsets down after several hours of transcribing, shouting, "I hate doing this!" Yet I even liked typing Fleury's tapes. For one thing, I like that I'm fairly good at it—I can, for instance, often engage in a little parallel processing, typing the sentence that just passed while listening to and storing the phrase that I'm currently hearing: I enjoy seeing how long I can go without resorting to the rewind half of the foot-pedal. But mainly I prefer doing tapes to typing handwritten documents simply because you can hear the dictator thinking. You can hear him groping for the conventional formula that will cover a slightly unusual case. You can occasionally hear undertones of irritation or affection. It is a great privilege to be present when a person slowly puts his thoughts into words, phrase by phrase, doing the best he can. Because you are traveling right along with him as he forms his sentences, making each word he says appear as a little clump of letters on your screen, you begin to feel as if you are doing the thinking yourself; you occupy some dark space in the interior of his mind as he goes about his job.

It isn't difficult to imagine an erotic aspect to all this. Sandi, a temp I discussed the subject with a year ago or so, told me she once developed an intense thing for a man she transcribed for. He was in personnel, and his job was to advise employees and retired employees on the best way to handle their pensions. He talked very slowly, she said, in an almost dreamy but loud low voice, with long bold pauses. She said he sounded a little like David Bowie in "China Girl." He very seldom resorted to the pause switch on his machine; he just let the tape run. And he talked a great deal in his letters about "invading the annuity." "If your husband predeceases you, Mrs. Plochman," he would say in a letter, "and you elect to invade the annuity . . ." "If, on the other hand, you both invade the annuity now . . ." So often repeated, this particular actuarial idiom began, as a result, to take on a special meaning for her. As she typed it, it was as if she were handling what he was saying, consenting to it, letting it run scarf-like through her fingers. "Please do," she felt she was whispering back to him by typing exactly what he spoke into her headset, "please do invade my annuity." They never did anything sexual, though.

In my own case, I often get thoroughly hypnotized by the tapes of women dictators. Women litigators, especially: when they say things like "Although there are no hornbook rules," my breathing elevates. And I already mentioned the strange thrill I felt when I heard in a credit update Joyce quote someone as saying that someone else "lied like hell." Gerard Manley Hopkins somewhere describes how he mesmerized a duck by drawing a line of chalk out in front of it. Think of me as the duck; the chalk, softly wearing itself away against the tiny pebbles embedded in the corporate concrete, is Joyce's forward-luring rough-smooth voice on the cassettes she gives me. Or, to substitute another image, since one is hardly sufficient in Joyce's case, when I let myself really enter her tape, when I let it surround me, it is as if I'm sunk into the pond of what she is saying, as if I'm some kind of patient, cruising amphibian, drifting in black water, entirely submerged except for my eyes, which blink every so often. Each word comes floating up to me like a thick, healthy lily pad and brushes past my head. And sometimes, especially if Joyce kindly lets me hear her hesitate (rather than clicking her recorder off to hide the length of her hesitation, I mean), the stretch of black still water between the intermittent green floating words can momentarily expand into infinitude. All the lily pads withdraw themselves from me. At those times I become amazed by the power I have: the power to lift my foot off the transcriber pedal at will and halt that sentence of hers right *there* for as long as I want in order to think about just where I am in it, and about what it can mean that this living, feeling creature is spending five days a week saying such things into a tape recorder, and about what her mouth looks like as she says them. I pause within her pause and float in the sensory-deprived lagoon of her suspended meaning. What is especially nice, in this state of "deep transcription," as I call it, is to look up and discover that cheerful, unmysterious Joyce herself is walking briskly somewhere, perhaps toward my desk, wiggling a pen in her fingers.

So there is, without a doubt, a strong chronanistic element to my doing of tapes. It may even be that if I hadn't spent so large a portion of the last ten years of my life transcribing words, starting and stopping so many thousands and thousands of modest human sentences-in-progress with my foot-pedal, I would have long ago lost the ability to drop into the Fold altogether. The daily regimen of microcassettes has kept me unusually sensitive, perhaps, to the editability of the temporal continuum—to the fact that an apparently seamless vocalization may actually elide, glide over, hide whole self-contained vugs of hidden activity or distraction—sneezes, expletives, spilled coffee, sexual adventures—within. "The mind is a lyric cry in the midst of business," says George Santayana, whose autobiography (volume one) I got out of the Boston Public Library yesterday; and it occurs to me that this aphorism illuminates the peculiar suggestiveness of the microcassette, and of all audiocassettes, in fact: these stocky, solid, paragraph-shaped material objects, held together with minuscule Phillips-head screws at each corner (the screws are smaller, incidentally, than the screws in the hinges of my glasses, so small that only SCARA robots could have twirled them in place in such quantity), with their pair of unfixed center sprockets left deliberately loose so that they can comply with slight variations in the spindle distances of different brands of machine—these chunky pieces of geometrical business within which, nonetheless, an elfin wisp of Mylar frisks around any tiny struts or blocks of felt placed in its path, minnowing the ferromagnetic after-sparkle of a voiced personality through whatever Baroque diagonals and Bezier curves it can contort from the givens of its prison.

This said, the surprising thing really is how little luck I have had using the foot-pedal of my tape-transcription machine to trigger a true Drop. I have thus far been unable to stop the universe using it, or using the remote-control PAUSE buttons of VCRs or CD players, which would seem obvious actuators. I had, as I mentioned, only a brief success in college with a garage-door opener. It may be that to engage time effectively and stop it cold, a mechanism has to have some quality that links it uniquely with me, with my own emotional life, which is why, for example, the toggle-switch transformer for my race-track only worked as a chronoclutch after my fallen hand brushed against it, discovering its warmth, in the middle of the night. This could also explain why the general trend in my Fold-actuators, with a few important exceptions, has been away from hardware and toward simpler, purely bodily spurs like a finger-snap or the pushing up of my glasses on my nose.

The most elaborate piece of fermational equipment I ever developed was a custom-made piece of machinery I called a Solonoid (with three o's). I had it built for me by an MIT undergraduate four or five years ago. I still have it, though it stopped working after a week of Fold-hours. It is very bulky and it made a loud chuffing noise when it was idling, although I'm sure it could be miniaturized and redesigned for quietness. All it did was stretch and unstretch three rubber bands oriented in the x, y, and z directions. I was able to tune the oscillatory frequency of each rubber band by pushing a rheostat on a small mixing board. I had it built simply because I knew one morning, just after I awoke, after many dry Fold-free months, that this design would work. My uncle loaned me fifteen hundred dollars (I told him that it was to take several months off from temping and see if I could get interested in my master's thesis again), and I put an ad in the MIT student newspaper and interviewed a number of students. I chose the sole woman respondent, naturally.

She used three small motors. I told her that I was a post-doc in philosophy working on a monograph about a turn-of-the-century American metaphysician named Matthias Batchelder, who had postulated that three India-rubber bands, when alternately stretched and slackened at a particular frequency in the three Cartesian planes, would insert null placeholders into the stream of Becoming, effectively pausing the universe for all but the operator of the mechanism. Though Batchelder had written to G. E. Moore, C. S. Pierce, and A. A. Michelson about his ideas, I said (scrambling for plausibility), nobody had exhibited the slightest interest, partly because he lacked institutional affiliation, and partly because he had an off-puttingly contentious personal manner. (I should stress that there was no metaphysician by the name of Batchelder—the rough design for the machine had simply come to me one morning—but for the sake of secrecy I needed to distance myself from it. I "lied like hell" to this young mechanical engineer—I had to, I'm sorry.) She—I'm ashamed to say that I've forgotten her name—built the machine in short order, and she did a very nice job of explaining its finer points to me, though I have forgotten them. To keep costs down, she was kind enough to use "takeout" parts ordered through the Jerryco catalog—that is, motors removed from used equipment, copiers and such. "Well, I got it to do what you said you wanted it to do," she said, in her serious way, as we stood in one of the mechanical-engineering labs (she was getting course credit for this project, it turned out, although she had hidden that fact from me), "but I've played with the frequencies and I can't get it to do anything. The rubber bands look kind of neat when they really get going, though."

I sat down in front of it. It was ludicrously bulky, definitely not portable. "You mean it doesn't pause the universe?" I said, chuckling with mock incredulity to indicate that I knew full well that Batchelder's ideas were a crock, and that I had gone through this whole exercise only out of kindness, merely to give this forgotten eccentric a belated chance to prove himself. "Well, I suppose I should try it myself anyway, for the old man's sake," I said. She pointed out the on/off switch, which I threw; I took a moment to adjust the stretching frequencies. (The rubber bands were chosen by me at random from a forty-nine-cent bag of Alliance rubber bands, PROUD TO SAY MADE IN USA.) As soon as I got the ratios right (by ear), the lab, the woman, Cambridge, and everything else, with the exception of me and the jouncing Solonoid, promptly went into suspension. I crawled behind the engineer and kissed the beautifully defined H shapes at the back of her thick knees, which are often the best feature on college women (she wore a jean skirt), and then took my place at the controls again and cut the power to the Solonoid.

"See?" she said. "Nothing." We shook our heads sadly, pitying poor deluded Matthias Batchelder, and I wrote her out a check for the full fifteen hundred and thanked her. (I keep my canceled checks; I must remember to go back and find out this young woman's name.) She asked if she could possibly have a copy of some of Batchelder's metaphysical writings, and I told her that for estate reasons I wasn't allowed to give anything out, but that I would definitely send her a reprint of my monograph when it appeared. That satisfied her. And for a few weeks after that, until my supply from that first bag of bands ran out, I was able to do a fair number of intricately filthy Foldy things. The nice unforeseen quality of that machine, now that I think of it, was that it had a high degree of risk associated with it, since a rubber band could snap suddenly, without warning, causing time to resume and potentially exposing me at a very awkward moment—the sex-in-public-places risk. But I was careful. Eventually I incorporated some redundancy into the design by stretching two rubber bands in each direction rather than one, even though it meant I ran out quicker.

This problem of remembering names, which just came up in connection with the MIT woman, is a particularly acute one for the career temp. I may work as many as forty different assignments in a given year—some for a week or two, some for a few days. At each assignment, there are typically three to five names to learn the first day (and occasionally many more); ten or more the second day. Depending on how heavy the phone action is, the number of names I end up finally mastering per job can go considerably over one hundred. Per year, I am being exposed to roughly three thousand names, of which (scaling back again) perhaps five hundred belong to individuals I get to know a little, talk to, work fairly closely with. Over ten years, that makes five thousand personalities, about each one of whom I must develop a little packet of emotion, a liking, a disliking, a theory about their feelings for some colleague, a mental note about their taste in clothes, a memory of how they like things done, whether they are of the opinion that state names ought to be spelled out in full or given the two-letter abbreviation, whether they like the document name or number included on the letter or think that this is a vulgarity, whether they want me to amuse myself when I've caught up with my work or prefer that I come bounding into their office asking for more to do. In college I was impressed by how well some very popular professors kept up with the particulars of their students' lives—but the fact is that I master just as much raw humanity each year as the most hotshot celebrity professor. And the difference is that in my lowly case, all these people, or most of them, continue to work downtown, just as I do. They aren't going to graduate and go away.

What this means, practically speaking, is that every few days I will almost certainly run into someone with whom I have worked closely at some company at some time in the past. And I will want so much to remember his or her name! They usually remember my name, and in some cases I can detect a faint hurt look in their eyes when they perceive, through my

joshing and bluster, that I don't remember theirs, since together we did work very hard and beat impossible deadlines
and joke around only six months ago, or a year and a half ago,
or five years ago. And—they and I both secretly think—they
were higher-ranking than I was, they were salaried, I was a
temp, so it is a duty in keeping with my subordinate station to
remember their names, while it is only noblesse oblige for
them to remember mine.

Yet if they took a moment to do the arithmetic of my work
life versus their work life, as I have, they would perhaps understand and absolve, for they see the same people every day,
their universe of clients and contacts and colleagues is relatively confined and stable, so that a new temp like me in their
office is a novelty, a topic of conversation, a person to whom
they can "give a leg up," an outsider in whom they can con-
fide hatreds and old wounds. I stick in their mind because they
are pleased that they were able to put aside class differences
and treat me as an equal. "Arno, hi!" And there I am, standing in front of Park Street Station, unable to reciprocate
properly, feeling like a waiter asked to remember an order
from a table he served months before.

The name problem is compounded by the fact that there is
apparently some vulnerability in my countenance that signals
to lost people that I should be approached for directions. I
have gotten good at sensing the lost now as they look over a
crowdlet of potential help at a stop sign: they spot me, and
though I'm wearing a tie like the other men, they seem to
smell that I'm a temp and must therefore be permanently
lonely and lowly, a sick caribou that the wolf singles out for
attention; they know that they will feel at ease with me about
admitting to being a stranger because I am going to welcome
any human contact, any indication that I'm established and

not transient. I go through periods when I am asked three times a day for directions. And these lost people are right—I do like being interrupted on the street, especially by women, but by men, too. I am poor at retaining street names, however, even streets that hold buildings in which I've worked in the past. For a while I deliberately studied maps of the business district in the evening, counting traffic lights and memorizing cross streets and helpful landmarks, so that I would live up to the expectations of unintimidating guidance that my face and features seem to create. (I find that the response is especially heavy if I am carrying some bulky item, like a bunch of flowers or a Wang VS backup disk.) As a result, I never know if the person coming toward me on the sidewalk and seeking eye contact is someone I worked with at Gillette or Kendall or Ropes & Gray or Polaroid or MassBank or Arthur Young, or whether he or she just needs to know how to get to Milk Street.

During the periods when I have full Fold-powers, however, these difficulties are easily solved. As soon as I hear an "Arno, hi!" I can do a Drop and check wallet or purse ID and then greet whoever it is properly. It makes such a difference. I don't feel cringey and can lose myself in the pleasure of the reunion: for I really do like most of the people I have worked with over the years; almost all of them have some lovable feature. And if someone asks me how to get to a place that I should know perfectly well how to get to and don't, I can freeze his inquiring expression and check a map. (I carry one in my briefcase, as well as my old bottle of contact-lens solution, in case someone finds herself in ocular distress.) Of course, I could pull out the map while he looks on, but I hate to see that shifty, clouded look come into his eyes as he thinks to himself, This guy doesn't have a clue—I should have asked one of the others. Also, when I pull out a map to help a tourist, especially an Asian tourist, I inevitably end up giving it to him, because impulsive generosity is such a high—and those maps are ridiculously expensive.

I'm not being quite fair to myself, then, when I say that the Fold is just a sexual aid. It is primarily that—my Fold-energies seem to be a direct by-product of my appetite for nakedness. I doubt that I would have wormed my way into the Fermata even once if I had not been motivated primarily by the desire to take women's clothes off. But I don't want to ignore or depreciate the range of nonsexual uses that I have put it to. I have, for example, relied on it for things like last-minute Christmas shopping; it's nice to browse in utter silence. When I'm irritable at work, and I know that the people around me don't deserve my misanthropy, I can stop them all until I'm fond of them again. If someone makes a revealing comment in passing, I can take time out to think about its hidden implications and check the expressions of others who have heard it, all while I'm right there and it is fresh in my mind.

I also use the Fold when I'm called on to come up with something especially understanding or sympathetic in a conversation and I want to be sure that my tact is exactly on key—although there is a serious risk in mulling over your kindness for any longer than fifteen or twenty seconds, because as you weigh and polish your response you can quickly lose your working sense of the immediate emotional flux. I've nearly derailed one or two important heart-to-heart talks by pausing so long to hone my tone that when I was finally ready to re-enter time I knew that I was going to be brittle and foolish and insincere, exactly what I'd Dropped out to avoid, and I had a very hard time working myself back around to the mood that had made the conversation seem important enough for me to have wanted to interrupt it in the first place.

Nonetheless, used sparingly, the Fold can really help with commiseration.

It is an obvious escape, too—though here again, I have learned to use it sparingly. I was given a temp assignment at the alumni office of a graduate school, where I was asked to roll up posters and stuff them in mailing tubes. I did this for four straight days. I would not have minded if the posters had not been so ugly. On the second day, I found it difficult to entertain the notion of rolling up one more purple-and-black poster—the waste of glossy paper, of post office energy, of university money, seemed too awful—and so I hit the clutch and took two non-hours to read some of Diana Crane's *The Transformation of the Avant-Garde*. In that case it helped a lot: the book was better, more licentiously toothsome, for being read *en Folde*. But there have been other times when, once I have lapsed into the timelessness of the arrested instant, the particular obligation or person from whom I have temporarily freed myself becomes more and more horrific, posed in its or his stalled imminence, and the idea that I will have to take up right where I have left off becomes unbearable, and I re-enter time's cattle-drive with a sense of defeat and unhappiness more acute than any I felt before I had ducked, or copped, out.

I think, too, that it is exceedingly dangerous to Drop when you are in any sort of depression about how bad the world is. A Fold then can deepen infinitely—since in a way you are now in control over whether all the world's continuing atrocities and tragedies should resume or not. You know that as soon as you give the go-ahead to time again, pets will not be given enough water, feelings will be needlessly hurt, killings, crashes, miscarriages of justice, bureaucratic harassment, infidelity, artistic disappointments, and worse will all go forward, and you begin to think that you will be in a sense their cause, you will be directly responsible for them, since you have a choice whether to let them happen, by opting to restart time or not. When I am in a Fold, I know for a fact that no woman anywhere is crying or feeling betrayed, and since I want above all for women not to cry, I can begin to believe, irrationally, that it is my duty to live out my entire life in this artificial solitude, eating canned foods. "He died suddenly," they would say on discovering my abruptly aged body. But when I died, all the misery-in-progress that I had so heroically held at bay for forty-odd years would resume anyway. I don't have any power to alter the fact that evils will do their work, only how "soon" they will. As a consequence, I have determined that my Foldouts should in general be short, recreational, and masturbatory, rather than deep and pained.

I should mention here, though, under the heading of nonsexual uses of the Fermata, one of my least attractive episodes. Three black kids, age eighteen or so, stopped me one afternoon and asked which way the Boston Common was, and when I put on my usual "Yes, I'd be delighted to help you find your way, and I will of course be discreet about your sketchy knowledge of this area of the city, and when you walk away you will be cheered by the conviction that you did the right thing asking me and not those other, less amiable people for directions" face, one of the kids placed a gun to my jaw (this was near the medical center downtown), and asked me to give him my wallet and watch. I timed out by pushing on the lead-advance button of my mechanical pencil (in my back pocket), and took the gun out of play. I was trembling, outraged that these kids would feel entitled to my wallet and watch and were willing to threaten me with death to get them. I was put in mind of the old jokey way of teaching genuflection: "Spectacles, testicles, wallet, watch." So I got some wire from the back of a New England Telephone truck that was parked nearby and tied all three of them by the balls to a nearby stop sign. It is a somewhat disorienting experience to be calmly winding telephone wire around the testicle-sack of a person who has just been in the process of mugging you. I taped their dicks up temporarily so that they wouldn't annoy me by hanging in my way while I wound. (Two were uncircumcised.) When all three of them were fully secured to the stop sign, the three wires exiting the backs of their pants through holes I had snipped with wire cutters, I stood back a few paces, turned time on, and, with pathetic bravado, said, "Come and get me, you little fucks!" Startled, they sized up the situation for a second, then lunged after me and fell forward at once, swearing with pain. I loped off, feeling increasingly remorseful, not to mention relieved that I hadn't in the first flush of my vengefulness cut off their balls altogether and dragged them to the emergency room; an option, I am ashamed to say, that I had briefly considered. (Can one bleed to death from castration? Probably. And it was doubtful they had medical insurance.) After that unsettling experience I spent an "afternoon" performing acts of lite altruism, wandering in the Fold through crummy neighborhoods collecting concealed handguns off anyone who looked under thirty, but the frisking was tiring and distasteful work, and I stopped after I had only forty-four weapons in my commandeered shopping cart, with the sense that I had done nothing of real value, and had possibly even destabilized a momentarily tranquil street scene. (Still under cover of the Fermata, I pushed the weapons into some newly poured cement at a construction site.)

4

B UT—I DO LIKE TRANSCRIBING MICROCASSETTES. I MENTION
this because only a few days after I wrote that very first *sur le
vif* chunk about Joyce's exuberant pubic hair, I was immersed
in one of her tapes, dog-paddling along in the moonlit scum-
less lily pond of her consciousness, my eyes fixed on the green
letters that she called forth from my fingertips, when I glanced
up to see her walking briskly toward me, wiggling a pen and
looking to one side as if preoccupied. I made a move to take
off my headphones, but she held up her palms, indicating
that I should continue transcribing, evidently feeling a twinge
of the guilt which considerate people often feel when they
drop off an unusual amount of work for a temp to do in a

short interval of time. Obedient, I kept on transcribing. "Subject indicated that high credit was in the low six figures," etc. Joyce meanwhile wrote something on a scrap of paper and affixed it with one of the rubber bands from my rubber-band tray to the cassette and put it on top of my monitor. It said, "No rush, thanks." I nodded, making my mouth into a downward U of conspiratorial assent. I didn't tell her that I was typing her own earlier tape. I let her walk away. And the sight of her diminishing figure, while at the same time her voice talked so tiredly and yet evenly in my ear of high credit and low credit (this bank job was beneath her, surely), made my interest in her, my love for her, flare up. I loved her, for instance, for not writing "Thanx" on her note and not using an exclamation point. I watched her go back to her desk and sit down and pull in her chair and pick up the phone. *She was a woman.* Though I'm thirty-five, as I seem to want to point out on every page, I am often surprised by the simple observation that there *are* women, that they wear rustly layers of clothing, that they have lips and teeth which on occasion they employ to smile at me. They take their existence for granted, but I don't, by any means. I think, too, in all modesty, that I have an unusually good instinct for detecting when an average-looking woman senses herself entering a new phase of attractiveness. I can detect better than others when a woman feels that she is looking unusually good that day, or when something like a new haircut, or the discovery of a store that has the kind of clothes that she looks best in, reminds her of the fact that romance and flirtation are part of life, too. Joyce is perhaps not, objectively considered, stunning, though she is pretty—but these happen to be, I think, miracle weeks for her, as she learns to her surprise how she can be beautiful in a thirty-year-old rather than a twenty-three-year-old sort of way. The French braid is part of it. I doubt very much that anyone at work has said that to her—"You are entering a new phase of beauty, Joyce"—but some of them must have noticed it, too.

Joyce had been eating something—yogurt, probably—as she dictated. Normally I am not fond of this practice. But when she said the word "unplanned" and I heard one of those odd palatal moments, most often associated with yogurt, in which the tone of her voice changed suddenly, went nasal on me, I simply could not believe I was this close to her. My head was practically in her mouth! I had a great deal of work left to do, though, so I snapped time off in order to have a few minutes of freedom to think about what I might do with Joyce if I switched off time in a big way. (I often do this: I Drop just to itemize all the neat things I could do if I did Drop right at that moment.) I could stay in the Fold for several years, mastering carpentry and other building trades, and construct an entire alternate city for her, a city with irregular spires and elevated walkways, where I would transport her, and then, turning time back on, I would wait in one of the deserted buildings I had built until she discovered me, and I would profess total bewilderment at how we had gotten there and why we had been left to fend for ourselves, and eventually she would get desperate and we would fuck sitting up at twilight, looking into each other's eyes, in the middle of a cobblestone street, each cobble of which I had laid by hand.

Or I could write her a short, immoderate, uncool letter telling her how wonderful it was to do her credit memos and how little I had expected to meet someone of her charm on this floor of the MassBank building, and how extremely glad I was that she liked my glasses, and I could paper-clip the note to the back of the papers I gave back to her. Or I could borrow her keys from her purse and go see what her apartment looked like. (I used to hang around cafés in Cambridge on Sundays, reading women's handwritten poetry journals while in the Fold, but the surprising thing was how little you learned about what the women were actually like, what their manner was like, by reading their poetry journals—though their handwriting told you something. Eventually I found that a more dependable way to get an idea of a particular woman without actually talking to her was by hitting PAUSE, finding her address, and borrowing her keys to see how she lived.) Or I could put one of my special homemade editions of a pamphlet called *Tales of French Love and Passion* in a trash can just as Joyce was tossing something out, so that she would find it and perhaps read it. Or I could ask her out to dinner. That seemed the most reasonable thing to do.

But in the end, needless to say, I borrowed her keys and checked out her apartment. I dropped into the Fold at around four-thirty. Fortunately for me she lived on Garden Street, one of the streets that slopes down Beacon Hill, a fifteen-minute walk, and not out in Brookline or somewhere, though I would have been willing to walk to Brookline, or at least borrow a courier's bicycle to get there, something I have done often enough when I have needed to get around while the universe is off. (The stopped traffic makes driving a car in the Fold impractical.) Joyce lived on the fifth floor, in a small oddly shaped studio attached to an incongruously long narrow sunporch, where she apparently slept. There were a number of flat canvas shoes, floral, turquoise, in front of her sofa, which was a faded blue foldout and looked second-hand. The floor was painted gray. A plastic tampon wrapper crinkled underfoot in the bathroom. Her makeup was thrown haphazardly in a metal box that had once held some sort of French biscuit. A Piazzetta poster was on one wall; a small framed illustration taken from some eighteenth-century textbook of perspective was on another. Her alarm was set to seven-forty. She was reading several books; the only ones I recall now were Mary Midgley's *Wickedness* and D'Arcy Thompson's *On Growth and Form.* There was a bottle of maple syrup and a copy of a Dover book, *500 Small Houses of the Twenties,* on the kitchen table. A cat, a lithe adolescent whose sex I didn't bother to determine, was estoppeled in the middle of jumping from a counter onto a chair. I tried to get some notion of what Joyce wore when she wasn't wearing work clothes, but as usual, when I hit the clutch to snoop, I couldn't: it is not intuitively obvious what items go with what others. But her mess was good—I love messy women. (On the other hand, I love neat women.)

The best thing about her apartment, though, in my opinion, was the mattress pad. It was one of those bumpy therapeutic ones, made of hundreds of rounded inch-high hillocks or pingos of foam, that people use to dampen the pressure points of too firm a mattress. I had never known anyone personally who used one. It gave me great pleasure to slip my hand under the disorderly blankets to feel it under the sheet. My fingers looked as if they were playing the piano as they passed over its repetitively dimpled surface. I pulled up a corner of the fitted sheet. The foam pad was a dark-yellow color; when I stared at it, the pattern of identical shadows tricked my eyes with false dimensionalities. I felt as if I were looking at a rough approximation, in foam, of time's true geometry. Everyone else stayed at the level of the sheet, and only I could drop below it.

Feeling Joyce's mattress pad made me want to kiss her. I not only wanted to kiss her, which I could do easily using time trickery—I wanted her to *know* I was kissing her and to want me to be kissing her, which was a great deal harder to bring about. I turned on one of her kitchen taps; a trickle of water came out (water pressure is never good in the Fold), and I drank a little from one of her kitchen glasses. Just before I left her apartment and walked back to work, I placed, under an antique glass bottle on the sill of her sunporch-bedroom, entirely out of sight, without knowing exactly why I was doing it, a folded fortune-cookie fortune that I had found in a bowl of forgotten things on top of her refrigerator. It said, "Smile when you are ready." Then I walked back to work. When I had put on my headphones and reassumed the lost, somewhat spiritual expression of the concentrating transcriber, I snapped everything back to life.

But I had entirely misjudged my capacity to handle the sound of Joyce's abruptly resumed business voice in my ears so soon after I had gotten such a huge and illicit idea of her apartment. The fact that she had no notion of what I had just done, that she did not know the full extent of my knowledge of her mattress pad, pained me much more than I expected—not because my unlawful entry was wrong, exactly, but because I felt that my fuller sense of her life was going to make it more difficult for me to ask her out, rather than easier. The more I learned about her, the more I liked her, with a friendly, almost marital sort of well-wishing affection; but also the harder it was to imagine my having dinner with her and pretending that I knew nothing except what she was willing to tell me. Her pubic hair, her braid, I could handle just fine: they were graphic sights and textures whose memories wouldn't get in the way of any later, more preliminary flirtation, but still-lifes like the maple syrup and the Dover book on the kitchen table made me imagine spending my life with her, and how could I possibly spend my life with her if I had to keep the secret of my Fold-proficiencies and activities from her? This sort of doubt was not entirely unfamiliar, but in the past I had simply concluded (most recently after Rhody broke up with me over this very issue) that I was never going to get married, and I was content with that conclusion. This time, though, I found it depressing to think that I had just been in her apartment, in her life, sitting on her bed, and yet that if I didn't act on my love—or whatever such a hybrid emotion should be called when you learn important things about a woman all in the wrong order—by asking her out, then I might not, in a year or so, if I ran into her on the street, even remember her name: I would have to use the Fold then simply in order to be polite to her.

5

OBVIOUSLY I WAS MISTAKEN IN PREDICTING EARLIER IN these pages that Joyce would play a minor role in my autobiography. I finished doing her tape and walked over to her office to deliver it, intending to ask her out. But she was talking to a witty charming SVP whom I found intimidating and didn't want to compete with. Instead, I just nodded at them both and gave her the papers. At five o'clock I left. I got to my place feeling extremely sad, hopeless, almost tearful. On my desk were three vibrating dildos of varying degrees of stylization, along with a woman-designed vibrating butterfly, and a Jeff Stryker penis pump. They were all "mint-in-box," as toy collectors say. I sat down in my chair and looked at them, feeling great waves of misery. I had ordered them from a company in San Francisco, paying extra for Federal Express delivery, in the momentary grip of the idea that I would be able sometime soon to watch Joyce use one or more of these devices on herself. I bought the penis pump as an afterthought, so that I would have it in reserve as a bargaining tool: "You go ahead and use these vibrating dildos for me, and I'll pump my penis for you with this penis pump." But I couldn't afford these machines—almost two hundred dollars' worth of sexual hardware—and it seemed pathetic and undignified for me to have them in storage in my life when I would never be able to use them with someone like Joyce. Sipping wine, with the radio playing some progressive jazz construct with the usual cleanly miked bongos and synthesized tribal flutes and pre-enjoyed Steely Dan chords, I filled out the return slip, wrote, *Nobody to use these with, unfortunately,* next to the REASON FOR RETURN line, and one by one I tucked them back in the carton they came in (they had been responsibly packed in recycled styrene), my self-pity mounting to impossible heights. I wanted . . . I wanted to tell Joyce my dream of a flying blue brassiere: that we would be stranded in a rowboat in the middle of a sulfur lake, and the only way we could escape is if she took off her shirt and removed her flying blue brassiere and kneeled in its cups and took strong hold of the straps and pulled up on them for lift, using them as a steering-bridle. I would ride piggyback, and she, noble bare-breasted horsewoman of Lycra, would lift us and swoosh us to verdant safety. I also wanted to tell her the dream I had many mornings just before I woke up, that my mouth was filled with an enormous wad of decayed Bazooka chewing gum: I had stuffed in eight or nine loaves of gum because the first taste was so attention-gettingly tart, but now it was changed for the worse—sticky and oppressive, almost doughy, almost friable, and I tried to hook its unpleasant mass out of my mouth with my finger and couldn't remove it, but on waking I discovered that the gum-mass was in reality just my tongue, which as I moved up toward consciousness had made its sluggish presence known against the reviving nerves of the roof of my mouth. I wanted to tell Joyce these dreams. But she wasn't my lover, and lovers are the only people who will put up with hearing your dreams.

I don't think that loneliness is necessarily a bad or unconstructive condition. My own skill at jamming time may actually be dependent on some fluid mixture of emotions, among them curiosity, sexual desire, and love, all suspended in a solvent medium of loneliness. I like the heroes or heroines of books I read to be living alone, and feeling lonely, because reading is itself a state of artificially enhanced loneliness. Loneliness makes you consider other people's lives, makes you more polite to those you deal with in passing, dampens irony and cynicism. The interior of the Fold is, of course, the place of ultimate loneliness, and I like it there. But there are times when the wish for others' voices, for friendliness returned, reaches unpleasant levels, and becomes a kind of immobilizing pain. That was how it felt as I finished packing up the box of sex machines. I used a "tape gun" to tape it back up, just like the pros at Mailboxes USA. A tape gun is a triggerless machine with a handle that enables you to dispense tape from thick rolls one-handed. It has a set of sharp metal teeth that cut the tape at will, like the row running along a box of plastic wrap that can hurt your finger if you rummage overhastily in a drawer, but its whole function stands in swords-into-plowshares opposition to the gun—it is meant to seal, to mend, to hold together, rather than to injure and rend. I bought it at an office-supply store as a reward after an awful week working for the Department of Social Services typing Social Security numbers in boxes that were not spaced to fit either of the type sizes of the typewriter. Now, in my moment of despair, taping up the carton of sex toys, I lifted this nicely balanced tape gun and held it to my temple, and investigated my wish to die—and in doing so I immediately realized how laughably far I was from actual suicide, and how good, happy, lucky, fundamentally, my life was. The idea of trying to commit suicide over a box of vibrating dildos with a tape gun held at my temple struck me as almost comic. It got me over the hump of Joyce-loneliness. I decided that what I really needed to do was go to the library and get out some more autobiographies and read them, so that I would have a better idea of how to write this one properly. Before I left, I cut open the carton that I had just sealed up with tape and took out one of the vibrating dildos (*not* the Pleasure Pallas, a medium-sized Japanese-made one in the shape of Athena holding an oddly flamed torch of wisdom in her hands, the torch being in fact a pliant clitoris-stimulating projection; but rather the Monasticon, which was a large twisting Capuchin monk holding a clit-nuzzling open manuscript), and put it in my briefcase. I brushed my teeth. Then I reconsidered, and put the hot-pink vibrating Butterfly in my briefcase as well. It would be a waste of life's possibilities to send them dolefully back, I thought, just because I might never use them with Joyce. Much more sensible to distribute them free at the library.

I was luckier than usual in finding the books I wanted. Maurice Baring's autobiography, *The Puppet Show of Memory*, was on the shelf, as was George Santayana's *Persons and Places*, *The Memoirs of John Addington Symonds*, and Jane Addams's

Twenty Years at Hull-House. I sat down at a large table and
looked my books over. The particular library table I had chosen with some care, of course: it had one other resident—a
petite woman in her late thirties with curly salt-and-pepper
hair, wearing a short-sleeved top and earrings made of cloudy
yellow glass. She was looking through several piles of microfilm copies, sorting them and circling paragraphs every so
often. She spun her pen gently, silently, on the table as she
read, as if it were a spinner in a child's game. Her eyes moved
with impressive speed over the chemical-smelling legal-sized
pages, but she looked tired from spending hours gazing at the
gray light of one of the library's horrible microfilm readers,
contending with the trembling magnified crotch hairs and
scratches on its screen. I stopped time to find out what she
had been microfilming: it turned out to be copies of *Harper's
Bazaar* from the late forties. I didn't touch her. I wanted only
to arouse her—or not even to arouse her, but simply to be a
subliminal part of her life. I wanted her to become vaguely
aroused, without knowing I was the source of her arousal.

She needed, it seemed to me, to see, or sense, my Moving
Psi Squares. I had in my briefcase three rarely opened en-
velopes. One held many one-inch squares of construction
paper, some black, some pink. The second held one-inch
squares I had cut out of fashion magazines and Garnet Hill
catalogs, just faces: beautiful, interesting, exotic, or otherwise
noteworthy women's and men's faces. The third envelope
held squares I had cut out of a flyer I had gotten in the mail
from a place called Elmwood Distributors, a somewhat low-
end distributor of porn films, most of which were compila-
tions, or "revues," of surprising specificity, with titles such as
*Double Hand-Job Revue, Brunette Lactating Hermaphrodite Blow-
job Revue,* and *Big Uncut Dick Facial Cumshot Revue.* Each film

was illustrated by a single one-inch-square still, some of which I had cut out. Now I arranged many of these squares randomly in a rectangle around the microfilm page that the woman was gazing at, took my seat, lifted my book, and snapped time on for a fraction of a second and then off again: snap snap. Then I went over to her and displaced each square in a counterclockwise direction, again took my seat, again snapped time on and immediately off. I did this repeatedly, dozens and dozens of times, wanting to offer her a pulsing marquee of images on the periphery of her vision as she read her forties *Harper's Bazaar*s. I must say, the work was tedious in the extreme—whenever I do my Moving Psi Squares I feel new respect for the most primitive of *Sesame Street* animated shorts, and I'm awed by Hanna-Barbera. (Sometimes, when I have less energy, I employ just one square, a face-square or a porn-square, something that I think, judging by the way the woman looks, might interest her, flashing it for an instant every minute or so in a different position on the open page of the book she is reading.) In the present case, the woman with the cloudy yellow earrings sighed and lowered her head for a moment. I stopped time and removed all the squares and put them away, then switched time on. She yawned, throwing her head back with her hands held behind her neck; then she pressed her thumb hard between her eyebrows. She thought she had been working too hard, seeing things—and in fact she had been seeing things: she had been seeing the little sex-squares that I was strobing into her life. I sensed her glance at me for a moment. I didn't look up: I was paging in a leisurely, preoccupied way through Maurice Baring's account of his years in Sweden. The woman yawned again and gathered her things. I had no idea what she was thinking. She walked over to the trash can beside one of the other tables.

Just before she threw out some of the *Bazaar* pages, I stopped time and put my Monasticon vibrator on the top of the trash, where she might spot it peeping out of a paper bag. She did see it: she lifted the bag and peered inside, looked to her right and to her left, checked the contents of the bag once more. What on earth, she was wondering, was a brand-new, mint-in-box, sealed-in-plastic vibrating dildo representing a Capuchin monk and his clit-fondling manuscript doing in the trash of the Boston Public Library? She stood there for a second or two, pondering what to do, frowning, and then the bagged vibrator went quietly into her Boston University book bag. She walked toward the exit. I blew a kiss at her back. Good luck to her.

That might have ended my generosity for the evening, since the library was closing, but for the fact that as I got in line at the checkout desk, a large tall woman appeared just in front of me. I am always glad to be in line behind a woman, because I can look at her freely without making her uncomfortable. This one had loosely arranged, very thick soft hair that was possibly dyed with henna—anyway, it was a deep red-brown color. She was the sort of plump person who people say carries it well. She looked great. She was wearing an indeterminate number of layers of very loose clothes with huge loose neck-holes that slumped overlappingly over one another like the eccentric orbits of several comets—one neck-hole was almost falling off her shoulder, exposing some sort of blue bodysuit strap that probably represented the deepest layer. It was a way of dressing and looking that I had never until then thought I liked, but on her I felt I could like it very much. The shoulder that was partially exposed had lots of sun freckles on it, which made it seem unusually smooth and touchable, like some sort of river stone.

But it was not until I noticed the book that she was checking out that I was completely captivated: she was on her way home to read something called *Naked Beneath My Clothes*, a fairly recent book by a woman stand-up comic. I've looked at the book since: it is a sometimes funny, okay little book—but the greatness of it for me then was its title. For years and years I had been amazed by just this obvious truth, that we are all naked beneath our clothes; coming across a woman in the library holding a book which announced the fact in its title made me get that so-sexual-that-it's-not-sexual melting feeling, as if my knees were no longer going to do what they were designed to do and my balls were going to droop past them like toffee and hang to my ankles, softened by the warmth of my longing. I knew that the woman had just wanted to take out this book because she wanted to laugh and she had been told it was funny, but it had this provocative title, and now she was, despite her relaxedness about sex, ever so slightly embarrassed to be checking it out of the library.

Her embarrassment was, it seemed to me, directed forward, at the man working the card machine—a spindly nice-mannered ugly man who shaved too far down on the sides of his beard. But she knew that someone was behind her as well, and she could be considering that my eyes were on the freckles of her shoulder, and she might be able to feel them moving down her arm to read the title of the book again, *Naked Beneath My Clothes*—a fact that, because she held the book, was being asserted not as a general truth but as a truth specifically about her and her alone, prefixed by an "I am." I very much wanted to see her naked beneath her clothes. And of course I could have easily enough. Yet I hesitated to drop into the Fold to remove all those layers, since I would have trouble remembering how they hung with such artful sloppiness over one another when it was time to dress her back up. (She wasn't, thank God, wearing those leggings that terminate in a bit of lace!) Every curve and movement of her body cried out, "I'm extremely single at the moment and I'm available to-night to have a drink or two with a nice man who will listen to me añd make me laugh." I knew that she was feeling that this interval in the checkout line was her last chance to meet someone, and I knew that I was at least a better catch than the library staffer with the unsightly beard.

But though I was, am, extremely single, and though I had suffered a serious attack of loneliness involving a tape gun only hours before, and was probably giving off the same rads of availability and generalized longing as she was, I didn't strike up a conversation with her, because I was smart enough to know by now to spare a woman like this my tentative but occasionally successful pickup technique, since even if we did go out to dinner a few times and have a few nights in bed, it would all be essentially sad, essentially wrong. I wasn't the sort of man that she really wanted, and she wasn't for me, either—there would be a temporary wonder and excitement in those loose neck-holes, and then the differences between us would doom us—and why do any of that, when all I really wanted to know was how, exactly, she was naked beneath her clothes? I could imagine some of the unseen her in advance, having undressed so many women on the sly in my life—I'm aware of certain connoisseurial correlations between the type of face a woman has and the type of back she has: in fact, I felt that I had a fairly well defined sense of how her back would look and feel, how high her hidden waist was. But breasts were always a wild card, and the ass, too (I mean the real-world ass, not the dirty-magazine ass), was a thing of a billion unique variations.

I wanted, failing knowledge of her nakedness, simply to

announce to her, in a quiet, serious voice, "I am, too." And when she turned her face to me in sociable puzzlement, I would gesture at her book and say, clarifyingly, "I mean that I'm naked, too, beneath. Really, I am." Maybe she would roll with this lameness. One of the very first times I ever made out with a girl was in a park when I was fifteen: we lay on a slight slope, among many short conifer trees. Eventually her hand undid my pants and went into my underpants, and she hoisted my moist troika out into the world and left it there. Neither of us looked down for a long time—I was concentrating on making her come without taking off her jeans, which was not all that easy. Finally we gave up, needing real privacy to make any headway, and then we both looked down, and there was a sight of my naked self that I had never seen, or never paid attention to—an almost shockingly awful sight: the ultra-pale skin of my horizontalized balls was stretched very tight, stretched to a state of egg-glaze glossiness (because the waistband of my too-small underpants was underneath them, pushing my balls up), and it was overwritten with many delicate, infantile blood vessels, as in a Lennart Nilsson photograph of the head of a developing fetus. And—adding considerably to the overall obscene effect—sparse hair follicles made little white bumps in the stretched skin. Though it was highly unpleasant, or at least unromantic, to look at (my girlfriend flinched, I think, seeing more of me than she had been prepared for just then), I couldn't help noting to myself with some satisfaction how surprisingly spermatious the ballhairs themselves appeared, with their long wispy tails and their ovoid follicle heads: hair-sperms surrounding the egg-like testicles, trying to fertilize them, as if my body were offering to anyone who cared to look its own magnified, three-dimensional representation of the task that my gonads were programming their product to perform.

The woman in front of me at the library, it now occurred to me, was older than that sixteen-year-old girlfriend of so long ago, and she might be willing to have the strange resemblance between ball-hair and spermatazoa pointed out to her—but then again she might not. So much depended, of course, on how you presented the information—a tone of self-surprised irrepressibility often worked best. My ex-girlfriend Rhody once had a barbecue and invited six or seven friends over. My job was to get the charcoal to light. Standing with my feet planted far apart, leaning over the small hemispherical grill, I fanned the coals so strenuously and rapidly with the Arts section of the *Globe* that my balls started flapping backward and forward in exactly the same rhythm as my arms. It was a unique experience, to be able to feel those cocktail onions to-ing and fro-ing with such gusto. I stopped to get my breath and as the flames grew looked up at the woman standing near me holding a drink (one of Rhody's friends from work), and I said to her, in an amazed voice, "My balls are actually *flapping*. It's a new experience." She nodded sideways, smiling, and sipped her drink; she didn't seem to mind my telling her that. I fanned the coals some more and then we talked briefly of barbecue starter-coils. "But you seem to like flapping," she said. "I wouldn't want to deprive you of that." God, how I treasure those little flirtatious moments.

The book-checkout line was not short, so I had plenty of time to think as many sexual thoughts as I wanted to while I looked at the blue shoulder strap and freckled skin of Ms. Henna in front of me. The title of her book was exerting ever more roentgenizing power over my state of mind; I was almost out of control. *Naked, naked, naked, naked, naked.* I wanted so *very* much to see her back and big soft buttcheeks. I imagined her face-down on a massage table, with her soft hair pinned out of the way, her eyes half closed, dreamy from the steam

room, a white towel over her legs. I would walk in bearing a
large white bowl with a green rim that was filled with quarts
of semi-cool tropical oil and a dozen or so stone eggs of
various marbled colors. I would set the bowl on a small rolling
table very near her head and begin to stir and tumble the
stone eggs slowly with my hands in the oil, like a sedated
saladier, so that they clicked and clocked against one another
and against the sides of the bowl, and then I would let my
hands close around two of them, a reddish one and a black
one with gray and violet markings, and I would press these
into the muscles of her back, on either side of her spine,
cupping them in my palms. I would work my hands alternately
as a purring cat works its paws, so that the stone eggs would
palpate themselves slowly down her back, carrying their own
oil with them. When they threatened to go dry, I would drop
them back in the bowl, and jostle their submerged forms
again with my fingers, and I would select two others; these I
would again hold against her, manipulating them with my
hand muscles so that they turned end over end under my
slippery palms. She would try to guess by feel alone what
colors they were: "Hmm, I think the left one is gray and white
stone shot with pink," she would say. But no, it was a quartzy
blue. I would help her turn over so that she was on her back
and I would turn the slippery eggs on her high thigh muscles
and on either side of her mound, and then I would have her
choose which two she wanted inside her. She would pick two
and I would palm the stone eggs in, so that I could hear the
muffled clocking sounds as one hit the other, and as I pulled
my hand away, she would bear down with her muscles and I
would see the skin of her vadge stretch as she gave birth to one
of them, like those wonderful midnight sea-tortoise egg-lay-
ing scenes on *Nature*, where you can see the tortoise's vagina

swell and stretch over the sand pit as another egg appears, and it would fall out all slick in my hand.

The more graphic and specific my sexual imagery grew, the more the relatively simple idea of strapping the vibrating Butterfly onto her became, by contrast, tame and gentle and uninvasive—the very least I could do for her. Her neck-holes, her back, had the definite look of a vibrator-lover, anyway. I let her check out her book (she and the library man had a moment of feeling eye contact, as I had expected) and walk out onto the street, and then I brought the universe down and got out the Butterfly. My plan was to put it on her as she walked home, because I thought that she would feel it less, perhaps, if she was in a state of movement than if she was sitting down. But I had to be sure that it wouldn't startle her—I wasn't interested in disturbing her or making her feel she was losing her sanity. Consequently I had to test the product out on myself: I kicked off my pants and underpants, and, placing a Handi Wipe between the pleasure-nubbins of the machine and my scrotum so that I wouldn't be exposing Ms. Henna to any of my germs when I did finally strap it on her, I stepped into its straps and pulled it snugly in place. I walked around the lobby of the library with it on, looking at the high corners of the room and concentrating on what it felt like. I was surprised to find that, though fairly tight, the black straps around my ass and thighs weren't perceptible at all as I walked. What was perceptible, unfortunately, was the width of the Butterfly itself between my thighs. Perhaps if the bulk of my genitalia weren't in the way the device would have nestled more comfortably, but even then it might be instantly apparent to the woman that something was there. I recalled reading a news item about a large woman who shoplifted portable TVs by walking out with them between her legs; but it wouldn't do here to have a shape that the woman could feel as she walked. But all was not lost—I found that when I was sitting down, even with my legs crossed, it was as if the rubbery shape of the Butterfly didn't exist. My body adjusted instantly to its presence. I put the two free Sonic-brand batteries in the pink plastic battery case and turned the dial until the vibration started. On full, the noise was appallingly loud. She would hear it. Even at the lowest level, which is where I would have it when I put it on her (so that it would remain below the threshold of consciousness, would be a vibration that was perceptible only as a change of mood, not as an actual physical signal), it made a sound that was not so much a buzz as a kind of low chuckling. My only hope now, I realized, was that she wasn't going to walk home, but was going to take the bus or the subway, where the transit noise would mask its noise. As for the feeling of the Butterfly on my own equipment: it was not positively unpleasant, but didn't feel at all wonderful, either (maybe the Handi Wipe was part of the problem), which I was on the whole pleased about, since it made the fact that women come so hard with vibrators all the more mysterious and womanly and different from male pleasure.

I got dressed, got back in line, flipped on the universe, and checked out my books, looking at my watch to make the checker-outer hurry. Outside, I spotted the woman at the corner of Boylston and Dartmouth, where she was waiting to cross the street. I loitered, hoping that she would go down the steps to the T, which, lucky for me, she did. I was observing her in the shadows; nobody could see me and so nobody would notice if I suddenly disappeared from where I was standing. I stopped time and caught up with the woman. Her name, I found, hastily looking through her purse, was Andrea Apuleo, a perfectly reasonable name, though like all names something of a surprise for the first few minutes if you have had the opportunity to develop an idea of the person in advance. She lived in Chestnut Hill. I hopped down the stairs ahead of her and took a seat on a bench on the platform, so that when I got on the same train as she did she wouldn't have any suspicion that I had been following her. (I was pretty sure that she hadn't gotten a good look at me in the library.) When a C train finally showed up, ten minutes later, she took one of the forward-oriented seats and I took one facing sideways. I had been worried about Andrea's bodysuit, thinking I might have to take it off or slide it to the side, but when I began putting the Butterfly on her in the Fold I found that it worked beautifully to hug the device tight against her inner drapery. It could be set very low and yet she would feel something. I shook the battery case to awaken it within the Fold and turned the dial and brought it down to the barest hint of vibration—and then I thought better of it: the first time I turned time on in this sequence, she should just have the device strapped on, unvibrating, so that her body would get used to its presence. Over a series of six or seven time-perversions I gradually increased its flutter-level. Pretending to read, I watched her. At a certain point, she made a peculiar expression that was clearly pleasure and covertly reached down to feel between her legs to find out what was going on (nobody was sitting next to her): just before she would have felt the shape of the alien Butterfly with her hand, I stopped time and removed it. Satisfied that there was nothing there, Andrea sat back, and when I had reinstalled the machine and gradually accelerated its vibration with the thumb dial, as the train accelerated between Copley and Kenmore, she let herself feel good, her hands resting on the back of the seat in front of her, her head resting on the black glass of the window. She wanted to look

as if she were having a long and complicated train of memories of something faintly sad and peaceful in the distant past,
as if her thinking were accompanied by a soundtrack of
Gregorian chant, but I could read through her veneer of
inner peace to the sexual fizz that was definitely there. Very
slowly her lips parted and her mouth opened, or almost
opened: her lips were only in contact in the very middle,
where there was a fuller part. By this time I had abandoned my
book, unable to keep from looking directly at her. The train
rhythm sounded like *appetitive, appetitive, appetitive, appetitive.*
In a book called *Love Cycles,* about hormonal rhythms, parts
of which I have read with great interest, Winnifred B. Cutler
(Ph.D.) cites a study by Sullivan and Brender in a 1986 issue
of *Psychophysiology* in which women were shown "sexually
stimulating videotapes" while their faces were wired with elec-
tromyographic sensors. Consistently their zygomatic muscles
(one of the several sets of smile muscles) contracted subtly as
they watched the tapes, an effect which the researchers took
as an indirect marker of arousal, like pupil dilation. Since
reading around in this book (and I must point out in passing
that Dr. Winnifred Cutler is photographed with a very slight
Mona Lisa-esque zygomatic smile in her jacket photo, and
that, according to the flap, the book's publication date was
October, the month, says Dr. Cutler, that male hormones
reach their highest levels), I had been on the lookout for these
secret zygosmiles, and had not noticed many—but I think that
between Copley and Kenmore Andrea Apuleo was offering
the world a stunning example of one right in the T.

Just as I resumed time after turning the Butterfly up almost
to full, she noticed me looking at her, and our eyes caught and
laser-locked; I tried to tell her with my look that I understood
how good it felt, though she was doing a tremendous job of

suppressing it, and that I was the only one in the train who could see what she was going through, and that I was very moved to be able to witness it and would make no sign to anyone else of what she was letting me see. I nodded, closing my eyes, and looked at her again: giving the nod to her approaching clasm. She looked away, up at the ads for temporary agencies over the windows, and then she looked back at me, and I watched her put her lower teeth over her upper teeth, her eyes getting bigger and browner and fuller—and (I am almost sure) she came. Then she took a deep breath and gathered her hair in an O made of her forefinger and released it and reached down again tentatively to her legs, so that I had to fermate quickly and remove the Butterfly from her and wipe it off (using several Wet Ones) and put it back in the case so that it looked unused. I put it in a blank manila envelope. Time rolling, I smiled at her again, in a wowed, foolish sort of way, and she smiled uncertainly back, not quite sure how to explain to herself what had just happened. At the Chestnut Hill stop she stood and passed where I was sitting. I said, "Excuse me?" and handed her the vibrating Butterfly in its envelope and then touched my fingers to my lips. I didn't get off at that stop because I didn't want to unnerve her or seem threatening; I reached home an hour later feeling that, in making gifts of two of my sex toys, I had turned the day around.

6

I HAVE WRITTEN ALMOST ALL BUT THE BEGINNING CHUNK OF this autobiographical work not sunk in the Fold but moving forward in "real time" (a term that Rhody, my ex-girlfriend, hated, though, let me tell you, substitutes are hard to come by), over two weeks of evenings, sitting at my desk in my room, smelling the smell of burning dust given off by my high-intensity lamp. I thought when I began this recital that I would write every word of it in the Fold, but, like most of the extreme ideas that I find so exciting when I first have them, I have had to abandon it in the execution. Writing is solitary enough (especially the way I'm writing now, which is with a set of earbuds in, listening to music, and thus existing unaccompanied in the very middle of a vast artificial stereophonic space, like one of those tiny figures, each accompanied by its perfunctory shadow, in a Le Corbusier drawing of an urban landscape) without intensifying the sense of solitude by stopping time. Also, the radio stations don't broadcast when the universe is stopped. And furthermore, writing takes a great deal of time. A paragraph can take an hour! I've already noted that I have spent close to two years in the Fold: which makes me really thirty-seven, not thirty-five, if you measure my age by my internal cellular time. Were I to add to that secret aging all the time I will ultimately spend writing this book, I might begin, would probably begin, to look noticeably older than my birth certificate says I am, and I have no interest in inverted remakes of *Dorian Gray*.

Reading over what I've put down so far makes me conscious of many imbalances and omissions, but there isn't too much I can do about them. I do, though, want to point out sooner rather than later that my sexual life has not been entirely made up of the sorts of Fermating activities I just described at the library. Rhody and I had good, friendly sex (though I tended to talk too much throughout, perhaps), real-time sex, and we were together for long enough, a little over sixteen months, that we were able to marvel at how many incremental variations a couple could come up with—variations so minor that they couldn't really be codified. It wasn't a question of distinct "positions" but of—I don't know—crystals grown in slightly different concentrations of a reagent, or grown in the presence of one or more trace impurities, or grown while subjected to faintly stronger or weaker gravitational fields. And we did even from time to time try *new things*, in the textbook sexual sense. I cut an unpeeled avocado in half one Sunday, along its poles, and pulled it apart so that one half held the blunt, slimy seed. Though not a devotee of food-sex mixtures as a general rule (not whipped cream, not peanut butter, not champagne), I do think avocado flesh is so extremely similar in its slippery bland softness to the labial rheology that it makes sense for a woman to cup half of one in her hand and press it against herself so that the big nub of the seed noses at her natcho. Rhody seemed to like it, and I was gung-ho, too—but while I was testing out our new guacamole recipe I had the further idea of cutting a small hole in the avocado skin and stuffing Rhody's electric toothbrush at an angle into the fresh flesh so that the brush head was buried somewhere near the seed. That was how she good-naturedly came, in fact, and came big, holding the humming toothbrush-driven avocado-half between her legs while I played with the wisps of hair at the nape of her neck. I record this here in passing so that I won't seem, with all of my somewhat aberrant sneaking and skulking in the Cleft, totally devoid of more typical sexual instincts.

And just what would other people think of the Fermata? What would they do if they were me? Although I have up to now been able to keep my powers a strict secret, I have gone through periods when I have been eager to get some idea of what others would do in my place. I am superstitious, though, about describing what actually goes on—fearing, even when I put it hypothetically, that if I conjure up the possibility in too complete detail for someone else it will no longer be my secret and hence my temporal competence will leave me forever—so superstitious in fact that I often instead ask about ideas in the neighborhood of my secret, such as what a person would do if he had X-ray vision. What would he look at if he had X-ray vision? I had an interesting talk with a man named Bill Asplundh about this. Bill is one of the few truly fast-typing non-gay temps I have run across—he types much faster than I do. He drifted into temping while working on a master's in something or other, as I did, and now he genuinely likes it. We were at a Chinese restaurant one time when I asked him what he would look at if he had X-ray vision. He was eating a yellow curry chicken dish. He said that the first thing he would do would be to look through the walls while the cooks were making up their curry powder, since it was extraordinarily good curry powder and he wanted to be able to duplicate it at home. Then he admitted that he would probably use it to look at women. "But what people don't think about when they talk about X-ray vision," he then said, suddenly animated, "is two things. First, what you're talking about is not a blanket sort of X-ray vision, where your sight penetrates through any substance, but a very specific sort of X-ray vision that only goes through clothes. Textile X-ray vision is what we're talking about. That's pretty obvious, but perhaps less obviously, think about what you're going to see when you see a woman who is wearing clothes but you can't see the clothes she's wearing. You have this idea that you're going to see her with no clothes on, that her breasts are going to be there looking the way they would look without a bra on, but remember, she *has* a bra on, you just can't see it, so you're going to see indentations where the seams are, and if it's a push-up bra, her breasts are going to look all squished out of shape, not the way you imagine them at all. And think if she's wearing some kind of support pantyhose, and it's tight—you're going to see all this squeezing around her rear end and stuff like that. You're going to see the panty lines there, red lines, but without the panties actually being there."

I admitted that he had a point, but countered that the sight of breasts in a bra, without the bra visible, might be kind of wonderful: if you could see her breasts moving as they would move in a bra and yet the bra was out of the picture it might be a totally novel kind of semi-constrained motion—not even the kind of motion you would expect in zero-gravity environments, because the undersides of the breasts would be held relatively firmly, within the limits of the give and take of that particular bra, but the top would shake a little more where it wasn't being held. Maybe the sight of breasts in invisible bras would be incredible. But he was probably right, I conceded, the nipples would probably have that flattened quality of faces pressed against panes of glass; and what makes the sight of kids squishing their faces against glass comic is that it takes away their "faceness" and substitutes a sort of monstrous nostrilly planar expression. It would be strange to see the shape of the bra outlined in indented plump back-skin. There might be some interest, we agreed, in seeing extremely saggy breasts hoisted up in an invisible bra, since the idea of sag is very stimulating, as is the notion of hoisting.

But, though it interested me, what Bill had to say about X-ray vision didn't really bear on the Fold, so I went ahead and described to him the possibility of halting the universe and remaining mobile oneself, as if the idea had just occurred to me for the first time. What would he do if he had some machine that could switch everything off and he was here in this restaurant? Bill answered without hesitation that the first thing he would do is go back to the kitchen and try to find and copy the curry-powder recipe. His voice went low and he said that he might even *take* a little curry powder, if there was a lot of it, home with him, looking awed at his own wish to thieve. "Okay," I told him, "but after you had all the curry you knew what to do with, then what? What would you do vis-à-vis that woman over there?" I indicated a blond woman in black whom he had noticed with approval earlier. "Would you go over there and check out her tits, or what?"

"Possibly," he said. He asked me a few more questions about how quickly he would be able to switch time on and off. Then he said, "No, what I would probably do is hide out so that I could watch couples I knew. I'd be very curious to see that." His idea surprised me, since I have almost no active interest in seeing couples I know have sex, or seeing couples at all. I have of course seen it from time to time, but only in pursuit of other sights or experiences. After Rhody broke up with me, in part over the very issue of time-perversion, she started going out with an older divorced man, and I did hide out behind the tired gold wing chair in her bedroom and watch them have sex once or twice (well, six times)—and the last time in fact I did a very very wrong thing. Rhody was on her knees, with her ass way up in the air, licking and biting the pillowcase of the pillow she held, which was *our* favorite way for a while, and I felt violated and hurt that she would be doing this now with him, with this divorced consultant who looked like the "before" sketch in a NordicTrack ad, so I stopped time with my fingernail clipper (each time I snipped a fingernail, time toggled) and pulled the guy off her and out of her and hauled him to the garage, where I tied him securely to a piece of plywood; then I stationed myself in exactly the same position that he had been in, with my cock inside Rhody, and clipped time on, and was pleased to hear her surprised change of tone: "Oh yeah! Wow! That's good! Like that!" I pulled out and let my cock rest against her tailbone and pressed down on it with the heel of my hand, which was something we used to do a lot that she liked, because when I shot she liked to feel the come-tangents reach up her back. I could sense her immediate surprise as I did this—*Could it be?*—and just before she looked back to see if it was really me, I stopped everything and got the divorced guy out of the garage and put him back where he had been and stuffed what was left of his erection back in.

"What's wrong?" Rhody said, as soon as I clipped time on.

"Nothing," said the divorced man. He tried to pretend to be fucking her with abandon, but he was almost completely limp by now.

"Something's wrong," said Rhody. "What's wrong?"

"I had the *strangest* hallucination," he said. "I thought I was tied up against a board, looking up at the skis in the ceiling of the garage. Beyond weird. Sorry, baby."

Rhody comforted him. Lying on the bed with his hands doing unpleasant things with his own chest hair, he began describing the "incredibly vivid" out-of-body experience he had just had of being tied up, staring at the skis. Eventually the two of them tiptoed giggling off to the laundry room to find some rope and the ski boots. I left soon after.

Another person I asked, a guy who worked for Boston University, said that, given time-perverter powers, he would wander through women's locker rooms for a while; then he said, after much hemming and hawing, that he would "probably want to see people I knew." This was after I had described a hypothetical scene in which someone is watching a rented copy of *Metropolitan* on his VCR and he really loves it, but he needs to piss extremely bad, and he points the remote at the machine and hits PAUSE, but finds that instead of pausing *Metropolitan, Metropolitan* continues and the entire rest of the world is in a freeze-frame—so that the remote-owner has however long it will take for the movie to finish playing to run outside into the suspension and pry and peep to his heart's content. As I mentioned earlier, I have never had any success with remote-control keypads, which is exactly why I used a remote PAUSE button in the scene I offered him—it felt far enough removed from things I had actually done. I asked one or two women as well, and one of them said she would be eager to see her friends having sex. "I'd probably be grossed out, but I'd want to see it anyway." I felt a little sad that I didn't have this temptation in common with my respondents.

One other woman, a paralegal at a small firm in a building with a statue of Edward Coke in front, gave me a long and interesting answer to my question one evening, when we were working late assembling the documents in a huge real estate sale-and-leaseback agreement. Her name was Arlette. We walked around and around a conference table, piling one copy of some ancillary agreement on top of another in a soothing rhythm, and eventually I asked her for her thoughts on what she would do with a PAUSE button that stopped life rather than videotapes. Let me try to record what she said exactly—I took a few notes at the time. "Well," she said, "I think first I would just sit and think for a while and try to comprehend the fact that I was the only person around who was able to move. Then I'd plan out the little revengeful things I could do. I'd bring it to work, definitely. I could put some of those Dennison colored dots on Stephen Milrose's evil face, one by one. While he is sitting there at Tuesday Conference, making his nasty little comments, shooting every-one down, ridiculing people for no reason, I'd pick a word, some harmless word that he says a lot, like for instance 'back-side.' Every time he said that some deal or some client was going to 'turn around and bite us in the backside,' I'd hit the PAUSE button and stick a yellow dot on his face. I would *love* to do that! They would add up, too! That would give me enormous satisfaction, to see his face fill up with a rash of dots. Nobody would say anything, but he'd be covered. He loves to say, 'Time out, time out.' I'd be merciless—every time he said, 'Time out,' making that T with his hands, I'd time-out for real and stick a little green dot on his face. It would be such a screech to see his evil little face get totally covered with yellow and green dots. So that kind of thing is number one— performing little pranks like that on the top two or three true assholes on this floor. I'd have to get that out of my system. But then I would have to think, I'd have to think . . ."

I didn't say anything, because I didn't want to prejudice her response in any direction.

"Well," she said finally, with some decision, "what I think of is going over to Mark Thalmeiser and chitchatting with him about something or other, and while he's looking at me and blinking innocently, I'd pause him right in the middle of one of his blinks and stand over him and take out my boobs and sort of fluff them in his eyes. First I'd take a big powder puff and get them all powdered up, and then I'd fluff my nipples in his eyes. That would be fun."

"Would that be classed as an act of revenge, or an act resulting from sexual attraction?" I asked her.

"Both. Mark is sex on wheels, in a way. His wife is sex on wheels, too." She looked at me significantly.

"Yes?" I said, stretching the word out.

"Yes. I don't really like Mark, I like Mark's wife. Well—I like them both. She has the best *mouth*. It's sort of like Leslie Caron's mouth. No—here's what I would do if I had a remote that freezes the world. I'd be in a florist's shop, and Kari Thalmeiser would come in to get some cut flowers. She dresses beautifully, in an expensive loungey way—yellow pants and that kind of thing—but she pulls it off. She would lean into the flower-cooler to smell a bunch of flowers, cold flowers, and I would pause her as she's smiling, with her eyes closed, breathing in the scent of some really filthy-looking flower. Or no, better yet, some bunch of nice simple pretty flowers, like carnations. Whatever the flower is, I move it aside after hitting the remote, because it's *my* turn, Kari Thalmeiser, and I adjust the wire shelf on the cooler so that it's just below her chin, and I like climb up on it, get up on my heels, and spread my big solid mega-thighs wide open for her, so she's half an inch from this giant, sopping, sloppy, juicy, dripping flowerbox of mine. I can feel that I'm dripping all over the blossoms that are in the vases on the floor of the cooler. The metal is cold on my ass. I see her mouth, that Leslie Caron mouth, smiling at the smell of the flowers, her eyes closed, and that makes me jill at myself really fast. When I'm just about to flip and I can't stop myself, I hold the back of her head and I jam her face into my juice-box and I hit the remote so that time flashes on for her for just a half a second. Too quick for her to know. As I start coming I'm merciful and I pause her again and I just come and come and come against her beautiful lips—and even against her nose, her nose would be just right for my clit. Yeah, I'd hold her earlobes and pull her face into me until I'd humped every little come-kick out of my hips, and then I'd climb out of the cooler and put everything back where it was, all the nice pretty carnations and baby's breath and shit, and I'd carefully dab at her pretty face with some floral tissue, because we wouldn't want pretty Kari to look like she'd been eating a watermelon. I'd spend a couple of minutes fixing her lipstick. Then I'd start things up again and I'd go, 'Wull, Kari Thalmeiser, how are you!' "

"Interesting!" I said, enjoying Arlette's filth. "Couldn't you spread those thighmasters for me? Show me that big fat Georgia O'Keeffe?"

"Never," said Arlette. We laughed because it was so obvious an impossibility. Neither of us wanted the other, but we did want to get close to what we really wanted by talking about it. I pushed my glasses up on my nose Clark Kentishly, forgetting that I was in a period where pushing my glasses up actually did trigger a time-stopping Drop. Out of curiosity, realizing I'd triggered a Drop, I slipped my hands under immobile Arlette's skirt to see if talking about Kari Thalmeiser had made her detectably wet. It had not. Her idea was to her at that moment no more than a verbal flourish, a rhetorical bit of self-display—her exuberant pleasure was in being cheerfully shocking as much as it was in really feeling the sexual charge of her flowershop-idyll. But I had the strong suspicion that there would be a residual effect—that when she got home from work she would think again about Kari and the flower-cooler and, without the distraction of my being there as an audience, *would* allow herself to become worked up by it, and I found that I wanted very much to see that happen.

So I followed her home, pushing up on my glasses when it was necessary, as when I slipped past her as she was frozen in the act of opening her door. Standing silently in out-of-sight corners and closets, I watched her take off her work clothes and sit at her kitchen table in her sweats eating a bowl of rice with soy sauce while she watched the news. When she had finished her rice, she began tugging and twirling her pubic hair. She tapped her middle finger to her opening and smelled it. And then she went to the bedroom. It was almost dark by then. She had a solidly sexy field-hockey-playing sort of body. No snake tattoos anywhere; no pierced body-parts. She made herself come twice, first with her fingers, wrongways around in the bed with her feet on the wall, one fingernail tickling the frustum of her ass, and the second time with her

Hitachi vibrator—and the second time her eyes were closed in bliss and her left arm was thrown sideways on the bed, so that her hand, palm up, was out in midair, looking as if it wanted something to hold. I pushed up my glasses, stopping events in progress, and emerged from the shadows of the open closet and knelt so that my big silent dim-witted dick hung near this upturned palm. I wanted to close my hands around her hand, around my dick. It was as if her description of what she would impermissibly do with Kari Thalmeiser made it okay for me to give her a handful of myself unasked, though of course I knew that it really didn't. There is nothing so sexy as seeing a solid young dyke coming with her legs bent in a diamond shape, feet together, and one of those Hitachi camping flashlights, those Hitachi huge-eyed deep-sea exotic fishes, doing its blunt tireless thing in her Marianas Trench. I risked being seen, emboldened by how loud the vibrator was, timing my mastur-strokes to the shaking of her knees and the somewhat Zen-like whooshing of her breathing, and when she began to come for the second time I did in fact stop time for an instant and laid my dick in her palm and closed my fist around her fist, and squeezed on it so tightly my knuckles turned yellow, sliding within my skin in and out of her grip. As the inexorability of my clasm began I pulled down on my glasses so that she and I were living coterminously, and as she came I released one-liners of sperm up her forearm and then squeezed the last semi-painful droplets of my orgasm out on her curled fingers. I let her just begin to register the fact of my cooling slime on her arm after she finished coming herself before I stopped time and toweled her off and left. The next day she looked at me oddly—she said, "Were you . . . ?" and "Did you . . . ?" and then stopped. I said, "Was I what?" smiling innocently. She didn't pursue it.

Now that I have recorded it here, it seems to me that Arlette's flowershop story and my behavior in her apartment afterward may mark the end of one phase of my Fold-life and the beginning of another. I was always, or almost always, quite careful, even painstaking, in my sexual adventures in the Fold up until then, but Arlette's recklessness liberated me, at least to a degree. I still revere the word "painstaking," as I always have—I pronounce it and think of it as if it were divisible into "pain" and "staking," because the "staking" contributes a tweezery sort of push-pinned delicacy to the connotation and is in its pointedness the secret reason for the word's success, even though technically it merely means taking pains, or exerting oneself. But sometimes when I'm recording detailed notes as I remove a woman's clothes ("left bra strap fallen" or "panties inside out and worked partway into asscrack") so that I will be sure to replace everything perfectly, just as it was, I feel a gurgle of Arlette's joyful who-gives-a-fuckness working in me, and I want to strip the entire city of Boston and mound all the clothes together in the middle of Washington Street and dance on top of them screaming, "We're totally fucking naked, we're totally fucking naked!"—or failing that (since sudden widespread big-city nudity could lead to rapes and other unforeseen turbulence), I might want to strip everyone in an idyllic small town like Northampton and see how they would adjust to it. That actor on *Unsolved Mysteries* could do a nice twenty-minute segment about the event—the Quiet Little College Town That Stripped. Nobody would connect it to me and my Solonoid. Since Arlette, I have taken many more risks; I have increasingly wanted to give the world something to digest—something big and anarchic and sloppy but not (I hope) harmful or even particularly embarrassing in any permanent way to the individuals concerned. Probably my decision to assemble something on paper about my life flows in part from this urge.

But I do have limits and hesitations. Only a few days after my evening chat with Arlette, I was waiting in the lobby of the same building for a cab to show up. It was about eleven at night. A Hammermill box full of backup documents was to be put in a cab to go out to a partner's house. (The partner was sick but, good man, planning to work all night.) The cab was delayed. Every so often I spotted a rat moving fast across the plaza in the dark. The security guard was in a chatty mood. I knew him slightly. He was in his forties, with some serious dental problems. Once, when I had stopped to say hello for a second, he had raved about a piece of music on his radio—"Listen to this, I just love it! I wish I knew what it was. It's mint!"—proud of himself for his sudden affinity for what he took to be Rachmaninoff or Bruckner or somebody. I listened for a phrase or two and inquired whether it wasn't the theme from *Love Boat*. His face went through a male menopause as he realized that I was right and that his attempt to demonstrate his culture had betrayed him into humming enthusiastically along with a tired old TV show. So in a general way I thought I liked him. While I was waiting for the cab, I decided to ask him what he would do if he had a remote-control device that, instead of pausing a video, froze the entire universe. He understood the sexual implications of what I was asking immediately.

"What would I do?" he said. "I'd find the nicest, best-looking chick I could find and rip her clothes off and plank her right there."

I was a little taken aback. "But she wouldn't be moving. You would really fuck her?"

He said absolutely he would. "I'd find the nicest, mintest

chick I could find and carry her off to an alley and rip her clothes off and start hammering the shit out of her."

"But she wouldn't be responding!" I again protested.

"So what? I'm talking about a mint chick now, a really mint chick. If she was mint I wouldn't care if she was moving. Or, okay, if she wasn't moving, I'd just click the remote on for a second, and she'd start fighting a little, and then she'd be moving, and then I'd turn her off and I'd hammer on her some more."

"But then she's fighting you," I said. "That's rape."

"Well, yeah, it's rape, I guess," he said. "Call me a sick fucked-up guy, but that's what I would do. Now my friend Jerry, he's a ladies' man. He probably wouldn't shove it in and start whaling on her. He'd probably eat her out, suck on her tits and all that."

"But that's not really right, either," I said, feeling increasingly confused and unhappy.

"I know," he said. "Or—maybe he'd just look at her, I don't know."

"I suppose it's all basically equivalent," I said, thinking out loud. "I mean, unbuttoning one button is just as bad, since it's done without her say-so. But I don't really believe that, for some reason. I think there are levels to it. I personally would just undress her."

"What, undress her and pound your pud, man?" he cried. "You'd just unbutton a few buttons and catch a bit of tit and go, Oh, sorry I had to lay a hand on you, and then you'd fucking *masturbate*, man? What a waste! I'd fucking jump in there. I'd fucking yank the remote from you and start whaling on her. What's the difference? As far as I can see there's no difference between just tearing her clothes off and hammering on her."

"I guess not, essentially," I said. A brown and white cab drove slowly by but it didn't stop. "Still—there she is standing there, in a certain position, not moving. She's dry! How could you possibly want to fuck her?"

"Easy, I'd just move her arms around, adjust her legs."

"But, I'm telling you, she's dry!" I was trying to give him every chance to reconsider and retract.

"All right. Say I see this incredible chick coming out of NAPA."

"Out of what?" I asked.

"Out of NAPA. Auto parts. I haul her to the alley, I rip her clothes off, and I try to stick it in her, and she's a little dry, right? Then I notice that there's some fucking grease in the bag she's carrying, this tube of axle grease she's bought for her husband, right? I squeeze some of that on my cock and I fuck her with the help of that, and then I leave her there, and she wakes up, and she goes, What the fuck? Or no, I dress her back up, and I put her back where she was in front of the store, and I take off, and I click the remote, and she's there on the street, and there's this tingling in her cunt, and she goes to wipe herself later, and this fucking black *grease* smears all over her hand, and she thinks, What the fuck is going on here?"

"I don't understand why you have to haul her off to an alley," I said. "Why not right there in front of the NAPA store?"

He looked at me as if I was unable to understand the obvious. "I could *never* do it on the street. I couldn't do it in public. Even though everyone's frozen stiff. With my luck, one guy's eyeball would still be moving around, and he'd see me and he'd be able to give a positive ID. I'd haul her off somewhere secluded and hose the shit out of her until my dick was

NICHOLSON BAKER

sore. Then I'd start thinking about some banks." He got a
faraway look, imagining it all. "Ah-hah, but what if I click on
the remote while I'm fucking her, so she fights me a little, and
she sees my face? What do I do then, huh? What do I do
then?"

"You don't mean you'd kill her, do you?" I said, with some
actual horror in my voice. "Are you married?"

"Yeah, I'm married." On cue, he brought out a family
photo of his wife and one blond kid and one infant and
displayed it proudly. Then he said, "No, I wouldn't kill her.
Actually you know what? I'd rather be invisible, then I'd jump
on the chick and hose her while she was fighting me the whole
time. I wouldn't care, why would I care?"

"That's rape," I said again.

"Right," he said.

"Okay, but now, say it was someone you knew."

"A chick I knew?"

"Right," I said. "Someone you really thought was beautiful."

"Someone I'd always wanted to fuck and she'd turned me
down?"

"Okay, yeah," I said.

"I'd probably kiss her before I hosed the shit out of her. I'd
hit the remote and I'd say, 'You turned me down, but you're
my puppet now.' " Then he had a further thought. "No, okay,
say if she was a *nice* girl, a really nice girl. Say I go after her,
thinking I'm going to hose her, and I hit the button on the
remote and freeze her, and then I'm starting to grab her tit or
something, and something comes over me, and I can't go
through with it, even though I want to so bad, and a big tear
runs down my face, and I say, 'I could have had you, but I let
you go.' Right? That would be a real tearjerker. And I take off.

But first—*mint!*—this would be mint!—first I write my phone number on her tit. Right? That's what I would do in my imagination, but I'm telling you what I would do for real, right? I'd go after somebody I always thought was great-looking, like this chick I know from high school, Christine—her mother is fucking fantastic. Her mother is *nice.* Yeah, Wheelers' is probably the first house I'd go to—I'd hose the shit out of Christine's mother, then I'd hose the shit out of Christine."

I was distressed by this conversation with the security guard. I felt that he and I were radically different sorts of people (a realization that can be in itself dispiriting, because you want the rest of randomly encountered humanity to be comprehensible), but at the same time I felt that a case could be made for our fundamental likeness, and I really didn't want to be like him. Morally, I *am* different from that security guard— no, let's not mess around: morally, I'm a little better than he is. I am. But I acknowledge that some of the things I have done are—let me just say it—rape-like acts that some observers would condemn more vehemently than they would condemn the security guard's offhand remote-control fantasies, because I should know better, and because, in my own case, they really happened.

But I mention the security guard, and Arlette the paralegal, and my friend Bill Asplundh, not so as to raise the fretful subject of rape theory. I just want to point out what I think is my own oddity: unlike any of those I questioned, what I want to do, and what I in fact end up doing, in the Fold is to live out my perennial wish to insert some novelty into the lives of women. Arlette wanted to mash her clit-folds into the life of a woman; the security guard wanted to insert his small-minded dick into the lives of women; but I don't want to be quite that direct. Instead I replace the white chalk in Miss

Dobzhansky's hand with blue; I put the fortune-cookie fortune under one of Joyce's bottles; I leave the vibrator where the woman in the library can find it. I am still imposing my will on their lives, of course—but I want to arrange things so that they discover my imposition, and I want the imposition, however calculated, to have an element of simulated fortuity. I'm captivated by the simple idea of putting something in the path of a woman, so that she can choose to look at it or read it, or, on the other hand, choose to walk on by. In college I bought four brand-new copies of *Kinflicks* and left them one by one on a sidewalk near a gingko tree in front of one of the freshman dorms so that women on their way to class would see them and bend to pick them up and take them off with them. (A woman in my own dorm had told me that the book was very "orgasmy"—I hadn't read it then, and still haven't.)

Which brings me at last to my own self-published erotica, or "rot." A while back, while I was lying out in the sun in my yard on a beach towel, I became interested in the idea of using the Fold to have a woman encounter my very own words. Too undisciplined to write simply for the pleasure of writing, I nonetheless felt able to write as long as it served some specific sexual end. At first I imagined hovering at a bookstore a few shelves away from a woman who appealed to me: as she pulled a book off the shelf and began to flip through it (something like Eva Figes's *Light*), I would fermate and inscribe dirty messages in the margins, like "I need a big jumping clit under my tongue right now!" Then I'd watch her read my annotation and shake her head with disgust and replace the book. But maybe she wouldn't replace the book; maybe she would buy the book anyway; maybe she was in fact in the bookstore looking not for a copy of Eva Figes's *Light* but for a live nude tongue on her jumping clit; maybe my marginalia would be taken by her as a portent of sexually fructifying times to come.

Oddly enough, I didn't act on this rather crude idea until quite recently, because the thought of vandalizing a trade paperback with pornographic graffiti made me sad: a wheel-chair-bound art-history teacher in college once gave an impressive sermon out of the unparalyzed side of his mouth on the viciousness of writing in books one didn't own, and I took it to heart. A few months ago, however, I tried the idea out one evening at the Waterstone's bookstore on Exeter. A finely constructed woman of thirty in a black curl-necked cotton sweater with gray sleeves stood in the fiction section and pulled a copy of something called *Paradise Postponed* by John Mortimer off the shelf. It was a red paperback. I hadn't read it, though I'd heard of John Mortimer. She glanced at the back, then flipped to the first page, then skipped to some-where in the middle, where a scene caught her eye. She read for a few seconds, and then she did what I was hoping she would do: she curled the corner of the page under her finger-tip so that she would be able to turn to it immediately when she needed to—thus signaling to me that she was definitely going to look at the next page. I snapped my fingers to invoke the Clutch and gently removed the Mortimer novel from her hands and wrote on the page that she would be turning to, in as elegant a cursive as I could muster, *I need to pop my nuts on a pair of small sexy tits right this second!!* I snapped out of the time-clutch and watched her from a safe distance as she turned the page and read what I had written. She did an almost imperceptible double take, then flipped around in the book to see if there was anything else handwritten. She looked about her, noticed me absorbed in a copy of *The Princess of Cleves*, and, because (though somewhat rough-hewn) I look "intellectual" (the glasses), she was reassured that whoever

had written that desideratum in the book she had picked up
had done so a while ago, perhaps months ago, and was in any
case no longer in the store. Then she sighed conclusively and
put the book back on the shelf and inspected something by
Muriel Spark called *Loitering with Intent*. Titles are so important to lonely browsers. I could of course have written something dirty in that book, too, but I resisted the urge, not only
because it would have made her fearful that someone was
singling her out somehow, but also because I couldn't for
some reason make myself write nasty things in a book written
by a woman. I could deface John Mortimer without compunc-
tion, but not so Muriel Spark. I hovered there until the
woman in black cotton finally left (with *Breakfast at Tiffany's*),
and then I bought the Mortimer myself, since I had ruined it.
I still have it; I mean to read it someday.

Many, most of my fold-adventures are like that—inconclusive; wastes of time by some standards. But I like when my little
schemes don't really work out—I still feel that I have created
some bond between myself and the woman with whom I have
decided to meanwhile away the time. The woman in black will
eventually forget about the writing I did for her at the top of
the page of *Paradise Postponed*, since it is difficult to retain the
active memory of minor incidents which are in a small way
inexplicable and random-seeming, and yet for a short time
that evening, for a few hours, she might possibly have enter-
tained herself by speculating about what sort of person would
browse Waterstone's writing apostrophes of smut in modern
English novels. She might have brought it up that weekend at
a dinner party—maybe someone was talking about the history
of the Waterstone's building and she would be reminded of
the oddity I had given her and start to tell the story and realize
that she would be slightly embarrassed to repeat in company

what I had written, and then someone else at the table, a catty gay man, would say, "Oh, come on, Pauline, you can't bring us this far and not finish us off, we're grown-ups after all," and she would repeat to the dinner party, in her own thoughtful, even voice, surprising herself that she did in fact remember the text, "Well, I believe that it said, 'I need to pop my nuts on a pair of sexy little tits right now.' Exclamation point." And there would be whooplets of mock-shocked mirth. All because of me, all because of me.

7

LET US, THOUGH, BRIEFLY RETURN TO THE TIME I WAS OUT-
side on the beach towel in the yard, since I did go on to
imagine writing more than mere expostulations in paperbacks that morning, and the manner in which events developed as a result of my imaginings is quite typical of my
Fold-life. (Maybe *interlife* would be a good word for the portion of my life I spend between-times, in the Fold.) I turned
over a number of distinct thoughts that morning, but mainly
I thought of writing a brief amateur sex story of my own and
planting it where a woman might find it. I envisioned becoming a writer of private erotica—a rotter, a secret member of
the literoti. Specifically I envisioned dashing off something

about a woman on a ridem lawn-mower that I would print out, staple at the corner, and put in a plastic food-storage bag with a twist-tie closure and bury in the colder, unsiftable sand just below where some warm-skinned sunbathing woman was idly digging as she lay face-down on her towel on a beach somewhere.

I was during that period without Fold-powers—I had not, as a matter of fact, been able to disrupt sidereal time at will for eight full months, a fairly long fallow period for me, and while at first I had as usual been relieved not to have the distracting option of stopping all the clocks whenever I wanted to think or spy or feel, I was now really quite desperate to get back some of the old magic. What if I never accomplished a successful Drop again? Horrible. I wanted immediate controlled nudity. The calendar, the year-at-a-glance wallet calendar I carry around with me, that marvelous invention in which twelve locomotive-shaped months in series pull the miscellaneous freight of a full year of days along, had become my enemy. What had I done with all that free time? What had I done with my life, my interlife? Often on my mind was the slogan devised by some self-helper about ten years ago—"Today Is the First Day of the Rest of Your Life." It is a good, exciting, up-revving slogan. But it was beginning to occur to me to wonder what the person who thought it up had done with the rest of *his* life, following the momentous minute when he first conceived of it. Has he been himself helped by his own snappy bumper sticker? Has he done anything else of note aside from writing it? Is his mightiest accomplishment going to be merely the invention of a memorable formula that urges others to accomplish something? And was the world any better for his having written what he had written? The world has recognized its inspirational value and fully metabolized it;

individual lives have perhaps been in some cases improved as a result of its existence—high school homework may have been done that wouldn't have been done, new leaves may have been turned over, difficult phone calls may have been made— but now its own big moment of efficacy is finished, it can no longer surprise us into sudden effort, and yet the person who thought it up is almost certainly still with us, living out, not Day 1, but Day 1,234, or Day 3,677, of the sadly anticlimactic rest of his life—repeatedly experiencing, as we all do, those brief calendrical regrets when it is no longer the toddlingly innocent fifth or sixth of a given month but somewhere early in the teens, midway down, and then suddenly it's the twenty-sixth and the month is going forever, the one and only October you will be given that year, and the false optimism of a new young month is about to begin, like a stock split that without changing any fundamentals makes the price per share look alluringly cheap all over again; and then the "3" of the new month's date again slides into the "5," and the "5" mutates into the "12," each of the thirty or thirty-one successive numerical dates carrying with it, regardless of what actually happens on that day, a default mixture of emotions that results simply from its location on the scaffolding of the calendar—a specific ratio between the residual determination to get whatever difficult or distasteful things there are outstanding done in the days of the month that remain and the growing despair at the many difficult or distasteful things that simply cannot get done in the days that remain and must be carried forward to the next month. The calendar was my enemy because I had no control over it anymore, no option of postponement, no eject button, and I had not been in control of it for over eight months.

On the other hand, my coordinator, Jenny, had not had any

work for me that day, so I was free. I had been assigned to work at an architectural firm in Cambridge, but then they called and canceled and nothing else had turned up. I lay in bed for a while, took a shower, and wandered out to the back yard (my landlord's yard, really) with a large heavy dry beach towel. I don't know now what the date was, but I do know that it was early in the month, when I still felt full of hope (or perhaps it was so late in the month that I felt the undisturbed and imminent hope of the next month in full force), and it was sometime in the late spring. It was one of the first times I had gone out to lie in the sun that year; it was a clean, bud-popping blueout of a temperate-zone Boston weekday. A hundred very small hippopotamus-shaped clouds were on the march overhead, and though I like and respect a rigorously cloud-free morning as much as anyone—when the only possible seconds of shade you can expect out on your towel are those strangely paranormal ex-machinas when a high cruising bird (a gull on its way to inland Dumpsters) or an almost inaudible airplane comes momentarily between your eyelids and the sun, raising your consciousness of the conical geometry of umbral coincidence—given that there *were* all these evenly spooned-out clouds, regularly dispensing an ideal interval of coolness every five minutes or so, during which the trees regained their green depth and I had the opportunity to appreciate the heretofore-unnoticed sweat on my stomach, and given that I was nothing but a temp and lacked for the time being the one thing that kept my pride intact, which was my fermational gift, I was nonetheless quite happy with what the day had to offer. I invariably feel lucid and pleased with life after a shower anyway (there is an illusion of mental acuity that accompanies a thoroughly moistened and rejuvenated sinus-system and the sensation of wet hair-ends on the base of the neck), but seldom more pleased with life than when I can go directly from the tiley shower out to a clean warm sunlit beach towel on the lawn. I took off my watch and my glasses and set them on the edge of the towel, next to the Fieldcrest label; I took off my T-shirt and laid it gently over the portable phone, lying nestled in the grass, to keep it from overheating. I extended myself stomach-down on the towel (a blue-and-white-striped towel; the blue stripes were detectably warmer than the white ones) and let the weight on my ribcage produce a moan of utter contentment.

No thoughts of unclothed women disturbed my awareness; and it was not so late in the sunny season that lightweight, mothlike hopping creatures were liable to land annoyingly on my legs; I felt only how lucky I was that after a little rooting around, a little trial and error, the groundward side of my face was able to find, within immediate neck-flex range, as it always eventually did find, a conjunction of several sod-humps or dolmens that cradled my cheekbone fairly comfortably through the insulation of the sun-warmed towel. As when I took a seat in the older-style dentist's chairs and discovered that the weight of my entire head was to be supported by two swiveling occipital cups that determined exactly how far back I would have to slide my ass, so my location on the lawn now became with this satisfactory cheekbone settlement suddenly unarbitrary: I was home, my eyes closed, breathing easily because of the recent shower, still damp here and there not yet with perspiration but with cleanliness, and able to hear, if I concentrated, pressing my headbones deep into Fieldcrest's plush-blurred pattern, the lonely toils of a beetle or a grub somewhere very near my ear, chewing and pushing on some futile mission in the thatch. Was the weight of my head making life more difficult for the grub? Was there a grub there at all, or was it only the sound of the untenanted thatch itself adjusting to my weight? I couldn't know, but I was sorry if I was causing trouble for any living thing. I plucked a few blades of grass with my fingers; I heard the muffled sounds of the breakage transmitted through the underreaching rhizomes. I felt calm, thoughtful, at rest—serenely unproductive.

In my idleness I had of course the option of letting my thinking drift in a number of mildly erotic directions at any time, but it seemed important to resist that lure for the moment. It would have been so easy to imagine three women in white bathing suits lying on white deck chairs on a pale-blue cruise ship with their heads poised in different directions, each with one knee up and with her eyes closed, each holding a forgotten bottle of sunscreen that was the color of those older Tercels and Civics whose owners had used their garages for storing other things than their cars and whose paint had consequently oxidized into states of frescoesque, unsaturated beauty, like M&Ms sucked for a minute and spit back out into the palm for study. It would have been so easy to think hard about those leggy thighs flowing into the leg-holes of those white bathing suits; about one of the women straightening one thighy leg and bending the other; about how good the sun made them feel. But I wanted to steer clear of the leg-holes until at least twelve-thirty, preferably one-thirty if possible, because it was so very delightful out in the sun, and there was, after all, an infinitude of complicated and intellectually rewarding ideas in the world that I might use my morning of *otium liberale* to consider, helped toward states of scholarly attentiveness by the intrinsic good of the blue sky, and if I gave my hindbrain the slightest opportunity to work up a comely sexual shape, my meditative range would inevitably narrow, the sex-thoughts would replicate busily, they would begin to polymerize, forming short, slippery narrative chains which would bind with other formerly innocent images and voluptualize them, contorting themselves like lipoproteins into self-contained masturbatory sub-realities, and from there into fully realized frigments of my invagination, and I would find that I had turned over onto my back to let the sweat on my chest declare itself, and I would bend one knee and perhaps reach tentatively inside my bathing suit to make sure everything was shipshape, and five minutes later I would be inside my apartment, where my eyes weren't adjusted to the dimmer light, and where it was dissatisfyingly cool and unsunny, and I would send forth four gray stripes of fatherhood and fatherhood by-products onto a tree-patterned paper towel that was guaranteed to be made with more than seventy-five percent post-consumer waste, each stripe shorter and more albuminous than the last. And after that, the rest of the day would itself take on a post-consumer-waste sort of tone, an after-the-grand-fact tone, as when, on Saturdays, the mail was delivered unusually early and I would drive home from an errand in the late afternoon looking forward to it in error, thinking, Well, this was certainly a dud day, but at least there's still the mail to come, until I slumpingly remembered that the mail had already come—the usual bulk-rate packets saying "To Be Opened by Addressee Only" or "Sexually Oriented Material Inside" or "Over 70 Brand Spanking New Items!! We Command You to Order Today."

So I tried to draw an impermeable mental oval around myself with a kind of fantasidal foam, meaning to keep all sex-pixxxels, all prelewds, all floptical jillusions, outside its perimeter—much the way a lovely double-bass player I once knew in Santa Cruz practiced all one afternoon in her apartment in cutoffs with a big white circle of anti-bug foam sprayed on the carpeting around her so that sugar ants would not keep crawling up her tanned and defiantly unshaved legs and up the pin of her instrument and up the tripod of her music stand. She had been very nice, very nice—a nice person to know, with a pair of gorgeously autonomous Jamaicas. I had spent one afternoon lying beside her on the beach eating vanilla cookies with her, and at one point I impulsively put one round cookie on each full turquoise cup of her bikini top. She made a tolerant warning sound, lifting her head for a moment, and ate both the cookies; I then brushed a crumb lightly from a breast, saying simply, "A crumb." But we had never had sex, she and I. And when I brushed away that crumb, I did it with such a light, shy touch that I'd felt only an inanimate bikini seam, and none of the insurgent nipple-crowned weight beneath. Such a tragic loss of a chance! (This was when I was in my junior year, a Foldless time for me.) But that of course was why I remembered her now with such longing, rather than remembering any of the women with whom I had had sex or the hundreds I had surreptitiously undressed. So I should feel thankful that I'd been so shy in brushing away her crumb, since I had her to think about and miss and want now—except that, I reminded myself, I was not supposed to be thinking in sexual directions at all.

I tried to concentrate on the brain-muffling texture of the towel against my ear and cheek, and on its clean smell, and on how little I required female nudity in order to be happy with my life. Just the idea of how clean this beach towel was, how fast it had spun for me in the laundromat's washing machine a few days earlier so that I could lie on it now, was more than enough for me. I recalled John Lennon announcing to the world that he could get high just looking at a flower. I didn't need big breasts, big jeroboams of titflesh, big hot fleshpots shaking in their self-serve tit-boosting black breastiers—no, I could get high just lying on a towel. Towels, though, were unfortunately not an entirely uncharged subject for me: they were closely associated with my second successful fermation, a year after I had employed the time-transformer in Miss Dobzhansky's class—and perhaps I should describe that early episode for the record right now.

(I have to say, as I spring around this way, that I can't understand *how* real autobiographers like Maurice Baring or Robert Graves do it. How are they able to move so smoothly and so casually from *a* to *b* to *c*? I'm humbled by the difficulty of presenting one's life truly without seeming to be a proponent of overfamiliar nonlinear orthodoxies. It isn't that I think my disorder so far is in any way swanky or artistic; it's that when I try to be a responsible memoirist and arrange my experiences in their proper places on a timeline, my interest in them dies and they altogether refuse to allow themselves to be told. I find that I have to submit to every anecdotal temptation just as it arises, regardless of temporal priority, in order for it, for me, to flower adequately into words.)

So: chronofugation. The summer after fifth grade I used to go down the clothes-strewn stairs to the basement (the basement stairway was our dirty-clothes hamper) and spend major portions of the afternoon observing my family's sheets and towels and clothes toil and spin. There was a safety interlock, a hinged inward-swinging tab, that cut the motor if the lid was opened during the spin cycle, but it was a simple matter to disable it: I just jammed it open with a pen. I stood at the washing machine for many hours, refining my appreciation of centrifugal force.

At its peak speed, the basket of a clothes-washer turns at something like six hundred revolutions per minute. Towels, which are ordinarily the very soul of magnanimous absorbency, are at six hundred r.p.m. compressed into loutish, wedge-shaped chunks of raw textility, apotheoses of wadded- ness, their folds so conclusively superimposed, and their thousands of gently torqued turf-tassels so expunged, or exsponged, of reserve capacity, that I feel, after the last steady pints of blue-gray water have pulsed from the exit hose and the loud tick from within the machine signals some final disengagement of its transmission, and the spinning slows and stops, as if I am tossing boneless hams or (in the case of washcloths) little steaks into the dryer, rather than potential exhibits in a fabric-softener testimonial. Often the spun goods display on removal a pattern of raised dots, where the fabric has vainly tried to pour itself out of the holes in the spinning basket in the wake of the water it has just reluctantly released.

At first that summer I watched the wash with the lid up just because I enjoyed it—I liked imagining myself as an agitator, shouldering the water powerfully back and forth with my fins; but eventually I began to suspect that untapped temporal powers resided in the spin cycle. Nothing that could safely displace articles of clothing in a circle that fast could fail to be of help to me in my effort to discover a second way, after the race-track transformer, to remove the clothes of girls and women without their knowledge. There were words molded on the tops of the agitators' spindles—ours said SURGILATOR— and one day I let my fingers rest lightly on this rotifer of meaning as its final acceleration began. The word, made slightly slippery from residual soap, circulated progressively faster under my touch until, vibrating into unreadability, its letters merged into a whirling probabilistic annulus, and I felt that the secret of spin had been communicated from the machine to me.

And I was right—the secret of spin was indeed at my fingertips—but it took a while for me to discover how exactly to put it to work. At first I thought that *I* had to spin. I went outside at twilight and practiced whirling with arms outstretched, not too terribly troubled by the possibility that I might remind an onlooker of Julie Andrews in *The Sound of Music,* trying to get my red blood cells to crowd down my forearms with such force that the tips of my fingers would blow off and I would hemorrhage triumphantly over the pachysandra. But of course my fingertips held and time ticked on. (Fingertips are *so* durable. They don't even explode when you use them as temp shoe-horns; they just tingle for a second as your impassive heel forces itself past.) Even so, I knew I was on the right track experimentally when, just around that time, I came across a paperback about UFOs in a carousel at a Mass Pike gift shop. It was a collection of letters from the general public to the air force describing flying-saucer sightings, interior layouts, and so on. One of the letters was from a man who thought that UFOs were generating the antigravity forces on which they supposedly hovered by spinning quantities of loose dirt and boulders in a doughnut-shaped inner ring built into the per-imeter of the spacecraft. The author of the letter supplied a rough illustration which showed the rotating fill and the re-sultant lift. I knew that his idea was flawed and foolish, but I also knew that he had rightly sensed, as I had, centrifugation's evocative peculiarity, its possibly mystical potential. It wasn't the pull of gravity that spin would neutralize, I felt; it was the pull of time.

The longer I studied our washing machine with the lid open, the more I realized that "for best results" I would have to be directly linked to the unnatural forces that my clothes were experiencing. But I hesitated to climb into the clothes basket. I had heard stories of broken fingers and dislocated shoulders. I thought, however, that if I had a way of plucking something of my own abruptly from a state of extreme spin and putting it on while it was still damp, time would be shocked to a stop until my garment dried. It was worth a try, anyway. Just at the close of a rinse cycle, I tied a length of brown twine around a dripping dark-red T-shirt as tightly as I could and tossed it back in the machine. When the spinning began I stood on a chair and held the end of the twine above the basket so that it could bobbin freely. At the right moment I jerked hard on the twine, shouting, "Now!" My red T-shirt flew twirling into the room like a flushed duck. I put it on and ran outside, full of hope. But the two-tone leaves were aflutter on the lindens and I could hear the usual traffic, so I knew that I had failed. I liked letting the shirt dry and its color lighten on me, though.

A few days later, when there were enough dirty clothes to make another load, I hammered a finishing nail into the table next to the washing machine and mounted a spool of heavy-duty thread onto it. I wound the end of the thread clockwise around the spindle of the washing machine at the commencement of spin. Thread transfer proceeded with increasing speed. The little spool wobbled wildly as it was stripped of its cotton integument. I grabbed the spool and held it tightly, so that the thread being drawn into the machine had to snap—at that instant of rupture I expected time to be all mine. But time wasn't mine even then; I still, it seemed, wasn't connected intimately enough to the pure state of spin.

As so often happens, success finally came through the convergence of several independent paths of research. There was a long rope swing in our back yard. I had been climbing this swing a little higher every day, on the hunch that something unusual might happen when I was able to make it all the way to the knot at the top, which was perhaps thirty feet off the ground. The rope was smooth where we normally held it to swing (sitting on a rolled-up remnant of industrial carpeting tied in place and launching ourselves from a wooden refrigerator crate), but the higher I climbed, the rougher its hempen texture became. Every day I got a little stronger, in my stomach muscles as well as my arms, and I also got better at relieving some of the burden on my arms by winding the rope around one leg and clamping it between the top of one sneaker and the sole of the other. My hands burned more each time. I opened and closed my fists when I was safely back on the ground to make the pain inside them go away. After a week and a half, I finally reached the knot at the top and slapped the finely cracked bark on the load-bearing bough, amazed and even somewhat terrified that I had been able to work my way up so high. I expected, after that conquering slap, to return to earth with new powers, but in fact I had no new powers: I only had fourteen or fifteen excellent oval calluses on my fingers, of which I was very proud. In private I pushed at these calluses while I was thinking.

One weekend during this period my father took me to the hardware store. A man we called the Needle Man was in the parking lot. The Needle Man was deaf and dumb; he went around the city selling packets of sewing needles for a living. He was a short, toothless person of about sixty who always wore a baseball cap; there was something wrong with one of his knees, which bent sideways when he put his weight on it. He approached us and went into his silent sales pitch: he flashed the packet of needles, shrugged, looked away, flashed the packet of needles again, licked his thumb and tested the wind direction, smiled, gummed, shrugged, looked away, looked at us. My father gave him a dollar for the needles. The

Needle Man nodded and left us. He never showed gratitude.
I connected him with Rumpelstiltskin and with Gollum in *The
Hobbit*. We already had five or six packets of needles that we
had bought from him, so my father handed this one to me.
"Maybe you can think of something to do with them," he said.

And I did think of something, as a matter of fact. I got a
fresh spool of thread from the sewing basket. I opened the
packet of needles, which had a convenient front flap like a
book of matches. The needles were arranged by size and
resembled the pipes in a pipe organ; they were pinned with
exactitude through two folds of blue foiled paper—a hand-
held cathedral. I chose a medium needle, threaded it, and
spent most of the afternoon sewing my rope-climbing calluses
together in various ways. When the needle was partway
through a callus I tapped its tip to feel the tension within the
thickened skin; the sensation was usually painless. I waggled
my fingers with two needles poked into them in the mirror,
pretending I was being tortured. When I had pushed a needle
all the way through, the thread that followed was almost ticklish; my nerves were being stimulated in a way that left them
uncertain about what was inside and what was outside. It was
as if I could hear the thread tugging through the holes in my
skin rather than feel it. I sewed all eight fingertips in series and
walked around the house moaning and looking for an audience; then I played something very simple by Bach on the
piano—the additional presence of the thread in the moment
of contact with each piano key, and the restricted range my
fingers had, made the music seem unusually pointed and
intelligent and pure. I played better, more high-steppingly,
more like Glenn Gould, with sewn hands (though with many
more wrong notes)—just as show horses were (I had read
somewhere) made by unethical trainers to strut prize-win-

ningly with mustard and chains in their fetlocks. I was my own marionette. I stopped the Bach in the middle and closed the piano lid. And as I closed the lid I knew what I was meant to do.

I snipped all the thread from my hands and amassed a load's worth of dirty clothes from the floor of my room (supplemented by several towels) and I started a large warm wash with the lid open and the interlock jammed. While the wash churned through its preliminaries, I chose a new needle, threaded it, and pushed it through the thus-far-unsewn callus at the base of my left hand's middle finger. I put the spool in place on the nail and wrapped the loose end of the thread around the post of the washing machine. Now, as the spin cycle began, it pulled the thread through my callus, through a part of me, in winding it onto itself. The thread tugged through the hole in my skin surprisingly easily, faster and faster. My hand lay on the sill of the washer, face up. The heat of the friction began to hurt; when it became almost unbearable, and I was on the verge of closing my fist on the thread to snap it, the event, or non-event, happened. Everything stopped. I looked into the tub of the washing machine and was thrilled to be able to see and even touch that fiction of the physical sciences, centrifugal force. Without suffering harm, I could now reach in and hold clothes that were in the midst of spinning at six hundred r.p.m. I put my hand in the machine. The remaining blue water, immobilized in its turbulence and yet still wet to the touch, was especially beautiful. The world was again available for undressing. But I knew that if the thread that ran through my callus broke, time would resume. So I was unfortunately tethered to the washing machine.

Over a period of ten minutes I laboriously paid out the thread through my callus so that I could walk upstairs and out to the yard. A bird was out there, a robin, paused in the air, about three feet off the lawn—I touched its spread wings, though not hard enough to dislodge it from its pausal locus. I continued to unspool my callus-thread until I had reached the street. A woman was in a station wagon with her elbow on the door. I touched her shoulder with my hand, then reached into her blouse and went under her bra and felt her hot heavy ostrich egg of a breast. Her nipple was amazingly soft. Her hair was motionlessly wind-fluffed; the speedometer said thirty miles an hour. That soft unselfconscious nipple I touched (my very first after infancy, recall) was driving down the street at thirty miles an hour while I, caressing it at leisure, stood in place! When I had learned enough about the weight and highly advanced mobility of her entire Jamaica in my coarse and threaded hand (joggling it reminded me, to my surprise, of the variable heft of a Slinky toy as you let its arched length recoil back and forth from palm to palm), I went back to the sidewalk so that I wouldn't be run over, and I yanked on the thread until it broke. I pulled it from the hole in my callus. The station wagon sighed promptly by—I saw a flash of the woman in profile, then the back of her car, her meaning-lessly specific license plate, then her turn-signal light blink-ing, then she turned down Southland Street, gone. In the basement, my clothes took up with their spinning as if I were still standing at the washing machine looking in. Nobody in the cars that followed seemed to notice that I had just ap-peared next to a bushy spray of elm-stump suckers, out of nowhere.

My second successful drop-phase ended there, circa August 1969: it, like the time-transformer experiment that helped me into Miss Dobzhansky's shirt, was apparently induplicable, depending on exactly those particular clothes and towels, those calluses, and that specific new packet of needles from the Needle Man. Tethering oneself to a clothes-washer was in any case a somewhat awkward way of forcing time into remission; although as I thought that period over on the beach towel in the yard I remembered none of the awkwardness—only how leapingly happy I had been for the rest of the day because I knew then, after all my false starts and failed attempts, that there really was more than one way to trip the universal clutch.

Now, out in the back yard, because I was so desperate to stop the calendar, I considered trying something like it again: sewing through my fingers and washing the very towel I lay on. But the fact was that my adult skin was much too thin. Typing does not make for heavy callusing. (As I type I can feel the raised pleasure-dots on the J and F keys of the typical keyboard, molded there to let you know that your fingers are properly stationed in the "home" position, with something close to discomfort, so tender are my fingertips.) Perhaps there was a way to trigger a Drop by pretending I was sick and going to Commonhealth, my HMO, and listing off lots of mysterious pains and moments of dizziness in the shower, so that the doctor would order some comprehensive blood work, and when the blood was sucked from my elbow and spun at six thousand r.p.m. in a bucket centrifuge in the lab to separate the yellow plasma from the red cells, that higher-speed self-centrifugation would re-create the conditions of the primordial washing machine, and I would, while the spin was in progress, be able to unclasp the Hispanic phlebotomist's bra while she posed in the Fermata, expertly tapping into someone else's vein. But I rejected the possibility, since even if a temporal hematocrit worked, it would be too unpredictable and impossible to control; I needed a way to switch time on and off quickly and easily.

But this notion of self-centrifugation did and does have a powerful appeal, and I sometimes have the distinct sense, as I hover in the middle of a page of this memoir, choosing which of my past Fermatas I will relate next, that in order to write my life properly I need the entire receptacle of my consciousness spun, as the ultracentrifuge's rotor spins its vials of biological freight, fast enough to conquer diffusion and impose some artificial order. I need to dangle in a severe vacuum from a one-tenth-inch-thick length of piano wire (like the rotor in the old Spinco Model E ultracentrifuge, developed in the fifties by Edward G. Pickels and his colleagues and still in use in a number of grant-depleted research programs in protein chemistry), while a xenon lamp flashes some unforgiving wavelength over my memory sample, rotating sixty times faster than the washing machine in my basement did—I want all of the semi-remembered images of half-dressed women, all these fragments of my voyeuristic history, that still remain in messy colloidal suspension to fly around at the speed of insight until they are compelled to file themselves away once and for all into neat radial gradients of macromolecular uniformity, like layered cocktails or fancy multicolored creations in Jell-O. I happen to know, from a three-week assignment in the research department of Kilmer Pharmaceuticals (for better or worse, an alert temp can pick up lots of stray knowledge), that biochemists routinely use the centrifuge (especially the low-end tabletop Beckman model called the Microfuge) to spin down, or "pellet," lengths of DNA in order to purify or clean them. And everything in the mind—that final triumph of protein chemistry—is likewise in helpless motion, afloat, diffuse, impure, unwilling to commit to precipitation: only an artificially induced pensive force of hundreds of thousands of gravities can spin down some intelligible fraction of one's true past self, one's frustratingly poly-disperse personality, into a pellet of print.

One evening after work very recently, needing to rev myself up to continue writing some section of this very document, I snapped time off and went for an indoor walk around the research buildings of Mass General, looking for ultracentri-fuges and for the breathtaking women post-docs who use them. I again vaguely envisioned centrifuging some of my own cells, this time for the pure ideational rush of it: I could devote a whole Pause to placing small samples of my blood (or possibly sperm, though that seemed a needlessly cruel thing to do to my sperm) in every Sorvall and Beckman and Hitachi ultracentrifuge in Boston and Cambridge and setting them all on top speed. I would be anemic and listless by the end, but I wouldn't care, because I would know that at that second my own perky little cells were being crushed into alter-native world orders of protoplasm by exotic megagravities in expensive vacuums in every high-powered NIH-funded re-search program in the area, and that trickster knowledge would power me upward into raptures of self-knowledge and self-abandonment. But I didn't actually do it, because I would then have had to clean all the bloody test tubes after their runs were completed, since I wouldn't want to leave something as unsettling as provenanceless yellow plasma around for re-searchers to discover. Fear is my least favorite emotion; I want to be responsible for creating as little of it as possible. I did look at a fair number of ultracentrifuges, however, and what I noticed was that the big floor-model machines, the ones built in Palo Alto by Beckman Instruments, bore a surpris-ingly strong resemblance to clothes-washers. They were a little wider, and they were blue (which should be a standard color for washing machines but perplexingly is not), and a close look at the control panel revealed, in addition to familiar words like SPEED, TIME, and TEMP, the less laundry-relevant terms VACUUM and ROTOR—but they still had an oval opening in the top that you closed after loading with a simple latch, and their direct-drive motor (I learned this from flipping through a textbook in one of the lab's libraries) operated on exactly the same induction principal as a Maytag's. The huge difference between these two consumer durables (and I think one of the best things about *centrifuge* as a noun is the ghost of the word *huge* it safely contains) was that the Beckman machine could turn a rotor, fitted with eight or even twelve little cuvettes containing some biohazard or other, at sixty thousand r.p.m. In other words, it could dependably spin, without flying apart, or overheating, or making disturbing noises (I noticed that it was quieter than a washing machine), at a rate of over one thousand revolutions *per second*.

I lifted one of the rotors from a shelf in one of the labs. It was not a light object. It was milled out of some kind of compressed titanium alloy and it was finished in an elegant anodized black. It looked like a forty-five-dollar dark-chocolate birthday cake, with holes for, say, eight unusually thick candles—but it weighed about as much as a bowling ball, or a human head. I'm seldom as impressed as I should be when I hear that a weightless entity like an electrical impulse can dash around in its silicon irrigation ditches a thousand times a second, or even a million times a second, because electricity is ungraspable; opposable thumbs are of no use in its presence. But when a California company manufactured a machine that could get something heavy, something that you might grunt gently in lifting, that would dent turf if you dropped it, to rotate a thousand times a second, the achievement seemed close enough to being conceivable that it became inconceivable. A head, spinning a thousand times a second! I was impressed when the little girl in *The Exorcist* spun hers around once. As I held the rotor, knowing myself to be the one unstill being in the center of a temporarily still universe, I began to want very much for my own head to revolve at ultracentrifugational speeds—I wanted to spin so fast my ears would rip off my head and slap onto opposite walls; I wanted my grotesquely elongated tongue, unretractable after I opened my mouth to utter the usual "Help!" of the Faustian inventor, to form a pink Saturnian ring or an Elizabethan collar before my brain finally blew. Not only could the human head not survive sixty thousand r.p.m., I thought, it could hardly survive thinking about sixty thousand r.p.m. And in fact, when I reflect on it now, I realize that my Foldouts are in many ways equivalent to centrifugation, since when I spend a few hours of quality time in the Fold I am in fact held in the vacuum chamber of a single exceedingly patient millisecond, potentially doing a thousand things, reading whole books, wandering through buildings filled with scientific instrumentation, and thus, from a bystander's perspective, moving over my closed loop at miraculous Spinco speeds.

8

To RETURN TO THE BLUE-AND-WHITE-STRIPED BEACH TOWEL
of last year, however. I again tried to tell myself how self-
sufficient I was stretched out in the Goldman Sachs sun, and
therefore how totally unnecessary any sort of time-perversion,
chronofugational or otherwise, was to me. I had a whole free
real weekday to do whatever I wanted; I could, for instance,
and should, read a book. I could go to a bookstore and select
a new beautiful paperback and buy it and put my nose in it to
smell the fine pukey smell that new books often have. If I had
clutch powers I could browse in a bookstore until I saw a
woman I liked . . . and here I came up with the aforemen-
tioned idea of writing a startling burst of filth in the top

margin of a book that a woman was considering. With an effort of will, I erased that phantasm: there were wonderful non-gonadotropic topics everywhere and I wanted very much to do them the courtesy of thinking about them—it was my duty as a conscious creature to think about them. The plastic arts, for instance. At random I thought of Sir Lawrence Alma-Tadema, how skilled he was at depicting clear water and wet tulle. It would be good to be lying on a towel on a beach while the Hispanic phlebotomist held flat the pages of a large-format edition of Sir Lawrence Alma-Tadema's paintings with her flatly sagging coconut-oiled breasts, so that the Caribbean breeze wouldn't make me lose my place. My eyes were still closed, the towel was still clean-smelling, I was still lucid-feeling, but I knew that I was almost ready to turn over on my back, and I knew that if I turned over on my back my bathing suit would come off a minute later (and who cared if anyone saw me—I wanted people to see me!—but I was pretty sure nobody was home downstairs anyway, because no cars were in the driveway), and once my bathing suit was off, my Juiceman would writhe and elongate against my thigh until, in attempting to rise and make a drunken statement, it would lose its balance and fall heavily back against my hipbone, where it would writhe some more. As a last resort, to remind myself that most of the world was asexual most of the time and well worth a close look even so, I opened my eye, the one that wasn't lost in the turf of the towel, and I saw, with nearsighted monocular vividness, my huge sunlit watch and my glasses. Through one lens of my glasses I could see the Fieldcrest label, or rather its verso inside, which was nicer-looking than the outside because you could see all the spendthrift lushness of soft thread that had been necessary to sew the little familiar logo and its trademark sign—though the sight of this made my Fold-urges reawaken, since time too was lusher when turned inside out. Beyond the sharp-edged inner bourne of my myopia I saw the macrophage of my T-shirt draped over the telephone, which would only ring if Jenny, my coordinator, came up with a late assignment for me, and I imagined the quick upward arpeggio of metallic clicks produced by the telescoping chrome antenna as I pulled it out roughly to answer a call, one segment reaching the limit of its slide and engaging with the next, and the same clicks in reverse order after I'd hung up and was pushing the aspirin-shaped end-bauble down. Time telescoped in a similar way; it would be most helpful if I could instigate a Drop whenever I pulled on the antenna of my portable phone. All things that came to mind suggested mechanisms of pausation to me; so much so that I began to feel that I was on the verge of regaining my powers.

I closed my eye and opened it again, and this time I looked only at my glasses, and it seemed to me then that the very best thing about sunbathing was that you could open your eyes at any time and see your own companionable glasses waiting for you there so close to your face, casting their sharp shadow: I could see with extreme clarity the thick opaque ground perimeter of the rimless lenses, and the side-pieces crossed at their kneelike earward ends, and the eyelash hair, whose curve enhanced my appreciation of the curvature of the prescription, and the dust that built up so gradually that I hadn't noticed it, and the nose-pods that were filthy but whose filth was irrelevant because nobody else could see it, and the paired reflection of some branchy blueness in the faintly scratched surface—all this nineteenth-century precision that I wore on my face every day, and never had the opportunity to study because all I did was take the glasses off at night and fold them automatically and put them by my bed and put them on again in the morning. No matter how often I closed my eyes, my corrective lenses would be there in the sun when I opened them again, waiting to be praised and seen, and seen more exactly and clearly than if I were wearing another pair of glasses to look at them, because my nearsightedness shortened the minimum focal length, making things even two inches away fully contemplable. I saw my own glasses better than anyone who didn't need glasses could ever see them. The word *clarity* struck me as very fine. My happiness had a clarity to it. My happiness was optical. My happiness was the direct result of my glasses. Should I do ten pushups to celebrate the innocent clarity of my happiness? Should I do ten pushups naked? I took off my bathing suit and did ten pushups naked, and each time I lowered myself trembling down to earth, and my down-hanging soft-serve nosed unprotestingly into the towel, I turned my head so that I could see my glasses waiting there for me to appreciate them. Possibly they seemed beautiful to me in part because they were hybrids, existing halfway between knower and known, between what I saw and how I saw. I felt as if I were looking at my own sense of sight, even at myself, when I looked at them.

A conviction began to grow in me that as soon as I put my glasses back on (the side-pieces and nose-pods would be quite hot by now—I liked being burned this way) I would again have control over time. Whenever I pushed them up on my nose with my index finger, time would immediately go idle. My wish to look more closely at something through them would be enough of a trigger. So sure was I that my glasses had become, through my having finally simply *seen* them, Fold-actuators, that I didn't even try them out at first: I lay instead recalling a time when I was at a beach with Rhody. I went out in the surf with her with my glasses on so that I could for once see the Hokusai trim-work on the waves. I knew that I was risking a major loss (I did still have my contacts, unwearably moldy, no doubt), but I foolishly thought that I would know how to keep above the breakers. Rhody said, "Are you sure about wearing them?" I said I would be very careful. After twenty minutes, the second of two big unexpected waves tumbled us both. When it withdrew, my glasses were not on my face. They were somewhere in the ocean. I was blind, standing in five feet of cold choppy salt water. Rhody and I groped in the sandy turbidity, laughing hopelessly. I began to adjust to the fact that I had been very stupid and had lost my beloved eyewear. But seconds later, amazingly, Rhody felt them brush past her leg, and she caught them and waved them in the air. I put them on and liftingly embraced her, as in a travel poster. It was the best moment of the trip; we fought on the plane ride home—mostly because I felt, like Tolstoy when he showed his rakish journals to Sonya after they got engaged, that I had to try out the idea of time-perversion on her (presenting it only as fantasy, of course). She took it very badly—and we broke up a month later.

I rose from the towel onto my knees and put on my glasses and my watch. I looked down at the shadow of my semi-stiff richard against the blue stripes. What else was there in the world beside masturbation? Nothing. I pushed up on the bridge of my glasses and verified that the wind and the clouds had stopped. In the Fold, singing "Back in the Saddle Again," I got my Casio typewriter and went out to Storrow Drive and pulled a guy off his motorcycle and drove it out to the Cape, between the lanes of halted cars. The beaches were not crowded at all, which was just fine; I walked for about twenty minutes until I found a woman, fairly nice-looking, lying on her stomach on a towel in a two-piece bathing suit the gray-green color of the plant called dusty miller. She was in the process of blindly digging two diagonal down-ramps into the sand on either side of her towel, which was what I wanted. Her top was undone, the straps lying endearingly untautly with their inner surface visible; her back was not very tanned, and in her application of sunblock she had missed a triangular place near one of her very expressive, well-made shoulder blades, which was going to be painful in a few hours unless I put a little lotion on it for her, which I did. I sat cross-legged next to her in my bathing suit and turned on my typewriter and began to write a story that I hoped would interest her on some more or less debased level.

Naturally I had no idea what she liked, whether she was a particularly sexual person, but she happened to be the person on the beach who was idly digging in the sand, and that was all I required from her. The rest was up to me. I wrote a story about vibrators and dildos. I worked for about seven hours (seven personal Strine-hours), perhaps longer. It was one thirty-eight the whole time. I didn't worry about getting sun-burned; you can't tan or burn efficiently in the Fold. When-ever I thought that my glasses were starting to slip down the bridge of my nose, I hurriedly pushed them up in place, not wanting my perspiration to restart time by mistake. I only took a few breaks; one to press her breasts gently from the side to be sure she had no implants (the knowledge that a pair of breasts are fake unfortunately kills my lust); and one to go for a swim in the motionless surf. Swimming in the Fold was something I hadn't done up to that point: the water's viscosity varied, areas of paused turbulence in a crashing wave dissolv-ing like lumps in batter as I swam through them. Shells and pebbles were suspended in the undertow like forest underbrush. I ran my finger along the quiet sharp crest of wave and flicked a hanging drop of seawater into vapor with my finger-nail. It was very tiring breast-stroking my way up and down the stiff-peaked pectinaceous swells. But I found the "swim" re-freshing (I wore my glasses this time as well, since I was in no danger of being thrown by any surf), and I further cleared my mind as I came ashore by pulling on the front of a bathing suit of a woman of fifty or so who was standing in an inch of water regarding her feet; I peered down it to see her fat low white breasts in the filtered light of her suit.

As a novice porniste, I meant only to dash something off that would have a reasonable chance of arousing the sun-bather beside me when she found it. (I knew at least that she could read—there was a James Clavell novel and a book on how to get a job in her beach-bag.) But as I wrote onward (about a librarian, a youthful next-door neighbor, and a UPS man, since, being a beginner, I thought I should at least make an attempt to follow the conventions), picking the setting and the physical traits of my few characters pretty much at ran-dom, I got interested in what I was doing and found that it was making me want very much to make myself come. In fact, for the first twenty minutes or so, every time I typed the word "she" or "her" I slowed way down to press the component letters, overcome in the act of placing a feminine pronoun on the page by an almost irresistible need to whale on my bone. But I denied myself; instead I took off my bathing suit and knelt, crouched over before the typewriter as if I were on a prayer rug, showing the ocean my open ass and udderously self-juggling balls. I was not then used to nude sunbathing, as I have said, and I discovered that the sensation of the halves of my upraised ass being out of contact with each other—the sensation of a slight evaporative outdoor coolness on my very ass*hole,* and on the usually damp stretched skin high up on the sides of my balls—was most interesting. I didn't want anything to go *in* my asshole, no, no, I just wanted it out in the open, sunlit for once, flaunting wavewards its showered cleanness, exposed in a way that was both lewd and vulnerable. In this devotional position I worked for several intense hours, writing.

Not that I thought what I was writing was necessarily by external standards good: it was simply that I was positioned right next to a woman who would be my audience, though she didn't know it right then, and I was in her immediate presence creating for her alone an alternative "she" character, who, in thinking exactly as I wanted her to think about dildos and vibrators, would possibly entertain the real random "she" beside me. Basically I was feeling for the first time that heady paired combination of satisfactions that the sexual proseur can encounter at the outset of a new enterprise, as his long-neglected artistic ambition, however tentative or internally scoffed at—the wish to create something true and valuable and even perhaps in a tiny way beautiful—combines with basic grunting cuntlapping lust, the two emotions reinforcing each other and making you, or rather me, feel almost insane with a soaringly doubled sense of mission. At one point, finishing a paragraph, I shouted, "*I* am a writer of fucking erotica!" into the still close air. It was then, in fact, that the first twinges of dissatisfaction with the word *erotica* asserted themselves. I ditched the word permanently for its abbreviated replacement, *rot,* and I have never regretted it. Yes, I was out on the beach on a rotter's retreat, with my cool and drying Arnus exposed to the sun, my cock as hard as an empty Calistoga bottle, but untouched for hours and hours. I was denying myself for my rot.

Whenever I hesitated and needed inspiration, I simply rested my hand on the ass of the sunbathing woman beside me, sometimes sliding the fingers under her leg-hole, sometimes resting my hand on the fabric; sometimes squeezing, sometimes lightly slapping. I tried putting the typewriter on her ass but found it was too unsteady to proceed. Once, though, I pulled her bikini bottom off and sat right down on her softness, looking out past her brown legs at the tableau vivant of the waves, ass to ass with my reader-to-be. It was pleasant to wiggle and circle arou.id, feeling our massed loose-muscled ass-flesh move as one over our deep bones: it was almost a form of communication. And if I knelt beside her and pushed outward on her asscheeks, I could expose *her* ane, and I did this more than once, getting a great deal of pleasure out of feeling my own plein-air Arnality bared to the sky and holding hers open at the same time. Hers was a fine brown dot, like a tiny asteroid-impact crater, which repaid close study. Women's anes never used to interest me in my teens and early twenties—I think that they are one of the true acquired tastes. They are discrete, singular, clearly bounded, focused, in contrast to the bounteous plied gyno-confusion of the vadge.

When I had finished a fair copy of the story, I put it in a plastic food-storage bag and closed the bag with a twist-tie. I excavated the sand below her right hand, where she had been digging, and I buried the bagged story there, packing the sand as tightly as I could and restoring the hole she had dug to the smooth contours that her idleness had given it. Her arm was warm. Her hair, by the way, was bobby-pinned up, blond with dark roots. I positioned myself behind a nearby sand dune and took hold of my glasses at the bridge and pulled them down, restarting the present for the first time since I had rediscovered my powers. Through the binoculars, I watched her imperturbably dig, as if nothing had happened. It is always a kick to see a woman come alive again after I've paused her for an extended period: she has no way of knowing that an instant of time has just passed that was hugely richer in content than any of the instants that immediately preceded it. An immense pale-blue Norwegian cruise ship of a millisecond has just docked and stout tourists have disembarked from it and bought straw hats and trinkets and they have all reboarded and the ship has backed its tonnage away, its propeller doming the water—and yet she thinks that all the milliseconds of her recent past are equivalently in scale, little skiffs and junks floating here and there in the harbor. And I, who have lived consciously through, even piloted, that enormous single millisecond, have forgotten to some extent how much better a woman is when she is *not* motionless, when her shoulder blades, for instance, can move subtly around in her back; her aliveness is always something of a revelation to me as well.

This woman's sand-thinned fingertips felt the unexpected slidey movement of the plastic bag after a minute or so. She raised her head to look over at what she had found, trying not to lift her upper body off her towel and expose too much Jamaica. She pulled my bagged story out of the sand and brushed it off and undid the twist-tie. And then she began reading it. I am not kidding—*she actually began reading what I'd written.* When I saw her slide the first page of my double-spaced typescript to the back of the pile, still lying on her stomach but with her elbows out, her chin on her hands, I wormed my fist into my swimsuit and took hold of my stain-stick. (I had of course put my suit back on, since the world was with me now.)

Here follows what I had given her to unearth and read, slightly edited (as op-ed pages say) for space and clarity:

9

MARIAN, A RARE-BOOKS LIBRARIAN, WAS MARRIED TO David, who taught journalism classes at the local rural state college. His own journalistic days were over and he had become kind of pathetic. He was addicted to a certain brand of nasal decongestant, and had to squirt up noisily every few hours, which Marian didn't really mind except when they had guests. She was an early riser, while her husband stayed up until two-thirty and three, reading magazines he had once written features for with groans of scorn. They didn't have a whole lot of money, because they were paying for David's son by an earlier marriage to go to Wesleyan. One Saturday they had a big argument after David went out to buy some plants and came back with a two-thousand-dollar ridem lawn-mower in his van. It was the neighbor kid's job to mow their lawn, twenty-five dollars each time, which wasn't unreasonable since there was a lot of lawn, so there was no need at all for this huge expense. David said that he had been compelled to buy it because it was a new model whose engine incorporated some innovation of the cylinder head that he'd read about in *Popular Mechanics* and it was their duty to support companies that continued to fund research and try new things. Marian was very angry and upset. It was like the time he had bought two pyramid-shaped beehives and a complete kit of beekeeping equipment for four hundred dollars. There had been engulfing flows of honey for one year, and then both hives had mysteriously and depressingly died. Also the honey had been "somewhat gamey," to use David's euphemism—meaning it tasted distinctly of cow. On the new ridem mower David defiantly mowed half the back yard (they had two useless acres), maneuvering around the two tarp-shrouded beehives, and then he came in to make some iced tea and kick back. Marian told him she wanted to be separated from him for a while, so he packed the top layer of papers in his office and some clothes and moved out.

Immediately Marian felt happier. Over the next few days, she got rid of the gigantic television, which had always bothered her, and she put away the two primitivist portraits of David's Connecticut ancestors. She dressed with more care, and when a man at the bank picked up a deposit receipt that she had dropped, she smiled at him in a way she hadn't smiled at anyone in a long time. She felt available.

The new ridem lawn-mower had to go back, of course. But because David had already used it, it was now officially a used lawn-mower. The guy at the dealer quoted her a derisorily low buyback price, and out of defiance she told him to forget it and walked out. Fortunately, when she told her mother that she had finally kicked David out, her mother promptly came through with a check for three thousand dollars. Money worries eased for the moment, she hired the neighbor kid to mow the rest of the lawn using the new green ridem mower. His name was Kev. She watched him from various windows as he jounced around on her lawn. He had ostentatiously deliberate rips in the legs of his jeans from which his brown knees protruded, and he was wearing brown work boots. His shirt was off. He was wiry; he had that adolescent ability to bend at the waist and not produce a little bloomp of waist fat. The small side muscles in his upper arms had a sort of a sideways S shape that called out to her. They were the muscles he would use if he were supporting his own weight over her.

She watched him lean into a turn up the slight slope toward the tractor tire in the middle of the front yard. The previous owner had put it there, painted it white, and planted peonies in it. David had insisted on keeping it as it was, he being one of those non-gay would-be camp enthusiasts who rave automatically over anything tacky, and now Marian, too, had grown to like it. She had never expected to be living in a house like this, on a rural highway a mile out of a town one town over from the town the college was in, getting sexed up watching a seventeen-year-old neighbor kid drive her lawn-mower around. His chest muscles were indisputably square and flat; the cord of his Walkman headphones looked frail and kinky against his skin. How could he possibly be hearing any music with the mower going? She thought of gently removing his headphones and his pants, and then of making some sort of herbal wreath for his young penis, mainly of Sweet Genovese Basil (a kind she had recently planted), like a laurel crown; perhaps as a final touch she could insert a short sprig of curly parsley into the opening of his urethra, so that when she slid and stroked his soft newborn sex-skin twistingly up and down, murmuring to him not to worry, that it was just nature's way, and he finally whimpered the conclusive whimper, the sprig of parsley would flip right in the air from the force of his clotted sperm. But wait, wait—she didn't really want to have sex with a seventeen-year-old kid; moreover she didn't like the boy's mother, who was a complainer and a conspiracy theorist and none too bright. So Marian just paid the boy the twenty-five dollars, plus a two-dollar tip.

"Next time," she said to him, a little shyly, "I'd like you to show me how to drive that thing." She noticed that he had been careful to put his shirt on before he came to the door to be paid—a considerate touch. He was a good kid. He said, "Sure."

When he had left, Marian did the dirtiest thing she could think of, which was to drive fast to the supermarket, buy a copy of *Cosmopolitan*, drive home, pull the shades, and squat naked on her living-room floor directly over the magazine, opened to a full-page head shot of Patrick Swayze. "Look at what I'm showing you, Patrick," she said, stroking the underside of her open thighs and pulling on a few pubic hairs to add a piquant sensation. Patrick's eyes gazed unblinkingly up at her from between her legs, half obscured by her bush. "That's right, look at what you're making me do to my big clit," she said. "Do you want to see my big fat cunt come? Do you?" Soon her eyes locked with Patrick's and she sat suddenly down on his nose and half-smiling mouth, making the doubly slick magazine buckle. It was all so out of character for her that she felt glowing and refreshed afterward.

The next week had a day and a half of rain, and the lawn needed a mow badly by Saturday. Kev couldn't come by until

three-thirty because of soccer practice. Marian spent the day
pruning several overgrown lilacs and reading some more of
the new biography of Jean Stafford. She felt, by the time Kevin
showed up, that her sexual energy was very much under control and that she wouldn't make some sort of regrettable pass
at him. He explained how to drive the mower, with many
apologies for the fact that he knew how to drive his own
family's mower better, saying that basically you did this and
that and you had to watch out for this and that. She paid him
fifteen for the lesson, which he at first wouldn't take and then
did take with fairly good grace, and she waved and began
mowing. It was exhilarating to churn through the grass, especially when she drove up the slight grade toward the house
and heard the engine strain a little. At first she mowed in a
kind of boustrophedon pattern, back and forth, and then she
changed to an Aztec square spiral pattern, homing in on the
white tractor tire. As she got more confident about turning
sharply and using the accelerator, she began to understand
why David had wanted to own this machine—the feeling of
being in control of it, cutting this wide swathe, was really
terrific.

Over time, though, she noticed that there was a powerful
distraction from the mere feeling of twelve-point-five-horse-
power empowerment, which was that the constant vibration of
the machine had gradually won over her clit-shaft—in fact it
had enlisted her entire perineum. She began to think of two
long, lithe men lying back with hiked-up T-shirts in Dying
Slave poses over the tractor tire, looking up at the sky and
slowly pulling on their Michelangelesque penises. She imagined herself lying naked on the fresh cool grass with a huge
slow wooden wheel suspended above her, and twelve nude
men tied securely to the spokes of the wheel, their heads

pointing toward the center, all of their testicle-sacks hanging halfway down their unsnipped cocks, all of them masturbating languorously with their one free hand. As the Catherine wheel turned above her, she felt the gaze of all twelve pairs of eyes admiring her hips and pubic hair, seeing her pressing her thighs together, which were right in the center, and as each man's cock ticked into position over her face, she opened her mouth and held her tongue out and closed her eyes and felt warm semenous splashes fall on her lips and neck.

By this time she was in reality driving around and around the white tractor tire, mowing grass that had already been mowed, near coming but not quite able to. She was glad young Kev wasn't in sight right now, or she might not be able to contain herself. She went inside, had a shower, and finally came harder than she had in quite a while, lying on her bedroom floor with her legs up on her bed, one finger polishing her nug, the other hand reaching around her leg and rudely giving herself the finger. She prolonged the aftergasms by squeezing her clit gently as if it were her nipple.

But when she thought it over an hour later, she was not perfectly satisfied. The orgasm itself, though it had unquestionably had a beginning, a middle, and an end, had lacked, despite its intensity, the lush greenery and winding roads and hot, fruit-filled bazaars that her hour of ridem mowing had led her to expect almost as her right. Perhaps she needed to do something to pep up her masturbational technique; perhaps her clitoris was simply tired of her own fingers after all these years. The vibration of the mower had felt so unexpectedly good. A year earlier, David's car had developed a problem with wheel alignment, so that the steering wheel started wobbling dramatically at about sixty-three miles an hour, and she now remembered that before he had gotten it fixed she had been obliged once or twice to pull over to the shoulder and get her orgasm out of the way so that she wouldn't be a hazard to others on the road. She simply needed more vibration, faster vibration, in her life—it was that simple. The idea of sexual devices had seemed faintly ludicrous in previous years, and when it stopped seeming ludicrous it began seeming too trendy—she couldn't escape the suspicion that the majority of vibrators were still given as joke gifts at office good-bye parties. But why shouldn't she at least try a toy of some kind? She had gotten rid of David, she was beginning her life afresh. She went back to her *Cosmo*, avoiding Patrick Swayze (who looked a little the worse for wear anyway), and found in the back pages an ad for a company in San Francisco, "women owned and operated." They rushed her a catalog, sensing her breathlessness, and a week and a half later the good old UPS man was asking her to sign on line 34 for a large white box that Marian expected to contain four hand-held devices and a container of Astroglide. The UPS man, she noticed with relief, was, though handsome, not perfect—with a slight double chin and a pleasant asymmetrical smile and a hint of David's incipiently stocky shape.

When she opened the box, however, she discovered that she had gotten only three toys, not the full four she had ordered. There was the startlingly realistic hand-painted slightly curving Arno Van Dilden Heavydick, with movable balls and suction-cup base; there was the Swiss-made TorqueMaja Desnuda, with its twelve special "power-frig" torque settings; there was the mixeresque Oster plug-in coil model with its little cabinet of attachments; but she was missing the forty-dollar, four-foot-long, double-headed Royal Welsh Fusilier with dual slidable foreskins—it was on back order, to be shipped in several days. At first Marian was irritated, wanting to have all four artifacts to try one after another, but then she found that the ones she had at hand were more than enough to get her through the next forty-eight hours. She became especially fond of the fast-humming and refreshingly un-penile Oster. She pirated the surge protector from her ne-glected PC and plugged it in below the plug from her washing machine (safety first), and plugged the clit-knobbed Oster into it, and, using it, came with mystical intensity sitting naked on the cold lid of the washing machine with the door to the nearby garage wide open, looking down at her trembling titfat, as all her bras and underpants spun around in damp darkness underneath her. And when the clock radio woke her at six-thirty on weekdays, she unplugged it from its extension cord and plugged in the Oster in its place, relishing the illu-sion that time could be stopped while she started the day right with a brisk coil-driven clasm.

She took a vacation day on the day the back-ordered vibra-tor was due to arrive. When the UPS truck hadn't shown by almost one o'clock and when Marian, already on her third pair of underpants, found herself holding a mother-of-pearl hand mirror up to one of her nipples and watching the au-reole get wrinkly backward and then trying to push her nipple through a buttonhole of her linen shirt, she decided it was time to *do* something—to mow the lawn, which did need mowing. She changed to a full loose gypsy skirt with nothing underneath and a ribbed black camisole with no bra and drove the mower out of the garage into the yard with her freshly batteried Van Dilden resting in her lap. She hopped off in the middle of the front yard, and in full view of the world (though too fast for anyone to see really what she was up to), with her back to the road, she licked the vibe's inch-and-a-half suction-cup base and stuck it firmly on the seat of the idling green machine and turned its little switch on. She regarded it trembling there on the seat, this enchantingly obscene blurred tube of realism shaken simultaneously by its internal mini-motor and the macro-motor of the ridem, and her slype ached to feel it push her open. She slapped it once; it flinched a little to the side but didn't unsuction itself. She wanted to mow *now;* she wanted to mow that fucking lawn like she had never mowed it before.

Planting her feet on the floorboard of the ridem, holding on to the steering wheel, she demurely flounced her skirt over the seat, and then, arching the small of her back and closing her eyes, she slowly lowered herself until she felt the buzzed brainless head of the Van Dilden nudge into her underthigh. She only had to readjust herself slightly, ticklish trickles moistening open her self-aware slypelips, and she was ready to be upfucked: she looked out smiling at the cars driving by and stamped on the throttle, and with a long groan that was masked by the sudden rev of the engine, her slopping cuntness was forced back and down on the full hand-poured width of the Van Dilden. She sat heavily down on it and mowed and mowed, and as she mowed it was as if the whole lawn was concertedly fucking her: every little hummock, every undulation of turf, every tough clump of thistle stalk was telegraphed directly via her autodick-fitted ridem directly into her boggled cervix, while all twelve pistoning horsepowers added their internal combustions to the party as well. She worked the lawn for ten minutes or more, risking a numb-out but successfully avoiding it, smiling again at the traffic because they couldn't know the supreme full-pelvic cuntfucking she was giving herself as she mowed. She was lowering her head forward toward the steering wheel, just on the point of allowing herself to crooningly come, when she noticed the UPS truck pull over to the side of the road. The driver waved his clipboard at her and walked up with a long oblong box, stowing his sunglasses in his shirt pocket. Marian straightened and tried to collect herself. There was no way to turn the Van Dilden off without pulling up her skirt. She was covered with sweat. Above human hearing, her nipples were screaming for any knowledgeable mouth. She signed where the UPS man pointed, line 27, hoping the idling motor would hurry him off, and he almost handed her the box, and then said something she couldn't hear.

He gestured to the front porch questioningly with the box; Marian nodded. She watched him jog to the porch. He ran like a coach. She hadn't noticed before that his eyes were attractive; his helpful hesitation was quite sexy when she was able to contrast it with the idea of the molded thing that was fucking her right at that moment. Nonetheless, she wanted him to drive off so that she could finish mowing.

He was halfway down the slope to his truck when he stopped and came back with a "May I trouble you for something?" expression.

"Yes?" she shouted.

He said something she couldn't catch. Reluctantly she cut the mower engine. "Sorry—what?"

"Oh, you didn't have to turn that off," he said. "I was just wondering if I could hose off my head. I'm burning up. It must be over a hundred in the back of the truck." Suddenly he frowned. "You hear that?"

It was the vibrator. It felt so good. She smiled and closed her eyes. "What exactly do you hear?"

"Is your engine still on?" he said.

"It's nothing," said Marian. "Go hose your head, by all means. The hose is right up on the side of the house. Oh, damn—I had to turn off the water in the basement because it leaks."

"Never mind then, that's okay." He was backing away. He did look uncomfortably hot. She liked the idea of his hosing off his head.

"It won't take a second to turn the water on, just let me get off this thing." Marian held out her hand and he steadyingly took it. "Oof," she said. She lifted herself carefully off the Van Dilden and dismounted from the mower. The gleaming cock-shape continued to buzz away trustily on the slick, and in places even frothy, seat. "Pardon me," she said, waving dismissively at the sight. "I was just experimenting."

"Is that . . . ?" he said, slack-jawed, pointing. "Did I deliver that the other day?"

"You did. Come on and I'll get the hose going."

"Wait." He took off his shirt and draped it over the dildo.

"Thanks," said Marian.

While the UPS man bent at the waist and spluttered and snorted in the cold hose-flow, Marian opened the new box. The lean double-headed length of the Royal Welsh Fusilier lay bent in half within.

"Is it what you wanted?" the UPS man inquired, wiping the water from his eyes. "If not, I can tape it up for you and send it right back now."

Marian held it up and experimentally slid its two foreskins back. "No, it's more or less what I expected."

"What do you plan to do with that? My name's John West-man, by the way."

Marian introduced herself and they shook hands. She felt his eyes flicking over her nipples. "I know what I'd like to do," she said, "but unfortunately I can't do it on my new ridem lawn-mower because what I have in mind needs a little more privacy."

"Well, what about the back of my truck?"

"I was just thinking that. You have to drive, though. I'm not going to have sex with you—is that okay?"

"Sure, I guess. I'm just intrigued. You've gotten me all intrigued."

Together they retrieved his shirt and her Van Dilden.

"Lick this, will you?" she said. He licked the suction cup and she affixed the dick to the metal floor of his truck. Boxes were piled high on wire shelves on either side of her. There was a narrow opening to the front seat. The UPS man got in the front and sat watching her. He was squeezing his crotch through his pants.

"No, just drive," she ordered, lifting her skirt and kneeling over the Van Dilden. "Find a dirt road and drive on it. I want this truck to bounce."

"My pleasure," he said. She turned the vibrator on to full and slid halfway down on it. While she squeezed Astroglide on the two ends of the Fusilier, he turned onto a dirt road in low gear. The truck rocked and lurched. "Oh, that's it," she said, feeling herself filled with unexpected lateral UPS-truck fuck-motions. Already aching from her earlier mowing, she was impatient. "Now stop for a second. I want you to stick one end of this in my ass."

She pulled her skirt up over her ass with one hand and leaned forward and passed him the double-headed vibrator. The head of the Van Dilden was still inside her.

"Should I turn it on?" he asked, examining the little remote controller.

"Yeah, I guess, but, mmm, the main thing is to stuff it in my ass right now." He turned it on, using the little control box.

The two buzzings were at slightly different pitches, wowing in and out of phase. Marian felt something hard push against the muscle of her ass. "That's it," she said. She relaxed against it and let its head go in. "Push it a little further. Wow. Now drive—oh fuck, just drive this fucking truck."

The UPS guy hopped back in his seat and put the truck in gear. Marian unbent her knees and sat flatly down on the Van Dilden with her legs extended in front of her. This had the effect of pushing the Royal Welsh Fusilier deeper into her ass. It was like a fleshy tail. "I've got toys up my cunt and up my ass," she moaned. The truck started bumping and jostling. She pulled the length of the Fusilier up against her tailbone and bent it around her hip and found that, as she had hoped, the other end easily reached her clit. She pulled back its "foreskin" and held the slick second head against herself. "Oh, fuck" she said, feeling all of her circuits starting to get busy.

"Is that about right?" called the UPS man. He was driving manfully from one gulley to the next, steering with one hand. His other, Marian saw, was in a fist, pounding up and down on his surprisingly meaty coral-gabled cock. His brown UPS pants were around his knees, the zipper splayed open and ready to rip. The dirt road sloped down.

"Starting to feel nice," called Marian politely. Then her voice changed to a command. *"Now pump the brake."* She held the hem of her skirt with her chin so that she could look down at her spread vadge. The road was pounding the Van Dilden's cockshape into her stinging cuntskin. She reached back and twisted the Fusilier in her ass. Her clit looked as if it were ready to jump up and propose a toast to old friends; the other end of the double-header was sitting solidly to one side of it, talking in the fast, even, confident nasty-rumor language that vibrators use with their clit-clients. She felt a gorgeous huge thick-muscled orgasm moving slowly up her legs and fanning out toward all orifices. She spat her skirt out. "Pump the brake harder!" she commanded again. "Oh shit! Oh God! That's it. Pump it. Brake, brake, brake. That's it, like that. FUCK ME WITH YOUR TRUCK! JACK THAT BIG UGLY DICK AND FUCK MY ASS WITH YOUR TRUCK!"

The UPS man, his leg pushing the brake-pedal in rapid rhythm to the long white-knuckled strokes of his fist, looked as if he couldn't hold back another second. The truck lurched and rocked. A box from Harry and David's tumbled over beside Marian. She grunted down against her toys, feeling them stretch her sex-holes to the point of pain. "Now watch me come!" she called to the front seat. "Keep pumping the brake and watch this hot little cunt come! I'M COMING! AAAAAAAAH, fuck fuck fuck, coming, I'M COMING!" She pressed the silicone snake-head harder against her clit and let the truck-chassied orgasm bump and grind through her.

The UPS man had his head cranked around and was watching her crammed crotch, pop-eyed. He made a vowelly groan and lifted his butt clear off the seat. "Oh, here it comes!" he said. With a final upward fist-stroke, his squat thick dick blew a united parcel of peckerpaste all over the sleeve of his uniform. "Ooh, yeah babe. Ooh yeah."

He put the truck in neutral and the two of them caught their breath. Marian stood unsteadily, smoothing her skirt. The Royal Welsh Fusilier fell out of her ass to the floor with a snakey thump. The UPS man sighed happily. "The tightest ship in the shipping business," he said, shaking his head.

"That's me," said Marian.

When the brakes had cooled, he drove her home. And for several months afterward, whenever John the UPS man delivered a white box and Marian the librarian was at home, he helped her test out the sex toy that it was certain to contain. Without him, too, Marian had large numbers of outdoor-gasms on her ridem mower, helped by several dilda, and when she was done mowing and coming for the afternoon, she often arranged a towel in the sun in the back yard and lay there for an hour or two with her glasses folded near her hand, smelling the smell of cut grass and gasoline and sex juice on her fingers.

10

As a piece of rot this was, I know, a smidge keyed-up in places, but for a first attempt I felt it would do. It was fun to write. But much, much more fun was watching my sunbathing companion read it. I had spent so much time alongside her that I felt she was an old friend, and yet I had no idea how she would react. I stared at her mouth through the binoculars. (She had put on sunglasses.) Every line that she read was a personal triumph for me; every time she moved to the next page I was in absolute heaven. This was a pleasure the likes of which I had not known. Even before she started reading, the sight of her pulling the bag from the sand and undoing the silver twist-tie made my heart swat in all directions, like the Cocoa Puffs rabbit. I wanted her to be holding and reading my home-grown smut so, so much! I so much wanted to have inspired a feeling of quickened curiosity in her. To have done just that—to have created an expression of puzzled curiosity in the universe, where before there had been only a woman lying in a green bathing suit in the sun on the beach, digging in the sand.

And—I wish I could whisper this for dramatic effect—*she did get a little turned on*—she did, she did. The first sign of it was when she glanced around to verify her dune-grassed isolation and then subtly lifted her upper body a little higher on her elbows so that her titshape elongated, and then when they, her two laggard cherubim, were hovering almost free of the earth, she moved her shoulders so that her nipple-tips grazed lightly over the open mesh-lined cups of her undone bikini top. I debated stopping time to hold them for a moment, but I decided that I wanted to see her reaction continuously, without interruption. A little later, on about the fourth page of my typescript, she scratched her leg for a long time, apparently forgetting that she was scratching. I took this as a good sign, a sign of absorption. Then she pulled her chin in suddenly, surprised by something, and shook her head. She looked around. She resumed reading. *Then* it began: the rhythmic antiphonal tightening of her butt-muscles began: first the left, then the right, left right, left right, so that her heart-shaped ass-curve systoled and diastoled before my eyes. I knew that these marching contractions were pushing her bush-bone hard into the towel and into the accommodating sand underneath, and the sight of this secret self-assertion got me so hot and frantic that to work off the energy I had to drop the binoculars and push up my glasses and sprint down the length of the beach, slaloming barefoot around the halted family groups and single shell-musers and grizzled voyeurs. On the way back, running more slowly, I hesitated before a tall girl of sixteen or seventeen in a blue maillot standing in an inch of water, recoiling from the cold, and I stopped for a second, panting, so that I could slide her tight shoulder straps off and regard her white, hippy, sexily imperfect body with her suit turned inside out on her legs. "You'll do just great," I said to her as I suited her back up. Then I resumed my binocular station near my assive-aggressive reader and let myself calm down. Strangely, I felt a little guilt that I had been unfaithful to her with the seventeen-year-old.

She read the entire story, and when she finished she put it back in the plastic bag and twisted the twist-tie around it and buried it in the sand where she'd found it, marking its existence with three little shells. Then she reached back and re-clasped her top and turned over. I watched her stomach rise and fall as she breathed. I fancied that she was breathing a little faster than she would have been if my words hadn't just gone through her mind. I was *in* her mind. There were things about what she had read that she didn't like, or that seemed dumb to her, but even so it was working on her and making her want to *go home*. She sat up, put on a loose faded shirt that went almost to her knees, unpinned her hair, and walked up a path to a set of newish condos on one end of the beach. I did the usual business of pausing her as she unlocked the door so that I could slip past her and hide somewhere in her apartment. I hate hiding in women's apartments when they are there, because I suddenly become in doing so an intruder, and all those awful hider-in-the-house movies inescapably come to mind, and the music threatens to turn tritonally ominous. The last thing in the world I want is to be seen as a threat.

But happily, I'm good at remaining undetected in close quarters with a woman. I have never yet scared anyone. And this particular woman's place was perfect, since it was all open and loft-like, with a bedroom supported by columns up a spiral flight of stairs. I sat on her bed listening intently to her putterings below, and when I heard her steps on the stairway, I stopped time and went down and past her (ducking under her arm) and sat on a chair in the kitchen. The tops of my ears were getting a little sore from all the time-pervertive pulling and pushing on my glasses, but it was a tiny price to pay. The water began running in the pipes, always a good sign. I pushed my triune crotch-lump against the cool Corian edge of the countertop.

Eventually I Dropped and went up to see whether it was the sink or a shower or a bath and found her bent over, naked, rummaging around in the back of a drawer, while the lower tap filled her tub. I studied her profile for half a minute: she had a lively, somewhat thin face, oily from sunscreen, with a high nose bridge, a nose that was more intelligent-seeming than her eyes, if that makes sense. (Though I have to be careful about evaluating the intelligence of women's eyes in the Fold, since a person's look varies so radically from instant to instant, and I could just be catching her at a moment of unflattering inattention.) The corners of her mouth were tight as she reached in her drawer. I couldn't see what her hands were searching for under her folded sweatshirts and leggings, but I had my hopes.

Just before a woman takes a bath, as the water is running, her nudity suddenly releases all of its charged ions of lewdness and becomes wholly artistique: she is naked in order to bathe herself, and *bathe* is such a smooth-surfaced, wide-voweled, modest word that you can appreciate the particulars of her beauty without any of your own erectile fierceness getting in the way. She is suddenly a modern dancer, a water-sprite, a wood-nymph, a naturist, her tits are not conceivably tits but breasts, and no matter how funkily they are shaped they appeal to the lovingly appreciative Ansel Adams in us rather than to the groper and pocket-pool player. This despite her manifest protosexual charms, her softly domey areolae, the Moorish arch her ass made in giving way effortlessly to her thighs, all of which I was able to review thoroughly for the first time with her up and on her feet. I didn't spend too long in that early Fold, though, eager for her to get on with her intention, whatever it might be. I got out of sight and turned time on and distracted myself by reading half an article in *Condé Nast Traveler* on a lake system in Canada (my bather's name, given on the magazine's address label, was Michelle Hoffman), and then, when I heard the water stop, I checked in on her again.

Her bath had begun. Her knees were above the surface of the water, the kneecaps flat and square, and the water was clear (no genitally irritating bubble bath for this woman), and she had just lifted one arm, so that long pale-green streamers and trailers of water poured stilly off of it. Her hand loosely held a red washcloth, soft with a surround of unfalling water. I could easily have knelt in the bathtub with her and jacked looking at the way the riverine trails of water joined at her elbow and fell off her, a little like those festive triangular vinyl flags hung around used-car lots.

(Actually no—they didn't make me think of a used-car lot at all at that moment; they made me think of the way a woman's urine falls from between her legs, confusedly, in a stegosaurian fan of hard-to-source cockscomb-triangles. I used to think that the reason why women's urination sounded so intricately different from men's had only to do with the end-points of this splayed outflow, since there were so many separate points of collision with toilet water, as opposed to the single focused plunge of the continuous male stream—but the other day, listening to Joyce pee in the ladies' room from the next stall, I realized that it isn't only that. The more important difference is that male urine *makes no noise* as it flies out of the penis-knob, because it has become, due to the inordinate length of the male urethra, a coherent, laserlike flow. The only noise that men make, then, is the noise their departed urine produces later, in colliding with whatever texture and substance it collides with. But women's urethras are not stealthy. They are short, since they are not needed to help pulse out a comeshot (I ignore the touchy subject of fejaculation, or ejillulation, here); their urine wings excitedly out rather than releasing itself in a single laminar column, and this exit-spraying itself makes a distinct noise, a likable, high whistle-warble-hissing that you can hear over the broadcast of complex terminal splashings. "Making water" as a euphemism applies much better to what women do than what men do.)

But I didn't want to come yet with Michelle—I was curious about whether she had any sexual plans herself. To be honest, my feelings had been a little hurt that she had not brought home the story I had written for her to keep forever—although I consoled myself by thinking that maybe she was just being considerate in reburying it, not wanting to interfere with some top-secret interlover dropoff. I did feel a little rejected, and I was hoping to restore my cheer by watching her do something all by herself that would serve as real concrete proof that I had gotten to her in an actively crotchy sense. Just a bath was not enough. Kneeling by the edge of the tub, I spotted something dark in the water near her feet. Her toes were curled around it. When I put my head very close to the surface of the lavishly chlorinated water, steadying myself on one of her knees, I determined that the object was, as I had of course hoped but hadn't really allowed myself to expect, a large black realistic rubber dildo. She was bathing with her rubber dildo—oh poetry! She was relaxing, letting her eyes close, not thinking about that single-minded submarine cruising around out of sight, beyond her bent knees, but because it was unquestionably there in the water with her, it was working under her thoughts and keeping her just on the edge of conscious arousal. It was time to take some chances with her.

I removed all the clothes from the tall wicker laundry hamper that stood under the bathroom window and piled them on her bed and got inside the hamper with a wrinkly dark-gray linen shirt of hers tied loosely over my face; though I was in something of a fetal position, and though I could not see all that well through the linen, I could at least get some notion of what was going on as she proceeded with her bath. I used my glasses to Unfold; at once her hand tightened on the red washcloth and lots of water fell along her arm. Then nothing much happened for a long time. She wiped beads of sweat off her forehead with the washcloth several times, and she sighed a total of three long sighs. There were splashes whose nature I couldn't determine. She shaved her legs for a while. She ran some more hot water and stirred it around. Once or twice she whispered aloud, going over fragments of remembered conversation, as far as I could tell. She did what looked to be a set of leg lifts. When the pain in my knees became too acute I Dropped, climbed out, and took a break downstairs, finishing the article on the Canadian lakes. I sang the Beatles song "Here, There and Everywhere," walking around in her living room. I left my clothes in a little mound on her coffee table and went back upstairs and stuffed myself back in her hamper with the linen shirt over my head; I knew good things were going to happen. After ten or fifteen minutes she stood, letting the water pour off her, and toweled herself. I was on alert to push up my glasses at any second if she decided to throw the towel into the hamper, but she didn't. After she dried her hair, she put the towel around her shoulders, and then she planted her hands on the edge of the bathtub and knelt with one leg in the bathwater and one outside on the floor. "Ooh that's so cold," she said, when her vadge touched the rounded edge of the tub.

I was too crumpled in the hamper even to think of doing anything physical with my richard, but all I wanted in any event was the sight I was seeing; the sight of her leaning forward on her hands and rocking the weight of her hips down against the edge of the tub. "Where is that cock?" she said. "I want to see that cock." She fished around in the water and pulled out the dildo and looked at it. She dipped it several times in the water and pulled it out, shaking it each time, evidently liking the way it glistened. Then she worked herself down the edge of the tub and suctioned the black dick onto the tiled shower wall at about her eye level. She moved her face over it, kissing it in the most wonderfully fetishistic way, and biting on it. "You like when I suck that big dick, don't you?" she said. She put two fingers down on the edge of the tub and rocked forward on them, so that her clit was straddled. She let the head of the rubberdick pass over her closed eyelids, and then she stood up a little, one leg still in the bathtub and one out, and stroked her slit very fast while she circled the wall-mounted dick with her nipples. When she had straightened her legs completely, she was able to lean herself against the tile wall with the rubberdick between her legs and move its resilience over her clit-lump. Her forehead and nipples touched the cold green tile. She kissed the towel on her shoulders once. I was dying with visual happiness.

"You want this ass?" she asked the dildo and seemed to get an affirmative answer, for she turned away from it with her hands on the edge of the tub, wiggling her ass back and forth in front of it. The suction base lost suction and the cock fell suddenly onto a scallop-shell soap dish. "Aw, did I shock you, honey?" she said. "Am I going too fast for you?" She dipped it in the bathwater again, shook it off, and, straddling the tub, stuck it back on the edge of the tub and sucked it. "See how easy it is to get you hard again?" she said. She stood over it, pulling up on her pubic hair so that she could see her clit, and she said to the dildo, "You ready to fuck this nice clean cunt? Because I sure am ready for you. I bet you are. Are you big and stiff enough to fill this hungry cunt?" She bent her knees until its rubber head found her, and then she sat down hard on it. She fucked it bouncingly for a little while and then got off of it and went to get a mirror and propped it up so she could watch her rubberman going in and out. She fucked it some more. In the haze of the shirt of hers that I was wearing I watched her finger orbit her clit-folds until I was ready to weep at the lyricism of it. Was Michelle this nasty on a regular basis? Maybe not. She'd really had to grope to find the dildo in her dresser in the first place. This was not an everyday sort of autofuck for her, I didn't think. My UPS truck might have had something to do with it.

I kept perfectly still, hardly breathing, while she came closer and closer to coming. She would stop suddenly just before she came, fucking slowly up and down on the dildo some more, then frigging for a while. She started making some incredible clenched-teeth noises, followed by pheasanty sounds so superb that I was surprised I had been able to live without them. Her little finger went into her asshole and she squinted, cleared for takeoff. She started saying, "Oh fuck this cunt, baby, fuck it, fuck this cunt," over and over. Then her face wrenched itself into a squinting accelerated grimace and I pushed up on my glasses, stopping her right in the middle of her dildorgasm.

I climbed out of the hamper, very slowly because I was stiff. I studied her climax-face from every angle, trying to record its transient extremity in my memory. I held her perky little finger, which was still hooked in her ane. I rested my ear on the edge of the tub about three inches from her open boat and stared at the finger that was bestirring itself around her bright-pink pumped-up nerve; and beyond it at the very soft inner skin stretched tight around my fellow American, my fellow rubber hider-in-her-house. I loved what I saw. I licked her knuckles; I tapped my dick against her breasts to see how they quivered; I straddled the tub just as she was straddling it, facing her, and beat my richard savagely until I was almost there. When I was ready I stood and said, "Let me be there with you, honey, you're so sexy, please let me come on your face," in a strange almost singsong pleading voice, and without waiting for an answer from her I let all of my burning bechamel jump out onto her tightly closed eyes, unable to resist doing so even though I knew that I would probably regret it afterward—not least because it would be so much trouble to get all of it off her eyelashes and eyebrows. When I was done I sat down on the tub for a second to rest. "Thank you," I said. I wasn't crazy about the way my come looked on her closed eyes, but the beauty of her ecstatic expression survived it; in fact the existence of the outcome of my orgasm on her still-coming face seemed entirely irrelevant, as it should have. I turned time on for the tiniest fraction of a second, so that she would have a tactile flash of the sensation of liquid warmth, in case it would add a novel touch to her clasm, and then I spent a good ten minutes tamping and gently rinsing every sign of my sperm off of her. I put her dirty clothes back in her hamper. I took a last look around to be sure I had left everything in order. I stood behind her and flashed time on again for a second or two to be sure that, post-orgasm, she didn't suspect that she had had company, and when I was convinced that she felt safe and unviolated I went downstairs and got dressed and let myself quietly out. It hadn't really happened.

I intended to leave my UPS story buried in the sand where she had marked it with three shells, in case she wanted it at some future date, but as I mounted my borrowed motorcycle, vanity overcame me and I hustled back to dig it up. Then, still in the Fold, I drove slowly home. I kept thinking of Michelle's bath as I cruised down the shoulder of Route 3; I ardently wished I had a picture of Michelle's come-face (before I had come on it myself, I mean): it was the kind of sight that could enhance your life for a decade. Sadly, Polaroid pictures taken in the Fold don't develop properly—I know because I've tried. There was a woman in an airplane bathroom once: I saw her flipping through a *Playboy* "Girls of Summer" issue at the airport gift shop and then kept tabs on her in the plane, and when she went to the bathroom I knew she would probably be coming and I Dropped and got a key from a pocket of one of the flight attendants and opened the door and found her with one heel in the steel sink and the other propped in the air where the door had been, coming stunningly, and I borrowed a passenger's Polaroid and took her picture, but through some oddity of Fold-chemistry that I will never understand, the greens appeared only very faintly, and the oranges and reds did not show up at all, so my own visual memory was all I had. It surprises me, incidentally, that nobody has launched a men's magazine called *O-Shots*, devoted exclusively to close-up photographs of women's faces in the midst of orgasm. At the end of each photo layout would be a little official-looking certificate of authenticity, signed by the model, that said, "I hereby certify and swear that I did reach one or more female orgasms during the photo shoot herein pictured and that my expressions are neither fiction nor semifiction but are the true, unsimulated result of my own pleasure and amusement." I would subscribe. Or perhaps an O-shot calendar— the March orgasm-face, the November orgasm-face?

The guy whose motorcycle I had borrowed was sitting sullenly against a tree near where I had dismounted him. The note that I had pinned to his leg was crumpled in his hand; it said, *I have borrowed your bike. Wait here and I will return it to you shortly.* Sensibly, he had waited, but he wasn't happy about it. I parked the bike in front of him and walked home and lay down on the grass. I took off my glasses and rubbed my eyes. Time turned back on everywhere. I was exhausted. The total elapsed Strine-time had been almost eleven hours; elapsed real time, a little over two hours. In the space of a single "day" I had become a modestly successful amateur pornographer. "Rot makes life," I sighed happily to myself, thinking of lonely old Henry James, and then I dozed for a while on the blue striped towel.

II

I'VE GOTTEN INTO A NEW AND BETTER WORK RHYTHM. I NOW spend every other twenty-four-hour period in Fold-furled isolation. I wake up at seven-thirty, and if it's going to be a Fold day I thick-fingeredly snap time off, shake my watch to unfreeze it, and spend the whole next twenty-four hours enclosed within the quiescent seven-thirtyness of my room, working on this book. I have weaned myself from high-volume earbuds; I can think now without hearing music on the radio. Rarely, I take short walks. I eat lunch and dinner and go to bed exactly as I would were time in effect, and yet I have a whole stilled writing day funded with early-morning qualities of light that help me concentrate. After a "night's" sleep, I wake the world with a second snap and have a shower and go to my continuing temp assignment at MassBank. It is not such a good thing for me to be spending half my life in the Fold, doubling my rate of aging, but I only plan to keep up this alternating schedule until I finish a little more of my autobiography. An unexpected benefit of the regimen is that real life, the life I spend in time's flow, feels not unpleasantly elongated, as if I were ten years old again; my privately interpolated "yesterdays" push real events of only two or three days ago into the middle-distant past.

Am I an alienated person? Some who have read this far might say so—some might say that a man who comes onto an unknown woman's ecstatically squinting orgasm-face without her being aware of it is definitely an alienated person—or worse. And temps are prima facie alienated by virtue of their vocational rootlessness. But I don't see that nasal, sociological-sounding word applying in any useful way to me. I get along well with people. I haven't perhaps done such a good job of establishing my sanity in this sketch of my life, since I have had to concentrate on the episodes of temporal distortion that make my experience unique, and they almost always embrace the controlled mental disorder known as sexual arousal, but I'm not by any means a crazy person. I don't have a flat affect. I'm friendly and likable. I go out on the occasional date. I have several male friends, even. I have had long-term relationships with three women, Rhody being the most recent. The only major difference between me and any number of residents of the greater Boston area is that I have been able to invent and make use of several sorts of chronoclutch. No, there is a difference, I think: I'm arrogant enough to believe, at least to believe sometimes, that the reason that *I* have been chosen over any other contemporary human to receive and develop this chronanistic ability (if there is indeed some supernatural temp agency doing the choosing) is maybe that I *can* be trusted with it—trusted at least not to do any real harm. Morals depend in part on consequence; consequence on time; and since my amoralities flourish and expire entirely in momentary pico-states of timeless inconsequence, the usual rules just don't have the same prohibitive force. Nobody else should be entitled to take off women's clothes at will, at the snap of a finger or the flip of a switch, but I think I should be, because, for one thing, my curiosity has more love and tolerance in it than other men's does. Before Rhody broke up with me, she once told me that the attraction to having an affair with a painter (a figurative painter, she meant) was the possibility that he would really see her and know all that was to be known about the shape of her body—when she undressed for him there would be a thrilling completeness to her undressing. To nobody else would her physical self mean as much as it meant to his eye, and so her own nudity would feel sexier with him than with anyone else. I'm not a painter, I'm only a temp and an occasional creative rotter, and yet I do contend that when I strip a passing woman on the street because her face or body calls out to me, I see more in her than others do. Of course there is plenty of self-deception possible here. But I can truthfully say that I'm never disappointed, never—I'm never able to feel anything but love and gratitude toward a woman when I secretly take off her clothes. Say there is a low cesarean scar that nobody but her husband has seen at close range. Say there is some part of her body that I will see that she isn't very proud of. In seeing it, I feel the goodness in me *blossom*—I know that she would be embarrassed about my having seen this feature, whatever it is, and I turn the knowledge of her imputed embarrassment into an upwelling of affection for her and her vulnerabilities.

I would condemn in the strongest terms anyone else who did what I have done. But the thing is, I did it, *I* did it, and I know myself, I know that I mean no harm, I mean well. I want simply to know what every woman looks like and feels like. I mean only to appreciate what the ribs of a complete stranger feel like under my hands, or to hold some hair I haven't held before, or to come in someone's face while she is paused in her own orgasm. And since in the Fermata I happen to be able to act on these wants without troubling her—without shaming or frightening her or interrupting what she is doing or thinking, simply by stopping the entire known universe for a few minutes or hours, I feel that what I'm doing isn't wrong enough for me to override my irresistible desire to do it. In fact, maybe what I'm doing is straightforwardly right and good! I never ogle or leer on sidewalks. The Fold has permitted me to perfect my surreptitiousness. Maybe every single woman I have stripped, if she knew me, if she could know now what my thoughts had been as I unzipped her dress and undid her bra, would want me to have stripped her and sucked her breasts and understood her body as it truly deserved to be understood.

Rhody, however, didn't view it that way. When I tried the idea out on her (on the plane home from our beach vacation), she was interested at first, and then later she turned against it, using awful and, in my opinion, off-base words like "necrophilia" to characterize it. Let me say that I am not a necrophile. The notion has no appeal. Liaisons among the undead are fashionable, but I don't have a drop of vampiric blood in me. (I did, however, once put a pair of "nipple nooses" on the famous Anne Rice at Barnes & Noble some years ago, when I was at the height of my mechanical-pencil Fold-phase. I clicked time on for a minute or two so she would have a chance to feel them while she signed my copy of her book, which was going to be a birthday present for somebody. Then I removed them. If she noticed anything, she was extremely cool about it and didn't let on.) The Fermata allows something to occur that is the exact opposite of the necrophilic ideal: it allows me enough time to take in a particular lived second of one woman's life, the incremental outcome of so many decisions and misfortunes and delights and griefs, while she is in the very midst of fleetingly bringing it into being. The ability to investigate all aspects of her careless aliveness, where her clothes stretch, her body's textures, her expression, her smells, the way she happens to be standing or moving, as they are fused in a single total instantaneous female delta-self, is the great lure of the Fold. The Fold allows me to do sexual justice to times when she is fully conscious, but not in the least self-conscious; "stalls," Hopkins might have called them, in the daily fluidity of her life whose specific complex of qualities would have otherwise gone unseen by anyone—unphotographed, uncelebrated, unvalued, unloved. It is their randomness and, often, their very lack of overt sexiness that makes these instants so erotically precious. My sense of sight is infinitely and lovingly promiscuous, and each time I Drop I get another chance to love a chosen body as it really is: to see a woman's ass, for example, when its owner-operator is talking at a pay-phone and thinking about other things than the fact that she has an ass, and her ass can therefore be completely itself.

(For example, once I noticed a woman washing the long stretch of glass in front of the freezer-counter in the ice cream place where she worked, in a mall—she worked the cloth so vigorously over the glass that her ass circled unrestrainedly clockwise to counterbalance her hard work. She was wearing extremely tight stretchy jeans of a sort I can't fully understand but can forgive, and I wrote out the equation I used back then to get into the Fold—an equation adapted from one I saw in a journal of mathematics—and I pulled her pants down and came into a sugar cone staring at the cleavage of her ass. But I see now that this isn't in fact a good example of my appreciating an ass while it is unselfconsciously itself, since the reason I was attracted to her was that I had been observing her for a few minutes beforehand, as she served a customer, and I had sensed how relatively unproud of her face and upper body she was, and how certain she was that her ass was her best feature, and how much therefore she had *wanted* to wash the glass boldly in front of her store, though it was quite clean, with her back to all the mall-boys. As their representative, on their behalf, I came.)

The point is, in any case, that I could never get interested in a woman who was passed out drunk, or was sedated, in a coma, or dead; for then she is unconscious of me, and what I want is to be with her when she would be conscious of me but for the fact that I have interjected myself into a chink of her day so infinitesimally brief that she can't know that I have come and gone.

The way the discussion came up with Rhody was that she announced, on the plane, apropos of tiny Latino swimsuits, that more and more she was interested in seeing naked men and their penises. She said she liked the idea of *semis*—by which she meant penises that weren't totally hard, since a hard straight line was unbeautiful against the human body, nor totally soft and wrinkly either, but rather loungingly, curvingly full and interested and ready to be teased straight—like

159

(she explained) Jimmy Cliff's penis in *The Harder They Come*. I got animated, because I love talking about sex, and I impulsively decided that this was the right moment to begin to confess my Fold history to her, couching it first as a hypothetical case. All right then, I said to her, what did she think of the idea of some sort of chord on the piano that whenever you played it, stopped time? Say back when she was at Tufts, her piano teacher (someone on whom she'd told me she'd had a crush) had been working on a conclusive edition of a piece called *Map*, by a once forgotten but now increasingly respected twentieth-century composer named Mascon Albedo. Say that, in comparing the microfilmed manuscripts with the 1903 Yates and Boling edition of the work, Rhody's piano teacher, Alan Sparkling, discovered a surprising number of significant errors and righted them. As his corrections accumulated, he began to feel not only that *Map* was a much greater work than anyone could have known, but also that he, Alan Sparkling, was developing a sure instinct for Albedo's style. And his instinct told him that there was one chord which, even though it checked out as correct against several of the relevant manuscripts, still sounded quite wrong, or at least incomplete. It didn't sound at all like the chord Albedo would have written at that moment in the piece. And it was a chord of crucial importance to the meaning of the work—a very soft chiming that arrived after a long stretch of murkier pianism that should have come off as strange and triumphant, but as it stood did not. The chord was surmounted by a fermata.

Sensing a major discovery that would crown his new edition, Sparkling went back to Sewanee University, where Albedo's manuscripts were kept, and looked again through some of the notebooks that the Master had kept during the time he was composing that particular movement of *Map*. Albedo's later life had been decorated with odd incidents and minor scandals—there had been actual rumors of insanity. In the notebooks there were tantalizing annotations over certain motivic scraps—things like "Oh God, yes!" and "And here the Field develops greater potency." Alan began to have the sense that *Map* had been more than a piece of piano music to Albedo; that it had constituted some sort of magic sonic recipe or spell for him. He also began strongly to suspect that the errors in the Yates and Boling edition had not been the fault of the publisher but had been intentional last-minute alterations on Albedo's part, meant to disable whatever powers *Map* gave its performer, so that he, Albedo, could remain in sole possession of them. Finally, in one of the notebooks he came across a heavily erased part of a page under a large fermata and, with the help of a magnifying glass, was able to read the chord written there. It was an incomparably finer variant of the wrong-sounding fermata chord in *Map*.

Deeply impressed with himself, Professor Sparkling took the last plane to Boston, sure now that he had a masterwork of twentieth-century music in his briefcase, polished, cleaned, restored, awakened from its dodecaphonic slumber by his profound scholarship and delicate musicological instinct. The next day was his day of giving piano lessons. Rhody was his very best student; and that morning she tore through the *Tombeau de Couperin* with such verve that, on a whim he didn't himself quite understand, he turned toward her with an expression of great seriousness and seized her shoulders and told her that she alone must work up the new authorized version of *Map*. He made a copy of his own corrections for her so that she could incorporate them into her score. A week passed. Alan, gloating over his discoveries, played bits and pieces of *Map* for himself, and listened to it skimmingly in his head, but he devoted most of his time to finishing his article about it for *The Quarterly of New Music*. Since it was a formidably difficult work, he did not make any attempt to play the whole composition through, even sloppily, from beginning to end. That was what gifted students like Rhody were for, he felt.

All that week Rhody devotedly practiced *Map*, conscious of what an honor it was to be the first person to reanimate the cleaned-up version. It soon became clear to her that Professor Sparkling's enthusiasm was justified: Mascon Albedo stood revealed as no mere minor-league friend of Luciano Berio, but as a leaping titan of pianism. Though the surface of the piece had struck her ear at first as knotty and over-intellectual, as she perfected her performance of it she found that on the contrary it had an almost disturbing secondary sensual appeal: it made her exceedingly aware of the physical reality of her own playing. If the piece required her to play a simple A-flat-major triad with her left hand, she would feel in doing so as if the black A-flat and E-flat keys were soft, low, tree-covered hills, smoothed by forgotten glaciers, and the C between them a fog-filled valley, over which her poised fingers were parachuting very early in the morning; an ordinary pile of perfect fourths and fifths would slice through her like the stave of a hard-boiled-egg slicer; she could sense the felt-covered hammers thumping gently against the piano wires as gently as the noses of sheep in pens or fish against glass; she felt with extraordinary vividness her right foot making its little jumps on the sustain pedal, hosing off any recent blendings and allowing a new concord to rise up clean from its mud-wrestling past. The piece seemed to rediscover the amazement every pianist should properly feel at the invention of the piano. Moreover, playing it did very odd things to her perception of time, though it did so only when she began right at the beginning and went straight through.

Another piano student, Paul Mackey, knocked on her practice-room door on the eve of her lesson with Professor Sparkling. He asked her what she was up to. She was evasive, saying only that she was doing an Albedo piece for Sparkling. Paul seemed impressed and asked if he could hear some of it. Reluctantly at first, Rhody began playing it. Paul paced in the tiny room as he listened; he had the distracting habit of doing laps around the piano while he listened to his friends play. But the music was so powerful that Rhody found that she could successfully ignore him, at least until something unexpected happened. She came to the emended chord, the soft one dangling like a trumpet vine under the fermata, and played it, holding the sustain pedal down, and glanced up at him to get his reaction, and saw that Paul was completely motionless, halted in mid-step in some sort of trance. The chord slowly faded; when it was inaudible, Paul abruptly looked at her and said, "Why did you stop?"

"Why did *you* stop?" said Rhody.

"What do you mean?" said Paul. "You just hit that weird staccato chord and then stopped playing."

"It was hardly a staccato chord," said Rhody. "It had a fermata over it, in fact. Look."

Paul examined the music and raised his eyebrows. "Well, you certainly played it like a staccato chord."

Rhody pondered Paul's reaction for a second and then began a few bars back and finished the piece. This time there was no unusual behavior from Paul.

That night she had a dream in which she did Kegel exercises with a vaginal barbell until her PC muscles were so strong that when she went onstage under black-light and inserted a red Swingline 99 hand-held stapler in her vagina, she could staple a glowing airplane ticket with it. Professor Sparkling was in the audience, watching her staple the airplane tickets that the other men shyly brought up and held between her legs. He had a tube of phosphorescent motion-lotion that he squeezed on the shaft of his penis so that, as he began to stroke it, it glowed with a pale blue light. He walked up the side stairs onto the stage and knelt before where she sat on a black Thonet chair. He held in one hand the manuscript of his paper on the history of Mascon Albedo's deliberate disimprovement of *Map*. He was almost invisible except for his semi-soft glowing penis, although the EXIT sign cast a faint reddish tint on his wild Dershowitz-for-the-Defense hair and hairy shoulders; he placed a corner of the manuscript between her thighs and she lifted herself off the seat of the chair and positioned the jaws of the Swingline around the paper and groaned like a weight-lifter and tightened her vaginal muscles as hard as she possibly could and successfully got the stapler to force a staple through all nine pages. There was applause. Professor Sparkling bowed and walked away, stroking his penis in a scholarly way. In the background, the whole time, the fermata chord from *Map* chimed and faded, chimed and faded.

Still under the influence of her dream, she went to her nine o'clock lesson in a state of disoriented, stumbling horniness. "This is a momentous occasion," Professor Sparkling said archly. He sat as he usually did on a low couch with one ankle on the opposite knee, a copy of the piece open beside him. "All right," he said and gestured to her to begin. She played. When she came to the fermata chord, she splayed her fingers to play it and brought her hands gently down and felt both middle fingers descend into the low white key-vales, curved as ballet dancers curve their middle fingers when they stand in second position. Relying on the sustain pedal, she looked over at Sparkling: like Paul the day before, Sparkling was frozen, staring, stopped dead in the act of scratching his upper thigh. She could make out the profane, broccoli-shaped outline of his cock and balls under his loose cuffed pants. Hurriedly, before the chord wore out, she lifted her skirt and slid first her left and then her right middle finger high up into her slot and tickled her cervix. Then she resumed playing the piece. When she finished, Sparkling applauded, as much for himself as for her. "Wonderful, wonderful," he said, standing. "It's a strange and moving piece, don't you think?"

"I do," said Rhody, looking down at her two middle fingers, which were still slick from her juicy insertions.

"My only question is about the fermata," said Sparkling. "I don't understand why you cut it so short. It's the highlight of the whole work. Let's try it like this." He put his fingers over her fingers and played the chord with her. He took note of something. "Why, may I ask, are your two middle fingers perspiring so?" he asked.

"They do that," she said.

"Ah."

He requested that she play the work through from the beginning, and this time he stood behind her, his arms crossed. When she reached the fermata chord, she came down on it a little harder than she had the first time, to give herself a longer fade interval. She twisted around to face Alan behind her, taking care to keep her foot firmly down on the sustain pedal. He was as still as a statue. She unzipped his fly and deftly hauled out his taciturn musky handful. She gave his cock three long stretching sucks. It was big and luncheon-meaty in her mouth; sucking on it was like sucking on a carnalized version of his voice or mind. She fully intended to put his dick away before the *Map* chord ran out on her, but her sucking took a little longer than she planned and she barely had time to turn back to the keyboard and continue playing to the end. She heard a little cry of surprise behind her and some hasty zippering.

When she was done she turned again toward Sparkling and waited silently for his reaction. He looked greatly discon-certed; he was trying to figure something out that couldn't be figured out; his obvious mystification and flusterment, so unusual for him, was endearing.

"Was the fermata a little better this time?" said Rhody.

"Yes, I think it was."

"It's a very powerful work," said Rhody, relishing Professor Sparkling's speechlessness. "It's quite different in effect from the published version."

"Yes, it is," Sparkling said.

And let's say that that was the end of the lesson (I told Rhody). And say that she made a tape of herself playing the fermata chord, shaking the tape recorder to get it to work, and say that she went to the sound lab and sampled this sound (which did indeed appear to be a staccato chord to the lis-tener) and regenerated it, so that simply by hitting the PLAY button on a Walkman she could stop time for up to thirty "minutes." Wouldn't she, I asked her, take advantage of her freedom by hitting PLAY whenever she had the slightest incli-nation to check out the indolent dick-specifics of any man who caught her eye?

At first I thought she really liked the idea, because she said "Hmm!" to this with a certain amount of enthusiasm.

At one or two places during my hypothetical story (which I have jazzed up here a little for posterity, although it is in its main outlines as I presented it to her), she had gotten an interested glint in her eye. But to my dismay, the more she considered the whole concept of time-perversion, the more she seemed to turn against it. I tried to win her over to it with more examples: wouldn't it be even slightly interesting to her to be in some public place like Park Street Station, waiting for the train, and to be able to hit PLAY and go right through the crowd of men in their ties and jackets and briskly pull their pants down, so that their idiosyncratic idols peeped shyly out from behind their shirttails, available for all sorts of casual assessments and comparisons and cursory fondlings? Surely she would do that if she had the fermational power, wouldn't she? If she were in a certain mood?

An intensity in my gaze may have unsettled her slightly. The more her enthusiasm for the whole idea appeared to diminish, the eagerer I was to convince her that it had to be attractive to her. Any tiny Latino swimsuit was fair game, I said. Any penis-bulge *in the world* that she wanted to inquire into and even heft was hers to inquire into and heft. Right? But despite her having clearly said at the beginning of the plane ride that the idea of seeing naked beautiful men held more and more appeal, she now began to contend that really the sight of a penis per se didn't do all that much for her. Yes, possibly, she would investigate a crotch or two hands-on, if the crotch-context was truly extraordinary, but what she really needed was the possibility that a given penis could become aware of her and could grow and develop with the help of this knowledge. She needed to be in some sort of unfolding dramatic relationship with a specific penis for it to become a full-blown sex-object.

"But you're such a voyeur," I countered. "When we go for walks, you're always trying to get a look in the windows."

"It's foyerism, not voyeurism," she replied. "I want to look in windows because I like to see how people arrange their rooms, how they have decided to live. If I had a magical Tristan chord on tape that stopped time, I probably *would* wander through people's houses, if they were unlocked."

"Ah! Okay!" I said wildly. "Now we're getting somewhere. And if in your wandering you came across a paused couple having Sunday-afternoon sex, wouldn't you at least walk up and touch the man's flexed butt-muscle between her parted legs as he drives that dick home? Or if you happened upon a guy doing himself up right, pumping his fluke with two fists, his eyes closed, his face all slack from the pleasure, wouldn't you pull his hands away and give that fucking girder of a dick a suck or two, if it looked extra good and suckable? You would!"

Rhody thought. "I'm not ruling it out. But I need movement. What you're talking about is so static. I need to be seduced. That's what I really want. *I want to be seduced.*" She said this with such conviction that I dropped the whole subject. It was obvious to her that if the universe were stopped, any form of seduction would be impossible. I resisted the temptation to itemize the manifold ways in which a Fold-effect could make certain kinds of seduction possible, because I didn't want to seem to have given it a lifetime's thought. I just dropped it. I thanked her again for finding my glasses.

A week after that I had a revelation while browsing in Kibbeson's Discount House of Electricity on Mass Ave. after work. I realized that all I had to do was buy a handful of really cheap remaindered switches—perhaps the one-hundred-milliamp push-button switches with the twelve-millimeter bushings, which looked especially promising—and carry them around in my pants pocket. I had a hunch that if I held one tightly and pressed it with my thumb while thinking as hard as I could of an hourglass being spun in a centrifuge, I could easily force a minor concession from the elemental forces and descend into the temporal Cleft that way. Even if the switches burned out after only one Drop, as the race-track-transformer toggle had, they were cheap enough that I could afford it. I bought a bunch of different microswitches and tested them out on the street, fumbling with them in my pocket as I frowned out at the traffic. None of the momentary-connection push-buttons worked, to my surprise, but an undistinguished-looking plastic sixteen-amp spade-terminal rocker-switch did beautifully. I bought a dozen for five dollars.

Rhody and I had sex that evening—not outré toothbrush-driven avocado sex, but not all that bad sex either. While I was fucking into her slowly from behind, she began to come, muff-finger flying. I still had a ways to go. I never liked coming after she did, because I could not convince myself that she was still interested. Hastily I fished one of the rocker-switches out of my pants pocket (fortunately my pants were right there on the bed) and envisioned a spinning hourglass while I tripped it. There was a smarting spark against my palm as time's fuse blew. I pulled out and looked at the alluringly open negative shape in Rhody's vadge where my cock had just happily been—it didn't close on itself as it would have out of the Fold. I went and stood in the other room, looking through the frame of the open door at what she looked like as she was fucking me. Her glasses were on. Folds of the sheet were clutched in her hands. Though she was supporting her weight on her elbows and knees, her breasts weren't hanging straight down, as they would have been if she had posed herself in this position, but were shaped on the fly, the centers of gravity looming forward, because we had been slapping against each other quite hard and she had just begun a drive back onto my richard. She was looking down past her breasts at her own thighs or perhaps at my ballions swinging just below her tuft. Her face was very flushed, in part because her head was held down the way it was—there was a vein in her forehead that I could clearly see. My girlfriend! I pulled off my condom, disliking the wrinkly sounds it made as I mastur-worked myself. The coolness of the open air on my richard made it remember how good it was to be hard. I lay next to her on the bed, looking at her slung-forward drones and flushed face, and I imagined her imagining sucking her piano teacher's languid elutriator, or thinking about somebody or -bodies a great deal sexier to her than I was doing something nice and kinky, and in my anxiousness to catch up with her I almost went too far and came all alone—I clenched once in a false-dawn sort of pre-orgasm, which is a spasm (if I may be pardoned for an inelegant simile) very similar to the false flush-moment that can occur in a toilet tank if you don't hold the handle down quite long enough for the mechanism to confirm your unambivalent wish for it to go through a full flush cycle. I let my cock settle down for a minute, and then began driving up the grade again. It was now so mindlessly hard that the sensation of a pinchingly new condom being unrolled down its length was a matter of complete indifference to it. I pointed myself back inside Rhody and pressed the rocker-switch and, slapping against her as if there had been no break in the action, came just when she did.

I felt a little guilty about having thus engineered a simulta-
neous orgasm (and what if by some mischance she found the
second condom later?) and I lay there in the otherwise happy
post-coital calm, seriously weighing whether I should just go
ahead and tell her my entire history of time-perversion.

"What do you have in your hand?" she asked, undoing my
fingers.

"This thing? It's just a sort of charm."

She looked at the burned-out rocker-switch, which I stu-
pidly hadn't gotten rid of during our orgasm. "You were
holding on to this the whole time?" she said, looking at me
uncomprehendingly.

"I don't think the *whole* time," I said.

"Where did it come from? I don't understand."

"Well," I said, playing for time, "it's just that—I remembered I had a bunch of rocker-switches in my pants pocket
and grabbed one when I was going at you from behind. That
was *great*, by the way." I needed twenty minutes or so to think
about how I should answer her, and whether I should tell her
about the Fold, but I couldn't very well reach for another
rocker-switch while she lay on her side, propped on one
elbow, looking at me with such a troubled expression. I had
to go with my flash assessment, which was that this was not in
fact the time to tell her about my Fold-life after all. I disliked
how strange I must be appearing to her.

She said, "While we were making love, you reached in these
pants and pulled out a piece of electrical equipment and held
on to it? *Why?*" Now she was sitting up, wanting very much to
get an explanation from me that would clear everything up.
Her breasts looked aggrieved.

"It's hard to explain," I said. "I guess I wanted to imagine
that I was an android." I laughed sheepishly to confirm my
fabrication. "An invincible hard-body android. It's stupid, I

know." I felt despair at how ridiculous this explanation sounded, but I couldn't bring myself to launch into the truth, fearing that she would take it poorly. "I hate these stupid condoms," I said fussily, tying a knot in the one we had just used.

Rhody shook her head. "I'm not very comfortable with this, Arno. I really didn't plan to be fucked by an electric motor this afternoon."

"I know. I'm sorry."

I hugged her guiltily. She lay on her back, thinking. "Let me ask you this," she then said. "Is your idea of the perfect life to be able to stop time anytime you want and take off women's clothes on the subway and feel their breasts?"

"I know what you're thinking," I said. "You think that I'm turning out to be some kind of techno-sex nutcase."

"Well? No, I'm just a little surprised at all this. First you tell me this long story about a piano chord, insisting that I must find aspects of the idea sexually exciting, and now you hold this thing in your hand—what is it?"

"It's just a plain-vanilla on-off switch, a rocker-switch," I said. I tried mild indignation. "It's nothing! Forget it. It's just a little sixteen-amp rocker-switch."

"Well, it seems a very strange thing to bring into the bedroom. You should have told me beforehand. If it excites you to make love to me pretending you're a machine, fine. But you have to include me in it. What I don't like is discovering that you're doing this somewhat odd thing literally behind my back."

"You're right, I should have included you," I said. "But you know—I tried to include you in something fairly important to me when I told you about the fermata chord, and I must say I got a pretty lukewarm reception."

"Well, right, it was a loveless fantasy. It had no love in it."

"But I meant it as an act of love to tell it to you!"

"No," said Rhody. "What that fantasy says is that your idea of heaven is being able to hit the PLAY button on a Walkman and take off women's clothes and feel their breasts. Right?"

"I don't think it's my idea of heaven, exactly," I said, with some awkwardness. I had in fact briefly undressed a beautifully bloused woman wearing a yellow 32-B Lily of France bra on the Red Line just the previous day, so it was difficult for me to react with the right level of blanket disapproval. "As you yourself said, it's hard to rule out completely the possibility of an occasional capitulation to curiosity."

Rhody didn't like being paraphrased. She got angry. She said she had been thinking over my story, about the fermata chord, and she had begun to feel that it wasn't a fantasy that appealed to her at all. Here is when she dug up words like "necrophilia"—or perhaps, to be fair, she only said "implied necrophilia." I felt as if my whole life were being called into question and I tried to defend myself: it's *just* an idea, *just* a fantasy, etc.

"How would you feel," Rhody asked, "if I stopped time one day, while we were waiting in line for a movie, pulled your pants down, and inserted a blue eraser in your anus? Think about it."

"It would depend totally, totally on your intent," I said. "If you put a blue eraser in my anus out of some combination of desire and curiosity, and you simply wanted to know what it would be like to do that, then I wouldn't object. Go right ahead. But if you did it out of a desire to hurt me and rob me of dignity in your mind, then of course I would object."

"That was a bad example," Rhody said, waving it away. "How would you feel if a complete stranger stopped time on the street and pulled your pants down and took your shirt off and made a minute inspection of every inch of your body?"

"Well," I said piously, "if all they were interested in was seeing what I looked like in greater detail, and the motive was attraction rather than hostility, I would be flattered and wouldn't mind in the least. Maybe there are things about me that I don't want complete strangers knowing at such close range, but as long as I knew that the person was doing it out of some kind of positive feeling towards me, so that whatever they saw would be interesting to them, rather than repellent, I would say fine, pull my pants down. Just so long as I don't have to know about it."

"Ah, but what if it was a man?" said Rhody. "What if a gay man stopped time, pulled your pants down, and gave you a long slow blowjob? *What if he had a mustache?*"

This idea took me by surprise, but I pretended it didn't. "I admit that's not something that appeals to me. I was thinking of a woman doing the inspection. But to be consistent, I suppose I would have to say, fine, if the gay man means well, and he wants to give me a blowjob without my knowledge, it wouldn't be the end of civilization. Let him. What you don't know can't hurt you."

"That's a ridiculously glib thing to say," she said, pulling on her socks. She was angry again.

"Why is it glib?" I said hotly. "The point is, the real point is, forget strangers. When I told you that story about your piano teacher, I was talking not about some total stranger developing that ability to stop time by playing a certain chord, I was talking about you and you alone developing it."

Rhody had finished getting dressed by now. "I think what you were really trying to do was to get me interested in your little dream of taking off women's clothes in public places and doing various things to them and not getting criminally prosecuted for it. And I'm sorry—I don't think it's a good dream." Saying this seemed to force her to some sort of decision. A week or two later we had another argument and she issued a fiat; soon we were no longer an item, which was too bad, since I did love her and really still do miss her, even now that (as I will go on to tell) I have gone out on a date with Joyce.

12

"I NEED TO BE SEDUCED." THE IRONY IN RHODY'S SAYING that, as an argument against fermation used for sexual kicks, is that I never would have gone out with her if I hadn't been able to rely heavily on the Fold for help. Before I spoke one word to her I had already taken off her shirt and looked over her small dear breasts, which had faint triangles around them from the edges of the bra. Her skin was very pale. This happened in a Thai restaurant off Boylston. I sat down and looked around and noticed a woman with very short black hair and glasses with round black rims, studying the menu. Her lower lip was somewhat fuller than her upper lip, like a Hapsburg, which is a feature that attracts me—though I also like when

176

the upper lip is fuller than the lower, too, come to think of it. She ordered dinner and asked the waiter to bring her a cup of hot water and unwrapped a yellow teabag.

While her tea was steeping, she pulled out a book. She seemed not to have a bookmark, and yet I noticed that she didn't have to flip around to find her place. (I learned later that Rhody always automatically remembered her place in a book. She was not good with phone numbers, and even her Social Security number gave her trouble occasionally, but the page number of her current book would just come to her without effort as soon as she held it and saw the cover. Sometimes, she told me, the number would even occur to her at odd times during the day, and she would think, Two hundred fifty-four, what a mysterious and suggestive number! It would take her a second to realize that the number seemed unusually fine simply because it was where she was going to resume her reading. Nineteenth-century novels were all-important to her. It wasn't a question of her liking them; they were a neurological necessity, like sleep. One Mrs. Humphry Ward, or a Reade, or a Trollope per week supplied her with some kind of critical co-enzyme, she said, that allowed her to organize social sense experience. It was nice if the novel was good, but even a very mediocre one would do; without a daily shot of Victorian fiction she couldn't quite remember how to talk to people and to understand what they said. I miss her.)

She lifted the teabag out of her cup with a spoon and bound its string tightly around the bag-and-spoon duo, squeezing most of the water that was left in the leaves out into the cup. I had never been exposed to this method of managing a used teabag before, and I was thrilled by it; and I don't need much more than this to fall in love, after my fashion. I wanted very much to know what book she was reading. I pulled out my mechanical pencil, which, though it had lost its efficacy as a stand-alone Fold-probe some months earlier, still worked in concert with the special equation that I had adapted from a journal of mathematics. I wrote it on the placemat: the Strine Inequality. I had come across the germ of it in the Birkhoff Library at Harvard on a Sunday afternoon in a state of Tourette's syndromish meditativeness that I knew by now often presaged a Fermata discovery. I opened an issue of *The Canadian Journal of Geometry* at random and was surprised by how many symbolic systems mathematicians had pressed into service: Greek and Russian letters, of course, but the British pound sterling sign? Capital letters in a florid script that looked as if it came from a wedding invitation? From a short paper entitled "Minimally Gilded Hodge Star Operators and Quasi-Ordinary Handlebodies Within a Localizable 4-Manifold Whitney Invariance," I copied out an equation, as follows—

$$\left\| \to \overleftrightarrow{\underset{k=0}{\overset{\to}{\mathcal{Z}}}} \Big/_x \left(\left[\widetilde{\widetilde{C}}_{3r,\,\partial\Gamma} \right] \right) \otimes \forall_{\mathcal{N}} \right\|^{\perp} = \ddot{\mathcal{Y}}^{\scriptscriptstyle nd_t}_{\scriptscriptstyle >} \overset{\cdot}{\mathsf{H}}^{\scriptscriptstyle \varsigma}_{\scriptscriptstyle <} \left(\frac{\overset{\circ}{P}\big/_{\triangledown}}{T * \not{\phi}\, \{\underset{min}{\overset{\int\!\!\int}{\int}}_{\varsigma^{\sigma\wedge}}\!\![\![\mathbb{R}_{\bullet}^{\prime\prime\prime}]\!]\}} \right)^{a}_{2k}$$

Several hours later, at the Ritz Carlton bar, guided by a will greater than my own, I substituted several of the international textile care-labeling symbols for key variables in the original, and changed the equal sign to a less-than-or-equal-to sign. I felt as if I were speaking in tongues as I watched my possessed hand draw a crossed-out iron and a crossed-out triangle ("no bleach") and a stylized half-filled washtub with a large hand in it ("hand-wash"). When I had finished with the substitutions and the Strine Inequality stood complete on the page, there came a sound, a sound of distant chronic liposuction, of fine cosmetic work being done on the cosmos, nips and tucks tactfully taken, infinitesimal hairplugs of time removed from distant star-systems, where they wouldn't be missed, and arranged in quantity serially for me to live through. I was free once again to roam the Fold. To return to time I only had to erase the inequality sign, disabling its potency.

That was the formula I wrote down on the placemat at the Thai restaurant. When it had taken effect, I went over to Rhody and lifted her book from her hand. It was a green Virago paperback called *Lady Audley's Secret*, by Mary E. Braddon. The back cover said that *Lady Audley's Secret* had "shocked the Victorian public with its revelations of horrors at the very heart of respectable society and its most respectable women." Encouraged, I thumbed through it, reading things like "bonnet" and "gaudily-japanned iron tea-trays" and the sentence fragment "he amused himself by watching her jewelled white hands gliding softly over the keys, with the lace sleeves dropping away from her graceful arched wrists." I came to the inside of the back cover; on it, Rhody (or *Rhoda E. Levering*, according to the name inscribed in the book) had made several notes. Her handwriting had a self-assured intelligence. The only note that I could make any sense of, though, was:

Sexiness of men who take off their watches in public

She used, as I did, the back of her book to jot down passing observations. I put the book back in her grip, and I unbuttoned her shirt and found out what I could about her breasts. A slight asymmetry inspired instant fondness. (Women who read Virago Modern Classics almost always have fascinating breasts.)

I had planned to study a review of the new Mazda 929 in

Road & Track during dinner, but obviously that was not possible now. I was tempted to walk to a bookstore in the Fold and pick up some other Virago to show off to her, but I thought better of it: too aggressive a manufactured coincidence. Instead I erased the Inequality to end the time-transplantation and, once back in the swing, pulled out a turn-of-the-century biography of Edward FitzGerald by A. C. Benson that I had been halfheartedly reading; I held it open with the edge of my plate. The waiter came. I ordered dinner in a fairly loud, friendly voice in order to draw Rhody's attention. When I had handed over the menu, I dropped my eyes immediately to my book as if I were impatient to get back to it, and then absentmindedly began moving my watch up and down on my wrist. I knew "Rhoda E. Levering" was watching me. I turned a page, lifting the plate so that it would clear, and went back to playing with my watch. Suddenly I looked up, caught Rhody's eye, and gave her a friendly hello-look. I felt bad about doing this, because I know how hard it is to go back to a book, no matter how engrossed you were in it, when you are alone at a table in a restaurant and you become aware of someone else who may or may not be lonely, and may or may not be curious about you—suddenly, whether you welcome it or not, there is a fiery transversity connecting the two of you, where before there had only been a narrow rectilinear green-carpeted Thai restaurant that tolerated solo readers.

I returned to my book, deliberately making ugly lip-pursed faces to show that I was deeply caught up in *Edward FitzGerald*—and to release Rhody from the tyranny of the transversity if she wanted to return to *Lady Audley's Secret*. Without lifting my eyes from the page (though I was still sure that her black-rimmed glasses were flashing in my direction), I raised my left hand and very slowly and teasingly pulled on the flap of my watchband until the tiny gold prong of its buckle hung free of the slightly elongated second hole. Like a stripper delaying a moment of conclusive disrobing, I held the unbuckled watch in place for a time, turning my wrist slowly within its loosened embrace; finally I slid the buckle off the strap and caught the face of the watch as it fell from my arm. I did everything as smoothly and unsuddenly and strokingly as I could, not as if I were aware of Rhody and trying to entice her, but as if I were reading with such intense concentration that my unconscious watch-removal movements were being slowed to a fraction of their normal speed by the rapture of my literary appreciation. I set the watch down just above my open book, the two curved segments of the band forming a seagull shape. Then I looked directly and inquiringly at Rhody again. Her eyes fell to her page.

That was the big moment of the evening. We ignored each other from then on. Just after she asked for her check, she walked past me to the bathroom. I whisked out my mechanical pencil and restored the complete Inequality on my placemat and used the Fold's ideal privacy to count the number of tampons in her purse. There were five. I erased time back on and let her use the bathroom. When she emerged, I Dropped again and counted tampons: there were now four. Since I have had miserable luck befriending women at the height of their periods, I didn't try to say hello to her then. Instead, on my calendar I marked a day two weeks later, when she was likely to be at or near ovulation, and on that day I staked out her address on Marlborough Street after work. She got home around six-thirty. Half an hour later she reappeared in jeans. I followed her discreetly to the Harvard Book Store Café on Newbury. Just before she went into the store, I completed the Inequality on a pad of paper and slipped in ahead of her. I crouched in one of the aisles, near the Mrs. Humphry Wards, and erased my way into time. (I didn't want to seem to have materialized out of thin air to anyone in the store.) I stood up, holding a random book; I put the book away; and then I pulled a Virago paperback off the shelf. I heard someone step into the fiction aisle, and I was almost sure that it was Rhody, and it was. I turned and regarded her blankly, innocently, and then went through a pleased frown of recognition. She returned the favor. (Naturally I was holding the book in such a way that my watch was plainly visible.) I will skip the "Weren't you at the Thai Star a few weeks ago?" exchange that followed, since there was nothing newsworthy in it—I will just observe that, despite my having produced and directed the entire coincidence, I was as overjoyed and nervous and relieved when she started talking away about the subdued greatness of Mrs. Humphry Ward as if I really had fortuitously run into her.

"You know what really interested me about you?" she said several weeks later, after we had been on a harbor cruise and had had lunch twice. "You may not remember this, but while you were reading that time at Thai Star, you took your watch off and put it just above your book."

"So you *were* watching me!" I said. "I was very aware of you."

"Yes, I was watching you. You took your watch off, and you seemed to luxuriate in every tiny step of the process. I've always liked the sight of a man taking off his watch. It doesn't need to be an expensive watch, though I prefer leather to metal bands." She lowered her voice. "I like the rubbing of the wrist afterward."

"How interesting," I said. "It's just a habit of mine—I guess I started doing it in study hall in high school. It seemed grown up." (This was not altogether untrue.)

Rhody said, "I was enamored of this one guy, a physics major, in college who used to go through a ritual of getting set up to study at one of the tables in the library. He slipped off his shoes—he always had immaculate white sweatsocks on, and very clean pale jeans—and he arranged his watch next to his textbook, with one strap folded under the other."

"He sounds like a real catch," I said.

"But the interesting thing is that only a few days before I saw *you* take off your watch, someone at work did the same thing at a meeting, and I was reminded of how kind of . . . seductive it is, even though in that case I wasn't at all interested in the person who did it. Just in his wrist. In fact, I even made a note in back of the book I was reading at the time about how sexy it is to watch a man do that. So there. Isn't it weird the way things like that always happen in twos?"

I agreed that it was weird, and we got off into a discussion of Rupert Sheldrake and the morphic resonances that purportedly aid protein synthesis. That evening she brought me back to her apartment to show me the actual note in the back of *Lady Audley's Secret.* We ended up having sex for the first time. (There was a memorable moment when my hands were flat against a Sierra Club wall calendar as I fucked slowly in and out of her mouth. And there was another memorable moment when she put a cucumber in the microwave for a few seconds to take the chill off and I twisted the corkscrew we had used on the bottle of Cabernet into one end of it and she let me watch her cuke herself with it, holding it by its blond wooden handle.) I am not saying that it is a total impossibility that the two of us could have gotten together at the Thai restaurant if I had simply walked over to her and struck up a conversation. I might have cruised her successfully without subterfuge. But it's just as likely that she would have politely sent me away. I'm less suave with a woman when I haven't had a preview of her breasts. So the moral is: Rhody was quite wrong in assuming that the Fermata was intrinsically antithetical to seduction. I used the Fermata to seduce *her*.

13

I WAS IN A CERTAIN AMOUNT OF PAIN WHEN THINGS ENDED WITH Rhody. I had given her a glimpse of my inner life, and she had unambiguously rejected it. But I realize now, in putting Rhody down on paper, that good, tangible things grew out of our truncated relationship. If I had not seen and acted on that note about men and watches in the back of her copy of the Virago paperback, I would probably not have had the later idea of writing smutty expostulations in paperbacks just before women browsed them, and if I hadn't thought of *that*, I probably wouldn't have conceived of using the Fold as a rotter's retreat and leaving the outcome where a woman might find it. In a way, Rhody's spurning the glimpse I had given her of my secret freed me to investigate its potential further.

After the time on the Cape, I wrote a little more: one story about a naked woman suspended above one lane of the Callahan tunnel on a black rope trapeze net during rush hour, looking down through its square mesh at the cars filing slowly beneath her and pissing generously on them as their moonroofs slid open; one story about a man teaching a young woman to touch-type on his antique Oliver No. 9 manual typewriter, holding his hands over her hands and closing his eyes and feeling her fingers sink one by one into the deep counterweighted letters and knowing she was spelling H-I-P-S and being unable to resist putting his hands on her hips, then feeling her fingers type B-R-E-A-S-T-S on the round black cuplike keys and being unable to resist palming her breasts and pulling her back against him; one story about a group of scuba-diving Caribbean tourists corrupting the angelfish with aerosol cans of cheddar cheese, sometimes making cheese hearts in the water that the fish then momentarily echoed as they fed, sometimes squirting it on wet-suited arms or breasts and letting the fish nip it off; one about a woman letting her pet hermit crab walk lightly all over her back while she read *Barron's* and dreamed of blue-eyed men with tons of money; one about several caves of stalagmites, each one a different color, that, when broken off and inserted into a vadge, glowed, their stumps releasing bidet-like streams of warm subterranean mineral water.

I spent some personal time with Ami Pro and a copier and saddle-bound a number of copies of these several stories, along with the one about Marian and the ridem lawn-mower, in pamphlet form, using as a cover the pale blue cover of something called *Tales of French Love and Passion*—a heavily ironic reissue of a cheesy 1936 edition of several mildly risqué stories by Guy de Maupassant that I had ordered through the Archie McPhee catalog. I left my homemade booklet in lots of places—in copies of *Self* and *The American Scholar* just before they were shoved through mail-slots, in women's bathrooms at dance clubs, under the Gideon's Bible in several rooms of the Meridien Hotel, on coffee tables during cocktail parties, inserted in the library's *Encyclopedia of Philosophy* in the article on "Life, Meaning and Value of"—but nothing resulted from all this effort that was anywhere near as exciting to me as the simple sight of Michelle, the Cape Cod woman, dunking her dildo in her bathwater and shaking it off.

The peak of my life-imitates-rot phase came on the Massa-chusetts Turnpike one Saturday. I was out for a drive. It was autumn and hormone levels were rising. I was idly thinking of following through on my Northampton idea—the one about stripping everyone on Main Street and, if not mounding their clothes all in a single mound and dancing on it, then at least putting each person's clothes neatly in a plastic grocery bag in his or her hand—the idea of a naked town discovering that it was carrying its clothes around in plastic bags thrilled me. (The sight of naked middle-aged women in the steam rooms of certain country clubs carrying their jewelry around in droopy plastic bags, because they are afraid that it will be stolen from their lockers, thrills me, too; I have been in the steam rooms with them; I have touched their moist plastic bags of jewelry.) My ambitions are not global in scope—I don't think of nude nations or metropolises; but totally top-less Main Streets of small towns, especially small towns with classy women's colleges in them, yes. I decided that if I lost my nerve and couldn't go through with denuding the whole town, I could at least replace the *TV Guide*s in the rack at the

supermarket with my personal *Tales of French Love and Passion*
and watch how people reacted. But I never made it to
Northampton. I got severely distracted by a woman in a car
just past Worcester.

I was driving in the slow lane. My window was open; the car
was booming with air noise. My left (wristwatched) arm was
outside; I was making my hand into a wing shape to see
whether I could create lift, and making it dive and climb
against the wind. A woman driving a small blue car appeared
in the rear-view mirror. No expression is as impassive as a
woman's seen in a rear-view mirror: it has an impassiveness so
impartial and comprehensive that it cries out to be surprised.
She was going faster than I was and impassively began to pass
me; I lost sight of her for a minute as she entered that place
where passing cars don't exist—a kind of Fold-effect of the
rear- and side-view mirrors. I accelerated very slightly, so that
when she did pass, it would take longer. I had only seen her
face for an instant, in fact I had only had time to notice that
she was a woman of twenty or so with lots of thickly wavy
multihued fair hair driving alone, but my very sketchy simplistic sense of her windshielded face merged with my equally
simplistic sense of the headlights of her unflashy blue car to
turn her instantly into a well-developed character in my imagination. As she invisibly pulled closer to me in the fast lane
and I heard her tires singing and sensed how close she was to
me, the idea that she was soon going to pass me became
swoonsomely powerful: the steering wheel seemed to become
flexible and expand in widening ripples; I felt that I was a
glowing lump of something melting on the fly. I could not
believe that in a matter of thirty seconds or so this person was
going to pull up next to me and that I would be able to look
over at her; when she did I felt I would shout or weep.

At the same time I felt a blip of self-irritable disgust at the astonishing potency of these car-crushes and at how much mental air-time they consumed when I drove. It was *insane* to think that someone was more wonderful and mysterious just because she was passing me in her car. What could be more common than two people driving nearly side by side on a highway, one drawing abreast of the other? Why couldn't I just relax and let her pass me without falling in total temp-love with her? And yet that was what was going on—and maybe it was going on for her, too: maybe she was listening to Terry Gross on National Public Radio and barely registering that some car (me) was off to her right, but maybe her hopes were rising and crashing addictively each time she passed a lone man at the wheel—maybe she was trying just as I had done to piece together a sense of the lovability and marriage-ability of each person based on the ludicrously inadequate information available—that is, on the driver's head, on the state of origin of the license plate, on the general personality of the car (all cars are classifiable as cute/perky or elegante/mysterioso or Camaro/vulgaro), on whether one hand or two was visible on the steering wheel, and on the condition of the sheet metal. As her door-handle came in line with mine I tried to fight the desire to turn toward her but I couldn't; I looked blankly at her just as she was turning to look blankly at me; then we both turned back and looked straight ahead at our lanes. At that moment, we were driving at almost exactly the same speed. We were close. It seemed miraculous to me that we could be in such states of seated repose, and yet could be separated by the surface of the highway, which was moving between us so fast that if I opened my door and tried to walk over to her and get in her car, my feet and shin-bones would be sanded down to nothing. With tormenting leisureliness she finally pulled ahead and put on her blinker and smoothed her blue car-butt over in front of me. (It turned out to be a Ford Escort, which always makes me think of escort services when I'm driving long distance.) Then I saw something riveting—a Smith College sticker on her rear window, with a University of Chicago sticker above it. I didn't have to drive all the way to Northampton; Smith College was right here with me on the road! But I hesitated before I pushed up on my glasses, having never been through a full-blown chronvulsion in a moving car before. Would it be safe? Would my high rate of speed relative to the highway cause some unforeseen danger? Stopping the universe while driving at sixty miles an hour seemed an extremely rash and kinky thing to do.

I kept staring at her taillights. I saw her look up at me briefly in her rear-view mirror. Then she fluffed her massive coarsely wavy hair so that some of it fell over the whiplash projection on the back of her seat. The high small round chrome lock on the curve of her trunk looked a little like what I imagined her asshole might look like. I decided that I would survive whatever happened. I waited a polite interval and then pulled over into the fast lane and sped up to pass her. We were on a slight downgrade. As I came closer to her, the same swooning feeling as before swept over me, except that now I and not she was bringing about this unspoken thrill; when our profiles were even I didn't look over, knowing that she knew that I was passing her and wouldn't look at me, because the rule in highway flirtation was not to look on the second pass. Instead I hit the clutch pedal and glided freely for a second or two right next to her, setting myself up mentally for the disengagement of the temporal drive-train, and then very slowly I pushed my glasses up on the bridge of my nose; when I let go of them the Smith woman and I were still side by side on the

Mass Pike, but we weren't moving forward. My radio was silent.

My door was not easy to get open. I had to push with my shoulder to displace the jellied wind-flow. And the road surface around my car presented a strange sight: though motionless, it looked slightly foggy and indeterminate, as if photographed through a Vaselined lens; you couldn't focus on it properly. When I gingerly got out, leaving my door open, and tiptoed around the back of my car, I found that the asphalt was in fact somewhat resilient underfoot; its speed relative to the soles of my shoes apparently made it impossible for the two physical surfaces to interact normally, and gave the road the characteristics of some sort of dense, even spongy ground-cover, like moss. The other oddity was that I heard hooting and roaring noises in my ears when I walked into or away from the direction that I had been driving: I supposed it was something to do with vectors and frozen sound waves and the Doppler effect, but I didn't trouble myself over it. Instead I straddled the white line between the Smith woman's car and mine and extended my arms so that I touched both near doors, hers and mine, connecting us two. I held that quasi-crucifixional position for a time, looking out at the hills and the cars ahead, considering that if I pulled on my glasses right then to resume time, my car would race off driverless and would eventually crash, and I, left in the middle of the road, would almost certainly be hit by one of the cars behind ours. I looked through her window at her, my face inches away from her profile. I went around and opened her passenger door, which was fortunately not locked, and cleared off the junk on the seat (mostly cassettes and several books-on-tape from the library) and got in next to her.

I don't have to point out that cars are extremely private

places; the feeling that I was doing something of questionable ethics by entering this woman's small glossy blue Ford was more intense than I could remember in recent fermations. I was sweating with the almost horrified excitement of my wrongdoing. The soles of my feet were warm to the touch. I was in her car. "Well, here we are," I said aloud to myself. I couldn't bring myself to find out what was up with her breasts, or do anything more radical in fact than rest my hand lightly on her accelerator leg (she was wearing a huge thick pink sweater with roses woven into it, and faded jeans); I had a sense of being dangerously far away from home, perhaps because the steering wheel and brake pedal of my own speeding car were so nearby and yet so peculiarly out of my reach. What should I do? Should I simply jack in the passenger seat next to her? I don't as a rule like masturbating in cars. I could get out and stand in the road and jack onto her trunk lock or her driver-side window, or, having rolled down that window beforehand, I could jack directly into the interior of her car. But it would be rude to get my hard sauce all over the flowers on her sweater, which looked expensive and hand-knit, perhaps a favorite sweater of hers. Besides, my shoes might melt or catch flame.

What I really wanted was just to be alive in this woman's car for a second while she was driving it—so I climbed in the back seat and lay down and used my glasses to reactivate time for the quick count of five and then deactivated it again. It was wonderful to be riding in her car. She had some music going, something familiar, and I thought I could hear her humming quietly along with it. Her car was much quieter than mine. When my Drop was over I sat up and looked over at my empty car: it had drifted a little to the right (possibly the door's "sudden" opening and consequent slamming shut) but though driverless for a few seconds it had maintained course fairly well, just as I had expected.

I lay there in the Smith College woman's back seat for quite a while, my head resting on her overnight bag, playing with a wavy sprig of her hair and trying to think of some way that I could possibly become a part of her life. Some of her hair was held with a large toothed clamp. I grew curious about what she was listening to and climbed back up beside her and popped the tape: it was a Suzanne Vega called *Solitude Standing*. She had gotten only halfway into the first cassette of the audio version of *Gulliver's Travels* before abandoning it for some music. All at once I had conjured up a little plan. It would take time, but I wanted it to. She was worth it.

This is what I did: I walked for almost an hour until I came to a mall with a discount store, where I bought a fairly high-quality tape recorder and some cassettes and batteries. (Bought: that is, left roughly the cash to pay for it in the appropriate cash register along with a note saying that this money was in payment for item number, etc., etc.) I also assembled a festive picnic lunch for myself at a deli and left money there. Several Arno-hours later, I got back to my car and pulled out my *Tales of French Love and Passion* and sat in the Smith woman's passenger seat. The name I got from her wallet was Adele Junette Spacks.

"Hello and excuse me," I said into the tape recorder in a lower voice than I usually have, looking right at Miss Spacks. "With the help of my benevolent autokinetic powers, I have taken the liberty of popping the Suzanne Vega cassette in progress and placing it on the seat beside you. I have replaced it with a tape of my own, the very tape that you are listening to now. I would prefer to remain anonymous, but I will tell you that I too am currently driving west on the Mass Turnpike, and that you passed me a little while ago, and that, though you may not have been aware of it, during those few seconds when we were driving side by side, I developed one of the more intense car-to-car infatuations I have ever experienced. I've decided that this time I will act on my feelings for once by offering you this homemade tape for your diversion. Please feel free to listen to it or not as you wish. Feel free to press the eject button at any time if anything on it distresses you. It does contain nudity and sexual situations—in fact, it contains a great deal of nudity and sexual situations. But it's only words. I only mean to divert you while you drive. If my tape offends, please feel free to toss it out the window and accept my apologies. Please feel free, please feel free."

After this introductory spiel, I read aloud the story that I had written while kneeling next to the woman in the gray-green bathing suit on the Cape. Sitting so close to Miss Spacks in her car, in a silence thicker than any recording studio's, I started to feel a little style-crampingly self-conscious as I got into the more graphic sections of the text, and my narrator's voice began to lose authority; finally I had to transfer myself and the tape recorder from Miss Spacks's car back to my own, where, with a confidence born of distance, I finished reading the rest of it in one take, more or less, without too many flubs. It was good to be *making* a tape for once, rather than having to transcribe someone else's. Still, when I was done I was not completely satisfied. The one-hundred-and-ten-minute Memorex tape was not full, for one thing. And I felt ungenerous in offering this brand-new person my old rot. Indeed, I felt *unfaithful* to her, just as I had felt unfaithful to the Cape Cod woman when I had sprinted down the beach in the Cleft and checked out that girl. The old story had been part of an old seduction, and Adele Junette Spacks, who was unwittingly spending so much time "with" me, deserved something fresh in return, something rash, something more representative of what I was capable of coming up with right at that very moment on the road in her company. I ate lunch on the trunk of my car, thinking kink, kink, kink. Then I got out the Casio, which I had packed in my trunk, and in just twelve straight hours I wrote a second set of adventures for Marian the Librarian. I worked in a few of the sights I had witnessed in the Cape Cod bathroom. Here's how Part Two went.

14

TOWARD THE MIDDLE OF SEPTEMBER, MARIAN'S SEXUAL INTER-
est inexplicably abated. She put all her dildi and appliances
in the drawer that had once held David's sweaters. The last two
toys she had ordered—a tiny vibe, teasingly canine in appear-
ance but molded from an impeccably *comme il faut* piece of
pickled okra, and a giant Armande Klockhammer Signature
Model—she didn't even bother to try out before putting them
in storage. She felt a mild snobbish contempt for people who
devoted so much of their free time to solo sex-play. Her
perennial garden, for example, was far more satisfying than a
bunch of pastless, futureless orgasms. She read bulb catalogs
avidly. After much study she ordered several hundred tulip

bulbs from Mack's. When they arrived, via UPS, she gently deflected the eagerly scrotal leer of her friend John in the brown truck. It felt exciting and strange to be more than a sexual being, to have interests. As she looked over the boxes of bulbs, however, she realized that she would need help cutting the beds and planting them all, so she hired the neighbor kid, Kevin.

Ever since she had been mowing her own lawn, she had lost touch with young Kevin. He seemed to have grown an inch or two. He had gone out for the high jump, and he had acquired a girlfriend named Sylvie, whom he said was "a really special person." For a whole weekend and three cool late afternoons he and Marian worked together preparing the soil in the beds with bags of peat and then setting in the bulbs. The dirt was cool through Marian's gloves. After shyly asking whether she would mind, Kevin brought over his radio. At first she was a little irritated by the sound, which disturbed her bucolic alpha-state—but over time several of the songs separated themselves from the others. In one, a woman sang something about Solitude standing in the doorway. She sang, "Her palm is split with a flower with a flame." Marian kept time to this song, first with her troweling, and then with her chin. When she had heard it the second time, she asked Kevin (feeling a little shy herself), "Who does this song?"

Kevin looked up. "Suzanne Vega."

"Ah," said Marian. "I like it."

"Yeah, it's pretty good," said Kevin. He was impossible to read. He dropped another dark bulb in a hole and gently mounded soil around it. Marian glanced at him several times. He had a gray track-and-field T-shirt over a gray sweatshirt. When he pushed on the earth over one of her bulbs, she imagined the muscle in the side of his arm, as she had seen it when he had had his shirt off that day, long ago, at the beginning of summer, before she had learned to mow. And later, when the song came on again, he looked up at her and smiled and then went back to planting—and Marian noticed that his ears were quite red.

She watered the bulbs in and forgot about them. The ground began to look cold—three long beds of very cold bulbs. As winter hit, Marian became caught up in a battle with a developer who wanted to build another mall outside of town. It was going to be enormous and in its own way wonderful—but there was already a shopping center with a discount chain in it that was working under chapter eleven, and the downtown would suffer, as it always did. She went out on several dates with a man she met at the mall meetings, and while she enjoyed talking to him (he was one of those men who have a passionate interest in some particular writer which at first seems sincere, and then finally ends up seeming almost arbitrary—in his case it was Rilke: he seemed to be getting things from Rilke that he could have gotten from any number of poets, while missing whatever it was that Rilke had uniquely), she nonetheless didn't want to do anything more than kiss him cordially in her driveway.

When spring finally came, she went out every day to her tulip beds to watch for activity. It was an unusually dry hot spring, and she felt that she should water to give her beds a good start, but she despaired at her hose. The faucet still leaked tiresomely. The sprayer was rusty. What would make her bulbs really happy, it suddenly occurred to her, was if she could get a plumber to adapt her own Pollenex showerhead so that it would fit on the end of the hose. She needed a very light, very delicate but insistent spray for her tulips—no garden sprayer could offer that. She also thought that the hose water was much too cold—she felt that the bulbs would do better with warmer water. She realized that she wasn't thinking all that rationally, but her idea nonetheless was: hook up the garden hose to the shower-pipe, run the hose out the bathroom window, and fix the Pollenex showerhead onto the terminal end. Other ideas of interest followed on this one; she called a plumber.

The plumber was a thin derisive man with the usual plumber body-smell who rolled his eyes at her plan, told her she could have done it herself, but agreed, since he was there, to do it for her. He fitted the hose ends and the Pollenex with Gardena quick-clamp adapters so that they could be quickly reconfigured for interior showering or exterior gardening applications. The shower-pipe looked exotic when he was done, knobbed with hex nuts and adapters, but the system when tested worked quite well. And the plumber, as he cleaned up, was cheerful, pleased by now that he had built something he had never built before, and that he would be able to tell his partner about the nutty job this lady had gotten him to do. He even showed her how to use Teflon tape and was expansive about its merits over older kinds of sealant. He carried his heavy red toolbox out to his truck and drove away.

Over the next few days Marian took her early-morning shower and then opened the window, hooked up the shower-hose arrangement, and turned on the taps to water her tulips. She used only the fine pulse-mist settings, treating her plants as she would want to be treated herself. The tulips responded with enthusiasm—after a week her beds were popping with color. *They* knew the difference between water from a shower, meant for human use, and water from a crude leaky outdoor faucet. She sat on an aluminum chair with the sun on her legs, reading *The Machine in the Garden*. Every so often she glanced up at her tulips. She felt happy. She had planned this to happen and it had happened: she had delayed gratification and now she was getting the payoff. Young Kevin should see what they had done together, she thought, but when she called, Kevin's sour mother told her that he was at practice. Just as well, just as well, she thought. She began to give some consideration to her drawerful of dildae. But she didn't need any of that; no, she'd moved beyond that.

Just then Kevin's little gray cat with white paws showed up on her lawn, making untoward noises and acting oddly. Quite recently it, she, had been a kitten. Now she was clearly in heat, probably for the first time—and very irresponsible it was of Kevin or Kevin's mother not to have had her fixed! She crawled along with her forepaws very low on the ground, making low desperate mezzo-mewings, her tail jerking back, her little narrow feline hips flaunting and twitching in the air, her rear paws working with quick tiptoe steps. Marian could see her gray-furred opening; wetness gleamed from within. She went over and pressed her finger lightly against the cat's tiny slit; gratefully, the cat returned the pressure and tiptoed ardently in place. This was a cat in the grip of a new idea. Wiping her finger on the grass, Marian found that she had gotten hot looking at this creature's fluttery haunchings. There was a purity and seriousness to the cat's simple wish to be fucked immediately that Marian found refreshing. The cat didn't want love—it wanted cat-cock.

Marian was not a committed zoophile, though—at least she didn't think of herself as one. True, she and her best friend in sixth grade had made her friend's black Labrador shoot two quick clear squirts of come once by gently squeezing his dense buried bulb as he lay on his back with his legs open and his eyes half closed, but one swallow doesn't make a summer.

Marian was a fan of human cock, for better or worse. (Dog-dick did still have a certain appeal to her, in part because when it emerged it had a clitoral, almost hermaphroditic quality: something bisexual in her was triggered by the sight of it.) Mentally she again reviewed her dildos—how could she have (one or two late nights excepted) snubbed them all winter? The idea of running herself a bath, and then strad-dling the cold edge of the tub so that all her weight was on the soft place between her vadge and her ass, began to seem attractive. She could take one of the middle-sized dildi and swish it around in the bathwater and shake it off, so that it waggled obscenely, and stick it down on the edge of the tub and squirt Astroglide all over it. She could arrange herself over it, supporting herself with her hands on the edge of the tub, looking down past her hanging breasts at the slick dildo as it slowly disappeared into her sex-hair and found its thick way up inside her. She went inside to do just this, but by the time she had actually drawn the bath and gotten into it, she was much too aroused to do tame things in her bathroom. She got out and dried off and slipped on a dress. She had a new plan. She wanted to have a full-fledged Betty Dodsonian PC-muscled clasm outside in honor of her tulip garden.

She went out in her bare feet, scouting a location. Kevin's cat had disappeared. After some pacing and gazing, she picked a place between two of the tulip beds, near where she had seen Kevin's ears get red when they had talked about the "Solitude stands in the doorway" song. The problem was, what could she use as a stable base to affix her dildos to? The grass blades would be a ticklish irritant. Back inside, she tried a rectangular black lacquer tray in the kitchen, but it had a raised edge that, when she put it on a chair and experimen-tally sat down on it, hurt her butt. She considered a Thanksgiving serving platter but didn't like the idea of its breaking; she pondered a small plastic plate left over from a premium frozen dinner, but it wasn't heavy enough. Finally she went into her dining room and took the tea service off of her grandmother's brass tray. The tea service itself was undistinguished, but the tray was a Viennese beauty, chased with circles of bouquets and thick-scaled fish and pine-cones and mythical panthery creatures in high relief. In the middle was a very stylized sun—it looked like a fried egg—and this proved to be the perfect surface on which to fix a dildo's suction cup.

The famed male dancer at the Golden Banana, Armande Klockhammer, Jr., had only once in his distinguished career consented to have a lost-wax mold made of the trilogy-in-flesh that had opened so many doors for him. Along the underside of the slightly upcurved and alarmingly lifelike high-grade silicone cock-stalk, Armande's own signature, taken directly from the licensing contract, ran, in such a way that the two bas-relief *m*'s of his surname appeared right over what would have been, had this been his actual dick, its most sensitive part. Marian arranged her virgin Armande Klockhammer Signature Model, along with many of its veteran colleagues, on a linen napkin unfolded on her brass tray and bore them out into the garden. She put the tray down in the thick grass in the chosen spot, leaving room on either side for her to plant her feet. There was a slight haze in the sky, so that it was sunny, but not uncomfortably so. When she moved the napkin aside, the light glinted on the tray's ancient pattern, and, once she had squirted copious Astroglide over its head, on the surface of her chosen dildo as well—which looked opulently nasty poking up from that heirloom.

Then, playing hard-to-get now that she knew she had Armande where she wanted him, she went for a blithe little walk.

She was wearing a jumper printed with big loose flowers and nothing underneath. She went to her mailbox, checked that the mail had been delivered, but left it in there. She nodded to a bicyclist going by—he was wearing a kind of skin-tight black cycling shorts that she normally didn't like, but now she didn't mind seeing his thigh definition. She stood at the end of her driveway for several minutes with her arms crossed, breathing deep breaths of spring air and feeling peaceful and content, or playing at looking like the woman out in the garden breathing deeply and feeling content, while actually part of her was thinking over what dildic wickedness was waiting for her in her back yard. On her way back, she bent and felt a leaf of one of the peonies in the tractor tire in her front yard, very casually, giving the road the chance to appreciate her shape under her dress, and murmured to herself, "Hmm, I think it may be time to do some watering." She went in and got the water temperature just right in her shower, and then drew the hose into the bathroom window and hooked it to the shower spigot. Outside, she turned the stopcock on (the plumber had fixed it so that she could turn the flow of water on and off at the end of the hose) and toured her side yard, sending a frolicsome misty spray from her mobile water-source over the grass and over the mock-orange leaves. She hummed "Private Dancer." She heard a truck drive past on the road.

When she rounded the back of the house, she surprised a deer who had wandered by, drawn by the tasty-looking tulip blossoms. It appeared to be licking the pink head of the Armande Klockhammer with its equally pink tongue. "Now, now, enough of that!" Marian called, and the deer sprang away. She glanced around to verify that she was indeed in private, and put her foot up on her lawn chair and hiked up her jumper, holding it in a one-handed bunch just below her breasts, and directed the crown of water-jets on her clit-site. The water was just right. "Oh, nice," she said, watching the flow disappear into the grass. The idea that she could carry her daily shower around with her, outside, pleased her quite a lot. She dropped her dress and began watering again, working up the nodding tulip beds. Her maraschino tingled. She pretended to notice for the first time something alien and fleshy sticking up, pinkly out of place in the general verdancy beyond the near bed of tulips. "What's this now?" She pointed the shower-water at it (making sure to rinse away any deer saliva). "What's this sex organ doing sticking straight up in my garden? Does it need something to fuck?" She pulled up her dress. "Is this what Armande wants?" Again she pointed the showerhead up between her legs, now turning it to PULSE. Big dick-shaped bullets of water thumped against the skin surrounding her clit-pearl, against her vadge, and, as she rocked her hips, tickled against the poor-relation sensitivities of her asshole. "Oh man," she said, loving it. "Listen you, if you liked that Bambi-tongue, you're going to *love* my hot little box." The dildo was unresponsive. She walked closer, confronting it. "Oh? So you're not sure? You're not even sure you want to be in my hot little *ass*? You're shy? Well, I'm sorry, you have no choice now—you're going to have to fuck me in the ass." She took the bottle of Astroglide from her jumper-pocket and slid it between her cheeks and squirted herself with it until it trickled down her leg. Then she put her feet on either side of the brass tray and slowly squatted down until she felt the Klockhammer brushing against her butt-muscle. She directed the showerhead back on her clit. She didn't care if her dress got soaked or not. Her thighs began to tremble with the effort of supporting herself over the dildismic pressure without sliding down on it. Finally she couldn't help herself, and she opened her asshole to its big head and sat all the way down on it, until her cheeks touched the cold ornate metal of the tray. She rocked on the feeling of a hefty dickful of pleasure up her ass, adjusting to it. Her drenched dress hung over her thighs. She was fucking Armande Klockhammer's autograph! God, it felt good.

"Hello?" came a voice. Marian looked up to see young Kevin and a girl standing hand in hand a little way off. She supposed the girl was Sylvie, Kevin's new girlfriend. Kevin was looking recently showered, spruced up and proud of himself, though momentarily puzzled. Marian saw his eyes skip down over her exposed, wet legs. The two of them were wearing matching red-and-white-striped polo shirts. Marian made a quick attempt to pull her dress down and over some of the sex toys next to her. She began watering the tulips with little flips of the showerhead, as if she were conducting a Sousa march.

"Hi," she said. "Pardon me, I was just doing a little watering. Come over. Let me turn this off. I had a plumber rig it up for me. Are you Sylvie?"

"Yes, hi," said Sylvie. Sylvie leaned and shook Marian's hand. She was a petite, perky, small-breasted girl with long light-brown hair and a pleasant sly sharp-nosed face. Marian liked her immediately.

Kevin said, "My mom told me you called, so we thought we'd come over and say hello."

"I just wanted you to see all these tulips," said Marian. "They turned out well, I think. Thank you for helping me with them."

Kevin nodded. "I like the crinkly ones." He turned to Sylvie. "Last fall I helped her plant all these."

"They're really really pretty," Sylvie agreed. There was an

awkward silence. From a distant part of the yard there came an odd hissing sound. Kevin's gray cat appeared from behind one of the mock oranges. A huge golden chewn-eared stray was on top of her. Kevin's cat crept forward a few inches and then stopped, and the gold cat, holding Kevin's cat down and biting her neck quite hard, made tiny jerks of its hindquarters, holding its tail low and fluffed. The two animals, who didn't seem to like each other much, stared at nothing at all while they fucked.

"Oh jeepers," said Kevin.

"You really should have taken her to the vet, Kevin," said Marian, though she said it gently.

"I was planning to."

"I can take a kitten if there are some," said Sylvie brightly, thinking ahead. "Maybe even two."

Marian smiled at her. "That's solved, then. Well!" It was time for them to be off. "I'm really glad you two dropped by. It's very nice to meet you, Sylvie."

"Nice to meet you. But can I ask you something?" said Sylvie. "What are all those?" She pointed to the sex toys laid out on the white linen napkin. Marian's dress didn't really hide them effectively.

"I don't know that we should get into that," said Marian.

"Okay, sorry," said Sylvie. "I kind of know what they are anyway—I mean, it's obvious, but I just want to know what you're doing with them out here. Are you planning on burying them or planting them or something?"

Kevin's ears were changing color. He was readjusting his notion of his employer. Sylvie just looked friendly and sly and curious.

Marian said, "No, I'm not burying them. I just thought it would be exciting to try out a few of them outdoors, and I wasn't sure which ones I would want. It seemed like such a nice setting, my own back yard, with the new parrot tulips."

"Can I look at one?" said Sylvie.

Marian passed her the most decorous dildo—a medium-sized clear Lucite thick-veined figurine that the catalog called the Ice Princess. Sylvie handled it carefully, using her finger-tips, not, it seemed, out of repugnance, but out of politeness for another's treasures.

"Sylvie," said Kevin in an undertone. "I think she probably wants us to go."

"She's welcome to take a look if she wants," said Marian casually. The Klockhammer deep in her ane was now begin-ning to reassert itself; it was silencing any objections she might otherwise have had to showing two teenagers wearing match-ing striped shirts her fuckable toys.

"Can I see that really long one, with the two ends?" said Sylvie.

"Ah yes—this is my Royal Welsh Fusilier. Here."

"Wowsers!" Sylvie held the two dick-ends together, jerking on them so that the movable foreskins wrinkled and stretched in tandem. She offered one end to Kevin, who inspected it with fascination in spite of himself.

"I don't exactly get why you would need something this long with two ends," he said.

Marian hesitated. "Any number of reasons."

"One of which is," said Sylvie to Kevin, "if you misbehave with Karen in any way ever again, I'll put one end right up your fanny and make you jump in your next meet with it in."

"Karen is over," said Kevin. Deferentially he thanked Marian, handing his end directly back to her. "Where did you purchase all these things?" he asked, with an air of serious inquiry.

"Oh, from a place in San Francisco," said Marian. She was using every ounce of willpower she had to keep from announcing to the two of them that she had a massive dildungs-roman installed in her butt.

"Maybe sometime you could give us the address," said Kevin, still very serious, very grown up. "We might want to order something or other. Right, Syl?"

"You never know," said Sylvie.

Marian looked at them both and laughed happily. "God it's nice to see young love," she said. "Are you two lovers, then?"

They both nodded. "We've made love thirty-two times in two months," said Sylvie proudly. "In fact," she continued, putting a fond arm around Kevin's waist, "we were just going out for a little 'drive,' because Kevin's mother doesn't like us going up to his room anymore—which I can understand."

"Ah, a little 'drive,' " said Marian. She looked at Kevin with amused surprise—the employer surprised at the precocity of the employee.

"Yeah," Kevin agreed, gesturing vaguely in the direction of the road. "We'll probably go on over to the fish hatchery."

"Well, terrific," Marian said. "Have a glorious glorious time, you two. I wish I could . . . I mean, I wish you well." She shifted a little on the brass tray and felt the thick steadfast dilderstatesman issuing official pleasure-briefings down her legs and up to the warm unforgotten Fijis of her nipples. It was so fucking *hard*—so hard to keep from saying the things she wanted to say with it deep in there: she wanted to yank up her wet dress for them and say, "Go on and fuck each other silly! Take a good look at this monster cock jammed up my butt! I want you to look right at my asshole crammed with this big fat *dick* and then go out and fuck and suck each other and slam your bodies together!" Her skin prickled with the almost irresistible wish to be obscene. But all she said was, "I must say, I envy you both a little. I'm just sorry I can't get up and see you off . . ."

Sylvie was immediately full of concern. She touched Marian lightly on the arm. "Are you okay? Can we help you up? You know your dress has gotten a little wet."

"I know, I know," said Marian, "I've been watering everywhere."

"Everywhere?" said Sylvie. "Isn't it kind of cold?"

"The water's warm. It's from my shower. Feel." Marian turned the stopcock on and whisked the showerhead spray once over Sylvie's outstretched hand.

"Feels really nice," said Sylvie thoughtfully.

"The tulips love it," said Marian. "In fact, will you two do me a favor and pick some for each other before you go? As my present to you? Pick the ones you like most. The Etruscan Prune variety is my favorite at the moment, but choose whichever ones you want."

Sylvie and Kevin liked this idea a lot and set to work assembling reciprocal bouquets. Now that their eyes were off Marian, she was free to move on the tray again and make pleasure noises in a whispery undertone. She watched them circle her beds. She imagined them all breathless and loving and wide-eyed in a shady spot near the fish hatchery. They were beautiful—fit, healthy, incredibly young—so inexperienced that they thought that their two-digit courtship, or coitship, made them seasoned fuckers. She knew so much more than they did. She lifted the sodden hem of her dress just a little and pointed the showerhead between her legs and let it flood her twat-cleavage. "That's not nearly enough, Kevin—pluck more!" she called gaily, wanting to risk his hearing the irrepressible vulval surges and catches in her voice.

When they stood in front of her again, holding their tulip bunches out to her for her admiration, she pronounced both arrangements equally lovely and told them to give them to each other. This they did with great ceremony.

"Thank you!" said Kevin to Sylvie.

"Thank you!" said Sylvie to Kevin.

They kissed. It appeared that their mouths were a good match. Marian, who normally felt squirmy and put off when she was a witness to heavy public pair-bonding, watched this particular kiss with nothing but good feeling. She *was* the public, after all. There was some tongue-action, but it had the license of youth and looked like it felt better than it looked. They hugged each other hard; Sylvie's heel went behind Kevin's and she used the leverage to press her blue-jeaned mound into him.

When they stopped, Marian said, "What a great kiss! You two are obviously *great* kissers. You must be beautiful when you . . . make love. Your bodies fit together so well. I wish I could—" She shook her head ruefully, her hand on her heart, and let them laugh at the impossibility of what she was thinking, so that they could start to get used to the idea. Then she slapped her hands on her legs and said, "I tell you what. If you would like to borrow any of these toys, feel free. Really. I don't make any great claims for them—I'm sure you can do without them, but who knows, just for fun . . ."

They looked indecisive.

Marian exerted the slightest additional pressure. "Pick one—or a few, even." She felt a trickle of sweat on her back.

"What do you think, Kevin?" said Sylvie.

Kevin shrugged. "Sure, I guess, yeah."

Sylvie and Kevin knelt, not minding apparently that their knees got instantly soaked in the wet grass. Sylvie's face, though averted, was very close to Marian's. "Which one would you recommend?" the girl finally asked, having touched them all lightly.

"Mmm, well—" This was just too much for Marian. She felt her resistance give way completely. "My current favorite is one I just got," she said. "It's called the Armande Klockhammer. As you may know, Armande Klockhammer, Jr., is, or was, a male stripper at the Golden Banana. It's kind of big, actually. Almost too big, depending on where you need it to go."

"Which one is it?" Sylvie asked.

Marian cleared her throat. "I'm afraid I can't show it to you right now."

"Why not?" Sylvie looked at her with innocent curiosity.

"I just can't."

"But why?" Sylvie insisted. "Where is it?"

"It's in use," said Marian. She looked at her two young friends and then down at her wet dress.

Kevin looked surprised. He had finally pieced it together. "You mean that all the time we've been here it's been . . ."

Marian took a deep breath. "Up my ass, yes."

"Up your . . . It's not in your . . . it's in your . . . ?" Sylvie, pointing to parts of herself to clarify her exclamation, looked genuinely surprised.

"It feels super, I must tell you," said Marian. "But that's not the crazy thing. The crazy thing is how badly I want to show it to you. While it's in there, I mean. I'm doing everything I can to keep from hauling this dress up right now and leaning back and showing you how good it feels stuffed up my tight butt. Oh man! Just thinking about it gets me going. Are you repulsed?"

They continued to look a little surprised, but not repulsed.

Marian went on. "I'm afraid you caught me at a particular

moment. Kevin, you can attest to the fact that I don't normally talk this way."

"She doesn't at all, no," Kevin agreed.

"It's dildo talk, frankly," Marian went on. "It's the way I talk when I'm sitting on a big fat artificial dick. What can I say? My butt is stretched so damn tight right now—I wish you could see, I really do. I wish I could show you, and I wish when you saw it in my ass you'd take off all your clothes and make love for me right here. Is that so unthinkable? I don't think it's so unthinkable. Kevin, I was so good last summer. Do you realize that? I thought about your cock quite a number of times, I thought about sucking it and jerking it off—I even thought of putting a sprig of parsley in your tiny little cockhole, and yet I never once did *anything*! And now you've found Sylvie, this wonderful friendly open person, who probably sucks your cock beautifully, and it makes me feel so good that you've found her—it makes me want to *see her* suck on your cock. God, I wish I could show you what I have up my ass right now. It feels so fucking hot." She paused. "See, that's a sample of dildo talk."

Sylvie was the first to speak. "You can show it to us," she said. "We won't mind."

"Really?" said Marian. "Well, you take off all your clothes, then, both of you. I'm not going to show you anything until all your clothes are off. Take them off."

Obediently Sylvie and Kevin took off their pants and under-pants and pulled off their matching striped shirts. When the dangling and tugging and hopping had ceased and they stood naked in front of her, Marian couldn't help whistling in amazement. Their bodies were so simple and perfect. Sylvie's flattish slanting breasts, with sharp confident little suck-tips, were especially good for the soul. Kevin's white straight penis

lobbed and loitered below his tight brown balls; he had a
Dennis-the-Menace touch of hair around each of his nipples.
Marian had to turn the Pollenex on and point it up her dress
in order to recover her seducer's concentration.

"Now show us," said Sylvie challengingly, conscious that
her revealed beauty gave her power. She ran her fingers over
her stomach and brushed the side of her hand casually against
Kevin's cock. "Show us what's up your . . ."

"Ah, you're such a beautiful couple," said Marian. "You're
made to fuck each other. I'll show you when it's the right time.
Right now, I need you to show me how pretty you are together.
Show me how you like to suck cock, Sylvie honey. I want to see
your pretty lips on that hot cockmeat. Kiss it for me."

Sylvie, compelled by the conviction in Marian's voice, knelt
and kissed a path down Kevin's cock until she came to its
head, and then she opened her lips and let it fill her mouth.
As he watched her and moaned, Kevin's mouth mirrored
Sylvie's. He was standing with his hands crossed lightly at the
wrists behind his back, his hips pushed forward, looking down
at his girlfriend. As he firmed up, Sylvie's jaw was forced open
wider and her tongue was pushed down, and Marian was
pleased to see her develop a cocksucker's temporary double
chin, which, because in reality the girl had nothing approaching a double chin, only made her face look younger and more
captivatingly innocent.

"That's so nice, so pretty, that pretty sucking," said Marian,
letting her showerhead do the talking for her. Areas of grass
near her legs were getting a marshy gleam.

Sylvie turned and looked at her. Her eyes were dreamy with
confused arousal. "Please show me and Kev what you have up
your fanny," she said again. She added rhetorical weight to
her request by stroking three times on Kevin's cock.

Marian pulled her dress up so that it was very high on her thighs, but not so high that anything was revealed. She lifted her weight onto her hands for a moment and then swiveled her hips. "It's all slicked up with lubricant. It feels so snazzy in there. I want it in there always. I want to show it to you as it fucks my butt, but I need some inspiration. I need to see your cute little asshole first, Sylvie. That's only fair. Squat right over my feet—I want to see your beautiful back and your open ass and your hot little asshole while you suck your boyfriend's cock."

"But—" said Sylvie.

"You know you want to show me everything about your body. You're not ashamed of anything, are you? You're proud of your body. You know you want me to look right at your ass while you suck that luscious dick. Don't you?"

"Yes," said Sylvie. "I want you to watch me sucking on Kevin." She planted her feet on either side of Marian's ankles and squatted, her back to the older woman. Marian twisted the showerhead to PULSE and aimed the spray in circles over Sylvie's ass globes.

"Pull your cheeks apart—I can't quite see you, and I need to see you," said Marian. Sylvie got two handfuls of her ass and pulled up, and Marian saw the dark little dot where they met and joined. She pointed the water's pulse straight at it. Sylvie arched her back to get a more direct hit; her breaths began to come harder and more irregularly through her nose. Her hair bobbed as her mouth emptied and filled with cock.

"*That's* what I like to see," said Marian. "Kevin, I wish you could see how beautiful Sylvie is when she sucks on your cock with her sexy ass all open and clean." Kevin looked up at her as she said this, and Marian, as she continued to murmur encouragement, gave him a brief secret show, looking straight at him as she jogged her tits under her dress and pinched her nipples through the fabric. Her fingers were wet, so they left dark marks where they had been. Then, when she knew she had his allegiance, she said, "Kevin, do you mind if I tickle Sylvie's pretty butt with the flowers she gave you? You want her to feel good while she sucks your big dick, don't you?"

"Go ahead," said Kevin thickly.

Marian leaned forward and brushed the tulip heads across Sylvie's shoulders and down her back. She slapped them lightly back and forth on the insides of the girl's fine thighs and up against her popped-out clit. "Ooo, she likes it," she said. Then she turned the tulips in a circle over Sylvie's asshole. "Do you like my flowers tickling your pretty butt? I bet you do."

Sylvie said something affirmative and sucked some more. Then she stopped. She didn't let go of Kevin's shiny cock, but she said, "Could I use your bathroom for a second? I'm dying."

"Sure," said Marian. "But you don't have to. Why lose time? Just let it go. I'll spray it away. Piss it right out on my feet."

"Pee on your feet?" Sylvie exclaimed. "No way! I can't do that."

"Of course you can," Marian said. "What's the harm? Just keep sucking that tasty dick and relax. When I have a big rubber dick up my asshole I like to see everything. I *want* to see it. I want to feel it spray out all over my feet—warm up these lonely toesies." She played the showerhead spray insistently over Sylvie's clim-folds. "Suck and push, honey," she urged. "It'll feel good, believe me. Arch your back so I can see."

Sylvie resumed sucking Kevin's cock.

"Push for me," said Marian. "Push that piss out." But nothing happened.

"I'm really sorry—I can't," said Sylvie. "I'm a little shy about that in front of Kev."

"Ah, I see. Kevin? You don't mind, do you? Of course not. In fact, you know what? I'd love to see a little dribble of piss come out of that big friendly cock. I bet that would help Sylvie relax." Marian moved one of her feet out where Kevin could see it. "Let her hold your cock and jerk on it a little and then point it straight at my feet and push and let go. I bet you can do it."

"Really?" said Kevin. He held his dick for Sylvie to aim it.

"Of course!" said Marian.

"Okay," he said. Sylvie gripped the base of his cock and Kevin's stomach muscles tightened and he pressed his lips together and forced out a curve of hot piss that momentarily reached Marian's foot.

"That's the way!" said Marian. "How did it feel?"

"Felt good," said Kevin. "Kind of burny." He wiped the tip of his dick with his palm.

"Of course it did," Marian said. "Now, Sylvie? You know how badly you need to let it go. You know what's up my ass. How could you possibly be shy?" Again she tapped the flowers against Sylvie's cunt. "Push and piss it out for me."

Sylvie gave it a second try. She pushed very hard. After a moment, her tiny urethra opened and a clear spurt flared out. The flow stopped almost immediately.

"Good!" said Marian. "More!"

"But," Sylvie objected, "I'm pushing so hard I'm afraid something else might happen." She stood up. "I really *need* to use the bathroom—I'm not kidding."

"Oh, but I want to see that, too," said Marian. "I want to see everything you can do."

"Gross, no way!" said Sylvie.

Kevin decided that it was time for him to intercede. "I really don't think she can do that," he said. "I mean, I wouldn't mind at all if she did, but . . ."

Marian pulled off her dress in a quick motion. "Look at this dick up my ass." She leaned back on her hands and lifted her knees back against her body. "See that butthole? See how nice and tight it is? Look at that tight skin. You can look for as long as you want. Look at me rock on it. Can you see it moving in and out? Foo, that's nice! I like to see your eyes on it." She looked at them both and shook her tits for them. "Now, Sylvie, it's your turn. I've showed you, now you show me. Show me that tight little butt of yours again. See, I had no idea you were as full as I am. I want to see that ass open right up, just like mine is. Suck that cock of his and push it out for me. Once you do that, you'll feel free to do anything that feels good, anything you want, and you'll come extra hard, and that's what I want—I want you to come extra hard, because you can be damn sure that's what I'm going to do."

"I really have to go," said Sylvie. "I'm not kidding."

"I know you do! Squat down just like you were and suck that cock. I'll spray you clean, don't worry. Pull up on your cheeks so I can see. Push and let it go."

Sylvie took up her cocksucking squat. She started sucking more Kevin-dick, but faster than before. She pulled one of her cheeks open. Her asshole looked exactly the same—tiny, sexy. Then suddenly her piss gushed out everywhere.

"Ah, that's it!" said Marian, frigging her clit. "Show me how you let it all go. Release it. That's it. Let it all go. Feel it relax." Marian whisked the linen napkin out from under her toys and held it at the ready. "Let that lovely butt open right up for me."

Sylvie made a moan of warning. Her asshole domed out into a doughnut shape and began to open.

"Good!" said Marian. "Now stop! Tighten back up on it."

Sylvie made a straining sound. Her hips rocked, and her asshole slowly closed.

Marian was frigging faster now. She let the spray drive into Sylvie's ass. "That's right, honey," she coached. "Keep sucking that dick. I know you need to let it out. Push on it."

"It's really going to come out this time," said Sylvie, somewhat frantically. "I can't hold it."

"I know you can't hold it. I just want to see your ass open one more time. It's *so* sexy to see it open up. Let it go. Push now. Give it to us. Come on, push."

Sylvie moaned again. Her asshole domed and opened wider, and a big dark hard dickshape began to push its way straight out. Marian held the napkin underneath. "Oh yeah. Keep pushing baby. Push it all out." She felt the weight drop in her hand and immediately folded the napkin over it and sprayed Sylvie clean. "*Now* we're ready!" she said. "We're ready to fuck, kids. Come on, Sylvie, get on your hands and knees over me. Open that cunt for Kevin's cock. I want to see Kevin's hard dick up your cunt while I pinch your nipples. Come on. I want to see some good hard fucking!"

But Sylvie didn't obey immediately. She had rights now. She was free to do anything she wanted. Boldly she lifted one of Marian's juggy tits and bent to slap it around with her tongue. Then, bringing her blond cunt-site close, she brushed Marian's nipple-tip over her neglected clit. "Could you hold those tits tight and point them right at my pussy?" she requested, with the zeal of a convert. "I think I've got a little pee left over for them." Sylvie pushed and let a brief spurt spray over Marian's mildly surprised breasts. "Let me hose it off," she said, and she took the showerhead from Marian and sprayed her mentor off.

"See?" said Marian, recovering quickly. "You can do anything now."

"Yeah, and *now* I'm ready for some cock. I need to be fucked good, Kev. Give it to me good."

She arranged herself on her elbows and knees over Marian's legs. Marian grabbed the girl's asscheeks and spread her open. Kevin got behind Sylvie; he stared at his girlfriend's impish twat as if he'd never seen it before and pumped his dick in his fast fist. It was a handsome dick, no question; watching him, Marian felt she needed to hold that purple stanchion for herself at least once. "Sylvie?" she asked. "You won't mind if I make sure your lover is good and stiff for you, will you?"

"No, just do it fast and get him in there!" said Sylvie, kissing her own bicep muscle. "Either that or shove one of those big dildo-dicks up my cunt and jerk him off onto my asshole. Your choice. But get something big up my cunt now!"

"I'll get him nice and fat for your cunt," said Marian. She surrounded Kevin's cock with her right hand and registered its warmth and livingly resistant rigidity. It felt, she found herself observing, extremely realistic. She steered its head toward the opening of Sylvie's pink slot and jerked its stem fairly hard in place a few times. "Feel the big head?" she said. "Wiggle a little for him. He's almost ready." She looked up at Kevin and mimed a licking mouth to show him how she would lick his dick if given the opportunity. He was aroused and slit-eyed, and, she noticed, he was gazing fixedly at her breasts.

"Could you please put him in now?" urged Sylvie.

"He's going to push it in now," Marian said, giving his dick a few last jerks. "Push that cock in her, baby," She held his shaft for as long as she could until it disappeared into Sylvie's cunt; Sylvie was very tight but equally wet, and the dick's length slid in without bending.

"Oh, fuck, that's good," said Sylvie, sighing with relief. Immediately she and Kevin started slapping fast against each other.

"Oh yeah! I like to see that boy-dick slapping in there!" said Marian, turning the showerhead on her clit. "I can feel it in my cunt just looking at it! Yeah! My cunt is so empty and yours is so full of that sweet hot dickmeat!"

As they fucked, Sylvie focused on the dildos, which lay tumbled on the grass. The girl turned so that her face was close to Marian's. Her hair was in her eyes. In an uneven whisper, she said, "I need one of those. Pick one and put it in my ass, will you? Please?"

Marian brushed the tulips down Sylvie's back and tapped them against her asshole. Then she replaced the flowers with her middle finger, resting it lightly on the opening. "Is that where you want something? Right in there?"

"Oh," moaned Sylvie, "I want what's in your ass."

"Honey, I've got something much better than that for you," said Marian. "Kevin, look where my finger is. Isn't that a pretty little asshole? Has your cock ever been in there?"

Kevin shook his head no. His hands were on Sylvie's hips, and he was pushing with a circling motion of his hips, making gravelly grunts.

"I want to see that dick up that gorgeous little butt. That okay with you, Sylvie? You want your honey's big burning dick up your ass? Believe me, it'll feel good. You know you want it, don't you."

"Yeah I want it, I want it," said Sylvie.

"You want it straight up your ass, don't you," Marian repeated.

"I *need* it up my ass," Sylvie pleaded. "Kev, I need it up my ass!"

Marian grabbed the four-foot-long Welsh Fusilier and turned it on. She whispered to Sylvie, "Slide this up my cunt." Sylvie fumblingly obliged. "That's good. I want our slutty cunts to be connected while you get fucked up the ass for the first time," Marian said. She handed her end of it to Kevin. "Pull out of her, baby. Push this in instead." Kevin's long glossy dick emerged from behind the horizon of Sylvie's ass-curve and with evident reluctance he fed the end of the double-vibe where he had just been. Sylvie made a surprised shout and arched her back and started fucking against it.

As soon as Marian saw Kevin's cock reappear, she knew she had to suck it. This was her one chance. "Oh, God, that's a pretty cock," she said. "I need a real dick in my mouth for a second, just for a *second*. Come over here for a second, baby. Sylvie, he needs to be super stiff for your tight little butt. You don't mind if I get his dick good and stiff for you with my tongue, do you? I'm sorry, but I just have to suck on this dick."

"Suck him!" said Sylvie. "Ooh, God, suck him stiff for me. Just hurry and get something big up my ass. I'm so hot for it." She circled Marian's clit with her end of the Fusilier, gazing at the base of the Klockhammer buried in the older woman's ass. Marian, her mouth stuffed with purple cock, groaned and opened her legs for the pleasure. As Sylvie felt Kevin jabbing the other Welsh-head in and out of her own buzzing cunt-lips, she reached back and spread her asscheeks open and said, "That's enough. Stop sucking my boyfriend's dick and get it in my ass!"

Marian pulled her mouth off of Kevin's dick. "Okay,

sweetie, it's ready for you." She squirted lube on Sylvie's asshole. The squirt bottle made rude noises, but nobody cared. She pulled Kevin into position by his cock and tapped the head of his dick on Sylvie's now-sloppy asscrack, circling it over the opening. Then she pointed it and held it still. "Okay, push in slow, Kevin. Open up for him, Sylvie. He's going in."

"Push it in me! Fuck this ass!" cried Sylvie.

Marian held Kevin's cockshaft while it began to drive slowly in. It bent a little as he put his weight behind it; then, as Sylvie relaxed for him, it straightened out and filled her.

"There he goes," said Marian.

"Fuck me with that dick, oooooooo!" said Sylvie. Kevin began making very slow long strokes.

"That's it, Kevin—fuck straight into her perfect ass—you're getting it." Marian took hold of the end of the vibrator in her cunt and started pulling it in and out in rhythm with Kevin's steady dick-thrusts. Its length curved up and disappeared into Sylvie's clim. She kissed Sylvie on the shoulder. "God, I like being connected to your sexy pussy, sweetie!" she said. Sylvie was looking straight ahead, taking little breaths as she pushed back on Kevin's thickness. "You like him in your ass, don't you?" Marian asked her.

"I like him to fuck me hard!" said Sylvie. "Fuck my hot ass, Kev. I'm getting closer to the smiley face!" She looked at Marian. "That's what we say when we're going to come soon," she breathlessly explained.

Marian sprang into action. "Hold on, though—one last thing." She picked up the little okra-sized dildo and slipped it over her middle finger and squirted some Astroglide on it. "Can I put this in Kevin's ass?" she whispered. "I want to feel him fucking you when you come. Can I?"

Sylvie blew up on her bangs and nodded. "Just hurry."

Marian flicked the okra-dick over Sylvie's nipples and then dragged it down Kevin's ribs and slid around to the base of his back and gripped the near cheek of his ass, so that her four fingers were near his asshole.

"What are you doing?" Kevin said, freezing suddenly.

"I'm putting some okra up your ass so you won't feel left out," said Marian. "I want to help you fuck Sylvie. I want to feel you fucking her ass, and I want your asshole to feel you fucking *her* asshole. Don't trouble yourself—just let it in and keep fucking."

"Let her do it, Kev!" Sylvie called earnestly.

Kevin overcame his uncertainty and resumed his slow, deliberate ass-fucking. But now, each time he pulled out for the next thrust, Marian drove the okra-dick a little farther into his reluctant male hole. He seemed to like it more after a minute or two, and as he began to get his own butt in gear, Marian started urging and guiding his movements, making him go a little faster, getting him to angle his thrusts, the way she knew Sylvie wanted it. Every push he made made his high-jumper's maximus-muscles bunch memorably under Marian's cupping hand. "See how she likes it faster?" Marian said. "Fuck her like this." She controlled his pumping torso with the okra-plug like a puppet-master and he said, "Oh, jeepers! Get it up there!"

"Pinch my nipples hard!" Sylvie ordered Marian in an urgent whisper. "I'm right *at* the smiley face," she called to Kevin.

"Let's get off together," said Marian, pinching as she was told. "Come on. Come on, come on. Fuck her, Kevin! Shoot that come in her. Look at this cock up my butt, Sylvie. Come over me. Oh! Oh fuck!" She let go of Sylvie's nipples and held the Welsh-head tight to her love-bean as her orgasm gathered the necessary signatures. The autographed Armande had been in her ass for so long that she felt the biggest climax of her life had to be well on its way. But she wasn't quite ready for it. She pushed her breasts forward and said, "Suck my titbags for a second, Sylvie. Suck them hard, bite them, bite them. Oh shit! Now come for me. Come around that hot dickmeat."

"Oh, God!" said Sylvie. She tried to suck Marian's nipples but couldn't concentrate on them and arched her neck, staring forward at the invisible pleasure in her head.

"That's okay—come for me baby. She's starting to come, Kevin! Shoot that hot juice up her ass for her! Fill her ass with that burning come!" Marian finger-fucked the okra-dick faster in and out of Kevin's asshole, and he leaned forward to take it and then straightened up, lifting Sylvie by the hips right off the ground and pulling her back against his cock. "Now, Sylvie?" he said.

"Oh, fuck me good, Kev! Fill my fucking fanny!" Sylvie shouted, looking in Marian's eyes and then down at her toy-filled fuckholes. "Harder! Oh, yes! Fuck me real good, darling! SHOOT THAT HOT DICK UP MY FANNY-HOLE! OH! OH!"

With an astonished expression, Kevin made one last long lurching shuddering push and started to come.

"OH YES!" said Sylvie, feeling Kevin's cock empty ounce after ounce of boiling scream-cream into her ass. "AH! I'M COMIIINNNG!!!!!" As pagan pleasures wracked her body, she did indeed make a huge grimacing smiley face.

It was Marian's turn now. She allowed the idea of Kevin's squirting dick in Sylvie's ass to merge with the sensation of Armande Klockhammer, Jr.'s in her own. She conjured up the sight of the dollar bills stuffed in his asscheeks as he danced with his back to the audience. She thought of the shouting women; the whomping music; the sight of him turning on the stage and tossing his heavy live meat around inside its black silk pouch as he looked out at all his women. All these memories were *up her ass.* She opened her eyes and said evenly, "Please watch me come, now, you two. Watch my asshole and cunt come around these huge horny cocks!" Then she threw herself back on the wet grass and lifted her legs and rested her feet on Sylvie's back; she let them watch whatever they wanted while the brutish, hunky orgasm ennobled her body. "Oh nice . . . so nice . . . so nice . . ." she sighed as the clit-twitching ebbed.

When the three of them had recovered a little, Marian rinsed off Kevin's softening cock and lifted herself off the Klockhammer and sprayed it fresh.

"Can we pick some more of your tulips sometime?" said Sylvie sweetly before she and Kevin, dressed once again in their matching outfits, left for the fish hatchery.

"Anytime you want," said Marian. "I love young love." Naked, replete, she put her toys and her abandoned book on the tray and went indoors. Over the next year, with Kevin and Sylvie's weekend help weeding and planting and mowing, her back yard became the envy of her neighbors.

15

THAT WAS WHAT I FINALLY RECORDED ON THE CASSETTE THAT I put in the tape-player in Adele Junette Spacks's Ford Escort in place of Suzanne Vega's *Solitude Standing*. It—Part Two— was sixteen single-spaced pages long, and it took, in addition to the twelve long hours and two fiercely snuffling orgasms I devoted to its composition, another two hours to record on tape. (I let both of my comeshots hop out directly onto the hazily indeterminate Mass Turnpike, my bottom scooched forward on the hood of my car so that my richard made a sort of hood ornament. Unable to endure the physically paradoxi- cal contact of a surface going sixty miles an hour faster than they were, the sperm-drops began to sizzle on the roadway after a few minutes; they had vaporized completely in less than half an hour.) When I was done recording I didn't feel exhausted—I felt exhilarated. My right wrist hurt a lot—this marked, if I'm not mistaken, the beginning of my carpal-tunnel problem, which has bothered me on and off since. It isn't clear to me now why Marian's adventures ended up being so unremittingly ane-oriented in content—I like to think it was just a matter of mood. After all, I had never typed the word *butthole* before in my life. It isn't a word that comes up much in business correspondence. Private coarseness is a known high. What was just as important, I wanted to minimize the chance that this Smith College woman would find my audiotaped company tame, and an anus or two livens up any gathering. I wanted my rotterly imagination to feed rather than limit hers, to extend without strain as far as hers would go; and I hoped that whatever she didn't like she could filter out. I hoped that she would realize that I was an unusual man, possibly worth knowing.

I didn't leave my gift in her player right away, not wanting to be seen driving right there, brazenly next to her, when it came on. I started up time, accelerated, and moved a few cars ahead, then jogged back on foot to her car with the universe on pause and switched the tapes. Consequently I didn't get to see her initial reaction. But I drove annoyingly slowly, forcing the buffer cars behind me to pass; very soon I had Adele in my rear-view mirror again. I put on sunglasses so that she wouldn't be able to see when my eyes were flicking up to the mirror at her. I saw her doing something, leaning, examining: I guessed that she had ejected my tape and was checking for identifying marks. (It said only MARIAN THE LIBRARIAN on the label.) Then there was a long period where she—I'm fairly sure—listened to some or all of it. She passed me again, paying no attention to me; I Dropped for a second to verify that my tape was in her player and then let her proceed. We drove for quite a while together, over an hour, although I don't think she noticed that I was keeping discreetly close to her. She fluffed her hair several times. I looked for signs of arousal: weaving, sudden slowing. There were none. I hoped she would be so aroused that she would have to stop at a motel very soon.

To my surprise, she drove right past the turnoff for Route 91 and Northampton. She continued to drive west. Was she on her way to Chicago? That made sense. She was probably in graduate school there. (The University of Chicago sticker on her rear windshield was above the Smith sticker, arguing for Smith's temporal priority.) I wasn't sure that I wanted to drive all the way to *Chicago* with her, but presumably she would have to stop somewhere for the night. And even if she hated my tape, she was still driving, and driving allows for a great deal of idle thought, and idle thought is the perfect medium for the accelerated transmutation of remembered distastefulness. By the time she turned into a motel that evening, some image off my cassette might be soaring through her sensibility, robed in urgency and fire. And regardless of how she felt about my tape, she would almost certainly come in her motel room, since what else is there to do in motel rooms?

As I drove, I worked out an elaborate plan of how I would proceed if she did check into a motel. As soon as she entered the parking lot, I would stop time and pull in ahead of her and park in an out-of-the-way spot. I would restart time. She would park and go into the office for five minutes and then reappear and walk to a room, say room 23. As she was pointing her key at the doorknob, with a semi-blank set-mouthed face that no actress could duplicate because it was so wholly

a product of the certainty of her unobservedness, I would
pause her, go back to the office and get the spare key for room
23 from the key drawer, and enter ahead of her. It wouldn't
be a bad room, a little on the brown side, but there would
probably be no good place for me to hide to watch her undress. I would be deeply sleepy by this time. My yawns would
be coming every thirty seconds. It would be about seven in the
morning Strine-time, counting my lengthy on-the-road Foldout, but I would still be needing some moment of closeness
with this total stranger, who had become my chosen traveling
companion. I would notice that in her room there was a
locked door that led to the adjacent room. This would suggest
some possibilities to me.

Still fully fermational, I would leave her standing at the
door with her key out and I would walk out and "buy" (in
the usual informal manner) fourteen dirty magazines from a
newsstand a quarter of a mile down the road. I like wandering around newsstands in the Fold and looking at people
looking at magazines. Sometimes it's just as you would expect: the thirteen-year-old kid with a fine little mustache
looking at a shelf-ful of gory horror-film mags, etc. But
often it isn't so simple: it isn't like the cartoon cliché about
how people resemble their dogs. The man at the rack of
computer magazines is someone you couldn't have pre-
dicted would be there; likewise the woman looking at the
sailing magazines and the man reading at the antiques rack.
You can't necessarily match people up with the periodicals
they flip through. Perhaps this is because people who spend
time in newsstands aren't representative of the people who
are deeply interested in a given hobby or subject—the real
enthusiasts are out on sailboats or at antiques auctions,
rather than reading about them; or more likely they are

leafing through the magazines at home, where they can really study them, being subscribers. Some of the true hobbyists disdain the magazines because they have studied them for so long that the level of repetition in the how-to articles has begun to tire them. It might often be that the inhabitants of a newsstand are those who want a taste of what it would be like to have a certain interest without actually having it. But then again, some are probably true aficionados of their particular realm who are drawn to the newsstand precisely because here they can see their specialized sub-passion on display near all others: model rocketry right on an equal footing with *Metropolitan Home;* the science fiction magazines only a few feet from bodybuilding, or from those flimsy how-to-write-an-effective-query-letter writers' magazines. Unlike a bookstore, a newsstand unifies its huge range of subject categories by its overriding sense of nowness. It is a Parthenon of the immediate present, a centrifuge of synchronicity. Each magazine is saying, This is what we think you want to know about our subspecialty right this second, in (you scan the covers) July July July July August July July July August August July. My Fold-powers are replenished by trips to newsstands; I find that the longer I spend in one, the more cleanly and responsively time stops for me the next time I trigger a Drop.

So I would go down the road from Adele's motel and buy fourteen men's magazines at a newsstand, and I would walk back and arrange them on one of the beds in her room, room 23, covering its objectionable pink and brown coverlet with a superior quilt of plush womanflesh. I would get a washcloth from the bathroom and drape it on the edge of the bed, as if to catch the scumsquibs that were imminent from my bloated factotum. I would make sure that I had stroked past the point of caring at the moment I adjusted my glasses. Immediately thereafter, I would hear Adele's revitalized key in the lock.

When, on the threshold of her own motel room, she caught sight of me inside, looking up at her with surprise, she would say, "Oh, sorry!" and close the door. It would not be too difficult for me to act flustered and embarrassed. I would genuinely *be* flustered and embarrassed. "I'm terribly sorry—one moment!" I would call loudly. "Sorry, sorry!" I would hurry outside, doing up my belt. She would already be on her way back to the office. "It's my mistake," I would say. "I think I was given the wrong key."

"No problem," Adele would say crisply. "I'll get a different room." She wouldn't want to meet my eye.

"What I mean is," I would hastily explain, "I think I'm in *your* room. The man said room twenty-four, but then when I looked at the key he gave me it said twenty-three, so I just assumed that it was the room I was meant to have. Obviously I was very wrong. But if you hang on thirty seconds I'll be totally out of your room."

Adele would say, "That's all right—you're obviously already all settled in there." She would make a little laugh.

But I would be full of sincerity. "You mean the magazines? I can pile those up in half a second, really. I think that you should have the room you were meant to have, since it's my mistake. I haven't even used the bathroom. Well, no—I did use it." I would put my hand on my chest. "This is mortifying."

Adele would reassure me. "Don't worry about it, honestly. I'll get a different room. You stay in that room, and I'll get a different one. It's fine."

But I wouldn't want that to happen, of course. I would hand her my key to her room, the one I borrowed from the office while in the Fold. "Here's the key to your room," I would say. You get your suitcase or whatever, and I'll get the right key for my room, and then I'll be out of *your* room in two seconds. Okay?"

She could so very easily not go along with this and insist on talking to the man in the motel office herself, and it would not be at all good for me if she did: I would have to use the Fold to escape, and I would have to abandon her while she was in the middle of telling the person at the desk that there was someone in her room, and then he would tell her that nobody was checked into room 24, and she would be left with a mysterious and disturbing sexual event that she could not explain. The police would possibly get involved—awful to contemplate. But because I always mean well, despite my sneakiness, I would be flustered enough and genuine enough that she would believe me and accede.

I would check in at the office and request room 24 and get the key. Adele would be standing outside room 23 when I returned. The door would be ajar—I would have left it ajar—so she would have been able to glance at the arrangement of magazines and the washcloth on the end of the bed during my brief absence if she wanted to.

"There, all set," I would tell her. I would noisily slap all the magazines in a big pile and cover the top one with the washcloth and carry them out to my new room. Again I would say, "I'm terribly sorry for the dreadful mix-up."

"That's quite all right," she would say. She would be very unflappable and pleasant. We would wave good-night.

In my room, I would throw myself on the bed and sigh with relief—nothing bad had happened! I would think that I should ask her out for a bite to eat, since it was dinner time. I better ask her out right now, I would say to myself, before she gets undressed or has a shower, while we are both still in the ceremonially friendly mood-envelope. I would hop up—and then I would think better of it. The problem would be that I was right on the brink of being perceived as a threat by her, and I wouldn't be able to risk seeming sinister or sleazy by making any advances now. And I wouldn't have to. The fact that we were in side-by-side rooms would feel increasingly relevant as the evening progressed: time would be on my side. I would lie back on the bed with my hands on my forehead, listening to the sounds from her room. Despite the doors connecting us, her room would turn out to be surprisingly uneavesdroppable-on. I would hear her water run for a while—perhaps a very quick shower, more likely a face-wash and a toothbrushing. Fifteen minutes would pass. I would hear her unlock several locks and go outside. She would be on her way to dinner. I would wait and then Drop and hide behind a corner and watch her. She would decide to dine at the lugubrious woodgrain-Formica-and-waitresses-with-Early-American-bonnets restaurant that was linked to the motel, just because she was tired and it was close by. I would buy a local paper from a machine and go inside and take a menu and sit down somewhere, ignoring the PLEASE WAIT FOR HOSTESS TO SEAT YOU sign, and then I would stop meddling with time. I would be deep into menu-parsing when Adele walked in. There would be very few folks in the restaurant. The hostess would seat Adele at a nearby table. When Adele said, "Thanks," I would look up with pleased surprise. I would say hello. She would be carrying a copy of *Mirabella*, still wearing the pink sweater. When she sat down, I would lean over and ask her, "After you've read your magazine and I've read my newspaper, will you join me for dessert?"

And of course she would say yes.

The two of us would pretend that we didn't exist for half an hour. While I ate my pot roast, I would rattle the newspaper with a serious air and read it more thoroughly than I've read a newspaper in years. Finally there would come an indecisive moment after our dinner plates were removed. I would look up again and say, "Dessert time?"

She would get up and come over. "I shouldn't, but I will," she would say. "The list looks interesting." We would discuss what an apricot crumble might in reality be, pretending to be more in the dark than we were. Then I would apologize again for the mix-up with the rooms. I would say that it was pure absent-minded stupidity on my part.

She would say, "It's the second weird thing that has happened to me today."

"Oh?" I would prompt. "The second?"

Yes, she would reply. She would tell me that she had been driving along the Mass Pike a few hours earlier, minding her own business, listening to a Suzanne Vega tape, when all of a sudden this voice had come on the speakers saying that he was someone in a car that she had recently passed and that he had used his powers to replace the tape in her cassette player with the one she was hearing. She would report that the tape had turned out to be, as you might expect, pornographic. "Really kind of strong stuff in places," she would tell me. "Kind of disgusting, actually."

"How very lurid and suggestive and mysterious," I would say in reaction, making perplexed noises. I would question her further: did she have any idea how such an audiocassette could have made its way into her tape-player?

She would say that she had no idea. I would tell her that I was convinced that there were still one or more major phenomena in the universe that were as yet unknown or were radically misunderstood. "Are you a scientist?" she would inquire. I would say no, with a light laugh, and tell her that I was a temp in Boston, returning from seeing relatives in Pitts-burgh. She would say that she was doing linguistics at the University of Chicago. She would be interested in language acquisition in children from bilingual families. We would talk quite happily about language acquisition in children from bilingual families for a long while, since I am interested in that subject myself. She would let me pay for her dessert.

Before we left, I would take a deep breath and say, "You have to forgive me. I'm desperately curious to know what sort of stuff was on that pornographic cassette. Was it just him huffing and puffing?"

"Nothing like that," Adele would reply. "It was fairly elaborate. It was a whole story."

I would lean forward, intrigued. "Really?" I would watch her think over what she remembered of it. I would notice her mentally putting aside the first images that came to her from it because she didn't want to discuss them with me.

She would say, "It was about this woman who—well, there was a UPS man . . ."

"Figures," I would say dismissively.

"And a neighbor boy," she would continue, "and the boy's girlfriend. And a lawn-mower."

I would look alarmed. "Not something violent with a lawn-mower."

She would shake her head.

"So just your standard porn, basically," I would say.

She would think that one over. "I guess so. There were a great many dildos, which is fine, I guess—whatever. But then—I don't know—golden showers? Actual out-and-out defecation?"

"Yuck," I would exclaim.

"I don't mean," she would add, "that they were defecating

all over the place. It was done with some taste and refinement. But still, there was a general overemphasis on the anal side of things, in my view."

"Fascinating," I would say.

"And I'm not saying," Adele would open-mindedly go on, "that there isn't some merit to checking in on that part of the world from time to time. I know that it's richly furnished with nerve-endings. But to give it top billing . . ."

I would agree wholeheartedly and shake my head at the error of laying too much stress on that area. Then, however, I too would be forced to demonstrate my open-mindedness. "I mean, it certainly doesn't hurt to include it in the festivities from time to time, occasionally. But it's more to reawaken one's appreciation of the usual avenues than as an end in itself."

Adele would suddenly start laughing.

I would look inquiringly at her.

"Nothing, nothing," she would say. "Something just popped into my head and struck me as funny. It's nothing— it's not funny at all. It's just that ancient expression 'Hershey highway.' " Having said it, Adele would lean forward, her hands on her face, laughing hard. "Oh boy, sorry." She would lift her water glass an inch off the table and then set it down, clearing her throat, still laughing a little. "Sorry. It's just that if you could have *heard* this tape, on and on about 'up her butt' and 'in her ass' and 'show me that tight little ass,' God. Sorry."

I would laugh politely. "What sort of voice did the man on the tape have?" I would ask.

"A very sort of straight-arrow voice," Adele would say. "No Boston accent or anything. Maybe a bit like your voice. Quite deep, though." She would give me a look and I would have a feeling that she was on the verge of asking me if I had made the tape. (The stately pace of sound-waves in the Fold would further explain my altered timbre.) But she wouldn't ask. Possibly she wouldn't want to know that I was the Arno Van Dilden behind Marian the Librarian. She wouldn't want me to be a liar and a trickster and a sneak, but a genuine, somewhat-fun-to-talk-to one-time dessert companion, which is what I would genuinely want to be for her as well. We would walk back up the slope to the motel. Our respective keys would make jingly sounds. I would be so sleepy by this time that I would hardly be able to stand.

I would ask her, "Are you leaving at the crack of dawn or will you be able to have some breakfast?"

She would say that she would probably just get something at a drive-through.

"Well," I would say, shaking her hand, "good luck with your bilingual research." We would go into our rooms. I would take a shower and get in bed and fall asleep thinking about light-switches that go up and down without making a clicking sound. It would only be about eight-thirty, real time. The effort involved in trying to be likable, on top of the lack of sleep, would have completely wiped me out. Two hours later, the phone would ring.

It would be Adele. "Did I wake you up?"

I would say no.

She would say, "The reason I'm calling is, you know what? I think you unintentionally made off with my washcloth."

I would pretend to think back. I would remember. "Right, of course. I was flustered."

Adele would say, "I believe that you had it on top of that pile of reading material."

"You're right," I would say. "Do you need it? I'll bring it right over."

"Well," she would explain, "I'm thinking of taking a bath, and a bath is just not a bath without a washcloth."

I would indicate that I agreed wholeheartedly with this statement. "The washcloth is one of the more versatile things you can bring with you to the bathtub," I would say. I would tell her how much I liked it when I got soap in my eyes and I squeezed out the washcloth and scrubbed my eyes really hard with it, making the sting of the soap miraculously go away. Adele would tell me how as a child she had arranged her dolls at the foot of the tub and used wet washcloths as blankets, tucking them in. I would ask her whether she had raised her dolls bilingually. She would say that in fact she had developed several doll languages. We would share a few more thoughts on this rich and interesting subject.

"Well," she would finally say.

"How do you want to work this?" I would tentatively ask. "I could just bring one over. You'll hear a knock and I'll just hand you one. I took a shower earlier, but I only used one."

"I took a shower earlier, too," Adele would say. "But I can't sleep now." She would hesitate. "If you're not decent, or you don't want to go outside in the cold, I was thinking that there seems to be a *door* leading directly from your room to my room. I'll keep the chain on my side hooked on, because I'm not . . . well . . . anyway, you could just hand it through the gap in my door."

I would tell her what a good idea I thought that was. "Let me see if my side opens." I would undo the chain and the slide-lock on my side and open my door, revealing a second, knobless door on her side. "My side is open now," I would say. "I'll hang up and get the washcloth."

"Okay, see you in a second," she would say.

The white square of fabric would still be resting on top of the pile of dirty magazines. I would fold it up neatly, like a blank business letter, and knock once on her inner door. After a series of unbolting noises, the door would open a crack. Adele's eye and the corner of her mouth would appear. "Surprise," she would say.

"I'm so very glad to have found you at home," I would gallantly offer.

Adele would put her hand to the gap and I would stuff the washcloth through. "Have a good bath," I would say.

She would thank me and apologize for disturbing me so late.

"Don't be silly," I would say. "Do you read in the bath? I have the local paper. But I guess newspapers are not really bath matter. I do have, though, as you saw, a *stack* of dirty magazines. Ah, I forgot—you have *Mirabella,* so you're all set."

"I've already read everything in *Mirabella* except the horoscope page," she would say. "I suppose I could read it again. I do love to read in the bath. In that . . . pile," she would innocently ask, "are there any magazines that you could recommend?"

I would be taken aback by the idea of a recommendation. "To be quite honest," I would say, "I had just laid them out on your—on the bed in your room there, pretty much at random, when you unlocked the door and found me. I haven't really studied them. Why don't I drag them over now, and we can take a look."

"Okay," she would say, elongating the second syllable with a trace of doubt.

I would exaggerate the "oofs" of lifting the weight of fourteen magazines. It *is* remarkable, though, how heavy a pile of men's magazines can be. They would make a deep heavy rectangular sound when I let them drop from a few inches above the brown carpeting, a sound that would momentarily remind me of newspaper-recycling efforts and the closing of car doors. (It would make sense that dropped newspaper bundles and car-door-closings would be related, since car doors are in fact filled with old newspapers as sound-damping insulation.) With an air of bemused superiority, though with a distinct undertone of boyish excitement, I would read off the names of the magazines. "Let's see. There's *Celebrity Sleuth* and *Leg Show, Max, Fox, Lips.* What's this one? Ah, *Best of High Society, Assets, Club, Hooters, Velvet, High Society, Swank, Tail Ends, Gent . . .*"

She would ask, "Why in the world do you need so many?"

"I only do this in motels," I would explain. "I have to have the entire bed covered with open magazines. Ideally I'd have twin beds covered, and be able to pivot back and forth between both pictorial bedspreads."

"It seems a little excessive," Adele would say, justifiably.

"Does it?" I would ask.

"Expensive, anyway," she would say.

"This pile cost eighty-five dollars," I would tell her. "So it would make me feel much better, much less wasteful, if someone else besides me got some use out of them. It's like not wanting to drink alone." I would tell the story of how, when I was packing to leave for college and I had to get rid of all the dirty magazines of my adolescence, I couldn't bear to throw them away, so I took them to the park in a paper bag and left them in a place where drunks sometimes slept, figuring that they might have a second life there. "Now I know that there are bookstores that buy used magazines," I would say. "Ave-

nue Victor Hugo on Newbury. Now that's a great store. Have
you been there?"

Adele would say she thought she had, once. Encouraged, I
would tell her another story, about a time when I was in the
Avenue Victor Hugo one Sunday afternoon when a very serious Lebanese-looking man brought in three heavy boxes of
old *Penthouse*s. The used-book buyer looked at the boxes, but
he didn't issue store credit for them right away. Instead he
called out to an assistant, a woman of twenty, black hair,
glasses, who had been in the back shelving some old mint
Frederik Pohl paperbacks, each one in a protective plastic
collector's sleeve, and told her there were three boxes of *Penthouse*s. The assistant sat down cross-legged on the floor in
front of the boxes. I thought she was just going to count the
magazines. And she did count them. But as she lifted each
one, she flipped through it, opening it to its center-spread,
glancing at the picture, and then closing it back up and
putting it in a neat pile. I hovered near the fancy slipcased
editions of Poe, observing all this, trying to puzzle out her
behavior. The woman didn't seem to be motivated by a desire
to get a look at each *Penthouse* pet. ("Pet" *is* offensive, in my
opinion.) She sighed in a bored or perhaps resigned way as
she did it. Her movements repeated themselves automatically.
She didn't mind opening these magazines, baring them right
down to the bent ends of their center-spread staples in the
front of the store, in the presence of anyone who happened to
be there, but she did it not out of interest but because it was
simply part of her job. What exactly, though, was she looking
for? I wondered. And then I understood. The store was not
going to accept any magazine onto which someone had come.
Having been burned in the past by greedy unprincipled men
who tried to unload their utterly unresellable porn-libraries,

they now had instituted a firm policy of flipping through every issue to make sure that none of its pages were stuck together. The Lebanese man had stood uncomfortably by while all this was going on. Fortunately, he had not personalized a single page of his entire collection.

"Nor have you, I take it," Adele would say when I finished telling her my Avenue Victor Hugo story.

"That's right," I would answer. "Each of these magazines is as impersonal as the next. Which ones do you want to look at?" I would tell her that *Swank* was said by insiders to be temporarily in the ascendant and that *Leg Show* was interesting and funny at times. I would pretend to be more of a connoisseur than I am. Showing someone your pornography collection was, I would reflect to myself, a very straightforward form of exhibitionism: Here are my private sexual things, it said. Look at them, like them, hold them.

As I fed magazines through the gap in the door, Adele would leaf through them, at first attentively, then less so. She wouldn't react as I had hoped. "I don't know," she would say several times with different intonations. I would push a few more through to her. Finally she would say, "No. I don't go for this. The skin has an unreal look. All the women look the same. Why do men need so many identical pictures in one month?" She would finish flipping through the last magazine. "No. I just don't think I can take any of these to the bath with me; I don't think I can take seeing any more pictures of women's vaginas. I've never seen so many vaginas in my life. Here."

She would slip the magazines back through the gap in the door to me. I would pile them up neatly as they reappeared, two by two. I would try to recoup through explanation. I would tell her that bringing out all your magazines and ar-

242

ranging them on the bed was sort of like getting an erection. First your periodical pornography is folded away in darkness in a drawer or a bag or a box, stored in its most compact form, and then you *bring it out*, you flap it around in the light, you increase its two-dimensional surface area. I would grant her that there was a feeling of sameness at times, that sometimes I got surfeited, that my interest went through phases. (Which would be a true statement: I rarely used porn when I had Fold-powers, since all the world was a dirty magazine then.) But in general, I would say, men unfortunately *do* want the same thing over and over—a different woman identically posed is the only difference they need. I would tell her that each tiny variation between two women's bodies constituted a huge difference from a sexual point of view. The same body wearing different clothes or with different-colored hair didn't read as sexually different; it had to be a different body. I would tell her this not as if I were pleased about it, but as if it were simply the way it was. For some women like when men tell the truth about themselves.

"Since we're letting our hair down," Adele would say, "can I ask you something?" I would see one of her eyes peering in at me. Because she would be leaning from behind the door, it would be impossible for me to tell for sure what she was or was not wearing. I would have a strong suspicion that she had a towel wrapped around under her arms, and I would be glad if she did, because it was such a marvelously simple extension of the towel's utility (despite its visual overuse in made-for-TV movies), relying on the slightly moist post-shower plush of the towel and the swell of the Jams to keep the folded-under corner from slipping and freeing the entire wrap: its very tightness kept it tight.

I would put my face close to the door as well, and she and

I would regard each other eye to eye. "What's your question?" I would say.

She would ask, "Is the washcloth you handed me just now the one that was sort of hanging on the edge of the bed when your magazines were all spread out in here?"

I would admit that it was.

Adele would blink carefully. "Why was it on the bed that way? What were you planning to do with it?"

I would tell her that I had been planning to shoot onto it. "Or maybe I would have bundled my penis in it and muffled the explosion," I would say. I would reveal to her that my orgasms were almost always better when shot into cotton than into tissue paper. Then I would add: "I would have rinsed the washcloth out afterward. I don't think whoever does the room when I check out should have to deal with that sort of relic."

She would tell me that I was a considerate person.

I would lower my voice to a whisper and tell her how much I wanted to see her ass.

"That may or may not happen," she would say.

I would ask her what she had been planning to do with the washcloth in her bath.

"Wash with it," she would say. She would now be kneeling very close to the door. She was, I would verify, wearing a white towel. My face would be so close to hers that I would be able to hear every detail of her breathing, and yet we would not comfortably be able to kiss. She would be smiling, pleased that I was so obviously hers. I would be able to smell her lipstick. She would finally say, "I suppose I should take my bath now. The water is going to get cold."

"You've had the bath ready this whole time?" I would say, distressed. "I had no idea. And here I've been stuffing all of this month's pornography through the door at you."

THE FERMATA

"I'll add some warm if it's gotten cold," Adele would say. Then: "It's not that I hate those magazines, it's just that they didn't do anything for me."

"You know what I wish?" I would say. "I wish you would wash right here at the door."

"You do, do you," Adele would say. She would think. "Let me see you for a second."

Up until then, I would have been leaning so that my body was out of her sight-line. I would shift so that one of my knees was against the door, and one was just outside the door-frame. I would be sitting on my feet. All I would have on would be a pair of venerable 1984 red Calvin Klein underpants that had gone loose around the leg. I would pull one leg-hole sideways over my dick-bundle so that I was free to shake my yokel a little for her as it stiffened. "Will you wash your breasts for me while I activate this?" I would ask.

"You know that I'm not opening this door," she would say firmly. "The chain stays on."

"I know," I would say.

She would relax then, because she would see that we were both content to play by the same rules. "You'd be interested in seeing me wash my breasts?" she would ask. She would run her tongue over her lips. I would see her eyes go down my chest to my handful of dick. The speed of my fist-shuttle would say yes.

"Here's a suggestion," I would then offer, abandoning my cockwork to raise a finger. "Don't waste the bath, since it's already there. Sit in the bath for a minute or two, wash the lower part of your body or whatever, do half the job, not that it needs it. And then get something . . . do you have anything that can hold some water?" I would look around my room doubtfully and spot an ice bucket. "The ice bucket!" I would

245

cry. "Perfect. You could get your ice bucket and fill it with some of that warm bathwater and bring it over here and wash your breasts for me. You could dunk the washcloth in the bucket and hang your breasts over it and squeeze that warm water all over them. I want to see that so *much.* Please? I'll just wait here patiently stroking my cock." I would give her a querying look. "Do you have an ice bucket?"

She would crane her head momentarily. "Yes, oddly enough I happen to have an ice bucket. Tell you what. If I'm not back here in, oh, ten minutes, it means that I'm shy and I don't want to wash my breasts for you, in which case you've got plenty of magazines to tide you over. That's one thing I want to get clear, by the way. My body isn't exactly like the ones in those magazines."

I would tell her that she was absolutely right: her body was three-dimensional. "That third dimension can be pretty nice sometimes," I would say. I would tell her that I could already see some hints of her shape under the white towel, that I knew she was magnificent, that I was super-keen to see more, etc.

"Give me a few minutes," she would say. She would disappear from the doorway. I would put my ear to the gap and listen as hard as I could. I would hear her towel fall and some watery sounds.

"Are you in?" I would call, loudly.

"Sssh!" she would answer. There would be more watery sounds. I would let my forehead rest against the door, imagining her sitting in the bath. I would repose that way for a long time. Then there would be the unmistakable sound of someone rising up out of the bath. More watery sounds would ensue. The ice bucket would appear on the carpeting near the opening in the doorway. "I'm back," Adele would say.

I would ask her if she had had a nice bath.

"A little rushed, but yes," she would reply. On peering in at me, she would be somewhat startled. "We're rather rock hard, aren't we?"

"Are you still toweled?" I would ask rhetorically, since I could see that she was.

"I can not be if you want," she would say. She would pull near her shoulder; the tucked-in corner would give way and she would gather the collapsing towel in her hands in front of her, still shielding herself from my sight. Then, with grace, she would set it aside and look at the gap in the door where my eye was. She would have high round medium breasts and broad shoulders and smooth, solid arms and thighs. Her tan lines would be very faint, almost unnoticeable. Her thick disorderly hair would be just right for her body. To get herself over her embarrassment, she would say, "Now where *did* I put that washcloth? Ah, yes." She would hold the dry washcloth indecisively.

With my mouth very close to the door-frame, I would tell her that she was beautiful, perfect, amazing. I would tell her that I *loved* her breasts.

"Well, thank you," she would say, pleased. Her legs would be folded underneath her; she would be sitting on her feet (as I still was). Half seductively, half uneasily, she would run her hands up and down the tops of her long thick thighs. The way her squeezed thigh-flesh made an outward curve just above her knees, like the lid of a grand piano seen from above, would endear her to me.

"Why not put the ice bucket between your legs?" I would suggest.

"That's a thought," she would say. She would part her thighs and pull the bucket between them. I would see a brevity of light-brown hair. The ice bucket would be round and black.

She would remove its top. A little steam would plume up from the water inside. She would gather her hair and throw its mass behind her shoulders. "Shall I?" she would ask me, lifting the washcloth.

"It's the right thing to do," I would say. *"Dunk it."*

She would push the washcloth in the water. She would lift it, squeeze it, submerge it again. The second time she squeezed it out, she would let it fall open in her hand. It would be a fairly thin washcloth, as hotel washcloths often are—you would almost be able to see her shadowy fingers through it. She would look at me. Then she would bend forward and watch her hand as it surrounded her soft breast with the warmth of the white cloth. She would steady her breast from underneath with her other hand as she gently held it and circled it with the compress.

"What a beautiful sight," I would say. "Is it warm?"

"Very warm," Adele would say, squeezing and circling. "Very warm. I always wanted to do this with those hot towels they hand out in Japanese restaurants. Just lift my shirt at the table, you know? 'Why thank you! How very kind of you!' Mmm. Or at the end of airplane flights."

"The other one," I would breathe. "The other one's looking left out." Then I would have an inspiration. "Hang on, what am I thinking? I'll get the other washcloth! Don't move!" I would leap up and retrieve my washcloth from the bathroom. "It's still a little wet from my shower," I would tell her. "You won't mind?"

She would shake her head. I would poke the washcloth through the door. She would drop it into the ice bucket, squeeze it, and, leaning forward again, cup her other breast with it. Two hands on two washcloths on two breasts. I would make sounds of wonder and praise.

"I bet they'll stay on by themselves," she would say. She would straighten and let her hands fall to her sides. The washcloths would indeed remain in place. She would pull at their corners, neatening away the wrinkles. They would look like oversized pockets on a very sheer shirt.

I would ask her what it would feel like to hold her nipples through them.

"Probably it would feel pretty good," Adele would say. She would gently pinch her nipples through the wet plush. Still holding them, she would bow forward and shake her breasts so that the washcloths peeled off her skin and fell over her pinching fingers. Then she would drop both washcloths into the bucket. "You know how I might like to wash my breasts if I were by myself?" she would ask me, shaking the water from her fingers.

"How?" I would ask.

She would slide the ice bucket forward and lean her torso lower and lower over it, supporting some of her weight on one hand. She would allow one of her breasts to descend into the round opening of the bucket and then let it dip silently in the water. This would get me crazy. The chain on the door would start rattling.

"Oh, shit, that's so *fine*," I would say, thumping my fist up and down my gender-beam. "So efficient, so sensible. Can you do the other now? Can you dunk it for me?"

Adele would have both her hands on the rug now, and she would continue her wonderful alternating breast-dipping session: dipping one breast, lifting it, letting it drip a little, moving laterally, dipping the other breast. Watching her, I would get into such a froth of desire that I would find myself unable to say anything more than "Dunk that tit, dunk that tit, you're so fucking sexy, dunk that tit!" which wouldn't bother her. After a while she would bring her face close to the door-gap and look through at my jaction.

"It looks like that feels good," she would say.

"It really, really does," I would say.

"My nipples are all clean and hard," she would say. "Would you like to touch one?"

She would hold her breast to the opening and I would kneel forward and let my richard nose into it. Though this would be the first time we had touched, aside from shaking hands, it wouldn't feel wildly momentous, just part of the escalation. She would pull that breast away and would bring the other nipple close to the gap. The farther my yokel poked through the door, the more I would be able to feel the air of her room on it. The air would seem cooler. My dick, I would realize with surprise, was in her motel room! Her other hand would have found its way between her legs and would be unpretentiously polishing her Gummi Bear.

"I wish that I could give you a kiss," I would say. "I don't mean that you should unchain the door, I just mean I wish we *could* kiss."

"Let's see what we can do," she would say. We would get our heads as close together as they could be and we would stick out our tongues. Their tips would touch; the sensation would flow crotchwards. The chain on the door would continue to make its audible presence known.

"I wish I could see your ass," I would croak.

"Hmm." She would tilt her head. "I don't think our relationship is at a point where you can see my ass."

"No?" I would say, surprised.

"No," she would say. "Because you know what? Something tells me you want to see my asshole. Right?"

I would equivocate. "Not *just* your asshole. Ass and asshole together. In context."

"Right," she would say, "but I don't really want you looking at my asshole tonight."

I would not argue with this. I would say, "I accept that. An asshole is a very personal thing. I'd be perfectly happy just to see your ass. You could keep your cheeks together."

But she wouldn't go for that either. "I think not," she would say. "I don't trust myself. If I turned around and showed you my ass, my cheeks might fly open, and we wouldn't want that. What if I washed my breasts some more?" She would brush some of her hair over one of her nipples for emphasis. "Hmm?"

I would say, "That would be fantastic, of course, but— here's an idea. What if you took one of the washcloths and just *placed* it on your ass? Just placed it there. It would be a white square, a helicopter landing pad, but it would follow your shape."

"You mean like this?" She would wring out a washcloth and hold it as a loincloth over her bottom, and she would turn with her back to me.

"Yes," I would say, "in a way, but I guess I didn't mean quite so free-hanging. I think it might need to be wetter, so that it really clings, just the way it clung to your breasts. The way you have it now it's a little bit . . . centerfielderesque."

"Ah." Adele would dip her hands in the water and hold them on her ass to wet it, and then she would apply the washcloth to her skin and turn to show me.

"Perfect, perfect!" I would whisper-hiss. "Now I can see your sex-shape and yet your ass observes all the proprieties." I would shuffle my way as close to the door-opening as possi- ble and I would begin to jack frantically, my knuckles rapping smartly on the door. The lock's chain would clank and rattle with every stroke of my fist. "Can you back up towards the door a little more?" I would ask.

On her knees, Adele would back the white square on her ass towards me. It would follow the seam of her open peach faithfully; it would look oddly like an open book.

"Just a little more!" I would say. I would tell her how close my cock was to her ass, and how fucking incredible her ass looked. Just below the edge of the washcloth, I would be able to see four of her fingers fretting against the flushed cowling of her clit. I would let go of my cock and extend my hand through the door-gap as far as it would go; I would almost be able to reach her with my middle finger. "Back up just a teensy bit more," I would say. "I'm going to touch you."

She would let her knees slide farther apart on the rug and would push back with her hands, bringing her ass right up against the edge of the door. My fingertips would make contact with the rough damp texture of the washcloth. I would pull on one of the upper corners, which would have slipped down a little.

"Is everything still in place?" she would ask, looking back over her shoulder. "You're not seeing anything you shouldn't be seeing?"

I would let my fingers brush lightly down into her terry-cloth vale. Then I would go up the opposite slope a little way, then back down, tracing parabolas of shape-appreciation. I would know more or less where things were underneath, but I wouldn't be able to see them. "All is in order for the time being," I would say. "I'll keep a close eye on it, though."

"Thanks," she would say.

"Do you want to frig your pussy real fast?" I would inquire huskily.

Adele would answer that she *was* frigging her pussy real fast. We wouldn't speak for some time, mewing antiphonally.

The washcloth would be looser now. I would essentially be

holding it up for her with my finger. "It doesn't seem to want to stay put entirely," I would warn. "But I think I know a good way to keep it from falling. Shall I?"

"Yes, do it. Oh yeah. Do it." Adele would be lost in her onan-world.

"I'm going to push into the washcloth with my middle finger," I would then say. "Okay? Just half an inch. That will keep it in place."

I would find the right spot and I would push. White wrinkles would form in the fabric—a sort of plush white terry-cloth sphincter would gather around my stiff middle finger as I forced my way in.

"Eeeeeyeah!" Adele would say. "The texture of it!"

Carefully I would withdraw my finger, leaving the washcloth in place. "Now tighten it and make yourself come," I would say.

"It really tingles in there," she would say.

I would lean all my weight against the door and aim my cock through the gap. Adele would begin pushing against the doorjamb in a steady rhythm. This movement would finally make the washcloth slide off her ass-curves and hang down; but it would not fall to the floor, since it was still held tightly by her asshole. She would sense something amiss. "Oh no!" she would say breathlessly, alarmed.

"It's all right!" I would reassure her. "It's hanging there! I still can't really see anything. Just hold it in there real tight, don't let it fall, okay? I'm going to deliver a whole candygram of come right through this doorway any second."

"Ooh, you are?" Adele would say. She would be pushing against the door with her ass so hard now that she would practically be shutting it in my face. "Come on my wash-cloth!" she would call. "Squeeze it off on my washcloth!"

In my frenzy, I would aim wrong and release my first two smut-schnapps on the carpet and the door, but with the third I would manage to fling some fertile distillate on her upper thigh. Feeling it, she would give her commotion the final go-ahead—and the limply hanging washcloth, tightly cinched in her raving sphincter, would begin to move hypnotically, pulling in and out several times where it disappeared, making the free end gently lift and wag, like a handkerchief waved in farewell from an ocean liner.

She would turn and sit and look in at me. We would describe how pleasant it had been. "And see?" I would say. "The washcloth did not fall. Your modesty was maintained."

"Now I can sleep," she would say. I would refocus on her hair, which would look beautiful and thick and tossed around. Though we wouldn't be able to shake hands properly through the door, we would hook index fingers and shake good-bye that way. Her door would close and I would hear the lock on the knob turn and the bolt slide softly into place. I would close my door, too, and lock it, but I wouldn't reinstate the chain lock on my side—for it would seem to me that the sound of my chaining would constitute a faint rudeness after what we had done together.

The next morning, when I opened the door to the outside, I would find a small white bundle at my feet. It would be the Suzanne Vega tape wrapped in one of the now-stiffened washcloths, with a note saying, *Take care of yourself—A.J.S.* I wouldn't be sure if this gift was meant to show that she knew that I was the one who had switched the tapes in the car, or whether it was simply a friendly gesture. But I would take care of myself, at least twice, before driving back to Boston.

That was what I planned to happen. What did happen, though, is that after an hour and a half or so of steady driving on the Mass Pike, an hour and a half full of hope and keyed-up concentration, I saw a small twirling rectangular shape fly out of Adele's car window.

She hadn't liked it. How very sad and disappointing. Had she listened to all of it and then decided she didn't like it, or had she hated it so much that she had tossed it halfway through? I pushed up on my glasses and checked her car stereo: yes, Suzanne Vega was back in place. Nor were Adele's nipples noticeably erect under her pink floral sweater. Was she made of *stone*? Imagine her chucking my cassette right out the window! Hours and hours of work, all custom joinery, all for her, dismissed. Of course I had said that she should feel free to do that, but still, I hadn't expected her to do it. My pride was hurt. I paced around in the tall grass where I thought I had seen the tape land, but I couldn't find it. And I didn't want to spend much time out of the car, because the grass I walked in had the same disturbingly blurred quality that the road had—I felt I would inflict some rending injury to the network of cosmic wormholes if I walked on the median strip for too long. I started up time and drove slowly, until Adele was way ahead of me. At the next exit, I turned around and drove home. When I woke up the next morning, my Fold-powers were gone.

16

THE WEEK FOLLOWING MY FAILED DRIVE, I WORKED FIFTEEN hours of overtime at a consulting firm. I was bothered by a persistent tingly feeling in the base of my right palm and increasing pain in my forearm. I needed at least a week off from typing, but because my Fermatal visitation-rights were now denied, I didn't get one.

What was clearly a carpal-tunnel problem got quite bad over the next several months. An over-the-counter wrist brace didn't fit properly and made the pain worse. I was able to alleviate the symptoms a little by sleeping with my arm embracing a spare pillow. After a particularly trying stint typing an eighty-page price list, I went to Commonhealth and saw several nurse practitioners and doctors. Each of them tapped the inside of my wrist hard and asked what it felt like. Every diagnostic tap further injured the nerve, it seemed to me. I went up the chain of specialists until I reached the in-house repetitive-motion expert, Dr. Susan Orowitz-Rudman, a short cheerful woman of forty. I told her that I was a career temp and that I really had to be able to continue using the keyboard. She was full of ideas and theories. I found her hyphenated name powerfully attractive.

"Is there any other related repetitive motion that you engage in?" she asked. "One patient of mine was a legal secretary and a fanatical bicyclist on weekends, and it turned out that it wasn't the typing but the combination of typing and pulling on the hand-brakes of her bicycle that was causing the carpal flare. She switched to swimming and took a week off from work and she was able to keep her job and not have the operation. I'm happy to *do* the operation," she added. "It's not a big deal, it's just a matter of making a little incision right here—but I'm just saying that sometimes there are ways to make the problem go away by itself."

I told her that I snapped my fingers to music sometimes, and that I did some writing of my own in the evenings and on weekends which added to the overall amount of typing I did.

"What sort of writing do you do?" she asked politely, noting this down.

"Just stories. Nothing published. But I get caught up in it and I keep typing and typing and typing. The whole wrist problem has gotten much worse since I've started doing it."

Dr. Orowitz-Rudman talked about alternative keyboards and about dictating my own writing and then having a friend transcribe it. She suggested two weeks off from work. She also spoke highly of manual typewriters: since they took more muscle strength, they seemed to bother the nerve less. Some anthropology professor at Harvard had gone back to his old Olivetti portable and been cured completely. She described some research she was doing: "I'm interested in developing a wrist sensor," she said, "that will work as a biofeedback device, signaling the user when a motion is in progress that is likely to further inflame the nerve, based on certain correlations. But what I'm doing now is not that advanced, although it's quite interesting—I mean, of course it is interesting to me, but it can also be interesting to my patients, and helpful. I'm trying to develop a set of MRI motion studies for various characteristic motions, such as typing a particular letter of the alphabet, opening an oyster, salad prep, and so forth. We use something called a fast-pulse-sequence echo-planar MRI machine, which essentially shows the nerve responding to the motions as they proceed. Would you be interested in taking part?"

"Remind me what MRI is?"

"Magnetic Resonance Imaging."

"Oh!" I said. "Big time!" Extremely flattered, I said I probably would like to take part. We made an appointment. Then something suddenly occurred to me that I couldn't resist bringing up.

"What I still don't understand," I said, "is why it's all happening exclusively in my right wrist. Shouldn't I have a touch of it on the left side?"

"Are you a heavy user of the backspace key?" she asked. "Several of my patients have reconfigured their keyboard so that they controlled the backspace key with their left hands, eliminating that constant reaching up with the little finger as they corrected their typos, and they improved immediately."

"Interesting. Maybe that's it," I said, nodding thoughtfully, signaling that I was thinking of something else. "Maybe that's it."

"Well? What were you going to attribute it to?" the doctor asked.

"How shall I put this? The stories I write are quite—they're pornographic stories."

She took this in. Her face was sensual and intelligent and canny. "I don't see why what you write would make a bit of difference to your wrist. A letter *f* is a letter *f* to the nerve concerned, no matter what risqué thing it happens to be spelling."

"That's right," I said eagerly, "and yet the letter *e* is the most frequent letter in English, right? And the letter *e* is a left-hand letter. So it should be as much a left-wrist problem as a right-wrist problem!"

"That's why I mentioned the backspace key," the doctor explained patiently. "Or it could easily be the cursor keys, or the mouse. The mouse gives people terrible trouble."

"I use hot keys almost exclusively," I said haughtily.

"All I'm saying is, you have to look very carefully at how you really move at the keyboard and make some subtle changes. People think they can install a wrist pad or do a few exercises and everything will be hunky-dory. It doesn't always work that way."

I looked at her name-tag. I liked very much that her first name was Susan. I said, "I'll do that. But—what just occurred to me is—well—I write *pornography*."

"I know. So?"

"Well, as I write I often find that I get myself in something of a lather. I imagine someone reading it, you know, a female someone reading it, and I find that . . ." I held my hands out as if what I was going to say was self-evident.

Suddenly she understood and laughed. "Ah, ah, ah. You're just trying to tell me that you masturbate while you write."

"Exactly," I said with relief. "With my right hand."

"Constantly? Are you constantly masturbating while you write?"

"Not *constantly*, no. I'll type, say, a word or a phrase and then masturbate a little, and then another phrase, masturbate a little more, like that."

"Are these alternating sessions protracted?" asked Dr. Orowitz-Rudman, after a pause.

"Sometimes. I once wrote a story on the hood of a car for twelve straight hours."

"Masturbating intermittently the entire time? I take it you were in a secluded spot."

"It's a spot that's accessible only to me."

"Good."

I gave her an inquiring look. "Is this an area that you would be interested in studying?" I asked her.

She looked skeptical at first, and then more interested. "Well, you know, I have to admit that in the past I've had some fleeting suspicions in that direction. I mean, why shouldn't frequent or prolonged masturbational episodes aggravate, or even cause, CTS? But until now, no patient has spontaneously suggested it as a cause, and I've been reluctant to mention it. It's definitely worth looking into. Perhaps we could scan you as you . . ."

"Really?" I said. "You'd have me pleasure myself in one of those gigantic magnets? The ones like iron lungs, that take pictures of brain tumors?"

"Well, why not?" she said. "And you'd use our dummy keyboard, too. We're trying to simulate real-life conditions. We unfortunately can't use real keyboards, because we can't have any ferrous metal within the magnet. . . . Now, you don't habitually masturbate wearing a studded cock ring or ball separator, do you?"

"God no."

"Fine, because that might create real problems in a magnetic field of thirty thousand times earth gravity. So—I don't want to put you on the spot, but are you sincerely interested? I'm thinking out loud now, which I don't normally do, but my sense is that this could be an important new line of research. Who knows—you might make *The New England Journal of Medicine*. Anonymously, of course."

"Well," I said, pleased, "I suppose if I can be of some small help to others . . ."

A week later, I showed up at the MR wing of Commonhealth's hospital at a quarter to six in the evening, after an untaxing day at an accounting firm. My arm hurt, which pleased me, because I felt that I wasn't wasting anyone's time. In a conference room, Dr. Orowitz-Rudman explained in her friendly, faintly ironic way what was going to happen to me: some reference dots were going to be painted on my arm and penis, so that the imaging system could keep a fix on these two elements as I moved. She said she wanted me to type and masturbate just as I would in real life. She got up, and then remembered something.

"One thing I do have to ask," she said. She looked through some drawers in the back of the room. "I'm looking for something with a particular shape," she explained. She held up a tongue depressor, but rejected it: "A little unromantic. I should have thought to bring in a prosthetic penis-form of some kind."

"I could just show you mine," I suggested.

"No—no—then we have to get observers in here and worry

about all sorts of things. Thanks for offering, though. Ah! This will do." She brought out a stick of lipstick from her purse and handed it to me. "Can you hold that and show me roughly how you masturbate? I realize that it's a little smaller than you're used to."

I held it and stroked it several ways.

"Ah," said the doctor, "so you use both a fist grip and a finger-and-thumb grip. That's what I wanted to know." She tapped her lip, thinking. "I don't want to prejudice you in favor of either one. I'm going to have to ask you to announce when you've switched from one to the other. It will make it easier for us to get the imaging system to keep up with you, and eventually, of course, to isolate which particular grip is distressing your nerve. In fact, do you think you would be able to offer a kind of running commentary as you masturbate? You could tell us what you are doing, what hurts, what doesn't hurt—whatever's going through your mind."

I said that I would certainly try. She led me to an examining room, where I changed into a hospital gown. Two nurses or technicians or post-docs painted rows of silver dots up my forearm. They painted a silver square over the inside of my wrist. Then they lifted my gown.

"Should we trim him a little?" one of the technicians asked the other. She looked at me. She was Chinese. "We're going to trim your pubic hair."

I looked down at it. "It has gotten a bit unruly." I couldn't remember the last time I had trimmed it; it could have been a decade earlier. They pulled on the thick tufts and snipped them off. Then one stretched my penis and painted a silver dot on its circumcision ridge. Paintbrush hovering, she became uncertain. She called in Dr. Orowitz-Rudman. The three of them conferred in low tones.

The doctor put a hand on my arm and smiled at me. "Will you masturbate just a little now?" she asked. "Don't go hog wild. We just need you to be fully erect to get the reference dots on your penis spaced properly."

"Oh, sorry. Sure. Just take a sec."

"Fine." Dr. Orowitz-Rudman left.

I stroked my yokel while the two attendants waited. I noticed with some satisfaction that they seemed to appreciate its size and girth and garish coloration. (It is, I think, a more handsome penis than I deserve.)

One cradled it gently while the other painted the silver dots down the underside and the top, measuring their distances carefully. The soft contact of the brush was soothing.

They brought me through the control room to the door into the scan room. "Good luck," said Dr. Orowitz-Rudman, waving. She sat at a table with two monitors on it, a three-ring binder open before her. A window looked through some sort of fine-mesh screen into the room with the magnet in it. The technician stopped me. "Your watch has to come off." She pointed to a poster with a number of forbidden objects pictured with red bars across them—fire extinguishers, pacemakers, watches, steel skull-plates, anything metallic, evidently.

The scanner stood in the middle of a large empty room. It was an enormous white edifice, like a very thick wall, with a large hole running through it into which patients were slid on a gantry. Something was making a great deal of fairly unpleasant noise. I removed my gown and lay down on the pad. A dummy computer keyboard was placed on my stomach and I was slid headfirst into the bore of the superconducting magnet.

"Can you hear me, Arno?" I heard Dr. Orowitz-Rudman say through the intercom.

I said that I could.

"Good. Give us a few minutes to get things set in here before you start. Are you comfortable?"

"I am. It's *very* vaginal in here, doctor, in a smooth-muscle sort of way. Is the magnet on?"

"Yes, it's always on," she said.

"I expected to feel claustrophobic, but oddly, I'm not. There was this guy in college . . . excuse me—I'll shut up while you get set up."

"No, go on," said Dr. Orowitz-Rudman. "The technicians are getting set up—I'm just observing at this point."

"What is all this tiresome noise?" I asked.

"That's the coolant. The magnet has to be kept very cool, and the coolant has to be pumped around."

"I see. Well, there was this guy in college—" There was this guy in college, I said, who used to mime inserting one finger in a woman's vadge, then two, then four, saying, "Yeah, baby. Really? More?" Then the whole hand would go in, then his arm up to the elbow, then up to the shoulder; then he would slide his other arm in, still saying, "More? You *sure*, baby? Okay." He would place his head at the opening of the imaginary vadge and strainingly push up, turning his face, and suddenly his grimacing head would slide in alongside his arms, and finally he would squirm as much of his body into the vaginal canal as he could fit. "I feel a little like I've just done that," I explained. "I'm in this huge electrovagnet. It isn't womblike," I babblingly hastened to qualify. "It's purely vaginal."

"Interesting," I heard Dr. Orowitz-Rudman say absently. She hadn't been listening. She said something I couldn't catch to one of her associates, then I heard her say, "We are? Okay." Then she addressed me in her pleasant Susan Stamberg voice: "All right, Arno. First we're going to get you to use the keyboard a little bit. I'm going to read you a sentence, and you type it. Ready?"

I said I was ready.

" 'The cure . . .' " she read.

I typed. "Okay."

" '. . . for the greatest part . . .' "

I typed. "Got it."

" '. . . of human miseries . . .' "

I typed. "Okay."

" '. . . is not radical . . .' "

"Yep."

" '. . . but palliative.' Period. Good. Thanks. That's our baseline sentence. Now, Arno, I want you to go ahead and use the keyboard for about five minutes to warm up the nerve."

"Just type anything?" I asked.

"Right," said Dr. Orowitz-Rudman. "I can read you something if you would like, or you can make it up. It would be nice if it were similar to the typing you normally do, but that doesn't matter all that much. It has to be in English, though."

"Why?"

"So that the letter-frequencies are representative."

"I see. No problem," I said. I began to type, in the self-conscious way people do when they're testing typewriters and computers at a store, though in my case the words I was typing were not being recorded anywhere. *It's strange to be typing here in this magnet,* I clicked out on the keys. *But I kind of like it. I've never typed supine before. I recommend it to all interested parties. This keyboard has a nice sloppy feel, probably because it's been messed with inside and doesn't work. Feels like some of the old Wang keyboards. Since it is dysfunctional, I suppose I can type anything I want. Doctor Susan could possibly follow my fingers on a video*

*monitor to find out what I'm typing, or study the tape later, but I
doubt very much she'll bother. She's cheerfully all business. She
really attracts me. That's not surprising—it is much more surprising to me when a woman fails to attract me than when she does
attract me. Very occasionally I meet a woman and afterward I think,
That's incredible—nothing about that woman attracted me. It almost never happens. All women merit love and constancy. That's
true. All women should be loved by someone good and dependable
and honest. I am good, I think, but I am not honest or dependable,
so I have to pass lovingly through their lives without their knowing
I have been there. Man I like Dr. Susan's tits under that lab coat,
with that name pinned on one. Short funny forty-year-old women
with big tits should reign supreme. Or if I could just cycle between
silky-voiced tall women with small tits and short happy women with
big tits—plus medium-sized affectionately sexy women with medium-sized tits and short women with small tits and southern accents, and medium-sized women with small tits and Hispanic
accents—now there would be a life. I like the fact that Dr. Susan
doesn't know that I'm typing how much I'd like her to squat over
me and rip open the white cotton crotch of her black pantyhose and
grind her salty puss into my face.* I stopped pretend-typing. "Is
that enough?" I asked.

Dr. Orowitz-Rudman said, "That's plenty. We've got a good
fix on your nerve now. Can you type the reference sentence
again? You remember?"

"Sorry," I said, "I think I forgot it."

" 'The cure for the greatest . . . part of human . . . miseries
is not radical . . .' "

" '. . . but palliative,' " I finished, eager to prove to her that
I was no clerical robot, but rather a typist who reflected on
whatever he was asked to type. "Got it."

"How about pain levels?" she asked.

I snapped my finger several times to test how my wrist felt. "I feel the usual tingling in the base of my palm and some significant forearm involvement."

"Fine," she said. "We can go back to the keyboard later if we need to. I want you to put it aside now. Good. Except for your arm pain, are you comfortable? Are you ready to start masturbating?"

I told her I was.

"Okay, in just a minute I'll ask you to start."

I lay at peace, with my hands resting on my chest. I heard some more murmured conversation on the intercom, then, "Arno, why don't you go ahead and start."

"Can I lift my knees?"

"Can he lift his knees?" I heard her ask. Then: "Better not. We lose you on one of the axial monitors. Is it going to be a problem to proceed with your legs flat?"

"Not at all—it's fine," I said. "Can you see me? I mean, not my nerves, but me?"

"Yes. We have several video monitors in addition to the MR image."

"Oh," I said.

"Be sure to let us know any changes in the pain you feel," she said. "Keep a running commentary, if you can."

I hesitated, then plunged ahead. "The problem is that the pleasure from one source masks the pain from the other source," I said. "I think that's part of the reason it's gotten this bad. But, okay, I'm touching my—penile organ now. I have it, as I guess you can see, in the thumb-and-finger grip that we discussed. We might call it the Kokomo grip. I'm beginning to tug on it slowly, using the Kokomo grip, and at the moment I feel no distinct pain—well, there is a warm twinge, but nothing bad." Since I had avoided all orgasms for three days, I expected to have little trouble getting hot and nasty, even enveloped as I was in an electromagnetic field so powerful that it could potentially suck oxygen tanks and scissors and other ferrous objects lethally into the chamber with me. When I was fully erect, I held my richard vertically for a moment by its base, wanting everyone in the control room to get an eyeful of it on the monitors.

"Hold that for a second," said Dr. Orowitz-Rudman, unexpectedly. "Don't move. We need to get a fix on those R-points. Just hold still. Good. Great. Good. You still comfortable?"

"I think so."

"Good. You seem comfortable. Now we need to get a few motion-profiles. This is an entirely new repetitive motion for the real-time tracking system, so you have to bear with us, please. The software is going to teach itself to follow your arm. Okay—first will you go ahead and masturbate slowly, just as you would typically do it perhaps in an early phase."

"In an early phase . . ." I mused. "Probably I would change to the tight-fisted grip. And probably I'd squeeze it hard while I pumped it very slowly up and down. Like this." I parted my legs, so that my feet rested on the curving, culvert-like walls of the magnet's bore, and pumped. "Ooo, I like to feel the little hole get pulled open when I pump."

"Great, thanks. Okay." There was more murmuring among the researchers. I loved being studied. I loved that my simple self-pumping pleasure was going to yield scientific results. Dr. Orowitz-Rudman came back on and said, "Arno, now could you stimulate your penis fast?"

"How fast?"

"As fast as you normally might. We want to be sure we don't lose the image when you get serious."

"I understand." I pounded my cock as if I were shaking a

daiquiri in a busy bar, as if I were applauding after a marvelous performance of Ravel's *Mother Goose Suite,* as if I were
playing the only maraca in a salsa band. My body bounced
and flopped on the vinyl pads.

"Whoa," said Dr. Orowitz-Rudman.

"Could you track that?" I asked.

"No way," she said. "Go slower. Slower."

"How about that?"

"Nope. Slower. Slower. Slower still. Slower. There! That's
the fastest you can go. Is that going to be fast enough?"

I made a doubtful noise. "That is awfully slow. Isn't that
about how slow I was going when you asked me to demonstrate my slow speed? I really honestly don't know that I will
be able to come going that slow."

There was some inaudible conferring on their side of the
intercom. Then Dr. Orowitz-Rudman said, "Okay, that's fine,
Arno. Not to worry. Give us a second. We're going to try
something different. Just hang on for a moment."

"On the other hand," I added in a thoughtful tone. "I
guess you don't *need* me to come, right? There is no real
reason why I need to come for this motion study. How self-
centered of me."

Dr. Orowitz-Rudman's voice came on. "On the contrary, I
think it's crucial for the success of this preliminary study that
you masturbate straight through. You yourself alluded to the
reason why just a moment ago. As you approach climax, you
will be feeling such pleasure and stroking your penis so fast
that you'll be much more likely to traumatize the nerve-
sheath without knowing it."

"You're quite right," I said. "I do have to come."

"Just give us another second to tune the gate-and-correlate
software. You see," she explained, "we have to be able to stay

fixed on precisely the same cross-section of one tiny region in your arm, no matter how fast you move or how you turn, which is no easy task. We do it with the help of an entirely separate optical tracking system. The optical system, by the way, incorporates some hardware that was originally developed by Martin Marietta for one of the Defense Department's target recognition programs. It does two hundred and fifty compares a second, which is very fast—it should be fast enough for this application."

"So I wouldn't be here naked, doing this, if it weren't for the Department of Defense?" I said. "There you go. Who says military research doesn't have humanitarian payoffs?"

"Bear with us for just a little longer, Arno," said Dr. Orowitz-Rudman. I gave my richard a couple of maintenance strokes every fifteen seconds or so. Finally I heard her say, "Okay, we're set. You may start actual masturbation at any time."

"Okay, I'm starting," I said. "I'm back to the Kokomo grip. It doesn't feel all that great yet—I'm doing it because I know it will feel good very shortly. There is some definite tingling-action in my fingers. I'll give you a play-by-play. This is great to be allowed to jerk off in a fucking mega-magnet like this. I just know I'm going to be a different person after I come in this big-mama magnet. Focus it right on my big dick. Pardon my language: if you want me to talk while I do it, I'm going to have to talk dirty. You know what it reminds me of? *Zardoz. Zardoz* is a movie with Sean Connery. These superior beings bring Connery into their ship, and the woman superior being who is in charge of researching him tries to find out what makes his heart beat faster. They project various sexual images on a screen in the spaceship to see how he will react—a pair of breasts being soaped up, for example. His brain-wave levels remain utterly calm and unmoved. And then Connery looks straight at her, at the woman researcher, and instantly the EEG oscilloscopes start hopping and beeping right off the chart. So it's the superior *being* who gets him wild. Now, it seems a little implausible to me that the soaped-up breasts would do nothing at all for Connery—they certainly did something for me when I saw this movie back in the seventies. I haven't seen it since and yet I remember it as the finest footage of soaped-up breasts I've ever seen, partly because it was so teasingly quick."

"Arno—the pain in your arm," said Dr. Orowitz-Rudman. "What is its status?"

"Sorry. I'm experiencing a little more pain just above my wrist, and a cold feeling in my hand. But it hurts good, it's well worth it. I'm going to shift to the fist-fucking grip. Yeah, *there* we go. Yeah! To come for you here this evening, I think I'm going to adapt that scene in *Zardoz:* I'm going to think of a guy who is asked to masturbate inside a huge magnetic tunnel while three women superior beings observe his carpal tunnel. They are interested in determining with scientific certitude whether his masturbation contributes to his nervous inflammation. It almost certainly does, but they want to capture the images of the poor frail nerve leading to his hand getting squeezed and traumatized as he gives himself pleasure. They are trying out some brand-new fancy software that focuses the magnetic field in a new way. This software uses some tricks refined over at CERN, in fact. But this new software has a bug; it has a serious unintended side-effect on this masturbating man. They trim his pubic hair, they dot his dick in a tribal pattern, they shove him in the magnet, and they tell him to start jacking off, and then, as his hand is shuffling smoothly up and down on his penis, some kind of bizarre, anomalous micro-funnel develops in the universal core of time. A chronomaly. Within the magnet, time is sucked in on itself and twisted and compressed in such a way that the man's nerve—which is where all the analytic strength of the resonating system is focused—his nerve acquires the ability to stop and start time's progress at will. What happens is: the man's arm heats up for a second, tingling, as if it's in a microwave on defrost, and then he discovers that he can put humanity on hold every time he snaps his middle finger. He lets go of his dick and he tries it out. Like this: *snap*."

I snapped my fingers. At once I was lying in complete euphoric silence. My Fold-powers were back.

I crawled out of the machine and walked naked into the control room, my weighty richard leading the way. Dr. Orowitz-Rudman was wearing headphones. She was leaning back in her chair, her hand resting thoughtfully on her mouth, frowning in concentration at a monitor that showed an image of me lying feet first, legs parted, with my hand clutching my erection. I'd never seen myself from that angle before. It was not a pretty sight. One of the associates was sitting at the other large monitor, which showed a long glowing thing that was apparently the nerve in my wrist done up in the usual intense greens and blues and oranges. The other woman, the Chinese woman, was standing behind Dr. Orowitz-Rudman, looking on.

I knelt and opened Dr. Orowitz-Rudman's lab coat and pulled her ribbed green turtleneck out of her pants. I bunched it up at her collarbone and pulled the cups of her bra down so her nipples popped out. They were erect, I was pleased to notice, and surprisingly dark, like two Raisinets. "I can't help it—I need to suck your tits," I said to her, and I did, tactfully, untheatrically. I wrote, "Thanks," on a white Post-It note and stuck it on her left breast. Then I put her clothes back in order and went back in the scan room and climbed into the magnet and resumed my former position. I snapped my fingers again. The noise of the coolant started back up.

Immediately I heard Dr. Orowitz-Rudman exclaim, "Whoops! Lost our fix. Arno, we lost our fix on you. What happened in there?"

"I snapped my fingers."

"Okay, look, please don't do that. There are limits to our tracking system. Just keep stroking your penis if you can."

"How much longer do you want me to continue?" I asked. I was jubilant at having my powers back.

"How much pain are you in?" she asked.

"Mmm, this is about as painful as it gets—tingling up my whole forearm," I reported.

"I think you should go ahead and climax soon. I think we've got enough now to generate quite a thorough neural conductivity profile."

"You want me to come for you?" The foul-patter urge was rising in me.

"Yes," she said neutrally.

"You want it? You want to see it? Oh, God, I want to give it to you. This guy, this guy who's in the MRI machine, he snaps his fingers and time stops. He understands what's going on, he's not freaked, because it happened once before when somebody put a sample of his blood in a centrifuge and spun it very fast and time was interrupted. So time is stopped, and he crawls out of the machine, naked, jerking on his big swollen dick-knob, and he scampers into the control room and he throws back the doctor's lab coat and pulls up her shirt and brings her tits out and he laps at them. That's what he's wanted from the moment he saw her, he's wanted to suckle those hard little nipples with his mouth—oh, man, ma-ha-ha-ha-han—"

"A little slower if you can, Arno," said Dr. Orowitz-Rudman gently. "The image is degrading."

"I forgot. I'll try. I'll try. And so then he puts her tits back in her bra and tucks her shirt in and scampers back into the magnet and he lies there on the pad just where he was and snaps his fingers, and time starts up again, and he lies there thinking of the tits he has just sucked on, how great they felt in his hands, and it's such a tremendous thought that he has to come, he doesn't care how much it hurts—oh, that's right. I want to come inside your magnet, doctor. It hurts, but I don't care. I like you to take all kinds of graphic pictures of my nerve while I pump this hot nasty piece of meat off for you. I like being hard and hot in your core. Oh, doctor. Doctor? I've got to call you Susan when I come. Sorry. Is that okay?"

"That's okay," said Dr. Orowitz-Rudman. "Just try to stroke a little slower, if it's at all possible."

"Oh, thank you. Oh Susan, oh Susan, oh Susan, *uff, uffuck.* Tell me you want to see me come. I want to hear you say it."

I heard only silence over the intercom, and then: "As I said before, I do think it's important for you to climax."

"I will climax, you bet, you got it. I'm going to think of your tits and climax. Oh, you gave me your lipstick to hold. That was so good of you. I wish I could've circled your lips and nipples with it. Oh that feels nice. Squeeze my meat, Susan. Squeeze it in your big magnetic hole. Open that hole up for me. Suck me in, baby. Oh God yeah. Tighten that force down on my cock, uffuck. Uffuck. Here it is: oh yeah, oh *fuck* yeah. Oh yeah! *Urrrrr!*" I let the comeshots jump up and land on my stomach muscles. I lay there for what seemed like a long time, breathing peacefully. "Am I done?" I beatifically asked at last.

"Almost," said Dr. Orowitz-Rudman. "Normally, at this point might you resume writing?"

"If I'd been alternating writing and jacking, yes."

"Then could you type the baseline sentence again?" she said. "It might be useful to have. Remember it? 'The cure...'?"

"Don't tell me!" I put the fake keyboard on my chest, avoiding the sperm, and typed the sentence from memory.

The technicians dragged me out on the gantry and handed me a brown paper towel. I sat up, feeling a little sleepy and dazed, and put on my gown. In the control room, Dr. Orowitz-Rudman met me and led me to the room where my clothes were.

"I think that went well, don't you?" she said.

"I'm sorry I fixated so totally on you."

"Don't apologize," she said. "We were fixated on you, you were fixated on us."

"It's just that a woman doctor asking me to masturbate is like a dream come true . . ."

"I understand—let's not belabor it. My only regret is that the imaging system couldn't quite keep up with you and I had to keep telling you to slow down. I hope you had an okay orgasm even so?"

"Oh, it was a dandy. No, that was *fine* that you told me to slow down—slow is good."

She told me that I could set up an appointment with her in several weeks to go over the nerve-profiles. "But from what I saw on the monitors, I would suggest that you switch to your left hand if you want to get rid of your carpal-tunnel problem."

"I'll begin tomorrow," I said. "Thank you, doctor." I couldn't quite say "Susan" at this point.

"Thank you for taking part," she said. We shook hands. Then, smiling, she snapped her fingers. "Just like that?"

"Right, just like that," I said, pleased. I snapped my fingers for her, and while she stood fixedly, still in the midst of her good-natured, faintly flirtatious leave-taking smile, I kissed her name-tag and removed the white Post-It note from inside her bra. It would only have perplexed and disturbed her to discover it stuck to her breast (that soft, heavy, somewhat sticky breast) that evening. And what if she took off her bra in front of her husband, and he noticed it there before she did—a note saying THANKS on her breast? It would have caused needless suffering.

To recuperate from the experiment, I spent the next five days snapped into the Fold reading Louisa May Alcott; I didn't go near a computer keyboard or my penis the whole time. My wrist pain, which at first was so bad I could barely open a piece of junk mail, moderated considerably. I borrowed a friend's Hermes manual portable and used it to do some of my creative rotting; the deeper keystrokes were, as Dr. Orowitz-Rudman had suggested, a kind of physical therapy. And I did briefly try to teach myself to jack ambidickstrously, but I failed: my left hand simply did not feel good enough. After a month, I called Dr. Orowitz-Rudman to schedule a follow-up visit. She called me back that evening. I told her that my wrist was doing a lot better, thanks to her. I asked her how the motion studies were going, and she said they were going well.

"We've decided to focus on keyboard problems for now, though," she said.

"Oh? But what about—other obvious causes? You were so enthusiastic. You were so—forgive the jargon—sex-positive." I couldn't help sounding slightly disappointed.

"We established the link informally and that's as far as we can take it for the time being," she said. "I want to concentrate on keyboard-related injuries for right now."

"I *knew* it," I said sadly. "I was too talkative in the magnet."

She said no, it wasn't really that. "It turns out that there are problems with doing sexual research. For some reason, the people who hand out research grants don't take what you're doing seriously if it's related to masturbation."

This sounded believable. I told her I understood; indeed, I used that three-word sentence that ends so many affairs of the heart: *I understand completely.* "Anyway," I said, "it certainly was a pleasant evening for me. Time well spent. That magnet really focused my attention on the problem."

"Good," she said. She wished me all the best with my pornography.

17

THUS BEGAN MY LATEST AND LONGEST FERMATA PHASE, THE loose, easy, finger-snapping phase, the phase I remained in until quite recently. I would now like to take a moment to say a little prayerlike thing about my life. I am so *very* fortunate to have been able to see all the naked women's breasts I have seen. That's what it really comes down to. I am just shocked by how lucky I am. No life could be finer than mine. No compulsively promiscuous actor or pop singer, no photographer for a men's magazine, has a better life, for I can take off a woman's clothes *en passant*, as a momentary diversion, without my tender strippage interfering in any way with her life or with mine. The average woman, the unexceptional woman, the interestingly ugly woman, I can stare at in a state of sudden nudity (hers and/or mine) on a sidewalk, or in the unflattering light of a record store, and nobody else can. There are whole phyla of breast-shape that the public at large doesn't know about, because the women who possess these breast-shapes do not ever bare them except to their lovers and spouses and radiologists. And these ever-hidden plenums, perfect in their indispensable imperfection, that by their hang-angle and scooped realism of curve sing out, "We two are quite modest breasts! We two breasts choose not to appear naked in public!" I get to fill my mind with until I understand them. I love modesty, or Modesty; I love to see and kiss Modesty and suck Modesty's nipples and whisper to Modesty how arrestingly modest she is. And I have been able to do that.

I haven't been punished for it, either. Dr. Jekyll, Faustus, Stravinsky's soldat, the ballet dancer in *The Red Shoes*, Gollum, Wells's invisible man and time traveler, Dr. Frankenstein, and a thousand more recent horror heroes all master some quasi-supernatural power and are punished for it, worn out by it, destroyed by it. How false and wearisome this outcome is. Why should a life with some unusual metaphysical feature built into it inevitably end in unhappiness and early death? Why should all the heroes have some fatal flaw that causes them to overreach and hence to self-destruct? It's too convenient. Even the two quieter (and surprisingly similar, one to another) literary artifacts that treat conditions of temporal halt which resemble my own private Foldouts—I am speaking here of Ambrose Bierce's "An Occurrence at Owl Creek Bridge" and Borges's "The Secret Miracle"—both punish their heroes severely: they end with military executions. I read these two stories in high school with a sense of deep personal dissatisfaction. Is this all a writer thinks a Fold-drop could be about?

Putting off death at the last minute? Where are the superven-
ient hebephrenias? Where is the life? *Where are the tits?*

In reality, I'm here to report, people very often get away
with things. I have not been caught and imprisoned for what
I have done; and besides, I am *not* Dr. Jekyll or Dr. Frankenstein and don't deserve torments and agonies. Even if I publish this memoir as a book, and someone recognizes herself in
it and prosecutes me for a relevant sex-offense (I have gone
through the manuscript, by the way, and altered a few names
and fudged a few dates to decrease the possibility of this
happening, but it still might), my life will still seem to me to
have been a good life and I will seem to myself to have been
a man who wanted to do no harm and who in fact did no
harm.

In part I am self-righteous-minded at the moment because
of some recent developments having to do with the all-important Joyce Collier, Joyce of the love-inspiring black pubic hair,
whom I had to abandon early in these pages in my eagerness
to get as much of my past interlife recorded as I could without
new preoccupying interruptions. On a Friday at work two
real-weeks ago, about the general time I was starting to write
about taking my watch off for Rhody in the Thai restaurant,
I looked over at the head of a certain squash-playing loan
officer named Paul at MassBank and suddenly felt that I
wouldn't be able to stand going to work that coming Monday;
moreover, I felt I wouldn't be able to stand going to work at
all until I had finished a good deal more of this memoir. I
called my coordinator and asked her for a whole week off from
the bank. (I couldn't afford more than a week.) And I
stretched that one unpaid week into twenty-three precious
days (counting the final weekend) of autobiographical solitude, simply by upping from one to two the number of per-

sonal Snap-days I inserted between every real calendar day. This meant that I was aging three times as fast as a normal human being, but I wasn't troubled by that. I did my errands every third "day," and because I was working so hard on this book, I didn't get as lonely as I would have expected in the interim; a moment of friendliness with a bank teller or a waitress on the calendar days was enough to carry me through the two interior Arno-days that followed. In taking that week off from MassBank, I was of course putting Joyce Collier off as well—I still wanted to ask her out, but I knew that any sudden hubbub or heartbreak concerning her would distract me from the Fold-adventures in my past. I also had a hope that if I was gone from Joyce's office for a whole week, she might notice that her working days felt different with me not there doing her tapes, and maybe that she looked forward to going to work a little less in my absence—and from there I hoped that she would move closer to a conscious realization that she really liked me.

Towards the end of this final three-week retreat, as I re-created for the record my magnetic-resonance scan with Dr. Orowitz-Rudman, I was visited by a little realization of my own. It will seem ludicrously obvious to the reader, but to me it felt like real progress. My realization was that I would have to tell Joyce about the Fold right at the outset, before I tried to fuck her even once. There could be no more secrets: if I was going to shock Joyce with my chronanism, I had to shock her from the start, and if I was going to seduce her with the Fold's help, she would, unlike Rhody, have to be a knowing party to the seduction. That decided, I discovered I liked the idea of finally telling someone. It might make me, "just a temp," a little more glamorous in her eyes.

The night before I was to see Joyce again, I couldn't sleep

for about two hours early in the morning. I Dropped during most of my insomnia, because I didn't want to waste the night in sleeplessness. I wanted to be fresh for her. I lay in bed in a paused universe with my hand cupped over my troika; every time I thought of telling her that I had tied her knit dress around her waist in the middle of the afternoon and touched her hips and felt her sparkling vafro, I could feel my malefactor come alive. I *wanted* to tell her the shocking thing that I had done. I wanted her to forgive me and love me for it.

Here is how I asked her out the next day. Around eleven-thirty, she came by to drop off a tape and waved. I whipped off my phones. "How were things here last week?" I asked. Joyce was wearing a green dress I'd never seen before; her black hair was loosely tied in back with the Cyrillic scarf. I took this as a good omen.

"I'm swamped with various disasters," she said. "We missed you. The person they sent to fill in for you was none too speedy."

"I'm sorry to hear that." I held out my hand and Joyce gave me the microcassette. "I'll have this done in no time," I said. "I've missed these tapes, you know. I like being in the middle of typing something you've just said into my ear and looking up and seeing you walk across the floor."

This took Joyce a tiny bit by surprise. "How was your vacation?"

"It was good, quite good. *Long*, though."

"What have you been up to?"

"I've been—this sounds insane—but I've been writing my autobiography," I said.

"Have you led an interesting life?" Joyce asked.

I leaned forward. "Well, you know—I have! I have. What about you?"

"No."

"That's unfortunate," I said. "What can I do to help?"

"Find someone to sweep me away somewhere. The problem is that I have no time to do interesting stuff, because I'm so busy doing stuff that's uninteresting. Actually, on Saturdays I go to a botanical drawing class at the Arnold Arboretum."

"Oh, well *there*, that's a positive step," I said. "I haven't drawn a plant in years. Is it fun?"

"Yes," said Joyce. "Plants sit still. It's like meditation, but it's better, because you're thinking about the plant, and not about yourself."

I shook my head sadly. "I wish I had more art in my life right now. I did allow some medical researchers to paint reflective paint on several parts of my body a few months ago. Does that count as an artistic experience?"

"I should think so," said Joyce. She asked what the researchers were trying to find out.

I told her it had to do with my carpal-tunnel problem. "They were trying to figure out how much of my problem was due to typing and how much was due to other factors."

"Like what other factors? You know I have a touch of carpal, too," she confided.

"I'm sorry. The other main factor was—well—it's this hobby of mine, something I do in my spare time."

"Oh?" she said.

"In fact," I said, "I have to talk to you about it."

"About—?"

It was definitely time to ask Joyce out. Her expression had identifiable elements of puzzled, provoked interest. Her eyes were—I think this is the only word for what they were doing—they were shining. Yet what would the look on her face be when she learned that I had already Dropped in on her apart-

ment? I needed a moment to collect my thoughts. Without
blinking, I softly snapped my fingers. I relaxed. The easy thing
to do would be to undress her now: if I undressed her now and
stood on the desk and touched the tip of her nose with my
erect stain-stick or stroked her cheek with it in a friendly way,
I knew that I would phrase my request for a date more confi-
dently. But I didn't want to cheat and do that. I could go back
to her apartment and lie on her bed and gain strength and
confidence from having been there again. But no—the whole
point of this date was for me not to trespass unasked. I needed
a distraction.

Still enFolded, I walked briskly all the way to the Gap clothing store in the Copley Place Mall and took off the shirt of
every woman in it (there were eleven women), singing the
country-western Gap jingle from the seventies: "Fall—in—
to—the—Gap." I draped their bras over their shoulders. With
no pants on, I walked around the racks of braided belts and
along the walls of folded shorts and overdyed jeans. I knew
from previous experience that there would be sand in some of
the pants pockets—not because that particular pair had been
worn to the beach and then returned, as I had once thought,
but because the pants were sand-washed before they were
sold. They came pre-supplied with their own memories of the
Cape. I twirled slowly like a compass needle in the middle of
the store, both hands on my tiller. I let my eye be surprised by
each topless woman in turn, saying, "And you! And you! I'd
forgotten about you! Wow, those are nice! Hi, how are you?"
Having filled my brain with a multiplicity of naked Jamaicas
(without coming, however), I redressed my wrongs, putting
everything back where it had been, and made my way back to
the MassBank building. At my desk, I snapped and emerged
from my personal Gap full of self-assurance, fortified by secret

acts of vulgarity, looking at Joyce, who, needless to say, hadn't moved during my absence.

"Would you like to have a snack with me sometime?" I asked her.

"What kind of a snack do you mean?" she asked.

"A dinner sort of snack."

"Oh." She smiled sideways.

"I need to talk to you. I've done you a wrong, and I need to unburden myself."

"I see," she said. .

"Tonight?"

"Hm." She almost went for it. But then she said: "No, tonight is bad. I wish I could, but I'm probably going to have to stay late. I'm going to have to go over the stuff in that tape when you get it back to me. Thomas needs to look at it tomorrow morning."

"If I have it back to you in ten short minutes," I said, "will you go out with me tonight?"

"There's an hour of stuff on that tape!"

"I know that. I'm just saying, *if* I get it back to you in ten minutes, will you go out with me tonight? I know it's a little strange, but it has to do with what I want to talk to you about."

"Okay, yes, sure," she said.

I took her to the restaurant at the Meridien. As we walked there, we followed some deep unwritten law adapted from business practice, a law that enjoins against any discussion of the main subject until a certain number of random-seeming conversational topics have arisen and been dealt with and a context of cool detachment thereby established. We talked about the rise and fall of shoe-store chains and the merits of various kinds of women's shoes and whether women's shoe salesmen were invariably fetishists. (Joyce's own shoes were great-looking gray flats with sexy side-buckles.) But as soon as we got some wine, Joyce said. "Now: I want you to explain to me in detail how you did that tape so fast."

"If I tell you, will you tell anyone?" I asked.

"You can't know this about me," Joyce said, "but I never, ever tell anyone anything that was revealed to me in confidence."

"Good—I want to believe you. I've listened to your voice so much transcribing your tapes that I think I have unusual insights into your character."

"You *should* believe me," said Joyce.

"I do. No—I think the problem really is whether you will believe me."

"The only way to find out is to try me," said Joyce.

So I told her that at various periods in my life, starting way back in fourth grade, I'd been able to disengage myself from time. I told her briefly about the race-track transformer, the thread going through my callus into the washing machine, about the rubber-band stretcher and the mechanical pencil, and about pushing up my glasses.

Joyce laughed. "And this morning? How did you do it this morning?"

"I just snapped my fingers. I won't do it now, but whenever I snap my fingers, the entire universe immediately pauses for me, like a stretch limo waiting for me on the street while I run some errand. I spent probably, oh, an hour and a half doing your tape, with the universe in pause-mode, and then I snapped my fingers to turn it back on again and I went over to your desk and delivered the work. And before that I'd snapped and taken over an hour to go for a walk. I went down to the Gap and browsed a little. So it's really around ten o'clock at night for me."

"You must be starving," said Joyce. "I know I am. Some bread?"

"Thanks."

Chewing, she regarded me. "Do you have more to say?"

"Yes." I had felt confident, even cocky, moments before, but I now noticed that my hands were unsteady as I stuffed a piece of bread in my mouth. "I've never told anyone what I'm telling you," I said. "I tried to tell someone obliquely, but it wasn't a success."

Joyce said, "Why are you telling me, then? I mean, I'm delighted that you are—I think. But don't you want to continue to keep all this to yourself if you've kept it to yourself for this long?"

I said, "I'm tired of having this big secret life and not being able to tell anyone." And suddenly I did feel enormously tired of it. I felt as if I was going to get slightly weepy, but fortunately I didn't. "I like you and I just want to tell you. I've written about it in the memoiry thing that I've been working on, and though I haven't shown that to anyone, having done that, gone public on the page, I seem able to accept more easily the fact that people will know. It feels inevitable now, though of course it isn't. It's the next step. Also, I've used the Fold to do things that might make you uncomfortable, if you knew about them, and if they are going to make you uncomfortable, I'd rather that happened now and not later."

"The 'Fold'?"

I went into the terminology in some detail. We ordered. I told her about the equation with the garment-care symbols, and about colliding with the parking meter and stealing two shrimp. I gave her a bowdlerized account of my experience in the electromagnet. Finally I worked up the nerve to mention that at selected times in the past I had used the Fold to take off women's clothes without their knowledge.

"Ah—*now* I see where we're going," Joyce said. "That's not so good. That is not so hot."

"I know, I know, I know, I know," I said, shaking my head. "But when I'm doing it it doesn't seem bad. It seems wonderful, good, positive—it seems like the most constructive thing I could possibly be doing. I just don't understand why it should be so bad and wrong for me to take a woman's clothes off, as long as she doesn't know about it. I mean really, what's the big deal?"

"How much of their clothing do you take off?" She sipped some wine, looking at me intently. Her eyes were the color of peat moss; her pupils were dilated.

"Oh, it depends," I said. "Sometimes I don't take any off, sometimes I go down to the bra, sometimes I do go a touch further."

"You've never told anyone about this practice of yours?"

"Not directly. I've come close several times, but no."

She touched her mouth with her napkin. Then she narrowed her eyes. "But now you've decided to tell me. And you know why? I know why. You're telling me because you took my clothes off, didn't you? Didn't you?"

"Yes."

She let her hand fall to the table. Now she looked sad—sad rather than shocked. "I can't believe you did that."

To draw her attention away from her disappointment in me, I asked, "You mean you can't believe that I am telling the truth, or you can't believe that I would do something that rude and crude?"

"Both," she said. "God, I'm so fucking *sick* of liars and sneaks and cheats and weirdos. God." She wiped her eyes and sniffed. "Last year I was in a relationship with a guy for two months, and it turned out that he was married. He simply forgot to tell me that he had a nuclear family in Washington, D.C. And now this."

"I'm sorry," I said. "But can I say that right now I'm the opposite of the married guy? I'm trying not to deceive you. I'm telling you right out that, yes, I took some of your clothes off. I assumed you wouldn't mind. If I had known as a definite fact beforehand that you would have minded, I wouldn't have done it. I know I was probably deluding myself. You looked wonderful. Your pubic hair was like a bicycle seat."

"Oh Jesus. When was this?" She looked up at me, as if establishing the date would help.

I took off my glasses and put my hands over my eyes to think. "It's hard for me to get dates right, because I've been spending so much time lately in the Fold, writing. It was the first week I worked at MassBank. You were walking across the floor one time wearing that blue-gray knit dress." I put my glasses back on, which made me remember that she had said back then that she liked my glasses. I felt there was still hope. "That is a really nifty dress. You had your hair in a French braid, if that's what they're called. You were carrying some files. And I just *wanted to see more of you.* What can I say?"

"Arno, wouldn't it have been just as easy to ask me out?"

"No! It was very, very hard to ask you out today. It's just not something I do lightly."

"Tell me exactly what happened," she said.

"When I took off your clothes? Do you really want to hear this?"

"No, it's hideous, but go on."

"Well—I just snapped my fingers and got everything to stop and I scooted over to you in my chair and lifted up your dress. It was so light, it felt so good, the knit. I lifted it up over your pantyhose and over your hips and made a sort of knot in it at your waist. Your legs felt really warm through the pantyhose. Pantyhose material is strange stuff, like a substance from another planet, unpleasant when you first touch it, and yet the warmth of your skin radiates through it and humanizes it. So I kind of whisked my hands over your legs and I felt your hipbones, and before you know it, I had pulled your pantyhose down and I had my hand in your pubic hair."

" 'Before I know it' is right," said Joyce, pointing her knife at me. "I didn't know it, Arno. I didn't have a clue that your hand was in my pubic hair. Doesn't that trouble you?"

"No, because I fell in love with you with my hand in your pubic hair."

Joyce made an exasperated sound. "Everything's ruined and out of order! I was really pleased that you asked me out for dinner tonight. Really pleased. And now it's all confused."

"I also went to your apartment. I borrowed your keys."

"No." Joyce was incredulous. "No."

"Yes. I've seen your mattress pad."

"Arno, this is terrible. I don't know what to think. First of all, I don't believe a word of it."

"Under an antique bottle in your sunporch, I put a fortune-cookie fortune I found in a bowl on top of your refrigerator. It says, 'Smile when you are ready.' "

"You need help."

"I beg your pardon! I'm not a bad person. If you ask me to go away now, I'll go away. I'm harmless. I'm just a temp! I was curious about your apartment, that's all." I waited for Joyce to say something, but she didn't. "All right. This evening has nosedived. Still, I'm glad to hear that you were pleased to be asked out. That's something. Would you like some more wine?"

"Just a touch, thanks. Ope, ope, that's plenty." She drank a little of it. I let her think things over. We were silent for a stretch.

"I should go," she said.

"Okay," I said.

Then she said, "Prove it to me. I want you to do what you say you can do right now."

"You want me to stop time?"

"Yes, I do."

"All right. I'll do it right now. Ready?"

She nodded.

I snapped my fingers. I sat still for a while, breathing softly, nearly as motionless as the rest of the animal and vegetable kingdoms. Then I began tapping my hand on my napkin. I refilled Joyce's water glass. I went to the bathroom and checked how I looked. I looked fine—a little sheepish and worried about the eyes. I sat down again and poked around at my plate, but I didn't want to eat anything without Joyce "there." I didn't enjoy the enveloping silence this time, as I usually did; it was like sitting at a table with someone who wasn't speaking to me. In fact, it wasn't *like* that, it *was* that. I didn't want to be under the Fermata at all just then; I wanted time to be rolling forward at a nice brisk clip, so that Joyce would get used to the things that I had told her and forgive me for them, if forgiveness was still a possibility. It might take weeks.

I snapped my fingers. "I just did it," I said.

"What did you do?" She looked quickly down at her dress and back at me. "I had absolutely no sense of anything happening."

"I didn't do that much. I was chastened by your reaction, so I took it easy. I refilled your water glass."

Joyce looked at her water glass suspiciously. "It was already that high."

"No, really, it was about a quarter full," I said.

"I'm sure it was that high. I've been drinking mostly wine."

"Should we debate water levels?" I said. "Or should you simply tell me what you want me to do, what will prove to you that I really can stop time, so that I can Snap out right now and do it?"

"You could . . ." Joyce looked around the room for inspiration. I saw her eyes alight on the waiter. "I don't know. Anything. What would you want to do?"

I leaned forward. "See those two men? I could switch their ties. But I don't really want to do that. I hate practical jokes. It's hard enough to tie my own tie. The Fold is sexual for me." I looked pensive for a moment, then brightened. "I could take off your bra and put it in your briefcase in the coatroom. I'd be happy to do that. Would that convince you?"

"Yes, it probably would," said Joyce. "But hold off."

I said, "If you could snap your fingers right now and stop time, suspend all cause and effect, what would you do?" I leaned forward again and began speaking in a soft coaxing urgent voice. "There's the waiter there. I saw you check him out. He's got a nice butt, right? Think about it. This entire room is *filled* with cock. There is cock in every direction. Prosperous cock, arrogant cock, dumb cock, smart cock, old-regime cock, new-age cock. What would you do?"

"At the moment, if I could stop time, I'd stop time and use the facilities. Excuse me."

While Joyce was gone I stared at the flower in the bud vase

and felt up the table under the tablecloth to discover what sort of surface it had. It had a rough surface. I didn't think; I just waited. Our salads came.

Eventually Joyce returned. "Hi." She swept her hand over the back of her dress as she sat down, so that she wouldn't make wrinkles. "You didn't follow me in there, snapping your fingers, did you?"

"No, I was out here the whole time."

Joyce's mood seemed to have shifted slightly. "I was thinking that this power you say you have would open up some interesting possibilities," she said. "At the bank, for instance, I could think of lots of things you could find out."

I told her I wasn't all that wild about white-collar crime.

"Or," she continued, holding up her hand, "it would be very handy for working mothers. Or forget working mothers. It would be very handy for me. I could take a whole day to catch up. A silent paradise. No phones. I need it bad. I'd fill four tapes."

"That's true," I said. "It's funny, though. The idea of having time to catch up sounds so luscious. But in reality I've found that big chunks of raw time don't help that much. Parkinson's Law becomes the dominant force. Parkinson's Law and loneliness. You have to time the time-outs, and mix them in with life—that's were the art comes in."

"Still," said Joyce, "I'd love to know what it was like, to wander around Boston when it was totally still. Nothing moving but me. Everyone like a statue. Are you really serious that you can do this?"

I nodded.

She put her napkin on the table and sat up straight in her chair with her hands in her lap. "Tell me what color bra I'm wearing. Don't take it off. Just tell me the color and the make."

"Frankly I feel a little weird now doing it," I said, flapping my arms to signal uncertainty and moral confusion.

"Go ahead!" she said. "I'm letting you. I'm still not sure I believe you anyway. You have to demonstrate you're not lying to me."

I snapped my fingers and went around to Joyce's side of the table and, after some groping, tore the small label off her bra. I also kissed her lightly on the mouth, so that I could tell her I had. I took my chair and turned everything back on. "You're wearing a red bra," I reported. "It is"—I peered at the label—"an 'Olga Christina.' It says, 'Gentle machine wash warm, wash with like colors, no bleach, line dry, no iron.' "

"It's my favorite bra."

"All I did was unzip the back of your dress and reach in. I want you to know that I didn't really grope at your breasts or do anything in any way proactive." I held out the bra label between my two fingers. She took it and set it down beside her bread plate. "I did also kiss you briefly," I added.

"Really? Where?"

"On the lips."

She made an mmm-expression with her mouth to see if she could detect any residual sensations.

"No after-tingle?" I said, feigning incredulity.

"Nothing," said Joyce. "How did it go, the kiss?"

I said that it had gone very well.

"I'm glad to hear it," she said.

By the time we had finished our salads there was a definite feeling of amity in the air.

"You know," I said, "while I was snapped out just now,

tearing the label off your bra, I thought of something. I bet there is a way you could experience the Fold-cleft with me."

"I doubt it," she said.

"Well, this is what I'm thinking, anyway. The Fermata seems to know that I am physically one individual, and it exempts me from the general freeze. But what if we confuse it? What if my naked penis is in your vagina when I snap my fingers?"

Joyce laughed a this-is-all-just-a-little-too-much laugh, but I could see that the notion wasn't inconceivable to her.

I went on. "I think there's a good chance, if we did that, that the Fermata would read us both as one single entity. We would have to be in a real state of union, though. I'd have to be *way* in there, and your legs would have to be really locked around me. We'd have to be holding each other extra tight, and probably we'd have to be kissing, too. We'd probably have to be in love. Our tongues would have to be chasing each other around, and your hands would have to be gripping my thrusting buttcheeks—"

Joyce raised her hands. "Okay, I got it, I got the general idea."

"I'm not saying that it's a guaranteed sure thing, but I do think it's worth a try," I said excitedly. "Are you with me?"

"When would this happen?" She had the same sideways smile she'd had when I first asked her out.

"We could set a date, if you like. Five minutes from now?"

"That seems soon," she said.

"I've lost all conception of what 'soon' means. Don't you want to lose all conception of what 'soon' means, too?"

"I do, kind of." She lowered her eyes.

Suddenly I remembered birth control. "Shoot, that's right. A condom is out, because there has to be total contact." I made popping sounds with my lips, thinking. "You're not on the pill, are you?"

"There's a man I see sometimes. So I still am technically, yes."

"You are? Oh—*great!* Perfect." I waved my hands. "Forget we talked about that. Let's talk about something else for a while." I asked her to tell me more about her botanical drawing class. She described the difficulties of rendering bark. She talked about her teacher. There was a nice moment when she finished saying something, and took a bite of bread, and noticed that I was looking at her with an odd, gleeful expression, and her face filled with friendly curiosity. It was time. "May I?" I said.

"May you what?"

"Snap my fingers?"

She drank the rest of her wine. "Okay."

I snapped my fingers.

I carried her down the stopped escalator to a sofa in the lobby and found a rolling cart that the bellhops used for suitcases. I went into the back rooms and found several blankets and pillows and padded the cart with them. I put her down on the cart, on her side, with her legs bent. It took me less than an hour to push her to her apartment. I stayed mostly in the middle of the street. It had begun to rain, but we didn't get very wet because we were only dampened by the drops that were suspended in our path, not by the ones above us, and even in a heavy rain, the number of drops per cubic foot is far fewer than it appears when the rain is in motion. I left the cart by the mailboxes and carried her upstairs and used her key. I laid her down in the sunporch, on her bed. I kept my eyes closed while I pulled off her clothes and my own. (I wanted to be able to tell her that I hadn't looked at her.)

I arranged the covers of the bed over her and then got in next to her. She was very warm. I lay there for a while with my eyes closed, letting my heart calm down. Her mattress pad felt terrific. I was tired and sleepy. I had a nap of maybe half an Arno-hour. When I woke up I thought to myself, I'm lying in bed with the woman whom, above all others, I want to be in bed with. I snapped my fingers.

Joyce began to say something that began with "Although." She stopped abruptly. "What happened here?"

"See how easy it is?" I said.

She turned her head on the pillow to look at me. "What did you do?"

"I brought you to your apartment and got in bed with you."

Her arm moved under the covers. "I don't have any clothes on."

"That's true," I said. "But I assure you, I kept my eyes closed while I was taking them off. I haven't done anything seedily voyeuristic. They're over there. I just wanted to be totally naked in bed with you." We were both lying on our backs. Our arms touched a little. The room was dim.

Joyce put her hands on her forehead and thought. "How did you get me here? Did you drive?"

I explained how difficult it was to drive during an estoppel, what with all the immobile cars. I described the luggage cart and the borrowed bedding. Then I said, "There's one serious problem, though, having to do with time, which is that as we lie here talking, our entrees may be being served, and the waiter may wonder where we've gone. I left my jacket there to show that we haven't skipped out, but I think we should find a way into the Fermata together as quickly as possible, before anyone notices that we've disappeared at the restaurant, and then once we've done that we'll have loads of time to talk, and we can stroll back in a leisurely way and finish dessert."

"You mean—-?"

"Yes, I think we have to make love right now, and we have to put off any foreplay until after we've Snapped out—assuming, that is, that we do successfully enter the Fermata together. But let's try."

"Couldn't we at least kiss?"

"Are you kidding?" I said. "We *have* to kiss. It's a necessity. We have to have a total mental and physical union for this to work. Try to feel as much love for me as you can."

So we put our arms around each other and started kissing. I think we were both somewhat surprised by how good it felt. Her mouth was the best thing my mouth had felt in quite a while. I guess I had simply forgotten that there is no satisfactory autoerotic substitute for a kiss. Our lips cooperated; they understood each other. In fourth grade I had a rubber stamp that said ARNOLD STRINE. I didn't like stamping it hard. I liked placing the fully inked stamp gently on the paper and rocking it back and forth as I pressed down, so that my name came out very dark, and the tops and bottoms of the letters flared. While Joyce and I made out, I closed my eyes and saw for an instant an image of my old rubber stamp being held in the air and brought together with a second well-inked stamp saying JOYCE COLLIER, so that our two names met face to face and rocked together, printing themselves on each other.

I'd also forgotten, I guess, that there is no substitute for the joy of first putting your arms around a woman's nudity—when time is unfrozen and when she answers your embrace by actually *embracing you back* and you can't believe how well naked seamless bodies can coincide, how accommodating they can be, even before erections have been manually confirmed and clitorises tested or tasted. And it isn't often that you *begin* making out with someone, for the very first time, in a state of total nudity, as Joyce and I did. As if it was all part of our kiss, as if our bodies were kissing, Joyce moved underneath me and opened her legs and as I let more of my weight press on her she brought me inside, past her lush black fur and into her hot Fermata.

I whispered to her how good she felt. "Ready?" I said.

"Yes." I felt her breath on my neck.

"Hold me really tight. Snap your fingers when I do." I counted off, "One, two, three." Then we kissed again and we snapped our fingers in unison.

It was difficult to tell for a moment if anything had happened. We looked at each other inquiringly, our eyebrows raised. Our slightest movement made my cock squeak with pleasure.

"Did it work?" Joyce asked.

I listened. "Hear that? It's totally quiet. That's the way the Fermata always sounds. It worked."

She sighed with relief and started lifting her hips up against me. "Good news," she murmured. "Good news. Can we do this for a while, though?"

"We can take as long as we want now," I said.

Several Arno-and-Joyce-hours later, we walked back to the Meridien, wheeling the luggage cart with us. I showed her the negative black paths our bodies left behind in the constellations of hanging, glinting raindrops. "So—while you're out on walks like this," Joyce said, "you just take off a woman's clothes, if she attracts you?"

I said I sometimes did.

Joyce tried it. She undid the black jeans of a motionless man in a leather jacket and pulled on his underpants and peered inside. She also unbuttoned a businessman's raincoat and reached her hand into his jacket and felt his chest. "Hey, I could learn to like this," she said. We took our seats at the restaurant and counted to three and snapped our fingers. The waiter appeared shortly after with our entrees. "The plates are very hot," he said importantly, holding them with a cloth. We had been gone for no more than five minutes; nobody had missed us. Joyce and I talked for another hour, and we drank some more and then had some coffee, and then I walked her home and kissed her good-night at her door.

18

MY FINGER-SNAPPING PHASE IS NOW OVER, MY FOLD-powers are currently gone. I assume I'll get them back sooner or later, but I'm never sure. What happened, as far as I can piece it together, is that one night, when Joyce and I were having sex, I unknowingly transferred all my fermational proficiencies *to her*. I had jokingly trotted out the penis pump and the Goddess Athena vibrator with the clit-stimulating fork-flamed torch of wisdom and told her that I'd bought them with her in mind, before we'd started going out. "I'm not a big vibrator person," Joyce warned. But she did pump enthusiastically away at my penis with the penis pump, sucking it up into the clear plastic vacuum chamber and watching its veins pop out. When my penis had had more than enough of that treatment, I pulled it out and substituted the Athena vibrator in its place. Joyce and I then pumped the vibrator with the penis pump for a while, sucking it in as far as it would go. And finally, after some cajoling, Joyce turned on the Athena vibrator and slipped it inside herself. The fork-flamed torch of wisdom took her polytheistic clit to new heights.

But what we didn't realize at the time was that the penis pump had somehow sucked all of my temporal powers out of me. Then, when the Athena vibrator went into the penis pump, the same powers were apparently transferred to it, and when the Athena vibrator muttered its way deep into Joyce, the powers entered her. As a result, the next time I snapped my fingers, nothing at all happened—or rather, everything kept on happening. But the next time Joyce clicked on the switch of her Athena vibrator, time dutifully halted for her.

I find I don't miss the Fold too terribly much at present. My self-discipline has improved. I'm still temping, but I've begun going over some of the notes for my master's thesis. (It's a history of Dover Books.) Joyce, meanwhile, is having a good time. She carries her vibrating Cleft-Goddess around with her in her purse and turns it on at will, as when she has an important deadline at MassBank that she can't otherwise meet. She strips pedestrians and tells me about strange genitalia she has seen and known. She talks of taking a jaunt down to Washington and sucking the presidential dick. Sometimes she uses Fold tricks while we're having sex: for instance, she will alternate her mouth and her vadge on my richard so fast that I feel as if I'm in both places at once—as if she's twirling over me. We've mentioned marriage as a possibility.

The other day I was in her apartment. I did some pushups on the floor. Then I sat on her bed. I called out, "Can I tell you about this great dream I once had about how you saved the two of us with your flying blue brassiere?"

"Briefly," said Joyce from the bathroom. She was unbraiding her hair.

"We were in a boat in the middle of this lake of sulfuric acid," I happily began, "and you were wearing your flying blue brassiere . . ."

Joyce has saved me, for the time being. I haven't taken a stranger's clothes off in weeks now. I'm trying to interest a publisher in my autobiography. But even if nobody wants to publish it, I could still have, say, a hundred copies made up. I'll typeset them myself. I'll get Copy Cop to bind them. I'll design a jacket that uses the logo of some flush, big-name publisher like Random House. Yes, I'll put that little stylized house on the bottom of the spine of my book. I'll use a color copier to make the cover. It will look like a real book! And then, assuming I get my Fold-powers back, I'll go to Waterstone's or the Avenue Victor Hugo and Drop and put this book in people's hands just as they think their fingers are closing on some other, real, book. They will read me. Word will spread. The Fermata, my Fermata, the keeper of all my secrets, will be a secret no longer.

ABOUT THE AUTHOR

NICHOLSON BAKER was born in 1957. He is the author of *The Mezzanine* (1988), *Room Temperature* (1990), *U and I* (1991), and *Vox* (1992). He has written for *The New Yorker* and *The Atlantic Monthly*. He is married with two children.